EMPIRE DISCOVERED
The Rutherford Chronicles
Part I

Michael G. Bergen

Second Edition

First published by Michael G. Bergen, 2020

Copyright © 2020 Michael G. Bergen

www.michaelgbergen.com

ISBN 978-0-620-90463-6

Cover Design and Typesetting by www.myebook.online

All rights reserved.

The moral right of the author has been asserted.
No part of this publication may be reproduced, distributed, or transmitted in any form or by any means, including photocopying, recording, or other electronic or mechanical methods, without the prior written permission of the author, except in the case of brief quotations embodied in critical reviews and certain other non-commercial uses permitted by copyright law.

*This book is dedicated to my late grandfather,
who kept his good humour to the end.*

*And for anyone whose ancestors fought
on either side of the South African Boer Wars.*

*A tumultuous family journey
through the 20th Century*

"Take a community of Dutchmen of the type of those who defended themselves for fifty years against all the power of Spain at a time when Spain was the greatest power in the World. Intermix with them a strain of those inflexible French Huguenots who gave up home and fortune and left their Country forever at the time of the revocation of the Edict of Nantes. The product must be one of the most rugged, virile, unconquerable races ever seen on Earth. Take these formidable people and train them for seven generations in constant warfare against savage men and ferocious beasts, in circumstances under which no weakling could survive, place them so that they acquire exceptional skills with weapons and in horsemanship, give them a Country which is eminently suited to the tactics of the huntsman, the marksman and the rider. Then, finally, put a fine temper upon their military qualities by a dour, fatalistic Old Testament religion and an ardent and consuming patriotism. Combine all these qualities and all these impulses in one individual, and you have the modern Boer. The most formidable antagonist who ever crossed the path of Imperial Britain."

Arthur Conan Doyle, The Great Boer War, Eight years after giving up medicine for writing, the internationally famous creator of Sherlock Holmes became Dr. Doyle once more as a volunteer physician in the Langman Field Hospital at Bloemfontein between March and June 1900 and subsequently wrote The Great Boer War.

PROLOGUE

What is it about the military that so fascinates the youth of every generation, inspiring young men to fight in the next deadly conflict, I ask you? Is it the uniform acting as an attraction to the opposite sex? Is the military offering a chance to see the world and adventure the lure? Or is the opportunity to kill or maim an enemy that offers a perverse form of satisfaction? In this modern age, is it only about young men?

As a boy, I was fascinated by the military and warfare. In my fourth year at school, I had a veteran of WW II as an excellent teacher who captivated us with stories about the Romans and their warfare skills to conquer the Mediterranean world and beyond. We built a Roman Fort in a sandbox at the back of the classroom and imagined ourselves as Roman hero generals. He told us about the horrors of soldiering and being a prisoner of war in the WWII Pacific Theatre. He caught our attention, and I became hooked on history through his exciting classes. That interest has never left me.

I knew that my father had fought and survived WW2 in Europe, and I learned that my British grandfather had fought in the South African Boer War and WW I, spending four years as a prisoner of war in Germany. Why did my grandfather join not one but two destructive wars? Why did my father eagerly join the Canadian Army at the start of WW II and witness the horrors of that war in the hard-fought Italian Campagne? As a 7-year-old, I met a cousin in England who was a sailor in the Royal Navy during the Korean War, and he became my hero and role model, setting me on a course to join the Sea Cadets, the Royal Canadian Navy during the Cold War.

Does this sound familiar? Has your family lived through such historical events? Have you had relatives who followed similar painful paths? I suspect many of you have.

So yes, I became such a young man, fascinated by my heritage military history and a student of conflict. And like so many before me, I couldn't wait to get into uniform and take part in a war!

That is long behind me now, but my interest didn't wane, so later in life, I embarked on a project to learn more about the wars and challenges my forbears and I had survived. They had left no written record and were loath to talk much about their war experiences. So, wanting to understand how they had lived and what they went through, the burden fell on me to research the significant conflicts of the 20th Century. That research provided the historical framework for this series. My imagination filled in the blanks they had left by not recording their personal journeys.

This book is the first of four describing a tumultuous family journey through the violent 20th Century. It began at the end of Queen Victoria's reign in 1899 and continued into the first years of the century on the vast, arid Highveld of South Africa. In that faraway place, an unexpected clash transpired between the mighty British Empire and two tiny Boer Republics at the bottom end of the continent. The British hero is an Irish-Geordie worker called Joe Rutherford from the shipbuilding yards of the River Tyne in North East England. Another hero of that clash is a young Boer son of a past President of the Orange Free State Republic who recorded his family's experiences in that war. Other notable characters include the young war correspondent Winston Churchill, the young Canadian doctor and poet John McCrae, a middle-aged Dr Arthur Conan Doyle, and soldiers from the far reaches of the British Empire, including illustrious generals from both sides of the conflict. Beyond this violent first part of the journey, Joe enjoyed a few years in a peaceful British India.

Part Two of my family saga, Empire and War, took me to the early trenches of the Western Front in France, the deadly 'Rush to the Sea' and three POW camps in Northern Germany in that horrific war.

Part Three, Empire and Tyranny, allowed me to discover my father's path as a Canadian soldier during WW2.

Finally, Part Four, Empires Lost: Cold War Empire, describes how I rushed to join the 20th Century's most protracted conflict, the Cold War, from a Canadian warship in the Atlantic and Mediterranean. I experienced and recorded near-catastrophic misses called the Cuban Missile Crisis and the Berlin Wall.

In this quest for my family history called The Rutherford Chronicles, I learned that war is frightening, painful and undesirable. So why do we keep falling into its dangerous trap? Why do we follow the politicians and the youths of every generation who rush into it? Why are we so fascinated by the heroes of these wars, and why does every generation forget about the mistakes of the preceding generation?

Those are some of the questions I seek answers to in The Rutherford Chronicles.

CONTENTS

Quote	v
Prologue	1
1. Storm Clouds Gather Over South Africa *September to October 1899*	7
2. The Storm Begins *October 1899 to January 1900*	28
3. Field Marshal Roberts in Command *February 1900*	68
4. Lord Robert's Perfect Storm *May 1900 to February 1901*	99
5. Weathering the Waning Storm *March 1901 to May 1902*	135
6. The End of the Storm *May to October 1902*	245
7. Beyond the Storm in India *November 1902–June 1906*	262
About the Author	323

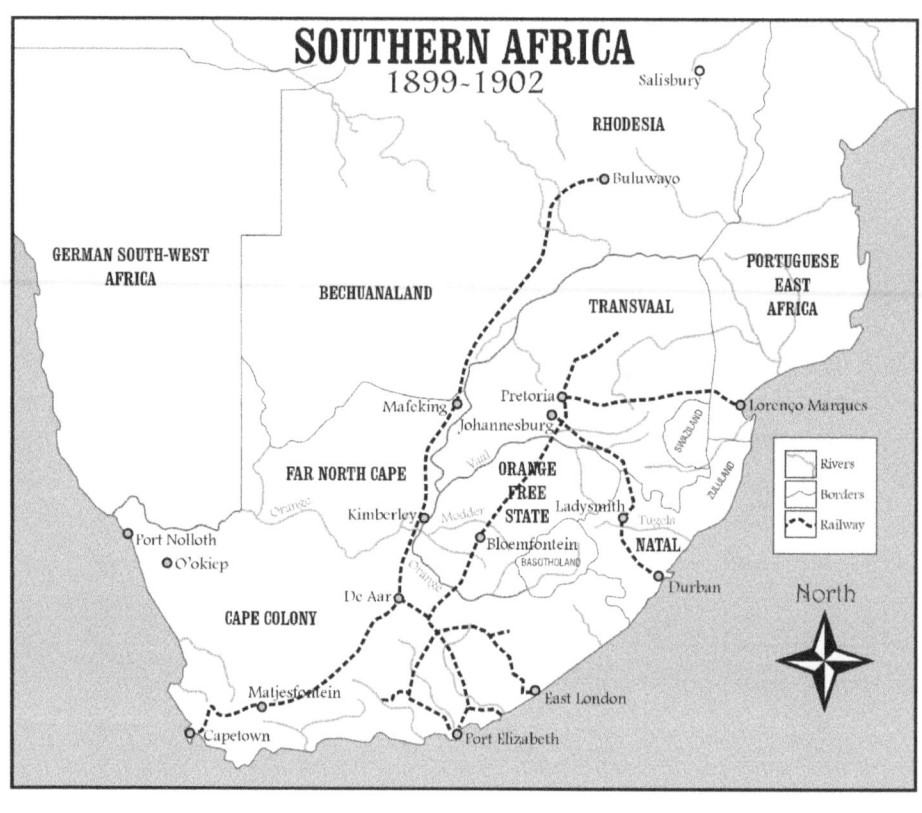

CHAPTER 1
STORM CLOUDS GATHER OVER SOUTH AFRICA
SEPTEMBER TO OCTOBER 1899

Tyneside—Introducing Joe Rutherford

Tyneside was never quiet at the turn of the Twentieth Century. Collieries, factories and shipyards on both sides of the River Tyne in North East England thrummed to the tune of tools and machinery day and night. Miners were blasting and extracting coal from deep below the surface, hauling it from the pits to the waiting ships and rail cars. The steel mills were rolling steel plates for ships' hulls, then cutting and hammering them into their designated shapes. The constant rat-tat of scores of striking riveters joined the steel sheets into place. Steam locomotives, weapons, and plate glass were taking shape in the Tyneside factories. Roaring furnaces billowed smoke into the skies above this bustling district while factories hurried to fulfil their orders to support Queen Victoria's imperial ambitions.

Tens of thousands of workers, the majority Geordies [1], filled the streets of Tyneside towns such as Newcastle upon Tyne, Gateshead, Tynemouth, Wallsend and Jarrow twice daily between long and hard-working shifts. None complained too much. They were the lucky ones to be working and earning an income. They emerged from their homes and walked to the pits and yards. And as severe as the work conditions were, they toiled the long hours and collected their modest pay every Saturday.

Besides the factories, the thousands of terrace houses of the families of workers belched a steady flow of yellow-grey smoke into the skies above Tyneside. The fog had moved in that night, muting the rumbling machines and trapping the smoke in its wet grip. One seldom saw a bright sky or a brilliant sun, never mind stars or even the moon, in the industrial areas of Britain. The air wasn't clean enough for unobscured sight, and a muted yellow orb glowed in the sky. But nobody there seemed to mind. They knew of nothing else. And they contented themselves with putting food on the table for their families and little else.

"Cheer up, laddies," called Joe to his marras [2] over the din, "only ten hours before we finish yet another working day."

"Aye, Joe," said Mike. "Another six days until pub night."

"Aye," said Billy, laughing, "My grandma has always said hard labour and avoiding the ale is better for a working lad."

"Well, they've blessed us then," called out Jack. "Still, we work hard and don't have enough ale."

They were far from alone. Joe and his marras were heading to work in the shipyards with several thousand other working Jarrow men; they shared the same routes every morning and evening at changing shifts. These men provided the muscle to expand the wealth of the British Empire six days a week.

"Look at that gadgie[3] over there," called out Billy. "What's a soldier doing here?"

"That's Danny's brother-in-law," said Joe. "He's home on a visit and walking Danny to work. Let's move over to them."

1899 was peaceful in Britain and throughout the Empire, with only a few exceptions. There were always uncooperative groups not happy with being occupied by a foreign power. And sometimes, they expressed their dissatisfaction in violent ways. The British had built their Empire through discovery and conquest for a few hundred years. Since the end of the Napoleonic Wars in 1815, Great Britain added 10 million square miles of territory and 400 million people to the Empire. Under Queen Victoria's rule, the realm experienced unprecedented expansion and accumulated unrivalled wealth. Despite isolated pockets of resistance, Britain's imperial nineteenth Century was known as the "Pax Britannica." It was an era of relative peace between the world's dominant powers, during which the British Empire became the foremost global power and adopted the role of a worldwide police force. The mighty British Army and the most powerful navy in the world enforced this unique role.

"Aalreet, Danny," called out Joe. "What's Patrick doing here?"

"Keeping my brother-in-law out of mischief," said Patrick on Danny's behalf. "My sister Susan asked me to watch over him, haha."

"Not that I need watching over," said Danny. "Patrick is a country lad and needs to see what real working men do."

"Aye, well, you are a smart-looking fellow in that outfit," said Joe. "Where have you been?"

"India," said Patrick, "with the 2nd Battalion of the Durham Light Infantry, and proud of it. Home on leave from Poona."

"Howay, man! Now that's what I want to do: Travel, see the world, serve our Queen and country."

"Aye, me too," said Mike. "Good luck to you, soldier. My name is Mike O'Brien, and we'll be joining you one of these days."

"I thank yee. And I'm sure you'll be most welcome," called out Patrick as he and Danny moved off in a different direction, "We've heard war is soon to start in South Africa. Why not join the fight?"

"I prefer his clobber to ours," said Mike.

"Aye, a British Army uniform is a fine clobber," said Joe.

"What does he mean by a war in South Africa?" asked Billy.

"Aye, I've read that," said Joe. "The Dutch farmers, or Boers as they call them, are preparing to fight the British Army."

"Are they mad?" yelled Mike. "Nobody can beat our army."

The British military forces recruited officers from the educated upper and middle classes. They sourced the rank and file, the nameless sailors and soldiers, from the working classes and the unemployed. As sailors, they crewed the mighty ships of the Royal Navy. As soldiers, they mounted the gangplanks of the vessels that took them from English shores to the farthest reaches of the empire. They raised these forces throughout the British Isles from various backgrounds and rural and urban environments.

Joseph Irwin Rutherford, the son of Irish immigrants and a shipyard worker, was eager to join the Army in October 1899, as were most of his marras. He was an example of the working-class upbringing of those who entered the lower ranks of the British Army of the day. On the 24th of November 1881, Joe was born in a town called Felling, between Gateshead and Jarrow, on the south side of the River Tyne in County Durham, North East England. He was a slight but sturdy, good-looking, young Geordie man of Irish descent, 5 foot 5 ½ inches tall, with black hair and a thick walrus-style moustache typical of most men in England then. Despite the harsh world in which he had grown up, he had permanent good humour and was a passionate raconteur.

"Aye, I'm just a working bloke on Tyneside," said Joe to his father and brothers at their local pub. "I've been keeping up with what's happening in the British Empire. I enjoy reading about the exploits of the brave men of the British Army, and I should be with them. But I can't now since my family says they still need me here."

"Aye, that we do," said Joe's father, Thomas. "Why do you need to read? As you say, you're a working laddie. So you need your arms and hands, not your head."

"Leave him, Da," said Joe's elder brother, William. "One of us should know what's happening in the wider world."

Joe and his family were the product of two consequential circumstances that had started in the early eighteenth Century and reached their climaxes in the mid-nineteenth Century in Great Britain: the Irish famine and migrations, known as the Irish Catastrophe, and the great British Industrial Revolution.

During the Irish Catastrophe between 1845 and 1849, one million people died, and a million more emigrated from Ireland. [4] The island's population fell by between 20% and 25%. [5] A census taken in 1841 recorded a population of 8,175,124. The census in 1851 after the famine counted 6,552,385, a drop of over 1.5 million in 10 years. [6] Of those emigrating, the majority travelled the scant distance across the Irish Sea to England and Scotland. Others went abroad to Canada, the USA or Australasia for a better life.

The Industrial Revolution fuelled rapid growth in specific regions of Britain, including the North East. County Durham included industrialized Gateshead, Jarrow, South Shields and Sunderland. On the other side of the Tyne were the industrial powerhouses of Newcastle upon Tyne, Wallsend and North Shields in County Northumberland. Rapid growth in the region occurred through the surge in coal mining, producing the fuel needed for the steam engines of the machines, railways, and modern steam-powered ships that drove the Empire's expansion. The engines furnished the means to transport goods from the industrial centres or the colonies to wherever needed. Coal was the only fuel of the nineteenth-century industrial world, leading to a twentyfold increase in coal production. By 1848, British coal production was two-thirds of the world's total. By the 1850s, the Northeast was the leading coal-producing centre in the world, with Newcastle, Jarrow, and Gateshead being the heartland of that industry. The number of miners doubled between 1840 and 1880. The mines used most of the working population of County Durham in the mid-nineteenth Century, with many pit villages founded throughout the County. The remaining workers were in such budding heavy industries as shipbuilding.

Joe's family was typical of the immigrant families of Tyneside. His father, Thomas James Rutherford, was born in 1849 in Cookstown, County Tyrone, in Northern Ireland, a descendant of the 17th-century plantations of Lowland Scots. His mother, Susannah Irwin, was born in 1850 and came from County Armagh. They married in July 1869 in Cookstown and soon emigrated. Upon arriving in County Durham, Thomas found a job in the pits since miners were in demand. In 1871, Thomas and Susannah lived at 171 Heworth Lane in Felling with their one-year-old first child, William. After William was George, Mary Ann, Margaret, Sarah Jane, Joseph Irwin, Thomas James, Susannah Balance, Eleanor and Elizabeth. Joe grew up as an Irish child in this sizeable family within an Irish immigrant community and had an Irish accent. But he and the other Irish-descended children of Tyneside assimilated Tyneside's local Geordie dialect through intermingling with the Geordie children at school.

Like most working-class people in the second half of the nineteenth Century, Joe's family lived in a rented terraced house, a so-called 'two up, two down,' or two bedrooms upstairs and two reception rooms downstairs. There was no bathroom, so they bathed in big metal tubs in the kitchen or backyard once a month. The outside lavatory was at the bottom of the yard - more convenient than the shared toilets of more impoverished urban families but inconvenient enough in winter.

The poverty-ridden areas of England were far, far worse. Hideous slums, acres full of crannies of obscure misery, comprised an enormous part of the cities of Britain. Thirty or more lodgers might live in a single room in once-grand houses. Many people couldn't afford the rent demanded, so they sublet space in their rented rooms to lodgers to cover the shortfall, the tenants paying between tuppence and fourpence a day. [7]

"Aye, we were well off compared to other marras," said Joe to his family many years later. "I went to school long enough to learn to read and write and add and subtract numbers," said Joe about his childhood. "My teachers said I was doing well, and I liked it. But we had to leave school and look for jobs from age ten to support the family. I worked as a coal miner with other children in the mines. They hired us to remove coal from the tightest passages as hurriers. This job was one of the toughest for anybody, let alone a child, to do. They equipped us hurriers with a wide leather gurl belt[8] with a swivel chain attached. After harnessing yourself into this, you attached the free end of the chain to a sled. Then, you made your way through the tightest passages of the mine. They were so small no full-grown man could fit, so they used us, boys. Or, I worked at the major coal face, watching out for myself among the older miners as these tough men threw the chunks and slabs of coal into my sled. Then, I scrambled and crawled back to the surface, pulling my load many times during a 12-hour shift. If I was lucky, I might get an even younger child to act as my thruster, pushing the sled while I pulled. And danger waits around every corner in that horrible work—quakes, rock falls, explosions. When I got home knackered, I could do nothing but sleep. But when two of my closest marras died in rock falls, I realized life as a coal miner could be short. So I looked for other, safer, work."

Along with coal mining, shipbuilding was one of the region's most important industries. By 1890, Britain had built ninety percent of the world's ships, dominating the world's shipping markets. The shipbuilders along the River Tyne had become its primary industry and work provider. The biggest shipbuilder in Jarrow was Palmers Shipbuilding and Iron Company, established by Charles Palmer and his brother George in 1852. By the mid-nineteenth Century, the British industry was booming, and labour was becoming scarce. Britain couldn't find enough workers for the expanding factories. So that was where the starving Irish came in, migrating to Tyneside's labour-hungry factories and yards. By the 1890s, Palmers had a complete order book and enough labourers.

"So, I escaped the dangerous coal mining work and found a job at Palmer's as a boy labourer," said Joe. "I later graduated to a full worker by moving to the Hawthorn Leslie Shipyard in Hebburn near Jarrow. Hawthorn Leslie was small compared to Palmers but still an important shipbuilder. They created

Hawthorn Leslie & Company from the merger of a shipbuilder, A. Leslie and Company, with a locomotive manufacturing company, R. and W. Hawthorn."

"At 13, I was helping the shipbuilders in their everyday tasks, positioning steel sheets and welding, for example. I worked long and hard but out in the open air. I enjoyed the company of men and learned the trade from them."

Joe was earning a wage and contributing to his family's upkeep. He dreamed of one day sailing to the far corners of the British Empire on one of the same ships he was helping to build. In the intervening years, Joe worked long hours but had developed his reading skills in the few hours he wasn't working, often by candlelight in the evening. He was an exception among his marras and family since he enjoyed reading and learning. He collected any print matter he could find to feed his curiosity. Joe had followed the war's end in Sudan when the Anglo-Egyptian Army, under its commander Sirdar Herbert Kitchener, defeated the Mahdists. He learned of many of the leading celebrities of the Royal Navy and British Army, and he followed their exploits. And he was reading the news of rising tensions in China and South Africa at the close of the Nineteenth Century. The newspapers in 1899 said that war was inevitable in both faraway places. But Joe couldn't enlist and followed events through the papers instead.

South African Highveld—Introducing Deneys Reitz

At the same time, a young Boer of Joe's age surveyed the endless grassy plains below him in South Africa before remounting his horse and continuing his journey. He had climbed the road to the top of a small group of hills eroded by the searing heat and powerful thunderstorms of the South African Highveld summers.

It was spring, and the shrubs were bursting with glistening young leaves and scattered blossoms under an azure sky. But since the rains hadn't started, the grasses that covered the plains were still in their golden winter colours. In the distance, he could see meandering lines of green riverbeds lined with evergreen trees and shrubs, splitting the flaxen plain as it faded into the horizon. He had observed this intoxicating scene often enough in his childhood, and to him, it was still every bit as enchanting as an ocean with its rolling waves. As a child, he had experienced the sea with his family at Plettenberg Bay and Capetown in the Cape Colony. But this golden plain was typical of the land of his birth, and he wondered when he might see the oceans of the Cape Colony again.

Commandos, organized groups of Boer fighters, had joined him along the way. Together, they were several scores, a loose gathering of fighting-age farmers called to action, mounted, armed and ready for war. Boer fighters didn't wear uniforms as regular armies do, wearing their working and hunting clothes in shades of brown instead.

These commandos had various destinations. One was heading northwest towards the South African Republic (SAR) and Mafeking on the British Bechuanaland border. Others rode to Winburg, turning east through the northeastern Orange Free State to Natal. Yet more commandos were heading from Bloemfontein to the Western Free State border with the Cape Colony near Kimberley, the diamond mining town and British garrison. Still, others, including Deneys, were aiming for Pretoria, the capital of the SAR. The commandos had a singular purpose: to protect their republics from the British preparing for war on their borders.

That evening, they camped at the side of the road and constructed a protective kraal for their horses out of branches with vicious-looking thorns. Such kraals protect against leopards, lions, and other unwanted predators in the bush. Then they pitched their tents, lit their fires and settled in for the evening. They roasted springbok, killed that day, on spits, meat being the primary diet of the Afrikander[9] Boers.

Deneys made new friends on this excursion, others he already knew. Most of the men knew of his father, and they talked and sang around the fire late into the night. When questioned by his comrades, he described his childhood as the son of a famous man.

"Tell us more about yourself, Deneys," asked one.

"What do you want to know?" asked Deneys, a slim man with a friendly, clean face and just the slightest hint of a beard running from his sideburns to under his chin.

"My full name is Deneys Reitz, and I was born on the 3rd of April 1882 in Bloemfontein. My father, Francis William Reitz, was a lawyer, a Member of Parliament of the Cape Colony and the fifth president of the Orange Free State. He was born in Swellendam in the Cape, and my grandfather was born in Capetown. Our ancestors were German immigrants but had assimilated the Dutch language and culture. Our family has five sons, two older and two younger than me, and we grew up in this wild paradise. My brothers and I learned to ride, shoot and swim very early. And we often escaped the town for the game-rich bush with our father and uncles for weeks, hunting, fishing and camping, only returning home when we became bored with this carefree temporary existence."

"My father took us with him on extensive tours into the outlying areas of the Orange Free State," recalled Deneys. "Besides more hunting and camping, we attended wappenshaws, held by the Boer commandos to honour my father. [10] [11] I consider our small country perfect. We are a peaceful community, hundreds of miles from the sea and the hustle and bustle of Capetown. There are no political parties, and our life here is protected from the outside world's noise. Nor was there any animosity between the Dutch and English, until now, that is."

Deneys noted the nods of recognition and agreement among his companions. They came from the same wild environments of the late-nineteenth-century Orange Free State, but that was where the similarities ended. Unlike the others, Reitz was from an elite family. His hands didn't have the thick callousness his fellow Boers had gained through hard labour on their farms. They were in awe of his family.

"Now there's trouble in the air," said Deneys, becoming stern and turning his voice an octave lower. "President Paul Kruger and Commandant-General Piet Joubert of the South African Republic often came to Bloemfontein on official visits to my father. Sir Henry Loch, Governor of the Cape, and Cecil Rhodes, a big red-faced wealthy man who cracked jokes with us boys, visited my father too. They were trying to prevent the Orange Free State Republic from allying with the South African Republic. They failed, though. President Kruger crafted a treaty with the Free State to stand by the South African Republic if war with England started."

Interest grew around the fire, with wonder and admiration because Deneys and his father had met and conversed with such famous men. They revered their President Kruger, whom they called Uncle or 'Oom,' while mentioning Cecil Rhodes provoked scorn and anger. While Prime Minister of the Cape Colony, he had been the wealthy instigator and backer of the failed Jameson Raid. He was a staunch Briton, a proponent of expanding the empire from the Cape to Cairo. Most Boers detested and mistrusted him.

"That man's a thief," said an older man. "A bloody troublemaker. We must get rid of this damned English!" Everyone agreed with him and cheered his comments.

"In 1895, my father's health failed, and he resigned," said Deneys. "So, my family went to live in Claremont, a cramped suburb of Capetown. While in the Cape, the Jameson Raid took place near Johannesburg. On our return to Bloemfontein, we found that tension had arisen between the English and the Dutch."

There were a few questions on the Jameson Raid, so Deneys explained in more detail. "The Jameson Raid was a bumbled incursion outside Johannesburg over the New Year's weekend of 1895 to 1896. British colonial statesman Leander Starr Jameson and his mercenaries attempted to trigger an uprising of foreign workers, known as Uitlanders in Dutch in the South African Republic, also called the Transvaal by the British. The raid failed, so no rebellion happened. However, the episode created more animosity between the British and the Boers. Deneys said the animosity between Boers and British caused by the raid spilt over into the Orange Free State, where differences had been previously unknown. People now spoke of 'driving the English into the sea.'"

"When my father recovered, he moved to the Transvaal and became Secretary of State under President Paul Kruger. By July 1899, circumstances had become so grave, and since the war with England by then appeared inevitable, my father ordered the family to join him in Pretoria. I've just returned to Bloemfontein with my brother for a brief visit. Having said goodbye to our home city, we left-behind the peace of our past life to face what?"

At seventeen, he was hurtling towards the growing turbulence on the republics' borders in those troubled times. With this thought in mind, he stared into the flames of their campfire and fell into a pensive silence, pondering his immediate future while others related their stories around him until late.

"We will push them back into the sea," said one of the Boers at the back of the assembled crowd.

"That we will," called another. "The British have no business in our republics."

"Oom Kruger will see to that," said another.

Such angry sentiments swept through the commandos, affecting those assembled there that evening and the many others around the Republics heading off to war.

At sunrise, they continued their determined journey across the plain. This vast, flat, grassy expanse at the southern end of the African continent sits a mile above sea level on the Highveld, a high, flat plateau extending over most of the Boer Republics. Clouds always gather in October over the Highveld, signalling the start of the rainy, summer growing season. But in 1899, the spring clouds coincided with the clouds of war. So, the usually joyous and promising time of year took on an ominous atmosphere for the Boers that year instead.

~

London—Introducing Winston Churchill

At the same time, twenty-five-year-old Winston Churchill rushed from one appointment to another in London, preparing for his trip to South Africa. His decision to join the dash to yet another British colonial war in the making resulted from a disappointing political defeat. Churchill's utmost ambition was to follow in his father Randolph's footsteps as a member of Britain's parliament. Robert Ascroft had invited Churchill to be the second Conservative Party candidate in his Oldham constituency, his first opportunity to begin a political career in parliament. But Ascroft's sudden death forced a double by-election with Churchill as one of two Conservative candidates. Amid a national trend against the Conservatives, they lost to the Liberals, who won both seats in July 1899.

Churchill looked around for something else to exercise his restless mind when he lost the election. He was forever impatient and needed yet another theatre of action. Churchill was no stranger to far-flung conflicts. In 1895, he travelled to Cuba to see the Spanish fight the Cuban guerrillas. There, someone shot at him on his twenty-first birthday. In 1897, he fought under the command of General Jeffery of the second brigade operating in Malakand, in the frontier region of India. He published an account of the Siege of Malakand in December 1900 as *The Story of the Malakand Field Force*, for which he received £600 (£95 000 today). Churchill wrote articles for *The Pioneer* and *The Daily Telegraph* during the campaign. His battle accounts earned £5 (£800 today) per column from *The Daily Telegraph*.

Transferred to Egypt in 1898, he visited Luxor before attaching to the 21st Lancers serving in Sudan under Major-General Horatio Herbert Kitchener, the Sirdar or British Commander-in-Chief of the British-controlled Egyptian Army. Churchill took part in a famous British cavalry charge on the 2nd of

September 1898 at the Battle of Omdurman commanded by General Kitchener. By October 1898, Churchill returned to Britain and began his two-volume work, *The River War*. This extensive work, published in 1899, is an account of the reconquest of Sudan and revenge for General Charles George Gordon's horrible death at the hands of the Mahdi warriors in 1885.

In September 1899, the war in South Africa was imminent and high in the British public's awareness. So, by mid-month, he arranged a deal with *The Morning Post* and was busy preparing for his departure to Capetown. He was to receive a generous £250 (£39,000 today) a month, plus expenses for a four-month assignment, and it was too good to refuse. Once more, it filled the young Churchill with anticipation. So, early in October, he visited Colonial Secretary Joseph Chamberlain.

"Hello, Sir. So good to see you again. I'm off to South Africa to cover the war this time," said Winston.

"My dear Winston, will you ever stop your travels?" asked Secretary Chamberlain. "Ah well, you've never been one to sit still, have you?"

"I wonder whether you could write a letter of introduction for me," asked Churchill.

"I will, with pleasure," said the Secretary as he scribbled on a sheet of his official paper to High Commissioner and Cape Colony Governor Alfred Milner. He recommended Winston as "the son of my old friend, Sir Randolph Churchill."

"Now look after yourself," said Secretary Chamberlain as Winston left. "Don't let one of those Boers shoot you."

"Thank you, Sir," said Winston with a grin. "I'll endeavour to avoid their bullets!"

Churchill had booked to sail on the *RMS Dunnottar* on the 14th of October 1899, bound for Capetown and hoping the war wouldn't start without him. With the letter, he could now take care of the rest of his last-minute arrangements.[12]

Jarrow—Serious Discussions at the Rolling Mill Pub

Back on Tyneside in early October, Joe attended a parade of the 1st Battalion of the Durham Light Infantry (1/DLI) in Newcastle. They were marching off at the start of their journey to South Africa to prepare for war, and it stirred a tiny, glowing ember in him into a bright flame. He overheard people in his vicinity saying the British Army had notified the 1/DLI that they were heading to South Africa early in September. They scheduled the Durhams to sail from Southampton on the 24th of October. After that, Joe followed their progress and developments in the colonies by reading everything he could find about South Africa.

Voyages of British troops posted daily in *The London Times* included the exact number of officers and men leaving and often the names of the officers. In October and November 1899 alone, two hundred and fifty military sailings left a dozen British Empire ports across the globe. More left overseas ports such as Houston, Texas, New Orleans, Italy and Spain with supplies. They carried vast quantities of men, horses, mules, weapons, cannons and other munitions. More transported wagons, steam traction engines, hospital equipment, tents, clothing and bedding. They brought food supplies for men and animals, including at least four-and-a-half million pounds of tinned meat from the United States. These ships had Capetown, Durban, or Lourenço Marques in Portuguese Mozambique as their destinations. An absolute avalanche of British and colonial forces and material descended on the tip of Africa to fight the defiant Boers. And that was just the beginning.

Joe, his father Thomas and his brothers William and George met on Saturday night in the Rolling Mill Pub on Western Road after a hard day's labour at the end of the week.

"I'm getting too old for this heavy work, boys," said Joe's father.

Thomas had arrived in Jarrow from Ireland in his early twenties and had adopted Geordie as his daily language. Although still active and very strong at fifty-one, he was approaching the end of his working usefulness and feeling the effects of thirty years of arduous labour and coal dust, visible deep in the creases and pores of his weathered face. His sons had grown up speaking Geordie. William was the first-born in England in Heworth nearby, now thirty. George, also born in Heworth, was 28. Joseph, the youngest of the boys, born in Felling, was almost 18 but had eight years of hard labour behind him.

"Aye, Da, it's hard work for an old man," said William.

"I didn't say I was old, Bill," said Thomas, somewhat peeved. "I said I'm too old for this heavy work."

"It's hard work for a young gadgie, never mind," said William, refusing to argue with his father.

"I don't mind working, except I find what I'm doing boring," said Joe. "Always the same thing day in and day out. I'm not learning anything new."

"Four pints of the best, Murphy," called out William, "You're lucky to have the work, Joe."

"I know and appreciate it, Bill.

The conversation moved to more pressing matters. "This new war in South Africa, have you heard anything?" asked Bill.

"I don't worry about such faraway matters," grumbled Thomas. "We have far more important affairs to worry about here. Where do we get our next meal from, for example?"

"Aye, I know, Da, but it's an enormous thing, you know," said Bill. "The Queen is sending a howfing number of troops out there, so it must be serious."

"Aye, I've seen that in the newspaper," said George. "It's an enormous thing."

"It is. I read that too," said Joe. "I'm considering signing up with the army."

"Are you mad, laddie? What the hell for?" said Thomas emphatically, leaning forward towards his youngest at the table.

"Da, I'm bored here," said Joe. "It's important for the Queen and our country, and I want to be a part of it. I want to see the world."

"Queen and country?" asked Thomas angrily. He was half-standing now and leaning over the table towards Joe, who was cringing under his stare. "Why support them? Did they support us in Ireland when we needed it? Nee! They let us starve. Why should we support them now?"

"Da, you came from terrible times in Ireland where you say you were starving. And you found work, food and a home here," said Joe. "The British have supported us, so why shouldn't you support them too?"

"Look at how we live, laddie," said Da, waving his arm around him. "Does this look like the Queen cares for us workers?"

"Nee, Da, but look at how you and your parents were living in Ireland — starving, friends and family dying," said Joe. "Are we not living better in England?"

Joe's brothers marvelled at their younger brother's courage to stand up to their Da.

"True, laddie, true," said Da as he sat back in his chair. "You have an excellent point there. But the British Government helped little. We are better off here because the pit and yard owners need our muscle."

"Well, I'd leave if I could," said Bill. "However, I can't any longer. I'm married now and have my wee bairn to look after."

"Aye, me too," said George. "I have my family to look after, too."

"Well, I've read that the Durhams are going to the Natal Colony in South Africa," said Joe. "They will soon fight against the Boers, protecting what belongs to England. I watched their parade in Newcassel the other day, and it was a magnificent sight and stirred me in my gut. If I wait much longer, they will end it."

And with that, the conversation moved elsewhere while Joe pondered in silence. He considered where he was in his life. Joe was approaching eighteen years old. He had a serious relationship with Ruth Anderson, a lovely Geordie girl with long ebony hair and a petite, shapely figure. She was quiet and introverted, and she cared for him. But Joe considered himself too young to settle and marry. He now had an excellent job at the shipbuilding yards and had become a full-time employee. Should he throw that up for an adventure in South Africa? But the army offered a decent job with a good wage and handsome uniforms. And he believed Ruth would wait for him.

So much to consider. For example, the pay of a soldier, at £1 15 shillings per month, he had heard, was low compared to the £4 he was earning in the shipyards. But then, soldiers didn't have to pay for their clothes, lodging or food, and "I take four quid for that alone" was an important consideration. Joe didn't drink that much, enjoying only a pint or two of Brown Ale on a Saturday evening, and he didn't smoke. So he could save his soldier's pay; how else could he spend it?

Then there was the travel and experience. By reading up on the British Empire, Joe knew of the places a British soldier could visit. He dreamt of travelling to far-off places such as Egypt, Sudan, Nigeria and the Gold Coast of Africa, India, Afghanistan, Burma, Borneo, New Guinea and South Africa.

"It appeals to me," he thought out loud.

"You're mad!" yelled his Da. "I won't hear of it."

So, with that last statement, all the talk with his father ended.

Once his father and brothers left, Joe joined his marras at their table.

"Ya'aalreet Mike, Billy, Jack?" Said Joe while pulling up a chair for himself.

"Aye, canny right, Joe," they said in unison.

"Sit with us for an ale," Mike offered, standing to fetch one.

"I don't mind if I do," Joe said, with no interest in an early night and needing to talk to sympathetic ears.

Mike O'Brien had the same pedigree as Joe—born in Jarrow of Irish immigrants. He was an intense, dark, curly-haired young man, amiable and loving, but he enjoyed a good scrap now and then. They had been in school, worked together, and were closest among Joe's marras.

Billy Wilson had red curly hair and a very nervous and retiring disposition. He was tall and thin, a lanky and awkward chap. Billy had Scottish parents but had grown up a Geordie.

Jack Williams was of Welsh descent but was pure Geordie, a blond, stocky, moody and introspective youth with possible Angle blood, who could be belligerent too and was always ready for a scuffle.

The marras had grown up with Joe and ended up in the collieries and shipyards together. They shared similar needs and passions but left the reading to Joe.

The conversation turned to football. Born in Felling, Joe couldn't decide between Gateshead NER and Jarrow F.C. Both talented teams, first in the Tyneside League and later in the Northern League, where Jarrow became champions in 1898–99. But his loyalties, as with so many others on Tyneside, were moving across the river to Newcastle United. The team had just joined the First Division of the Football Association, a more prestigious association than the Northern League. The team was gaining in popularity, even among the Jarrow boys.

"Newcassel United is doing great this year," said Billy. "Thanks to Jack Peddie."

"Aye, true," Joe said. "He's a grand player."

"We should finish better than the thirteenth position we finished at last year," said Jack.

"Aye, and Matt Kingsley will no doubt keep the balls away from the back of the net," said Joe.

Football was the dominant topic of conversation among these working men, and it was more important than work or women. But Joe was fond of Ruth, who was working in the grand house of a Tyneside shipbuilding baron. She was introverted and not very talkative but had a pleasant disposition, and she was an excellent companion for Joe.

"You're seeing that young lady often, Joe," said Mike with a broad grin.

"Not as much as I'd like to, Mike," said Joe. "She doesn't get much free time. And nor do I, so we can't spend much time together."

"What about the South African War, Joe?" asked Jack, keen to change the topic lest the talk of women turned to him.

"It hasn't started yet," said Joe. "But it might happen soon."

"Are they crazy?" asked Billy. "Taking on the British Empire?"

"I'm afraid so," said Joe. "They don't want the British or other foreigners in their countries. But the Army won't back down either."

"You seem to know a lot about it, Joe," said Jack.

"I read a lot about the empire, Jack. I find South Africa interesting and exciting, and I will join up, lads. Are you with me?"

"For sure," they said together.

"We have to sort out those bloody Dutchmen," said Joe. "I must sort out a few affairs with my family and Ruth first. Then I'm out of here."

"We'll be with you, Joe," they said.

Joe hadn't realized at that stage just how complicated the challenges with his family and Ruth would be.

"See you tomorrow afternoon with the other lads for our game of footie," Billy called out as they said their goodbyes outside the pub.

"Aye, that you will, Billy," said Joe, Jack and Mike quickly.

---

1. Geordie is a nickname for a person from the Tyneside area of North East England, and the dialect used by its inhabitants.
2. A marra is a workmate or friend in the Geordie dialect spoken in North East England
3. Young man
4. Ross, David (2002), *Ireland: History of a Nation,* New Lanark: Geddes & Grosset
5. Kinealy, Christine (1994), *This Great Calamity,* Gill & Macmillan
6. Woodham-Smith, Cecil (1991) [1962], *The Great Hunger: Ireland 1845–1849,* Penguin
7. Kellow Chesney, *The Victorian Underworld,* 1970
8. A leather belt with a swivel chain linked to the corf, a strong osier basket, for pulling from 4 to 7 cwt of coal.
9. Archaic term for Afrikaner
10. Deneys Reitz, *Commando: A Boer Journal of the Boer War,* 1929.
11. A wapenshaw, from the Old English for 'weapons show' was originally a gathering and review of troops formerly held in every district in Scotland, and had been adopted by the Boers to be an assembly amongst themselves, usually in the presence of a distinguished visitor
12. Roy Jenkins, *Churchill,* Pan Books, 2001

CHAPTER 2
THE STORM BEGINS
OCTOBER 1899 TO JANUARY 1900

Boer Fighters Assemble on the Borders

Deneys and his brother Joubert made the trip from Bloemfontein to Pretoria filled with apprehension. But since their arrival in Pretoria, the sense of unfolding events had exhilarated them. The Transvaal capital was an armed camp, and there was a busy atmosphere of preparation for the impending war. The businesses were at a standstill. Artillery batteries were riding through the streets regularly, as were commandos from the outlying districts on their way to the Natal border. The surrounding hills echoed with rifle fire as hundreds of men engaged in target practice. Trains left daily, packed with refugees fleeing the approaching storm toward Portuguese Mozambique.

Pioneer Voortrekker leader Marthinus Pretorius established Pretoria in 1855. The burghers named it after his father, Andries Pretorius, a hero of the trailblazing Voortrekkers after his victory over the Zulus in the famous Battle of Blood River. Andries had also negotiated the Sand River Convention of 1852, in which Britain acknowledged the Transvaal's independence. Pretoria became the capital of the South African Republic (ZAR) on the 1st of May 1860.

By 1899, Pretoria was a sprawling city of tree-lined streets, comfortable single-storey, painted tin-roofed homes with lush gardens. New multi-storeyed government buildings surrounded the heart of Pretoria, Church Square. This square was the primary gathering point for Pretoria's government and burghers on meaningful occasions.

Deneys and his brother were not Transvaal burghers, so they didn't call them up for service.

"Let's go to Father immediately and sign up for Natal," said Joubert.

"Yes, boet, let's go!" said Deneys.

But Deneys was seventeen and deemed too young to enrol as a burgher, so they turned him away. He then went to the government buildings, where he met his father, the State Secretary of the South African Republic, and the 75-year-old President Paul Kruger in the corridor. Deneys mentioned to the president that the Field Cornet's office had refused to enrol him for active service.

"Piet Joubert says the English are three to our one," said Oom Kruger. "Will you stand good for three rednecks?" [1]

"If I get close enough, Mr President, I'll be good for three with one shot," Reitz answered,

Kruger gave a throaty chuckle and said, "Well then, Mr Secretary, the boy must go. I fought younger than that."

Kruger then took Deneys to the Commandant-General's office close by, where Piet Joubert handed him a new Mauser carbine and a bandolier of ammunition, with which Deneys returned home pleased and proud. Piet Joubert was a famous Boer politician and administrator who led the Boer forces to defeat the British in the First Anglo-Boer War of 1880–1881. He ran for president of the Transvaal twice but lost to Paul Kruger.

Deneys and his older brother were ready to go, their horses healthy and their saddlebags packed. The authorities called up many country districts, but no

Pretoria commandos had yet left. But on the 29th of September, the first batch from the town was entrained for the Natal border. When Deneys and his brother heard of this, they grabbed their rifles, fetched their horses from the stable, saddled up and rode through the town to the *Raadzaal*, or Council Chamber, to bid their father farewell.

"We're on our way, Father," said Joubert.

"Look after your younger brother, Joubert," said the old man. "Both of you look after each other. I do not want to lose any of my sons to these damned English."

Then, the Reitz brothers boarded the next train to the frontier.

"We became soldiers of the Boer Army by throwing our belongings through a carriage window and clambering on board," said Deneys." [2]

Full of bravado and excitement, they were on their way to fight the British Army. But they had no way of knowing how challenging this fight would become. The journey east across the Highveld landscape was like the trip from Bloemfontein to Pretoria. Due to frequent winter grass fires, they travelled through flat or undulating grasslands devoid of trees. But the natural landscape was changing as the Boers cleared the bush and introduced more and more farms. They planted exotic trees to produce timber or for their gardens. The ancient treeless landscape of the Highveld was transforming, just as it had in Pretoria through its gardens. As they approached the Drakensberg Escarpment, the natural border with Natal, the flatness of the plains gave way to gently rolling hills.

After a tedious, often interrupted 270-mile journey lasting three days, the train reached a small station ten miles from the Natal border, where the burghers detrained. Scores of Boers from the outlying districts had encamped on both sides of the railway line. They dotted the veldt with tents and waggon-laagers everywhere. The wagon-laagers, also known as wagon forts, were mobile fortifications made of carriages arranged into a rectangle, circle or other shape and sometimes joined to each other as an improvised military camp. On the left of the track stood a large marquee tent over which the

Vierkleur [3] flag of the Transvaal flew, designating General Joubert's headquarters. Both he and his wife had arrived early, it being Mrs Joubert's custom to go with her husband into the field.

Although this gathering was much larger than in earlier conflicts with the native tribes or against the British during the First Anglo-Boer War, it was a well-practised and shared event for the Boers, who had faced many battles, preparing them for another fight with the British ahead.

Deneys and his brother off-loaded their horses and moved to their assigned position in the camp. They then removed their saddles, and after building fires and preparing supper, they spent their first night out in the open. For the next ten days, they lazed around, relaxed and were more or less oblivious to the imminent war.

One day, an old native family servant arrived, grinning from ear to ear at having found them. [4] His name was Charley, the grandson of the famous Basuto chief, Moshesh. Charley had long served as a family retainer, first in Bloemfontein, then Pretoria. White people find African names too complicated, so most Africans adopt a European label. He had been on a visit to Umbandine, King of the Swazis. But when Charley learned of the imminent war with the British, he returned to Pretoria. Deneys' father had sent him on to find his sons. Having just done so, from now on, he would cook for them and take care of their horses. He had brought a magnificent roan horse for Deneys from his father, who worried that Deneys' little Basuto pony could wither under his weight.

So, every morning, Charley, the grandson of a great African king, prepared their breakfast and fetched their horses from the grazing kraal—the irony of relationships between natives and whites then. They then rode out to visit nearby camps and laagers to see and experience as much as possible in those exciting times. The brothers surveyed the new contingents arriving daily by rail or on horseback from the local communities. They watched with fascination as long columns of shaggy men on shaggy horses passed. By the end of the week, they estimated that the assembled Boers were 15,000-strong horse riders ready to invade the British Natal Colony. They believed nothing could stop them from reaching the coast of Natal 300 miles farther east.

Boer intelligence informed them that the nearest British troops, 7,000 strong, were at the town of Dundee, Natal, 50 miles away. Farther south, at Ladysmith, there were another 6,000 or 7,000 British soldiers. But with fresh British troops landing every day, the Boers couldn't confidently estimate their enemy's strength.

On the 10th of October, they held a grand parade in honour of President Kruger's birthday. They had mustered the most extensive body of mounted men ever seen in South Africa up to that time.

Deneys was so impressed he turned to his brother and said, "Is it not magnificent to see commando after commando file past the commandant-general? Look how each man carries his hat or rifle according to his ideas of a military salute." [5]

"It brings a lump to my throat and tears to my eyes," said Joubert.

After the march-past, they formed en masse and then galloped up the slopes, cheering, to where Piet Joubert sat on his horse beneath an embroidered banner. He addressed them from the saddle, informing them the SAR Government had sent an ultimatum written by the State Secretary to the British. It gave the British 24 hours to withdraw their troops from the borders of the Republic. Failing this, they would go to war.

"Just look at that great throng of able men standing in their stirrups and shouting themselves hoarse," said Deneys. [6]

"We'll never see another sight like this for as long as we live," said Joubert, tears welling up.

Once the commandant-general and his entourage had pushed through the cheering crowd, the commandos dispersed. The jubilation continued deep into the night, and as the brothers and their recent friends sat around their fires discussing the upcoming struggle, they heard singing and shouting from nearby. It continued until the first light when they mounted their horses and set out for Natal.

~

The War Begins

And so it began. The British didn't respond to the ultimatum, and the Boers declared war on the 11th of October 1899. At dawn on the morning of the following day, the assembled commandos moved off, starting their first march. The Boer army poured through the majestic gorges of the mountains of the Drakensberg Escarpment into the Natal Colony to attack the British.

"As far as we could see, the plain was alive with horsemen, guns and cattle, moving forward to the frontier," said Deneys later with pride. "It was a stirring scene, and I shall never forget riding to war with that great host." [7]

The Highveld ends at the mighty Drakensberg Great Escarpment. This range of mountains encloses the central Southern African plateau, reaching its highest altitude of 6,600 to 9,800 feet. The mountain range stretches 600 miles from the Eastern Cape Province in the south to the far northeast of the Transvaal Republic. It forms the border between the British Crown colony of Basutoland and the Eastern Cape and the boundary between the Natal Colony and the Orange Free State and Transvaal.

As they descended into Natal, the landscape changed from pure grasslands into savanna grasslands, with more scattered trees and many acacias scattered here and there. It was teeming with quarry until the horde arrived. Deneys couldn't restrain his excitement.

The British and Boers began their preparations long before the actual hostilities started. These preparations occurred in the three centres of British presence surrounding the Boer Republics: Kimberley, Ladysmith and Mafeking. Kimberley, the British centre of diamond mining, lies just outside the Orange Free State in the northern Cape Colony. Lying just outside the South African Republic in the Natal Colony, Ladysmith was a significant

British garrison town. Mafeking was the capital and stronghold of the British Bechuanaland Protectorate to the northwest of the Republics.

At the war's outset, the Boer forces numbered 32,000 Transvaal burghers and 22,000 Orange Free State burghers. Six thousand from various other groups, including sympathetic Uitlanders, augmented these. The Cape Rebels contributed another 10,000 fighters. In the probable theatres of war, they amassed 21,000 on the Natal border, ready to attack Ladysmith; 8,000 Boers had gathered at Mafeking, and 6,500 were at Kimberley.

Since they expected the war with the Boers in June 1899, the War Office in Britain sent the first 15,000 troops to the Natal Colony. They assumed this force was strong enough to defend the colony until reinforcements arrived. Britain diverted soldiers returning from India to South Africa; they despatched others from the Mediterranean and elsewhere. The army appointed Lieutenant-General Sir George White to command the force in Natal. British troops numbered a mere 1,624 at Kimberley and 1,500 at Mafeking.

Back in Jarrow, Joe and his marras met as usual at the Rolling Mill Pub on the evening of Saturday, the 14th of October. The news of the South African War was gaining momentum.

"What's going on, Joe?" asked Mike as they settled into their chairs.

"The South African War started yesterday, Mike," said Joe, out of breath from running to the pub. "It started on Thursday. Boer General Koos de la Rey and his commandos attacked the British garrison at a railway siding outside Mafeking. They captured one of our trains that was carrying two guns to Mafeking. The Boers then surrounded our garrison overnight and laid siege to the town."

"That's it?" asked Mike. "So what's the problem? Didn't we fight back and recapture the train?"

"Aye, well, I read that the local people wanted no problems with the Boers, so they blocked any fighting. But Colonel Robert Baden-Powell had expected trouble and had moved into Mafeking beforehand, secretly building up his stores and means of transport within the garrison. He enlisted local men to help fight off any attack. But apart from the train I mentioned, the Boers didn't attack the town. But they surrounded it and blocked anyone from going in or out—the Army calls that a siege."

"That's it?" asked Mike. "That's the start of the war?"

"The army thinks so," said Joe. "They believe the Boers will try the same thing elsewhere. So, they are waiting to see what happens next."

"Howay, man," said Mike. "What are they waiting on, for God's sake?"

"Waiting to see what happens next," said Joe. "The Army knows that many Boers are heading straight for the Natal Colony, and they're expecting big trouble there. They're expecting trouble at Kimberley, where the diamond mine is, too."

"So, now we wait?" asked Jack.

"Aye," said Joe. "We wait."

For the time being, that topic exhausted, they moved on to the usual discussions on football and women. During the week that followed in Jarrow, everything was as usual, and the war wasn't uppermost in most people's minds.

Then, on the following Saturday, the 21st of October, they again met at the pub, where Joe updated them.

"Well, the trouble we were expecting happened this week," Joe began. "Today, the papers reported a battle in Natal at Talana Hill near Glencoe. The Boers fired on our troops from the top of the hill. And the commander, Sir William Penn Symons, was annoyed by the 'impudence' of the Boers attacking before breakfast."

"What the hell does impudence mean?" asked Jack.

"I'm not sure, but I believe it means cheeky," said Joe. "So our forces under the general attacked the Boers on this hilltop. They drove the Boers off the hill and won the battle, but they had many casualties, including the general."

"Is the general dead?" asked Jack.

"No, but seriously injured," said Joe,

The British left behind Symons and those with severe injuries with the Boers as they retired to Ladysmith; he died three days later as a prisoner of war. The papers announced General Penn Symons's death, the war's first high-ranking death. They also covered another battle at Elandslaagte near Ladysmith.

The following Saturday in the pub, Joe described that battle from a page of notes he had brought. "When the Boers invaded Natal," said Joe, "a sizeable force under General Johannes Kock of the Johannesburg Commando made up of Boer, German, French, Dutch, American and Irish foreign volunteers had taken the railway station at Elandslaagte on the 19th of October, 1899. Kock severed the railway line and communications between the main British forces at Ladysmith and a contingent at Dundee through this act. When they informed Lieutenant-General Sir George White of this, he sent his cavalry commander, Major-General John French, to recapture the station. Arriving at dawn on the 21st of October, General French found a large Boer contingent with two field guns. He telegraphed Ladysmith for reinforcements, which arrived by train soon afterwards. He then ordered the British attack."

"With Colonel Ian Hamilton out front, the principal attack moved around to the left of the Boers," said Joe. "Then the sky got dark with thunderclouds, and the storm burst as the British started their attack. The British soldiers couldn't see what was happening in the pouring rain and had to get over a barbed-wire farm fence. Several men got entangled in it and shot before they cut the wire and broke through the fence. They then took over the central section of the Boer position."

"Aye, aye, and then?" asked Billy.

"Well, even though a few small parties of Boers were showing white flags, the Boer general, dressed in a top hat and his Sunday best clothes, led an attack against our troops caught up in that fence. But our boys pulled themselves together. They charged again, led by a bugler of the Manchesters and a pipe major of the Gordons. They killed the Boer general, so we got ours back for General Symons."

"Good and not so good," said Jack. "What then?"

"As the rest of the Boers mounted their horses and tried to escape, two full squadrons of British cavalry charged and slaughtered many with lances and sabres," said Joe. "It was a good old cavalry charge with the traditional cavalry weapons. A nasty business, but we won that battle."

"Well, that sounds better," said Mike. "Did we lose any men?"

"Aye," said Joe. "We did. The report said we suffered 55 dead and 205 injured in the fighting."

"Lances and sabres!" said Jack. "A bloodbath?"

"Aye," said Joe. "That it was, they say. The cavalry lance is a 9-foot-long pole with a long metal spike at its end, and it's a lethal weapon at close quarters, especially when used on men on foot from a horse. But then the Boers were using their Mausers, so I guess we were even?"

"Tell me, Joe," said Mike. "Why does a Boer general wear his Sunday clothes and a top hat into battle? Sounds crazy to me!"

"Aye, it does," said Joe. "That it does. Maybe he knew he was about to die and wanted to look his best?" To which the table exploded into a loud chorus of laughs.

The following Saturday, the 4th of November, the marras met at the pub to listen to events of the last week.

"It's not positive news this week," said Joe. "Winston Churchill described these events in the *Morning Post*. He wrote in his words that the 'swift flame of war ran in a few days around the entire circle of the Republican frontiers.'

He described a battle at Tuli in the north, and in the west, King Khama III of Bechuanaland's territories under our protection feared invasion by the Boers."

"What's a skirmish?" asked Jack.

"Just a fight," said Joe, "Not a full-scale battle."

"I like that swift flame of war, as he described it," said Mike. "He sure has a way with words. I'll give him that."

"Aye, he does," said Joe. "Churchill wrote that the Boers had surrounded Mafeking, isolated and defending itself against continual attack. And its rebel burghers have surrendered Vryburg, south of Mafeking, to the Boers."

"Does this nasty news ever end?" asked Mike.

"No," said Joe, "Churchill said Kimberley is quiet, but they armed the southern frontier, expecting an attack at any moment. And he wrote that it's on the eastern frontier that the Boers have concentrated their greatest energies, and he said they had gone Nap to risk everything on Natal."

"What the shite is Nap?" asked Billy. "I understand so little of what that haughty man says."

"I don't know for sure either," said Joe. "I believe it has something to do with a card game. Churchill said this Natal border helps an invader. He explained the Boers could enter what he called the long tongue of plain running up into the mountains from both sides. The Boers could block communications with the garrisons, making a British retreat difficult. Should the British drive the Boers back into their own country, they only needed to retreat into the mountains where they could await the British at Laing's Nek Pass, the site of a battle during the 1st Anglo-Boer War. Churchill noted that the Boer leaders had gathered their largest contingent against the British in Natal. And that's where most of our troops are concentrating."

"That sounds highfalutin," said Mike. "I understand it, as they are beating us up everywhere!"

"Aye," said Joe. "That's what he is saying. On the 2nd of November, the Siege of Ladysmith began as expected, with Lieutenant-General Sir George White and his men trapped along with the townsfolk. Major-General French and his Chief of Staff, Major Douglas Haig, escaped east on the last bullet-riddled train to leave."

But that wasn't the end. Trouble started at Kimberley on the 14th of October. The Siege of Kimberley only began the week after the Siege of Ladysmith on the 6th of November. Joe recalled what he had read on the following Saturday at the pub.

"Mr. Cecil John Rhodes, who made most of his fortune in Kimberley and still owns most of the diamond mine," he began, "entered the town at the start of the siege, but he wasn't welcome because of his involvement in the Jameson Raid. He was one of the main champions of that conflict, so a real troublemaker."

"Well, at least he isn't on their side," said Jack.

"Aye, true," said Joe. "He doesn't get along with our military either. Rhodes always argues with them, but he is still necessary to the town's defence since he owns everything, including the workshops."

"The Boers shelled Kimberley with their best guns to force the garrison to surrender. In return, his engineers built a cannon called Long Cecil and used it against the Boers. So the Boers soon replied with a much larger French gun called Long Tom, manufactured by Schneider et Cie in Le Creusot, France. The barrel was 14 feet long and weighed 49 hundred pounds (cwt). Its carriage weighed 59 cwt and needed twenty oxen to pull the gun over the hard soil. Long Tom frightened the Kimberley residents so much that many took shelter in the mine.

"So, by the 6th of November, the war is three weeks old," said Joe. "The Boers have the upper hand. The papers are saying it's hugely embarrassing for the British High Command. The Boers raised 70,000 armed and mounted men to protect their Republics, and they have now surrounded three major British garrisons on their borders."

"This is a right bloody disaster," said Mike. "How can we allow a bunch of farmers to embarrass the British Empire?"

"Aye," said Joe. "You're right. They are fighting and beating the world's most powerful military force head-on with simple weapons and no military discipline. The papers say there can only be one outcome of this reckless action, and they should expect nothing less than a colossal British response to save the British Empire's reputation."

"Howay," called the others. "Who will sort this mess out?"

General Buller and Winston Churchill Arrive at Capetown

The *Dunnottar Castle* arrived in Capetown late in November 1899 with General Sir Redvers Buller and Winston Churchill onboard. With General George White besieged in Ladysmith, the British High Command put Buller in charge of this first relief campaign. An aristocrat from Devon, Buller was a seasoned veteran of the Second Opium War in China, the Canadian Red River Expedition of 1870 and the 1873–1874 Ashanti campaign in West Africa. In South Africa, he was in the 9th Cape Frontier War in 1878, the Anglo-Zulu War, and the First Anglo-Boer War of 1881. Buller went to Sudan in 1882 to command an infantry brigade. He fought at the battles of El Teb and Tamai and led the expedition to relieve Major-General Charles George Gordon in 1885, arriving in Khartoum too late to save the general. And now, at the end of October 1899, he must defeat the Boers in South Africa and restore British pride.

The following day, General Buller left the ship. Sir Frederick Forestier-Walker, General Officer Commanding (GOC) Cape Colony in command of Lines of Communication, South Africa Field Force, and acting as lieutenant-general, and his staff came to meet him. The sailors had decked the ship out in bunting, and a guard of honour of the Duke of Edinburgh's Volunteers lined the quay. A mounted escort accompanied the carriage, and an enormous crowd gathered outside the dockyards.

On the stroke of nine o'clock, General Buller stepped onto the gangway. He was a fine specimen of a British general, in full-dress uniform, his large walrus moustache quivering in the wind and his chest festooned with medals and orders. A large gathering of *Dunnottar Castle* crew gave three hearty cheers as he disembarked. Photographers arrived with their cameras and even a cinematograph. The guard presented arms, and the harbour guns thundered a salute. Then, the carriage drove into town through streets lined with cheering citizens waving flags. They celebrated Sir Redvers Buller's return to South Africa, where he had begun his distinguished military reputation and won his Victoria Cross during the Transvaal War twenty years earlier.

By this stage of the war, everyone tuned into the events building on the borders of the Boer Republics. They had waged several battles, won or lost. Mafeking and Ladysmith were under siege, and Kimberley was near to falling. The British citizens of the Cape Colony and the Empire's soldiers were full of anticipation of what the British Government should do next. Rumours ran amok. Theories from total defeat to master strokes of bravery and victory were circulating the streets of Capetown. The citizens assembled in droves for each ship that arrived. They embraced any opportunity to celebrate. So it was no surprise they received General Redvers Buller with great jubilation and honour. An established British war hero, he was to command a growing military force in Natal to chase the Boers out of that colony. Upon his arrival, they paraded him and his staff through the streets of Capetown with a local military escort to the sounds of military bands. While the parades marched through town, the disembarking troops prepared to leave for Kimberley and Mafeking. The Natal contingents continued their sea journey around the Cape of Good Hope and along the southeast coast to Durban. Those heading to the Republics continued by train through the interior.

Winston Churchill stayed for two days at the luxurious Mount Nelson Hotel in Capetown with his officer brother Jack, who was commissioned into the Queen's Own Oxfordshire Hussars in 1898 and signed up with the South African Light Horse. Winston then made haste to the central train station for his 1st Class trip to Natal—a ship journey would have taken too long for his impatience. Or was it the monotony of another sea tour or the curiosity of experiencing the South African interior? His trip took a few days by train to the eastern Cape Colony town of East London and another short sea voyage to Durban, where he immediately settled into work and adventure.

Winston Churchill and the Armoured Train Incident

As was his wont, Churchill was everywhere in the Natal Colony. He planned to experience as much of this war as he could. And he wanted to meet and engage with every officer, soldier, or other person of knowledge and influence he could find. Churchill, the correspondent, needed to gather intelligence and the ambience of the war encounters for his writings. In one incident involving a British armoured train early in the war, he got more than he had bargained for. Winston Churchill was to capitalize on the event as a public hero, and the story became one of the more exciting episodes of that early and darkest phase of the conflict heard by the British public.

The incurable adventurer Churchill occasionally caught a lift with an armoured train as it carried out its patrols deeper into the Natal hinterland and enemy territory. He noted the many defects in its construction and the dangers of such a "forlorn military machine," as he called it. These defects were so apparent that the soldiers nicknamed the train "Wilson's death trap" (Wilson presumably being the locomotive driver).

On Tuesday, the 14th of November 1899, the mounted infantry patrols reported that the Boers were approaching Estcourt from Weenen and Colenso. They believed that a sizeable Boer force was moving or was preparing to go southwards to attack Estcourt and Pietermaritzburg. They ordered the Estcourt armoured train to survey the line towards Chieveley farther up the rails.

The train comprised a locomotive, five cars, one small gun, and one hundred and twenty men. There was an ordinary truck in which they positioned a seven-pounder muzzle-loading cannon crewed by sailors, as was customary in this war. They came from HMS *Tartar*, a Torpedo Cruiser. Then came an armoured car fitted with loopholes containing three sections of a company of the Dublin Fusiliers. Two more armoured cars included another part of the Fusilier Company, the Durham Light Infantry, and a small civilian rail breakdown gang. And there was another truck carrying tools and materials for repairs.

Armoured trains saw use during the Nineteenth Century in the American Civil War, the Franco-Prussian War and the First Anglo-Boer War. They used the large-scale South African rail network in the Second Anglo-Boer War. Besides the horse, trains were the most effective means of conveying men and artillery along the main railway corridors connecting the major cities of South Africa. They were in constant use.

The train left at 5:30 A.M. the following day, travelling towards Colenso. But near Frere station, they encountered Boer patrols and exchanged fire. The train then reversed its direction to escape a large patrol of one hundred Boers. But after a short while, a Boer cannon on a hill fired on the train and hit it, damaging and derailing it, its cars rolling and scattered. The soldiers fought the Boers from under the overturned cars but surrendered when the odds looked too overwhelming. The Boers took the entire contingent prisoner.

Winston Churchill's arrest so early in the war was a significant incident and caused much active discussion at home and among the Boers. On the 15th of November 1899, Winston Churchill, 26, was a POW two weeks after arriving in South Africa, but not an ordinary one. He came from an elite family. And the Boers knew in him they had a valuable bargaining chip.

Years later, confusion arose over who his original captor was. Many, and Churchill himself, claimed it was the notorious and famed General Louis

Botha. But Louis Botha wasn't there, so was Jaap Botha, a member of the Commandos who captured him? Others claimed it was one Rolf de la Rey.

Once the dust had settled, they counted fifty-six survivors of the incident, now prisoners of war in the hands of the Boers. They were only the second group of British at war, the first being a small group from Kraipan. At this stage of the war, the Boers were ill-prepared to accommodate PoWs.

So Churchill and his fellows set off to the west, destination unknown. "We were a sorry gang of dirty, tramping prisoners, but yesterday, the soldiers of the Queen," bemoaned Churchill, "while the fierce old farmers cantered their ponies around the veldt or closed around the column, looking at us from time to time with irritating disdain and a still more irritating pity."

They marched across the bridge over the Tugela River and followed the road until they entered the hills through which they journeyed for several hours. They waded across the dongas[8], which torrential rains had turned into raging streams. Here and there, they met parties of Boers.

"There was much handshaking and patting on the back between the newcomers and our escort," recalled Churchill. "Once, they halted at a field hospital, a dozen tents and wagons with enormous red-cross flags, tucked away in a deep hollow."

They passed through Pieters without a check and on to Nelthorpe, where they approached the Dutch lines of investment around Ladysmith. A further march of half an hour brought them to a very sizeable picket where the Boers ordered them to halt and rest. Two hundred Boers swarmed around in a circle and asked questions of every sort at once.

"They are keen politicians and as curious as children, asking questions of every sort," said Churchill. "What did we think of South Africa? Would we like to go on an armoured train again? How long would the English go on fighting? When would the war end? And when I said, 'when we beat you,' they responded with shouts of laughter."

"Oh no, old chappie, you can never beat us," said one of them. "Look at Mafeking. We have taken Mafeking. You will find Baden-Powell waiting for you at Pretoria. Kimberley, too, will fall this week. Rhodes is trying to escape in a balloon disguised as a fine woman. What about Ladysmith?"

They reached Elandslaagte Station, 19 miles from Ladysmith, where a train awaited them. There were six or seven basic cars for the men and a first-class carriage for the officers and Churchill. Two Boers with rifles locked the doors and sat watching the prisoners.

The journey to Pretoria was slow and took several days. Along the way, they passed Majuba Hill, the site of the crushing British defeat in the First Anglo-Boer War. As they passed Majuba, it was early evening, and the light was fading. Churchill described the sight as "a great dark mountain with memories as sad and gloomy as its appearance." It stands still as a reminder of one of the Empire's worst military surrenders of the Victorian era. The Boers held this defeat over their prisoners as an example of their skill and prowess as fighters.

The trainload of prisoners reached Pretoria by midday. They pulled up in a siding which opened into the town's streets. It had an earth platform on the right side, where a crowd welcomed them.

"There were ugly women with bright parasols, loafers, and ragamuffins; fat burghers too heavy to ride at the front," remembered Churchill. "A lengthy line of untidy, white-helmeted policemen, too—zarps as they called them—lined up, looking like a worn-out constabulary."

As soon as Churchill reached Pretoria, he demanded his release as a press correspondent and a noncombatant. The others captured included soldiers of the Dublin Fusiliers and Durban Light Infantry and 8 or 10 civilians, including a fireman, a telegraphist and several men of the breakdown gang.

According to international practice and the customs of war, the Transvaal Government felt justified in declaring the entire group as combatants. But the Boers had too many prisoners to feed. So, as soon as they established their identity, they released the civilians and kept the military prisoners.

But in Churchill's case, they made an exception. General Joubert had read the emotional accounts of Churchill's conduct in the Natal newspapers. So, he decided that, since Churchill had been present during the fighting, they were treating him as a combatant officer.

They held officers at the State Model School in Pretoria, established in 1893, to train teachers. They interred the men at Waterval, north of Pretoria. On the 11th of October 1899, the school closed its doors because of the outbreak of the war. Then, the Boers held British officers captive in this building.

First, they served breakfast at nine in a stuffy room, with seventy British officer prisoners pressed together in captivity.

"A nasty, uncomfortable meal," recalled Churchill.

The prisoners then spent a dull morning filled with reading, chess or cards and perpetual cigarettes. Then they served luncheon at one, followed by an even longer afternoon, filled with rounders or pacing around the small exercise yard.

Later in the evening, they were allowed by special permission to read the *Volkstem*, "with its budget of lies," grumbled Churchill. *De Volkstem*, or *The People's Voice*, was the first Dutch newspaper of significance in the Transvaal, first published in 1873. It was anti-British to the extreme during both Anglo-Boer Wars. Few of the British POWs could understand the Dutch. They switched on the electric lamps at nightfall, and the courtyard lit up. Then the bell clanged, and they crowded the prisoners again into the oppressive dining hall for the "last tasteless meal of the barren day." Boredom and mediocrity were taking their toll on the British officers, accustomed to finer accommodation.

While Churchill was enduring his captivity, Buller left Capetown for Natal by ship on the 22nd of November to take command of the British forces arriving there. General Redvers Buller, an experienced and decorated soldier, seemed just the man to lead the British troops in Natal against a local Boer army of 21,000 men amassed near Ladysmith.

~

The 1st Canadian Contingent Joins the Boer War

The Dominion of Canada joined the South African war effort with its first contingent—the Royal Canadian Regiment. Their departure from Canada and arrival in South Africa show a different perspective through the eyes of a thirty-year-old Scottish-Canadian soldier.

His name was William Frederick Richard Hart-McHarg. He was descended from Scottish ancestry but was born in the barracks at Kilkenny, Ireland, on February 16, 1869. His father was stationed there with his regiment at the time. In his teen years, he emigrated to British Columbia, Canada, and joined his local reserve regiment. When the South African War started and Canada announced its intention to support the war effort, Hart-McHarg volunteered for the 2nd (Special Service) Battalion of the Royal Canadian Regiment. Unable to get a commissioned rank, he enlisted as a private.

The British High Command accepted Canada's offer of an infantry contingent of one thousand men. It was to be mobilized, equipped and landed at Capetown at the expense of the Dominion Government. The battalion would then be taken over by the Imperial authorities as a regular British regiment during the campaign and eventually returned to Canada. Steps were taken at once to mobilize. Each military district was asked to provide a proportionate number of men. These were raised by voluntary enlistment from the different militia regiments; the permanent corps also provided their quota. Recruitment stations were opened in all the principal towns. The new unit was the 2nd (Special Service) Battalion of the Royal Canadian Regiment of Infantry (RCR), and Lieutenant-Colonel W.D. Otter was given the command. Each company's staff sergeants and a colour sergeant were drawn from the permanent corps.

At the start of the South African War, mobilizing and outfitting the 'Royal Canadians' was immense. [9] Within sixteen days, the Department of Militia was required to recruit, organize, clothe, equip, arm and despatch the First Contingent to South Africa. It was a body of men equivalent to Canada's entire permanent militia. The Department of Militia also had to administer an expenditure equal to one-third of the department's annual budget. Securing suitable transportation to South Africa for forty-one officers, 978 NCOs and men, and seven horses seemed a tall order. The RCR carried the 55-pound Oliver equipment (overcoat, bandolier with 100 rounds, Lee Enfield rifle, 9 pounds, ball pouch with 50 rounds, water bottle, canteen, bayonet, haversack), equipment very hard on the men who damned surgeon J.W. Oliver, serving with the British Army in the Red River Expedition of 1870, who designed it.

The only available vessel of adequate size was the Allan Steamship Line's 425-foot-long SS Sardinian, which required extensive renovation to convert into a troopship. The officers and NCOs were quartered comfortably in staterooms on the main decks. Officers were housed in two per cabin, with separate toilets and mess rooms. Bunks and foldable mess tables had to be constructed on the steerage deck for half the soldiers. The other half were assigned closely-placed hammocks, attached to the bulkhead on the main level, with foldable mess tables beneath. Latrines, washhouses, a galley, a bakehouse, a canteen, two small rifle and two revolver ranges, and stalls for the seven horses were all constructed on the spar deck[10]. Electric lights and ventilation fans were installed throughout the ship, and it was repainted inside and out. All these renovations were made in Montreal and Quebec City quickly.

The mobilization took place in Quebec City. The last group of recruits from the far west reached the Citadel early Sunday morning, the 29th of October 1899. [11]

Hart-McHarg considered the ancient capital of Lower Canada the ideal place to see off the expedition on its journey. Throughout the streets decorated with bunting, "Gaul and Saxon vied with each other to cheer the departing troops." Proudly, he declared they would do their part in deciding who would prevail in South Africa—Boer or Briton. From the ship, they could see that every vantage point had been occupied: the Citadel, housetops, cliffs, Dufferin Terrace and the wharf. He noted that the weather-beaten ramparts of the Citadel, rising majestically above the town and surrounding cliffs, were re-echoing the cheers of the thousands of adoring citizens. A cannon fired a salute, and flags were lowered as the ship moved slowly downstream.

"All these left an impression on the mind not easily eradicated," he said. [12]

And so they were off on their journey from the autumn of Canada across the equator to the midsummer of South Africa. The trip would take thirty days.

On the 29th of November, the cry of "Land Ahead" went up around the ship, and shortly afterwards, the outline of the famous Table Mountain could be seen on the horizon. During the afternoon, they entered Table Bay. The harbour was filled with transports and other vessels, all of which blew their sirens and whistles, welcoming them.

They passed close to one vessel crowded with kilted soldiers, who repeatedly cheered; the cheers just as enthusiastically returned. They learnt, on landing, that they were the 1st Battalion of Gordon Highlanders, a regiment the Royal Canadians would march and fight with later.

The following day, the work of disembarkation took place. They marched out to Green Point Common, headed by the pipers of the Capetown Highlanders, through streets of enthusiastically cheering people.

The Dutch used the area of Green Point as cattle grazing pasture. After the British annexed the Cape in 1806, it became a common pasture, where they began holding horse races, and the area developed as one of Capetown's most popular social centres. During the South African War, the military used Green Point Common as an encampment for many transient British troops and Boer POWs.

They had barely pitched their tents and settled themselves when they received orders to entrain the following day for De Aar Junction. Valises and kit bags were all to be left behind, and the only things to be taken were overcoats, a shirt and a pair of socks rolled inside, and what articles could be carried in a haversack.

"We always needed to remember that room must be left in the haversack for one or two days' rations," McHarg pointed out. [13]

They were allowed one Canadian blanket per man, which was taken and packed away separately. These were very poor blankets compared to those of the British soldiers. The valises and kit bags, with all their belongings in them, were piled up in rows and left under an officer's watch. When they returned to the Cape, the Canadian soldiers found that everything had been rifled and most of the articles stolen.

"This was a most disgraceful state of affairs and one that could have been easily avoided," said McHarg [14]

On the 1st of December, they marched again through the principal streets of Capetown. They were met with an even more enthusiastic reception all along the route than they had received the previous day. They then entrained for De Aar in the Northern Cape Colony.

"Sir Alfred Milner, High Commissioner, the busiest of busy men, found time to come down to the station to see us off," said McHarg proudly. [15]

Joe Meets Fred McRae

On a day when a frigid wind and driving rain made life in the Jarrow shipyards a misery, Joe was looking for a sympathetic ear. There were few people with whom Joe could discuss his deliberations or plans, apart from his brothers, father, and marras. But none understood as much as he did, nor could they offer him relevant first-hand war experiences. But Joe discovered that a foreman in the yard, Fred McRae, had been to South Africa as a soldier in 1881 during the 1st Anglo-Boer War. He approached Fred, forty by then, taking shelter from the rain beneath a hull, and asked him to relate his experiences in the army.

"Aalreet, Fred. I'm Joe Rutherford, and I've heard you've been to South Africa?"

"Guid morning, Joe. I've seen you around and known of you for a while. I know your brother Bill. I'm pleased to meet you. Aye, I've been to South Africa. Why do you ask?"

"I'm thinking of joining the Durham Light Infantry and going there," Joe said. "What's it like, and what were your experiences there?"

"I tell you what, Joe. Let's catch up at the Rolling Mill Pub after work, and I'll tell you my story. I need enough time and a pint to ensure a guid chat."

They agreed to meet at the pub. Joe's working day in the shipyards started at 7 A.M. and finished at 5 P.M. They met that night just after 7 P.M. Joe bought two Broons—Newcastle Brown Ales. Then, they sat together in a stall.

"I started in the shipyards when I was 12, at Duthie Shipbuilders in Aberdeen," said Fred, "I worked my way up to junior labourer by the time I left in 1878 to join the Gordon Highlanders."

"I started at 12, too—at Palmers," said Joe.

"My first experience as a fighter with the Gordons was in Afghanistan during the Second Anglo-Afghan War," said Fred. "It was a bloody nasty wee war, but it went well for us."

The British Empire and the Emir of Afghanistan, Sher Ali Khan, fought the Second Anglo-Afghan War from 1878 to 1880. In October 1879, the regiment took part in the Battle of Charasiab, where they captured three hills. Major George White received the Victoria Cross for his role in the action. At the end of August 1880, the regiment was part of the force marching from Kabul to Kandahar. In the Battle of Kandahar on the 1st of September 1880, the Gordons, under General Frederick Roberts, were part of the 1st Brigade. Victorious in battle, the British made him General Baron Roberts of Kandahar.

"They supposed us to return to Scotland after that war. But our battalion commander, Major White, volunteered us to go to South Africa. So off we went to fight in the Transvaal War."

The British were governing the Transvaal then. They fought the First Anglo-Boer War, or the Transvaal War, from the 16th of December 1880 to the 23rd of March 1881.

"We moved around the Transvaal plenty in that war. And we fought three serious battles against the Boers. But the end came at Majuba Hill in the Natal Colony near Volksrust, Transvaal. It was a bloody massacre. They led us in our fine red and blue uniforms to fight the Boers so that the Boer marksmen could see us as colourful targets. And we didn't know what hit us. I was one of the lucky ones who lived to tell the tale."

"Tell me, Fred. What happened there?" asked Joe.

"Well, I don't like even thinking about it, but if you insist, Joe, I will tell you what happened. Our commander was Major-General Sir George Pomeroy Colley, who ordered us to occupy the summit of Majuba on the night of the 26th to 27th of February 1881. I guess he didn't think the hill was scalable by the Boers in an attack, even though we had scaled it. We were 171 men of the 58th Regiment, 141 men of our regiment, the 92nd Gordon Highlanders, and a small naval gunnery brigade from HMS Dido up there. General Colley had brought no artillery up to the summit, nor did he order us to dig in with trenches. I heard later that he expected the Boers to retreat when they saw the British positions on the Nek. But the Boers didn't retreat. They were hell-bent on destroying us and formed storming parties, totalling at least 450 men, maybe more, to attack the hill."

"My God, were you afraid?"

"Not yet, I wasn't. By daybreak at 4:30, our regiment covered the entire perimeter of the summit while a handful of men occupied Gordon's Knoll on the right side of the hill. We had the best position for a battle and enough men, too. And the Boers didn't know we were there until a few of our lads yelled and shook their fists at them."

"Well, at least they didn't show them their buttocks," said Joe, laughing.

"Aye, but it was like a red flag to a bull. Three Boer storming groups of 100 to 200 men each climbed the hill. As the better marksmen, they kept us at bay while other fighters crossed the open ground to attack Gordon's Knoll. At 12:45 midday, the Boers opened up an almighty fire on the exposed mound and captured it. General Colley was in his tent when they told him of the advancing Boers, but at first, he did nothing."

"How the hell could the general do nothing? And what was he doing in his tent, for God's sake?"

"Shock, maybe. We didn't understand it. He was a seasoned officer with a long military career in South Africa, and he played a significant part in the Second Anglo-Afghan War as military secretary and then as private secretary to the governor-general of India, Lord Lytton. I knew him from my time there. But I don't know how much actual battle experience he had."

"For the next hour, the Boers poured over the top of our line, and, avoiding close combat, they shot at us from a distance and picked us off one by one. Bushes and high grass were over the entire hill, something they hadn't trained us to handle, but the Boer fighters used it as cover, crawling from bush to bush and firing at will. They were slaughtering us, screams and moans of agony around us and across the entire summit! And we weren't getting enough of them. I was afraid for my life then. Unable to see the enemy without officers left to lead us, we panicked, many men deserting their posts. Then we saw even more Boers, scores of them, encircling the mountain, so many of our soldiers abandoned their posts and fled helter-skelter from the hill. We Gordons held our ground the longest but lost the battle once we collapsed. The Boers launched another attack, which shattered our crumbling line."

"My God, Fred. How did you survive that?"

"I don't know, Joe. Pure luck, I guess. Then General Colley tried to order a fighting retreat, but the Boer marksmen shot and killed him. The rest of our force fled over the rear slopes of Majuba, where the Boer marksmen, who had by then lined the summit, fired on us. Units of the 15th Hussars and 60th Rifles, who had marched from a support base at Mount Prospect, tried a rearguard rescue, but this failed too and made little impact on the Boer forces. When it was over, the Boers had killed 92 of our men, wounded 134 and captured 59. Among the dead were General Colley and Captain Cornwallis Maude, son of the government minister Cornwallis Maude, 1st Earl de Montalt. We killed 1 Boer fighter and wounded 5! It was a bloody tragedy! And an enormous blow for the British Army and Empire."

Even though Joe had become hardened to the descriptions of battles and their death tolls through his research, what he had just heard shocked him more. It was a far more detailed description of this famous defeat than most Britons knew, and he had heard it from a witness to the tragedy that had survived.

The Transvaal War was the first conflict since the American Revolution in which anyone had defeated the British. Boer leaders forced them to sign a peace treaty under unfavourable terms in 1883. The Battle of Laing's Nek was the last time a British regiment carried its official regimental colours into battle. Overall, Boer's fighting tactics, involving mobility, marksmanship, and their use of elevated defensive positions, proved far superior to their foes and ahead of the time. The British lost 408 killed and 315 wounded from 1,800 men. This loss compared to the Boers' 41 dead and 47 injured out of 7,000. It was a humbling experience for the British and one they remembered for a long time. Under Prime Minister William Gladstone, the British government understood that any expanded operations in the Transvaal risked significant troop increases. They recognized that the war would be costly, messy and lengthy. They were unwilling to get mired in another distant war, so they ordered a truce. The Boers had won.

Combined with the defeats at Laing's Nek and Schuinshoogte, this third complete defeat of the British at the hands of the Boers at Majuba drove home the strength and prowess of the Boers in the minds of the British. This recognition of the Boers' strengths may have influenced the British military during the Second Anglo-Boer War had they acknowledged it. "Remember Majuba" became a rallying cry. A few British historians claim that this defeat marked the beginning of the decline of the British Empire. Far-fetched? Not everyone agreed with that conclusion. But the British were about to be tested by the Boers in South Africa again.

"So that was my experience with South Africa, Laddie," said Fred. "It wasn't all that bad, and I enjoyed the rest of my time there. But after three years of service in two theatres of war and surviving a few battles, I left the army and returned to the shipyards."

"My God, Fred. What an experience. Did you regret your time there?" asked Joe.

"What? Not on your life, Laddie. Apart from Majuba, it was an impressive experience. I had been a young laddie when I joined up, so I had learned about life and matured. I saw the world beyond Scotland, and it was interesting!"

"Do you think I should go to South Africa and fight in this war, Fred?"

"Yes, why not?" said Fred. "It's a bonny country and different from that which you know. That will be a great education for a laddie of your age. But watch out who you get involved with over there. You don't want the same war experience I had with General Colley, or worse, ending up dead."

"Aye, I agree with that for sure. Oh, and Fred," Joe asked, "do you know this Winston Churchill, who the Boers captured?"

"I know of him, a right-haughty fellow, a British aristocrat in South Africa."

"That's right," said Joe, "Well, he escaped the Boer prison and is back with the British Army."

"Well, that just shows you how stupid those Boers are," said Fred. "They might be excellent horsemen and marksmen, but they can't keep a British upper cruster in jail."

With the beer and the conversation finished, they laughed and called it a night.

"For the morrow soon comes," said Fred.

Joe Visits Ruth

But Joe wasn't ready for sleep just yet. He found his way to the grand house where Ruth worked. She lived in a basement room at the front of the house, with a window opening onto the street. He tapped on the window, and after a few moments, a dishevelled Ruth appeared and opened it.

"Joe, what are you doing here?"

"I want to see and talk to you."

Ruth nodded approval and backed off while Joe dropped through the window feet first into the room. She didn't light a lantern, allowing the feeble light from a nearby gaslight on the sidewalk to illuminate her room. Ruth snuck back into bed and tried to adjust her hair. She was now wide awake and gestured to Joe to sit on the edge of the bed. Joe was dying to tell her about his conversation with Fred.

"You know, Ruthie, Fred agrees I should join the army and see the world before I marry and settle."

"Yes, and? Do you think I want to hear that?"

"I'm sorry, Ruthie, I know you don't, but..."

"... you have a problem," said Ruth, finishing his sentence.

"Aye, that I do. I am fond of you, hinny, and I will find it very hard to leave you. Even if only for a few years."

"A few years? You will go away for a few years?"

"Aye. I couldn't sign up for just a year or two."

"What about your family? Have you spoken to them about this?"

"I have, and my father won't hear of it. He is against this Queen and country; I think his Irish friends poisoned his thinking. But I don't see it that way. And nor do my brothers, and they're supporting me."

"What about your ma?"

"I've said nothing to her. And I don't know whether my Da has spoken to her, and he never does."

"Well, I don't think she'll be happy with it, Joe."

"She has to let me go. I'm old enough. And you, hinny?" asked Joe in a murmur while stroking her arm. Ruth then took drastic measures. She lifted her blanket and invited him to slip under it next to her. She then gave him a long and passionate kiss.

"That's how I feel, my man," she said. He stared into her eyes at length, then enveloped and kissed her again. Take off your clothes, my darling, and warm my body with yours."

Joe couldn't believe his ears but didn't resist her invitation. He ripped off his shirt and trousers and slipped under the blanket beside her naked body. Ruth was Joe's first experience with love. He was floating as he slipped out before dawn to avoid detection. But as Joe headed home to wash and prepare for another working day, he realized he had an even bigger problem. Joe was in love with Ruth, which further compromised his short-term plans.

Black Week

At the start of January 1900, Joe again arrived at the Rolling Mill Pub. This time, a larger group of family and friends had assembled to hear the latest instalment of events in South Africa. The whole of the empire was abuzz with the events unfolding at the bottom end of Africa. He didn't need to pay for his ale that night. This time, he spoke on the Relief of Kimberley—very much on the minds of British and colonial citizens. He started with the losses suffered by Lieutenant-General Paul Methuen, 3rd Baron Methuen. Born at Corsham Court, Wiltshire, in 1846, Methuen had served in the 3rd Anglo-Ashanti War in 1873. He served in Sir Charles Warren's expedition to Bechuanaland in the mid-1880s. In this war, he was the general officer commanding the 1st Division.

Joe took a seat, and a Broon appeared before him.

"Well, Joe, give us the news," said Mike, leaning toward his marra.

"Well, as you must remember," began Joe while checking a slip of paper on which he had scribbled a few notes, "General Methuen moved up the railway line last November under orders to relieve Kimberley. His orders were to move farther north on the line once they relieved Kimberley to do the same at Mafeking."

Someone asked, "What the hell do you mean by relieved, Joe?"

"Relief is a military word for breaking a siege and freeing the people trapped by the enemy," he said. "Relieving Kimberley means freeing it of the enemy. But events didn't go as planned. The Boers stopped the general's attempts to relieve Kimberley at the battles at Belmont first, then at Graspan, Modder River and Magersfontein."

"The Battle of Belmont was on the 23rd of November last year. There, they attacked a Boer position on Belmont Kopje—a kopje is what they call a hill in South Africa. One of the Boer's favourite tactics is digging in on the top of a hill and firing on us from above, as our army experienced in Natal."

"Bloody dirty fighting," called someone.

"Well, that's war," said Joe. "So, Methuen's three brigades of 8,000 men marched on Kimberley. But the Boers had entrenched 2,000 men on Belmont Kopje. So, General Methuen sent the Guards Brigade on a night march to get around the Boers. But because of faulty maps, the Grenadier Guards found themselves in front of the Boer position instead. He ordered the Guards, the 9th Brigade and the Naval Brigade to attack the Boers over open ground, which resulted in 200 casualties!" The audience grimaced at Joe's description of the battle so far.

"What happened then?" asked Mike.

"Well, just before our lads used their bayonets, the Boers galloped off and re-formed at Graspan. The same happened there on the 25th of November when we suffered another 200 casualties."

"What's wrong with our army?" called another from behind.

"Aye, well, what I've read is that the Boer way of fighting surprised them," said Joe. "Somebody else said it. They are using dirty tactics, anything to beat us. And our boys weren't trained for those tactics. But I'm sure they're learning."

"I bloody well hope so," said another. "We can't go on losing!"

"Well, we won the next battle. The Battle of Modder River followed on the 28th of November," said Joe. "There, Lord Methuen forced the Boers, commanded by General Piet Cronje, to retreat to Magersfontein. But again, we suffered massive casualties."

There was a pause while they organized another round of ales. Then, as the group settled again, Joe continued his narrative.

"After the fighting at Modder River and the Boers retreating, our army wheeled around to cross the river by nightfall. And there, Methuen's lads rested from the 1st to the 7th of December. They had expected General Buller to march on Ladysmith in northern Natal. They had hoped these two blows in the Northern Cape and Natal would end the war by Christmas."

"It got worse," he said, looking around at his audience for a reaction. "Much worse! It got so disastrous during the week of the 10th to the 17th of December that they called it Black Week. In that one week, the British Army suffered three terrible defeats by the Boer Republics at the battles of Stormberg and Magersfontein in the Cape Colony and the Battle of Colenso in the Natal Colony. We lost 2,776 men killed, wounded and captured in that one week!"

"I don't believe this," yelled Jack. "What the hell are they doing?"

And the group surrounding the table echoed this sentiment. Their frustration and anger with the news was growing. Joe consulted his notes again.

"On Monday the 11th of December, General Gatacre's night attack into strong Boer defences at Stormberg had failed. Their enemy fighters are experienced and proven horsemen with modern rifles and the right artillery. So Gatacre lost two guns and 700 men, of whom 500 were now prisoners of the Boers."

The group around Joe had become silent and tense, choosing to shake their heads from side to side instead. And Joe continued with the sad news.

"Then Methuen's division of 15,000 frontline troops ran into dug-in Boers on the Magersfontein Heights on the 11th of December. The British artillery barrage warned the Boers of the impending attack led by the Highland Brigade. This brigade comprised the Highland Light Infantry, the Black Watch, the Cameron Highlanders and the Gordon Highlanders."

Billy, being of Scottish descent, breathed an "Aye."

"They had to fight through heavy rains in the darkness. And at dawn, a terrible crossfire caught them," said Joe. "The commander of the Highland Brigade, Major-General Wauchope, became another high-ranking casualty in that fight, costing us another 1,000 men compared to the Boers' 250. The Highland Brigade suffered the worst losses, and this defeat further delayed the relief of Kimberley. But they wiped out the Scandinavian Corps, a Boer ally."

The entire pub had grown quiet since many other tables had been overhearing Joe's story. He then pulled another piece of crumpled paper out of his vest pocket and concluded: "After the British defeat by the Boers at the Battle of Magersfontein, a Private Smith of the Black Watch wrote:

> *'Such was the day for our regiment,*
> *Dread the revenge we will take.*
> *Dearly, we paid for the blunder*
> *A drawing-room General's mistake.*
>
> *Why weren't we told of the trenches?*
> *Why weren't we told of the wire?*
> *Why were we marched up in a column?*
> *May Tommy Atkins enquire....'"* [16]

The entire audience had gone silent. But Joe had one more story to tell: the Battle of Colenso on the 15th of December 1899 in Natal. There was a loud scuffle as the group dispersed to buy another round of Broons. Then Joe continued, checking his notes.

"Although they only knew of his reputation as a great general in England, Sir Redvers Buller was negatively disposed towards the coming battle. On Friday, the 15th of December, he tried to cross the Tugela River. A sortie from Ladysmith might have taken the Boer pickets on Hlangwane Hill, but they also suffered another embarrassing loss. We lost 1,100 men killed and ten artillery guns in that battle. It was a disaster. They ordered a retreat at nightfall even though half the army had not yet engaged the enemy. Lord Roberts' son was among those killed. Buller advised Ladysmith to surrender, but General Sir George White pledged to continue fighting."

General White's promise aroused muted approval from a group left in shock by the stories of Black Week. However, Governor of the Cape Colony Lord

Milner's assessment of the crisis developing in South Africa conveyed to London that they needed 70,000 British troops to win the war. Milner's concern over losses mitigating success on the field had caused a rethink of the conditions in the Transvaal.

The British government changed their mindset after the Black Week disaster. They realized that this Boer War was not to be a comfortable victory or won by Christmas. They made many changes in the military, including more personnel, better mobilization and better modernization to match and surpass the Boer troops.

After Black Week, the government called "for able-bodied men willing to abandon their homes and families and risk their lives to serve their country." Even with the negative news and the dangerous task before them, many still volunteered for the regular army or shorter enlistments. But Joe was still not among them.

Keeping Up with the News and Churchill's Escape

Joe had become an avid collector and reader of newspapers and periodicals. He gathered them daily, whether spending his spare pennies or finding discarded papers here and there. He then studied them by candlelight in his bed every night.

One day, when visiting Ruth at the mansion where she worked, Joe noticed a large stack of newspapers stored in a shed at the back of the house. He asked Ruth why she was keeping them, and she confessed that she hadn't found the time to get rid of them.

"May I take them, hinny?"

"Sure, Joe," she said. "Why do you want them?"

"I'm looking for anything I can read on the South African War," he said. "I saw papers in that pile I find hard to get. I've started a scrapbook on the war, using clippings from the papers."

"Well, Joe, by removing them, you will help me too," she said. "The masters have read and discarded them, so you can have them."

"Champion!" said Joe.

So now, with Ruth's help, he had expanded his collection and could read Winston Churchill's despatches from the war in the *Morning Post*. Joe carried his stash home and glanced through them. On the top of the pile was a *Morning Post* of Tuesday, the 24th of January 1900. To his joy, inside, he found what he was looking for: an article entitled *"How I escaped from Pretoria, and my subsequent adventures on the road to Delagoa Bay"* by Winston Spencer-Churchill, our war correspondent. Delagoa Bay is in Portuguese East Africa.

Joe read through the article, filled with anticipation.

It began with "How unhappy is that poor man who loses his liberty," lamented the captured descendent of the Iron Duke of Marlborough. "What can the wide world give him in exchange? No material comfort, no consciousness of correct behaviour, can balance the hateful degradation of imprisonment."

But Joe discovered that Churchill resolved to escape from the first day of his imprisonment. He was observing the details of his environment non-stop, developing and testing escape plans, rejecting the infeasible ones over an entire month.

One evening, as Churchill was leaning over the railings, a short man with a red moustache walked by in the street, followed by two collie dogs. As he passed, but without changing his pace or looking towards him, the man said: "Methuen beat the Boers to hell at Belmont." This small snippet of positive information and excitement lifted Churchill's and the other prisoners' spirits.

Even in captivity, Joe could interpret from reading that Churchill maintained his naturally arrogant nature towards his tormentors. And they might have hated it but gloated instead over the fact that they had such a famous British aristocrat behind bars. He continued protesting his imprisonment and wrote letters to the Secretary of War and General Joubert, but without success. So, being Churchill, he persevered in another way. He filled his idle hours looking for escape routes. He developed plans, but most, upon closer examination, he rejected. He thought of nothing else for the entire month of his captivity, intent on fulfilling his goal. But every plan appeared too dangerous or difficult.

The reports in *De Volkstem* didn't help. Every day, they read of British defeats. "Hideously exaggerated and distorted," complained Churchill. But as he pointed out, no matter how much they might doubt and discount these reports, they had a strong emotional effect on the prisoners. "A month's feeding on such literary garbage weakens the constitution of the mind, and we wretched prisoners lost heart."

After long and careful observation, Churchill developed a workable plan of escape by scaling the school walls at the right moment at night when the guards were not watching.

Motivated by the supposed defeat of the British at Stormberg and against the odds, Churchill escaped on the 12th of December under the darkness of night during a brief period when the POW camp had no visible guards. He had clothes and a hat that made him appear as a Boer. He then went undetected on a long, arduous, suspense-filled journey by train to Lourenço Marques in Portuguese East Africa.

Once there, he found his way to the British Consul, Mr Ross, who at first mistook him for a fireman off a ship in the harbour since his train journey had covered him in coal dust. But they soon welcomed him with enthusiasm. He bought clothes, washed them, and settled into a dinner with a tablecloth and delicate glasses. He was a cheerful man again. And he was even more determined to return to the battlefield to witness the thumping of the Boers.

As soon as the news of his arrival spread, he received offers of help from the English residents. He sent the despatch on his escape to the newspaper by telegraph from Lourenço Marques. Then, a dozen local gentlemen armed with revolvers escorted him to the steamer Induna in case any Boer agents tried to recapture him in the neutral territory. And the ship left that very night for Durban. When the news of his escape broke, the British hailed Churchill as a hero across the empire. He lived off this episode and regaled eager listeners for many years. He undoubtedly enjoyed many invitations and introductions, not to mention free drinks. And the Boers offered a reward of £25 for recapturing their well-known prisoner, dead or alive.

"What a story," thought Joe to himself. "Into the heart of the lion's den and escaped! What a hero. At last, a haughty toff I can respect." He resolved to relate the story to his marras on the following Saturday.

Joe spent hours that night combing every newspaper, reading and cutting out the relevant articles and adding them to his scrapbook. It was as if he had discovered a stash of treasure. He asked Ruth to keep the newspapers for him henceforth. The house master had *The Times* and the *Morning Post* delivered daily from London and the *Newcastle Evening Chronicle* and *The Shields Gazette*. The master scanned them, but his father, a retired widower, devoured the newspapers daily to offset his boredom. Before this find, Joe had had no problem finding the *Shields Gazette* and often came across the *Evening Chronicle*, but he only saw a London newspaper on rare occasions at the train station. These newfound papers were a gold mine of information on the war.

"These are great," thought Joe. "Finally, I have a constant news source on the war and want to know everything about it. I'll be a labourer by day and a student at night."

Joe had become absorbed in this distant war. But he was not alone. Across the British Empire, young men and old were buying up news media and debating the pros and cons of British involvement in the conflict. The 2nd Anglo-Boer War was the first major conflict to occupy public consciousness since Britain had achieved widespread literacy. Massive growth in the number of newspapers and periodicals available satisfied the public's newfound appetite for information. The biggest sellers concentrated on the armed forces and Britain's conflicts overseas. Learning of British achievements in a foreign land allowed the people back home to wallow in glory. In the weeks before the war, *The Times* kept its readers informed on preparations for the inevitable conflict with detailed maps and articles on developments in South Africa. That the newspaper favoured military action wasn't surprising, the directors being active Cecil John Rhodes supporters.

The Times newspaper was not the only publication to arouse "aggressive nationalistic feelings" among its readers. Most papers backed military action in South Africa, and the *Telegraph* summed up the prevailing attitude. "Kruger's asked for war, and war he must have." Newspaper editors were experts at manipulating public opinion to suit their directors' viewpoints. They published special war editions to encourage anti-Boer feelings. The demand for patriotic literature skyrocketed.

Once public interest in South Africa was widespread, editors spared no expense to offer the best coverage. They assigned 300 well-paid correspondents to report back from the frontline. These included Edgar Wallace and G. W. Steevens of the Daily Mail, Melton Prior of The Illustrated London News, H. S. Pearce of the London Daily News, Leo S. Amery of The Times, a young Winston Churchill of the Morning Post, and many more. The typical layout of the war section comprised small articles from correspondents covering various aspects and theatres of the conflict. Telegraph technology allowed journalists to file reports for printing the day after the events, keeping the news-hungry public up to date.

Joe caught the events of the day as the papers reported on them. He had become a layman expert on the war and kept his brothers and marras current on the events unfolding in South Africa. He did so at any opportunity to discuss it and receive feedback. His monologues echoed the styles and terminology used in his reading material. He related the war stories to anyone interested, but his brothers listened again today.

"Guess what," he announced to his marras at his pub in March. "I've found another source of the latest news on the war. Winston Churchill is one of my favourite reporters to read, and many others. They are following every movement and every battle, and now I can keep you updated better."

Another pint of Broon appeared before him, so Joe gave his account of the Relief of Kimberley.

---

1. Deneys Reitz, *Commando – A Boer Journal of the Boer War*, 1929
2. Deneys Reitz, *Commando: A Boer Journal of the Boer War*, 1929
3. Four-colour flag: the flag of the Netherlands with the addition of a green vertical band at the hoist.
4. Deneys Reitz, *Commando – A Boer Journal of the Boer War*, 1929
5. Deneys Reitz, *Commando: A Boer Journal of the Boer War*, 1929
6. Deneys Reitz, *Commando – A Boer journal of the Boer War*, 1929
7. Deneys Reitz, *Commando – A Boer journal of the Boer War*, 1929
8. A dry gully, formed by the eroding action of running water.
9. Carman Miller, *Painting the Map Red, Canada and the South African War 1899-1902*, Canadian War Museum Publication, 1993/97
10. In larger vessels during the age of sail, spare spars could be roped together to provide a temporary surface known as a "spar deck." These served as jury-rigged repairs for permanent decks, or as an additional platform under which to shelter goods or crew.
11. William Hart-McHarg, *From Quebec to Pretoria with the Royal Canadian Regiment*, 1902
12. William Hart-McHarg, *From Quebec to Pretoria with the Royal Canadian Regiment*, 1902
13. William Hart-McHarg, *From Quebec to Pretoria with the Royal Canadian Regiment*, 1902
14. Ibid
15. Ibid
16. Pakenham, Thomas (1979). *The Boer War*. Jonathan Ball. p. 201

CHAPTER 3
FIELD MARSHAL ROBERTS IN COMMAND
FEBRUARY 1900

"After our Magersfontein defeat, our forces licked their wounds at the Modder River for two months. They brought reinforcements forward from Bloemfontein during this time," said Joe. "Then, in February, Field Marshal Frederick Roberts took personal command of a much larger British force of 45,000 soldiers. The next battle was at Paardeberg, or Horse Mountain, on the 15th of February. It was a major battle fought near Paardeberg Drift, a shallow crossing of the Modder River near Kimberley."

"Whey aye, man! 45,000 British troops," called Mike. "Now those farmers are in for trouble."

"Aye, the Boer army of General Piet Cronjé was retreating from Magersfontein towards Bloemfontein," said Joe. "However, Major-General John French, whose cavalry had moved around the Boer positions towards Kimberley, had cut its communication lines. The Boers had just fought off an attempted direct assault by Lieutenant-General Herbert Horatio Kitchener. The British caught up with Cronje's column at Paardeberg, where the Boer general surrendered along with his 4,000 men. With that surrender, the 124-day siege of Kimberley was over on the 15th of February, the first of two major victories in February. Cecil John Rhodes, South Africa's richest man, was freed by this victory. Only just arrived from Canada, the Royal Canadian Regiment played an instrumental role in this victory, including moving in at night towards the enemy lines, entrenching on high ground a mere 65 yards from the Boer lines."

The Battle of Paardeberg

The Battle of Paardeberg is the best-known Canadian engagement of the South African war. Canada's first contingent held its own and helped the British Army achieve its first Boer War victory. What follows is a description of that battle from the perspective of the Royal Canadian Regiment by William Hart-McHarg[1]:

"Anyone attempting to give a description of an engagement in which he was actively engaged finds himself very much handicapped and can only speak from personal observation of that portion of the battlefield where his regiment found itself placed. However, A few remarks on the general scope of the action under review can be added so that the reader may understand what the engagement was like.

"Our regiment, having marched from Klip Drift along the south bank of the Modder River, arrived at Paardeberg Drift at about 5:30 A.M. Sunday morning, the 18th of February. The head of our column reached there at 4:15 A.M. It was apparent that we had come up with Lieutenant-General Kelly-Kenny's 6th Division, as a large amount of transport was spread about all over the place, and troops could be seen moving in all directions. The 65th Howitzer Battery was in action to our right front on a small ridge, shelling the riverbed higher up, and the distant rattle of musketry could be distinctly heard. We were exhausted, and the reduction of our rations to three-quarters of a pound a day was making itself felt, but the sound of the firing and the chance of finally getting into a 'scrap' put new life into us. At about 8:30, our brigade received orders to go into action.

"Every man must experience different feelings when ordered to go under fire, which will vary according to his temperament. A nervousness to a greater or less extent is, I think, felt, just as singers say they are nervous while waiting for their turn to go on the stage; but, like the singer, once the soldier gets fairly started, all nervousness is a thing of the past, the only result of its temporary presence being a bracing and nerving up of the whole constitution for the great work that lies before him. This nervousness is probably less apparent when first going under fire than on subsequent occasions. There is always a keenness on the part of the untried soldier to get into his first action; he thinks less of its pains and penalties than he does afterwards when experience has brought them home to him.

"There was no mistaking the temper of the men of the Royal Canadian Regiment on the morning of the 18th of February. It was three months and a half since they left Canada; they had been in South Africa since the 30th of November. Their great fear had been that they would not be given a chance. 'Colonials will only be put at garrison work and on the line of communication,' they argued, and 'we shall go home without getting under fire and be more laughed at than pitied.' But all these fears were things of the past. Men could be seen going about with contented smiles, congratulating each other on realizing their hopes and aspirations. True, one company had received its baptism of fire and done the most outstanding credit to the regiment at Sunnyside, but it was only a tiny part of the regiment, acting as a detached unit. The men who composed it were as anxious as others to see the RCR take part in a titanic battle.

"Eliminating the kopjes, which stood back some distance from the river, the battlefield was a good deal like the western prairies of Canada. The Modder River cut its way through the open veldt in a sinuous line, the upper parts of the trees that grew between its banks just showing nicely above them. There was absolutely no cover for the attacking force, and what made the job all the more complex and deadly was that the ground inclined slightly towards the river. Across this open ground, towards the big bend, we steadily advanced. It was not the battlefield one's imagination leads one to expect—not a living creature could be seen—but the rattle of musketry which we had heard all morning now became loud and fierce, and an occasional volley, intermingled with the independent firing, told us that some British troops were in front of us. We formed our opinions of what was before us entirely from what we heard, as we saw nothing except the fringe of trees we were approaching. The bullets were whizzing past us and throwing up little sprays of sand in all directions as they struck the ground. We were well into the fire zone in a few minutes and were ordered to lie down. All around us were men of the Black Watch and Seaforths, the supports of the firing line about 300 yards farther on. These men were lying perfectly prone, taking advantage of every inch of cover, the bullets finding them out even there, as one poor fellow I passed close to eloquently proved with his upturned face and glassy eyes.

"The order was then given to the leading companies to advance by alternate sections at the double. This was a mistake, as the advancing unit could not be covered by the fire of the others, the Highlanders' firing line intervening between the enemy and us, and one section getting up at a time naturally drew a concentrated fire on it from the Boers. Three or four rushes brought us up to the Highlanders, and we extended their line on the right and left, some of our men joining in with the Scots. We reached the firing line with few casualties by expanding comprehensively and advancing rapidly. As we had shaken well out on the right, we completely enveloped the western end of the Boer position, the right of our line resting on the bank of the river.

"There we remained. Through the fierce heat of the morning and on through a cold rain in the early part of the afternoon, with nothing to eat or drink except the odd bits of biscuit in our haversacks and the water in our bottles, we lay prone and fired into the trees in front of us. Not a Boer could be seen. We only knew where the enemy was by the incessant rattle of the Mausers and the endless procession of bullets striking all about us or passing overhead, one of which now and then claimed its victim.

"We had to be careful where we fired because it was impossible to know where our other regiments were. We knew they were doing much the same work as ourselves on the other side of the river, and orders were continually being passed up and down our line, first from one end and then from the other, to cease fire. The 82nd Battery was shelling the river bed in front of us, enfilading it from the left at long range, preventing any advance up the river between the banks. However, it was at first attempted by a detachment of Highlanders but quickly abandoned.

"Our casualties were mounting up. Our firing line had been swelled too much by bringing up three companies—a dangerous proceeding, except at long range, especially when the attacking force is entirely exposed, and the units being attacked were completely hidden. Captain Arnold of A Company, the brave and the kind, had fallen mortally wounded while sitting up trying to locate the enemy in the trees through his field glasses; Sergeant Scott, the celebrated oarsman, had dropped with a bullet through his brain at the head of his section. Altogether, some thirty or forty had been put out of action, and the moaning of the wounded and the cries for stretcher bearers went on incessantly in all directions. The wounded had to lie where they were, the men next to them doing what they could in the way of first aid. Stretcher-bearers could do nothing in that firing line, as the Boers deliberately turned their fire on them as soon as they got up and began moving about. Three men were struck down carrying Captain Arnold to the rear.

"Drill-book formations were more or less discarded; companies were mixed up. On the right, small parties of three and four men could occasionally be seen dodging from place to place to get into better positions. Some men were sound asleep. Others would fire a few shots and then turn and chat with whoever was beside them. Highlanders, Canadians and Mounted Infantry were all mixed up together.

"As the afternoon wore on, the rain ceased, and the sun came out again and dried our clothes a bit. Was nothing going to be done to drive those Boers out of the position in front of us? Were we to lie there till dark and then retire, gaining nothing? The answer to these questions was not long in coming. The Cornwalls had been brought across the river to support us and soon made their presence felt. Colonel Aldsworth, D.S.O., formed up two companies some little distance behind our firing line and ordered them to charge. The first intimation we, on the right, had of what was happening in our rear was the sound of hoarse cheering. Looking around, we saw the Cornwalls coming up at the charge. There were cries on all sides to fix bayonets and join the oncoming line. We jumped up and joined in the mad rush when it reached us. Cornwalls, Highlanders, Canadians, and Mounted Infantry, all in one grand melee—went yelling and shouting for that hateful line of foliage which had been spitting out death and destruction at us all day.

"It was costly work, but it was exciting to a degree. Poor young Todd, an American veteran of the Philippine war, yelled, 'Come on, boys; this beats Manilhollow.' He never spoke again. The fusillade that met us from the repeating rifles was terrific. The whole air seemed to be filled with lead; we were shot at from the front and enfiladed from the donga at the bend of the river on the left; it is a mystery that so many reached the bank. As we approached the river, we found that a state of things existed, which was impossible to know from where we had been lying all day. Close to the river, the ground sloped rapidly down. The trees, which had seemed to us to be equally on both sides of the river, were all on the other side, and so were the Boers, still invisible, while the river was practically unfordable. The charging line broke in two; the right half, seeing some small bushes near the water which would afford a little cover, made a dash for these, while the left half, seeing nothing except an absolutely coverless slope between them and the water, threw themselves down and again opened fire. But their position was not enviable, as owing to the sloping nature of the ground, they were more exposed than before. Nor had we, on the right, improved our position. The cover was scanty, and we were more or less at the mercy of the Boers, who knew exactly where we were while they were all invisible to us. The small bushes that afforded us some scant cover were cut to pieces with the lead the Boers poured into them. We were also in great danger from our own artillery, which was still enfilading that part of the riverbed from the left. The Boers drew in their western end a little because of our advance. All we could do was hang on to the ground we had gained. This position remained unchanged until darkness set in, when the Boers had vacated that part of the river and withdrew some distance around the bend.

"We then had to do what we could for the wounded. No one knew where the field hospital was. It was not anywhere within two miles—that was certain. No stretchers could be got. The only thing to do was turn to and render what assistance was possible. The work by some of the men that night was magnificent; it would be invidious to mention names, but there was one man who may be said without fear of anyone feeling slighted. I refer to Rev. Father O'Leary. He tended and soothed the wounded throughout that bleak night on the battlefield and carried comfort and solace to the dying. His work was not finished until the following day when Canada's honoured dead had been gathered together and placed in their sandy grave in a little grove of trees some distance from the banks of the fateful river. In hushed accents which sent a thrill through everyone within the sound of his voice, he tenderly committed them 'to the keeping of God's angels.'"

The Painful Relief of Ladysmith

Joe enthralled his audience with his tale of the Relief of Kimberley. He had a natural gift for recounting such gripping stories with wild gestures and expressions. Joe was becoming a favourite storyteller and entertainer at the pub and elsewhere. Everyone asked him not to forget them the next time he was to give an update on the South African War.

Then, Joe wrapped up the evening by relating another positive story from South Africa, the Relief of Ladysmith.

"In Natal, the British suffered pain at the Battle of Spion Kop (Spy Peak) on the 23rd and 24th of January, caused by a terrible military blunder. The fight started as 1,700 British forces, under the command of Major-General Sir Edward Woodgate, marched towards the town of Ladysmith," said Joe. "They couldn't move straight into the township without passing a row of four hills—Groenkop, Conical Hill, Spion Kop and Twin Peaks. And there again, the Boers were dug in along Twin Peaks, Groenkop and sections of Spion Kop itself. Woodgate believed Spion Kop was the key to winning Ladysmith and that his troops could climb a face of the hill in silence and aim artillery and infantry attacks into the exposed Boer positions."

"The general aimed to reach the southern crest, then push towards the northern end. Once there, the British troops could open a flanking fire on the Boer lines which run east and west."

"What the hell is a flanking fire?" asked Mike.

"Good question, Mike," said Joe. "I asked that one, too. It has an even fancier name of the enfilading fire, and it's when they shoot upon a row of soldiers from the side, along their line."

"That's a clever thing to do," said Mike. "If it works...!"

"The general believed Spion Kop was the key that would open the door of Ladysmith," said Joe while checking his notes from a report by a military reporter from the *Manchester Guardian* who had agreed with the thinking behind the assault. "Patrols reported only a few Boers were on it. So, he ordered the attack on the evening of the 23rd of January. Soon after dusk on Tuesday, a party made a night attack on the hill. There were Thorneycroft's Mounted Infantry, the Lancashire Fusiliers, the Lancashire Regiment, two South Lancashire Regiment companies and a company of engineers. It was a hand and knee march up the southern face—a climb over smooth rock and grass, so it was slow going."

"My God, it sounds like a real slog," said Mike.

"Aye, they say it was at first. Along the way, a Boer sentry challenged the advancing British, and they shot him on sight. Then, the Lancashire Fusiliers made a charge at the Boer line. But it proved to be only a tiny outpost. They didn't reach the crest until dawn. When dawn came, the British troops were in the clouds. They could see nothing but the plateau—four hundred yards across—on which it stood. They made trenches, but it was difficult to find the right positions. The Boers were invisible."

"Cut the suspense, Joe. Get to the point," said Mike.

"Aye, well, when the mist lifted, the curtain rose upon a tragedy. On another ridge of Spion Kop, the Boers fired upon our men, who weren't protected enough in their shallow trenches. The space was cramped as they huddled together."

Joe quoted from a reporter who described the scene as he saw it from below Spion Kop,

"I shall always have it in my memory—that acre of the massacre, that complete shambles. It lay at the top of a rich green gully with cool granite walls, reaching up to the mountain's western flank. It seemed our men were in a small square patch. There were brown men and browner trenches like an overripe barley field. The Boers had three guns playing like hoses upon our men. It was a triangular fire, and our men on the Kop had no guns. By the end of the day, they had lived a long life under that fire."

"So Spion Kop was the key that would open the door of Ladysmith?" asked Mike. "Who are they trying to fool?"

"This was a terrible loss for us," Joe lamented. "Thankfully, arriving reinforcements prevented the losses from exceeding the 332 killed."

The table fell silent despite the racket of the pub. Joe's brothers and Marras just stared at him. It was getting too much for them—one British disaster after another. Would it ever end?

One Mohandas Mahatma Gandhi, who had been in South Africa as a barrister and attorney since 1893 and was a civil rights activist on behalf of the Indians in British Natal, was at Spion Kop. In 1900, he volunteered to form a group of ambulance drivers during the Boer War. He wanted to prove that the British idea that Hindus weren't fit for manly activities involving danger and exertion was wrong. Gandhi recruited 1,100 Indian volunteers, and the army trained and certified them for medical service on the front lines. At the Battle of Spion Kop, Gandhi and his volunteer bearers carried wounded soldiers for considerable distances to a field hospital since the terrain was too rough for the ambulances. Gandhi would smile when someone said European ambulance corpsmen couldn't travel without food and water in the day's heat. General Redvers Buller noted the bravery of the Indians in one of his despatches, and Gandhi and 37 other Indians received the War Medal.

Joe continued with his story of the Relief of Ladysmith.

"After Spion Kop on the 3rd of February, the British Army crossed the Tugela River again. Then, on the 5th, more trouble descended on the British, at the Battle of Vaal Krantz where Buller's army suffered another 333 casualties."

"Will these British defeats and our embarrassment ever end?" asked Mike.

"Aye, but our lads of the 1/DLI performed like heroes," said Joe. Winston Churchill wrote of the 1/DLI at Vaal Krantz that they carried the hill at the bayonet's point. He said we lost seven officers and 60 or 70 men. But most of the enemy had quit before the attack, unable to endure the ghastly concentration of artillery which had prepared it."

"So, on the 14th of February, Buller launched his fourth attack to relieve Ladysmith. The army moved forward three days later and continued daily until the 18th. They defeated the Boers at the Battle of Monte Cristo. On the 20th, the 1/DLI occupied Green Hill and, on the 23rd, was waiting in reserve for Major-General Hart's brigade after crossing the Tugela. They relieved the Irish Brigade on Inniskilling Hill on the 24th and spent the rest of the day removing their wounded under heavy fire. Then, on the 27th of February, the 1/DLI took part in the important victory of Pieters Hill. They were decisive, and they relieved Ladysmith on the 28th of February, allowing General White and his forces to leave that town and join the rest of the Natal Army at last. After so many British casualties, we had won the battle. Ladysmith was free!"

Joe's brothers and friends were relieved by this positive news, which impressed them. They could not believe their labourer brother and marra had gained so much knowledge on this war. They had met no one with so much understanding of any topic other than coal mining or shipbuilding. From then on, they and others in the community developed a new respect for Joe. They consulted with him repeatedly to hear tales of the British Empire and its armed forces so far from home. None of them read well, and Joe was their only source of war events.

The defeats and sieges at the hands of a motley collection of farmers embarrassed the British High Command in London, and its Lords were fuming. Decades of colonial expansion meant the British Army was skilled in fighting savages and tribesmen. But the Boers were neither savages nor tribesmen; they were skilled horsemen and sharpshooters compared to the average British soldier. The generals struggled to understand that. They won back Kimberley and Ladysmith, but it had taken longer and cost more than they had expected. And Mafeking was still under siege. How much more would it cost to relieve that garrison, let alone the war? Were they using the wrong tactics against this enemy? The Empire had suffered 5,000 casualties in this war, with 1,000 captured or missing. Never in recent British history had the country experienced such losses and humiliation.

Along with another exceptional soldier, Lord Kitchener, Roberts arrived in South Africa on the RMS Dunnottar Castle on the 23rd of December 1899. General Buller's decisions at Ladysmith and the consequent loss of life and reputation resulted in him being sacked and replaced by Lord Frederick Roberts. It was the end of a brilliant career for the man the press now dubbed Sir Reverse Buller.

The troops knew Field Marshal Lord Roberts as Bobs, or Little Bobs, because of his 5-foot 3-inch height. But despite his diminutive stature, he had fought many battles for the British Empire over a distinguished career going back over forty years. They knighted and honoured him many times, and he became a member of several orders. The High Command tasked Roberts with sorting out the South African catastrophe and restoring the empire's reputation. With vast new troop numbers and enormous financial resources, Roberts set out to turn the tide and ensure a British victory.

When, in October 1899, the Boer War broke out in South Africa, the shipping magnate Bernard Nadal Baker from Baltimore, Maryland, immediately offered the British Admiralty the use of a vessel as a hospital ship. The American Ladies Hospital Ship Society based in London raised funding for the conversion headed by Winston and Jack's mother, Lady Jennie Jerome Churchill, Fanny Ronalds, and Jennie Goodell Blow. All were American-born socialites, and the effort raised money from Americans. While crewed by a British crew once handed over to the American Government, the ship was staffed with American medical workers. RFA Maine sailed for South Africa on the 23rd of December 1899, with Jennie Churchill aboard, and, after a stopover in Capetown, arrived at Durban on the 23rd of January 1900. One of the earliest beneficiaries of the ship was Jennie's younger son Jack, who was shot through the leg in February 1900 during the Battle of the Tugela Heights, part of the Relief of Ladysmith.

∽

The Arrival of More Canadian Contingents

The brigade artillery division in Canada's 2nd contingent for the South African War grouped together three batteries. Each battery comprised three sections, each of two 12-pounder breech-loading guns. The 12-pounders, however, were outranged by the Boers' field guns. Despite this handicap, the Canadian gunners held their own more than during operations in South Africa.

The batteries were designated 'C,' 'D,' and 'E' to signal the brigade division's link to the Permanent Force's 'A' and 'B' Batteries, Royal Canadian Field Artillery. There was, in fact, a core of permanent force artillery personnel in each battery. Additional members came from militia field batteries. 'C' and 'D' Batteries' militia gunners came from Ontario and Winnipeg units; 'E' Battery came from Quebec, New Brunswick, and Nova Scotia.

"D" and "E" Batteries arrived in Cape Town in February 1900 and took part in the suppression of the Boer rebellion in the western Cape Colony. "C" Battery, on its arrival in March 1900, went north to Rhodesia to join the Rhodesian Field Force, which then moved south to the relief of besieged Mafeking. The three batteries then continued to operate separately; even sections within each battery often acted independently with different forces, sometimes detached for months. The brigade division was only reunited at the end of its tour of duty and return to Canada.

When the South African War started in October 1899, John McCrae of Guelph, Ontario, decided it was his duty to serve in South Africa, and he requested a postponement of a fellowship in pathology that he had been awarded at McGill University in Montréal. He was commissioned to lead an artillery battery with 54 volunteers from his hometown of Guelph, which became part of D Battery of the Canadian Field Artillery.

McCrae sailed to Africa in December and spent a year there with his unit. In his diary, he wrote about his first battle on the 21st of July 1900, "In our baptism of fire, they opened on us from the left flank. One shrapnel burst over us & scattered on all sides. I felt like a hailstorm was coming down and wanted to turn my back, but it was over instantly. The only casualty from that battle was a horse."

For a year, McCrae and D Battery of the Royal Canadian Field Artillery took part in battles in the South African War. He was quickly promoted to captain and then to major. In one incident, McCrae nearly drowned while crossing a stream on horseback.

Although usually out of the limelight, the three Canadian artillery batteries saw much action. A section of "D" Battery particularly distinguished itself at the battle of Leliefontein on the 7th of November 1900. The Battle of Leliefontein was an engagement between British-Canadian and Boer forces at the Komati River 30 kilometres south of Belfast, Transvaal.

The 3rd Canadian Contingent also arrived in South Africa in February 1900, comprising the 2nd Canadian Mounted Rifles with 21 officers and 357 men and the 10th Canadian Field Hospital with 5 officers and 56 men. This battalion was recruited by the North-West Mounted Police. They were followed by the 1st Canadian Mounted Rifles (Royal Canadian Dragoons)

with 19 officers and 360 men in March and the Strathcona's Horse with 29 officers and 562 men in April 1900.

On the 10th of January 1900, Lord Strathcona and Mount Royal, the Canadian High Commissioner to the United Kingdom, offered to raise a regiment at his own expense for service in the British Army in South Africa. The Imperial authorities accepted his offer. Officially a British unit, it was recruited entirely in the Canadian West and equipped by the Canadian government, quartered in Lansdowne Park, Ottawa, and paraded on Parliament Hill. The soldiers wore wide-brimmed Stetsons and mounted on cow ponies with western saddles and lassos.

Sunday Stroll in Jarrow

One night, upon leaving the pub, Joe made his way to Ruth, and after talking and enjoying each other's company, he fell into a deep sleep, only waking up alone well after sunrise. He scribbled a quick note to her, then crept out of the room and scurried off towards home. Ruth was getting off work at noon, so they had made plans to spend the Sunday afternoon together.

Joe arrived at the mansion at noon sharp and waited on the street outside the elegant entrance. While waiting for Ruth's appearance, Joe walked around the large modern building to a side lane gate meant for servants and deliveries. He struggled to imagine what it was like to live in such a mansion. He admired its red brick walls rising three storeys with white wooden bay windows protruding on the third floor. The roof had black slate tiles, and a fourth-storey apartment embellished with an observation turret with enormous windows, allowing a 360-degree view of the town, river and shipyards. It was one of the tallest private houses in Jarrow. The entrance at the front of the house had a beautiful brick and wood portal protecting visitors from the rain.

Ruth emerged with her ebony hair arranged into a neat Pompadour, topped with a small straw hat. She looked adorable as she skipped up the lane into his arms. They hugged, and he kissed her quickly to avoid any undue notice from within the house. They then walked off, her arm on his, towards the centre of Jarrow. Ruth was a quiet lass with a man but showed comfort with occasional demure glances and radiant smiles towards him. Joe had dressed that day in his Sunday best woollen suit, wiped clean with a damp cloth. He wore a crisp white starched shirt and a black tie. On his head, Joe wore a simple straw hat. Ruth thought he looked handsome and was proud to walk at his side.

"You look fine in your Sunday best, Joe," said Ruth.

"You look beautiful, hinny," said Joe. "It's a pleasure to join you on this lovely Sunday afternoon."

Joe did most of the talking. He explained his work environment, describing the magnificent ships he had the pleasure of helping to build. Joe told them their purpose, whether they were freighters, liners, or warships, and their dimensions and fittings. He proudly described how modern ships had elegant light fittings powered by electricity. He spoke of the interior finishes and furniture at length and how opulent the first-class cabins were. Joe explained the size of the massive propellers and rudders and other essential aspects of the new ships by measuring them against buildings they passed. He avoided war and the army lest it spoiled the light-hearted spirit of their walk.

After a 30-minute walk, they found themselves at Jarrow Town Hall on Grange and Wylam Streets. It was late in March, and the weather hinted at spring, so the town centre was filled with people pouring out of church or walking arm in arm. Being Sunday, the shops lining Ormonde Street were closed, and they had no intention of shopping but glanced into a few as they made their way along the street.

Then, they encountered a shouting match between a dishevelled man and a well-dressed gentleman at a street corner. From his accent, they could tell that the person yelling was an Irishman; his clothing made him appear scruffy and unemployed. A group of curious and bemused persons observed the argument and snickered at his verbal abuses.

"We are downtrodden in this age of rich factory owners who exploit us labourers for a pittance," he shouted. "Look at you. Dressed in your Sunday best, pretending to be all happy and opulent in this decadent world."

"What about you, Bogtrotter?" called out an onlooker to support the gentleman. "For whom are you working?"

"I work for no one," said the Irishman. "These vile pigs will not exploit me!"

"Then what are you doing here, Paddy?" called another. "Go back to wherever you came from."

"I'm here, people, because I believe they are robbing you, men like this gentleman before me," he said. "Robbing you of your fair pay. Robbing you of your dignity and robbing you of your souls. Look at this fine gentleman. Does he look like he is suffering as you are? He doesn't look like you."

The gentleman he was referring to made a puzzled grimace in the Irishman's direction. Then, throwing his head up and forward, he hurried off to his destination, the crowd's gaze following him before returning to the Irishman. Then, at that moment, a soldier in uniform appeared within the group.

"Hey, soldier," called the antagonist. "What war are you rushing off to, South Africa?"

The soldier ignored him.

"People. Do you think it right that your Queen and empire can oppress the farmers of that country," he said, "the way they have oppressed us Irish for centuries? For them, Boers and Irishmen are nothing more than animals to be oppressed, just as you workers are here in England. Rise! Stop this exploitation!"

"So you're here to save us, Bogtrotter," called a bystander, to laughter from the others.

"Aye, I'm here to save you, swine," he said to the bystander and turning to the others, he cried, "You trash can laugh on the way to your early graves."

Then, a Bobby decided that enough was enough. He sauntered to the Irishman and said, "I'm sorry, Sir, but I must take you into custody for inciting trouble on a Sunday. Come with me." Then he led him away, protesting, while the crowd dispersed, muttering and laughing.

Joe ushered Ruth away without a word, and they continued their afternoon walk through the town centre, arriving at St. Paul's Monastery and Church. This ancient monastery at Jarrow was one of Europe's most important centres of learning and culture in the 7th century because of the scholarly writings of the Venerable Bede. Inspired by the scholarship and a new style of monastic life here, Bede dedicated his life to studying. He wrote over 60 works but is best known for the first history of the English, the *Ecclesiastical History of the English People* (*Historia ecclesiastica gentis Anglorum*). He died in 735. Joe and Ruth explored the grounds and ruins of the medieval monastery, taking in their mystery before entering the church during a service. They sat at the back of the church, enjoying the service and atmosphere of this centuries-old place.

After the service, they felt calm and cleansed of the anger they had experienced from the Irishman in town. They made their way home in no hurry.

Sanna's Post

Early in April 1900, Joe joined his marras again at the Rolling Mill Pub.

"What can you tell us today, Joe?" asked Jack.

"No pleasant news again, I'm afraid," said Joe. "Our problems continue in the Orange Free State. On the 13th of March, our forces captured and occupied the city of Bloemfontein, the capital of that Republic."

"That's excellent news," said Mike.

"Aye, and they were preparing to move north to Pretoria, capital of the Transvaal, under the command of Field Marshal Lord Roberts. He believed capturing the capitals of both Republics would lead to a rapid end of the war."

"Sounds good so far," said Jack.

"The Transvaal Boers announced that they would defend their capital, Pretoria, with any means they had," said Joe. "The Free State Boers, under the leadership of President Martinus Steyn and their foremost field general Christiaan de Wet, prepared to continue the conflict in their Republic and win back their capital. So, on the 30th of March, a 2,000-man Boer force led by General de Wet moved off toward Bloemfontein."

The audience suspected something ominous was coming and were on the edges of their chairs, so they kept quiet and held back questions. Joe continued the story without interruption.

"De Wet had found out that there was a garrison of British troops at a place called Sanna's Post, 23 miles east of Bloemfontein, where Bloemfontein's important waterworks are. A British mounted force under Brigadier-General Robert George Broadwood that had attacked Boer positions at Thaba Nchu was going there with two Royal Horse Artillery gun batteries with 12 cannons. Also, he had a mixed brigade made up of the Household Cavalry, the 10th Hussars, New Zealand Mounted Rifles and the Burmah Mounted Infantry (BMI), Roberts' Horse and Rimington's Guides, light horse units raised from English-speaking South Africans. The Burmah Mounted Infantry included a company of the Durham Light Infantry—our boys. The force amounted to 2,000 British troops. De Wet sent 1,600 of his men under his brother Piet to attack Broadwood from the north while he stayed at Sanna's Post with 400 mounted men to meet their retreat with an ambush."

"There they go again," said Mike. "Using dirty tactics to catch our boys."

"Aye," said Joe. "A famous writer called Arthur Conan Doyle claimed the Boers are masters of the ambush, and he said no other people he knows have shown as much ability as the Boers for this form of warfare. They have won this through a lengthy history of fighting with cunning African natives."

"As General Broadwood's men were breaking camp and preparing to move on early the next morning, de Wet, hidden in the wood, sprung his trap," said Joe. "His guns opened fire, and the result was a scene of complete chaos. Horses without riders and driverless wagon horse teams raced in every direction. Heavy wagons and carts filled with soldiers rushed to escape the firing but ran into the Boer trap in the woods with no idea that the Boers were hiding there. They poured into a drift across the Korn Spruit stream where the Boers commanded, 'Raise your hands!' They had no choice but to stop and raise their hands."

"Bloody hell... Shite bastards..." were the cries from the enlarged group around Joe at that point of the narrative.

"Wait, I'm not finished," said Joe. "The British officers realized that something was wrong in the woods, and one of their officers ordered that the troops return. But the Boers had already captured 200 of our men. Five of our guns and over 100 wagons were only 100 yards from the Boers on the banks of the spruit [2]. Two more of our guns were 300 yards away. Broadwood's troops tried to save the five guns, but they failed. They got the other two guns out of the Boers' reach, placing them behind the station buildings.

"A Colonel Alderson sent the Durhams and a party from the other two companies to the guns' aid. They galloped their little ponies to the station buildings through a herd of loose horses, dismounted and spread out to the right and left of the guns. The guns, meanwhile, were keeping up a constant fire. [3]

"Those men fought four hours in the open. The gun teams were falling, one by one, until only the battery commander, Major Phipps-Hornby, and a few of his men remained unwounded to fight with the guns.

"Having no choice, General Broadwood ordered a retirement to Boesman's Kop without guns. But Phipps-Hornby would not abandon his guns without a fight. They couldn't bring the remaining horses up from the wagon lines in the station's rear for fear of the fight killing them. But a few of Phipps-Hornby's men moved the guns 40 of the 70-odd yards between them and the station through brute force. It had exhausted them, so Phipps-Hornby called on the BMI escort for volunteers. Lieutenants Ainsworth, Ashburner, Grover and Way, Lance Corporal Steele and Privates Pickford and Horton of the Durhams answered his call immediately."

"I know a few of those guys," one onlooker said. "Me too," called another.

"They wounded Lieutenant Grover, who later died," said Joe. "They blinded Major Cruikshank with a bullet behind his eyes and wounded Privates Pickford and Horton. But when Phipps-Hornby's men moved the rest of their battery at a walk to the rear of the buildings, they reaped the rewards of their hard work and devotion."

"What heroes they were. What a fight they gave. They make us proud," called a patron.

"Aye. Sanna's Post might have been another of those so-called regrettable incidents that ruined the Army's record in South Africa," said Joe. "Had it not been for such brave acts. Everything else was distressing, and we lost control of the waterworks with the retreat.

"General Broadwood broke loose. Then, three hours later, the 9th Infantry Division, commanded by Major-General Sir Henry Colvile, arrived to relieve Broadwood's cavalry brigade. But in the meantime, De Wet's men had withdrawn to safe positions across the Modder River. The battle was over, and Bloemfontein's waterworks were under the Boer's control again.

"We suffered 155 casualties in this battle. They captured 428 men, seven field artillery pieces and 117 supply wagons. The Boer force had only three fighters killed and five wounded.

"Even more dangerous than the losses in action was the loss of Bloemfontein's water supplies. As a result, a severe water shortage developed, leading to enteric disease from contaminated water. Among the occupying British troops downstream, 200 more British soldiers died."

When Joe's story was over, the men thanked him for learning so much about the war and passing it on to them. It was closing time, and the pub emptied. On the street, the conversation between the marras continued.

"What a story, Joe. We've got to get out there and into the action," said Mike. "We're missing it all."

"Agreed," said Jack.

"I'm with you, too," said Billy.

"Aye, we must go," said Joe. But it's so difficult for me right now. It's so complicated with my family and Ruth. Go without me, and I'll join you when I can."

"No, Joe, I'm not going without all of you," said Mike. "I understand your Da is fighting this, but what is the problem with Ruth? You're not married, and you don't have children."

"A lot has changed in my relationship with Ruth," said Joe. "We have become so much closer."

"Oh," said Mike. "I get it."

"Let's just say I believe I love her. I don't want to leave her just yet," said Joe.

"You're in love with her," said Mike. "Well, don't let us pressure you, Joe. When you're ready, we'll be ready."

"Thanks, Mike," said Joe, "I'm working through it. Give me more time."

"We're with you the whole way, our marra," said Jack.

"Aye, we are," confirmed Billy.

And with that exchange dealt with, Joe scurried off to visit the lady of his affections, while his marras hoped he would get over her soon enough.

∽

Arthur Conan Doyle Enlists as a Medical Doctor

By December 1899, the recently formed Royal Army Medical Corps (RAMC) struggled to cope with the massive number of casualties in South Africa. Arthur Conan Doyle had attempted to join the British Army but was declined. So, hearing that his friend, philanthropist John Langman, was staffing and equipping a private field hospital to be rushed out to South Africa, Conan Doyle volunteered his services. Thus, eight years after he had written and given up medicine, the internationally famous creator of Sherlock Holmes became a physician again in Langman's Field Hospital.

On the 28th of February 1900, the 50 hospital staff gathered in the pouring rain on the Royal Albert Dock at Woolwich to board a converted P&O freighter, the SS Oriental. Once they were out at sea, Doyle was one of the first to volunteer to test the newly developed inoculation against enteric fever, a disease that had killed more British soldiers than bullets in the Boer War. The correct dose was yet to be determined. The inoculation made Doyle feel ill, but he recovered sooner than many others, and by the time the Oriental reached the Cape Verde Islands, he had recovered enough to play in the ship's cricket team. He was also writing the opening chapters of his history, *The Great Boer War*, confident he could finish the book before the war's end.

On the 28th of March, they disembarked at the port of East London and travelled to Bloemfontein, which had fallen to British forces under Commander-in-Chief Lord Roberts only ten days earlier. Bloemfontein lay 350 miles to the north, a journey that took four days and nights on a single-track railway line. They arrived just in time to deal with the catastrophic consequences of the Battle of Sanna's Post. More significantly, the Boers had seized control of the waterworks that provided the town with clean water. Desperately thirsty men had been drinking contaminated water from old abandoned wells and the River Modder. They arrived at the height of that city's typhoid fever epidemic, which raged from April to June 1900. There were nearly 5,000 cases of typhoid and 1,000 deaths, but official statistics do not truly reflect the magnitude of the suffering. Doyle argued that the British Army had made a major mistake by not making anti-typhoid inoculation compulsory. Because of the new vaccine's side effects, 95% of the soldiers refused immunization.

Within days, the Langman hospital tents, erected on the cricket pitch of the Ramblers Club in the centre of Bloemfontein, were filling with cases of typhoid. "The outbreak was a terrible one," wrote Conan Doyle, "We lived amid death—and death in its vilest and filthiest form." At the beginning of the third week in April, violent thunderstorms broke over the town. The tents stood in a swamp of mud and feces. Doyle and his colleagues listed their address as Café Enterique, Boulevard des Microbes. And in Kipling's poem *The Parting of the Columns,* the Tommies refer to the town as 'Bloeming-typhoidtein.'

Conan Doyle thought his own life had probably been saved in South Africa by his anti-typhoid inoculation. On his return to Britain, he campaigned for mandatory injection for all the armed forces, along with other preventive health measures such as the boiling of drinking water; he also campaigned for rubber life belts for sailors in the Royal Navy, most of whom couldn't swim, and for inflatable lifeboats for the ships they sailed in.

Sunday Visit with Fred and Mary

Joe had seen Fred often at work since their first meeting, and they became best friends. Despite the differences in their ages, a powerful bond was developing between them. Fred felt relaxed with Joe, too, and he could open up more on both the pleasant and the less enjoyable aspects of army life and the British wars in which he had taken part. So, Fred invited Joe and Ruth home one Sunday afternoon to meet his wife. He lived on the same street as Joe.

"The reason I'm here in Jarrow, Joe and Ruth, is because of this lovely woman," said Fred as an introduction, "Mary, meet my friend Joe and his lady, Ruth."

"Pleased to meet you, Joe," she said, "I've heard of you."

"Now, one day, Mary was in Aberdeen visiting an aunt of hers soon after I returned from South Africa," said Fred. "From the first moment I saw her, I knew her to be my wife."

"Aye, that you did, Fred. That you did," she said, "You told me that on our first meeting."

"So," said Fred, "I packed my kit, moved to Jarrow, and applied for a job at Hawthorn Leslie. Being prosperous times for the shipbuilders, and with my experience, I got the job. And I've been here ever since, a Scot in Geordie land."

Fred and Mary had no children, so they were just four. Mary had pulled out the stops and prepared a Sunday lunch of a roast of lamb with the complete trimmings for Joe's and Ruth's visit that day, which they ate with relish. As we know, Joe was now an accomplished storyteller with a permanent sense of humour.

"It's just us two here," said Fred. "Mary knows my jokes. So, it's good to have you both here with us. I hope you have a few new jokes, Joe."

After lunch, the men retired to a small lounge at the front of the terraced house. Mary and Ruth cleaned up the table and washed the dishes, chatting. Then they made tea.

"You know, Joe, the thing I admire most in you is your approach to life," Fred said. "Despite our hardships, you are always so positive towards life. I've never known you to be in anything but friendly spirits."

"Aye, thank you, Fred," said Joe. "There's no point complaining. Why complain when we should improve our lives instead? I believe a positive approach to life helps me. That's why I like your ideas on seeing the world and learning, and that's what I want to do."

"Aye, that's true, laddie, true," said Fred, "The problem is, most of us forget that when the going gets tough. Not you; you stay positive no matter what. I admire that in you since you are still so young, with your entire life ahead of you."

"Fred, can I ask you something?"

"Sure, laddie, shoot."

"As you know, I've been considering joining the army and going to the fight in South Africa," said Joe. "My father, who I respect, is dead against it. As an old Irishman, he considers fighting downtrodden people like the Boers wrong."

"Well, he may have a point there," said Fred. "Who are we to question that? There must be solid reasons our Queen and government believe we must be there."

"Aye, you are so right. And I have told Da, despite his birthplace, I was born in England. England has given us work and shelter and a much better life than the mayhem and famine he had in Ireland. And I was born here—it's my country!"

"I understand where you are coming from, laddie. I'm a Scot, and the Scots don't have the best history with England. But Scotland is part of the United Kingdom, and I fought for the British Empire, as you know, and that was not wrong," said Fred. "It binds us together to protect our homes, families and homeland, and the United Kingdom is our homeland now, and that is our solemn duty."

"I'm glad to hear you say that, Fred. Because I respect your opinion, and you have the experience and wisdom to guide me."

"I can't guide you, Joe. But I can give you my beliefs and opinions and tell you about my life experiences. But you must inform yourself and make the right decisions."

"Yes, Fred, you are right."

"You are young, Joe. You have a long life ahead of you. So you must experience as much you can now since it's not as easy once you have a family of your own."

"You're right," said Joe.

"It's an enormous world out there. You can't believe it—enormous. And exciting, Joe. I can't tell you what to do, but I can open your inexperienced eyes beyond walking this road every morning to the yards. Not that I mind that, Joe. Now I've got Mary to look after, and Mary to look after me; I do it with pleasure."

"What should I do, Fred, given my current situation? What do you suggest?"

"Well…" said Fred, "you could join the home volunteers?"

"Home volunteers?" said Joe

"Yes. If you were to join the Volunteer Engineers, you could learn what army life is and do a useful job here before going to South Africa or anywhere else. I'd look into it if I were you."

"That's interesting," said Joe. "What an excellent idea. Thank you."

And then, Mary and Ruth entered the room with a tray full of tea and biscuits. So, the talk of war and soldiering ended.

After visiting Fred and Mary's home, Joe called on the local Durham Light Infantry depot to understand the Volunteer Force better. He learned it was a militia comprising a part-time citizens' army, forming rifle, artillery and engineer corps. The government created it in 1859 as a modern movement throughout the British Empire, a home protection force to be called upon should an enemy invade Britain.

The force involved engineers preparing and handling defences in harbours and electrical engineers erecting and practising electric arc lamp searchlights protecting the British coastline. They launched and operated observation balloons, constructed telegraph lines for communication and supply, and conveyed and supported the army. The army involved the engineers in various aspects of railroads since they had become so crucial to the empire's war efforts worldwide. They used trains for heavy work within the shipyards. Joe had experience with the shipyard's railway. So he brought this experience with him, hoping it would hold him in good stead. He had learned aspects of laying and maintaining tracks and even had experience in locomotives' fuelling, firing and driving.

The next time Joe and his marras met at the pub, he informed them of his conversation with Fred and the results of his research at the depot.

"Lads, I have the answer," he began. "We can join the Home Volunteers and work our way into the army right here in Jarrow."

"Tell us more," said Mike.

"We can join the Durham Light Infantry Home Volunteer Engineers," said Joe. "We can use what we know from the yards and learn the job of soldiering, too." He explained what he had learned about the Home Volunteers and where they could enlist.

"Sounds good, Joe," said Billy.

"Champion," said Jack and Mike in unison.

They spent the rest of the evening discussing the possibilities of working for the army with the exciting promise of an alternative life, far from Jarrow, protecting the British Empire. They resolved to join at the next opportunity.

The following night, Joe visited Fred at home.

"I've joined the 1st Durham Royal Engineer Volunteers, Fred," he announced, "I'm now in the British Army. And my marras have joined with me."

"Well done, Joe," Fred said with a broad smile, "I'm sure you won't regret it. It will open your eyes to a whole unknown world. Good luck, Laddie."

"We start our training on Saturday when we will get our uniforms."

"That I've got to see, Joe."

He could see that Joe was very proud of his latest decisive move. It was an interim solution that would lead to Joe being sent to South Africa later, just as Fred had been twenty years before him.

∼

The Relief of Mafeking

Now that Joe had found his new raison d'être as a soldier and official raconteur, with a growing circle of admiring friends, family and the regulars of the Rolling Mill Pub, he couldn't stop. He was enjoying it. Joe poured over the newspapers and committed their contents to memory. He revelled in his ever more intricate and eloquent storytelling.

So, on the 3rd Saturday of May 1900, he again addressed an eager audience on the latest developments in this far-off British war, which had aroused widespread interest. Everybody was discussing it, but few workers followed it in as much detail as Joe. This time, Joe relayed the news from Mafeking, one of the most famous and celebrated British actions in the Second Anglo-Boer War. And it had turned Colonel Baden-Powell into a national hero.

Joe checked his notes.

"Even though 8,000 Boer troops outnumbered the garrison at Mafeking, the British survived the siege for 217 days," said Joe. "This was because of

Colonel Baden-Powell's clever military tricks." .

"Tricks? What tricks?" asked someone.

"They laid mockup landmines around the town, in full view of the Boers," said Joe. "Colonel Baden-Powell ordered his soldiers to pretend to avoid barbed wire that wasn't there when moving between the trenches. From a distance, the Boers believed what they thought they saw. Baden-Powell's men shifted guns, and a searchlight made from an acetylene lamp and a biscuit tin around the town to create the impression there were many more of them."

"Were the Boers tricked?" asked Mike.

"Aye, the tricks were so clever, he hoodwinked them," said Joe. "They did much more than tricks, too. They built a howitzer cannon in Mafeking's railway workshops. And they even put an old 1770 gun with 'B.P. & Co.' engraved on the barrel into service."

Joe had captivated them, ales in hand and puffing on their pipes or cigarettes, while they listened to his stories.

"The general had an armoured train loaded with sharpshooters and sent it along the rail line in a daring attack right into the heart of the Boer camp. They then returned to Mafeking without incident," said Joe.

"Ha, now that's one sharp soldier," called out someone.

"Tell us this has a happy ending, Joe," called another.

"Quiet," said Mike. "Let's hear what happened there."

"It was too well-defended for the Boers, so on the 19th of November last year, 4,000 Boer fighters moved off elsewhere," said Joe. "They left enough fighters behind to carry on shelling Mafeking, which continued for several months."

"Bastards," shouted a stocky miner across the room. "Cowards! That's it; I'm enrolling. I don't know why I'm not there."

Such sentiment was increasing across the whole of the empire. So, yet more men joined up to "punish the Boers."

"Then, in May, the Boers heard British relief columns were approaching," said Joe. "So they launched a final, heavy attack early in the morning of the 12th of May. They breached the perimeter and set fire to part of the town. But our boys inside put up a terrific fight and beat them back. Then, the cowards surrendered. The siege ended on the 17th of May when the British forces under Colonel B.T. Mahon of Lord Robert's army relieved the town. Among those troops was one of Colonel Robert Baden-Powell's brothers, Major Baden Fletcher Smyth Baden-Powell."

"Hurrah, hurrah, hurrah," called the assembled crowd. "Another Broon for Joe, somebody. Excellent news at last."

"Well, not only good news," said Joe. "212 people died during the siege, and they injured over 600. But for once, the Boer losses were higher than ours. The Relief of Mafeking was a decisive victory for the British and a crushing defeat for the Boers. Things are looking up for us."

Joe was revelling in using the unfamiliar words he had learned through his reading - such as siege, relief, garrison, daring attack, decisive victory, and crushing defeat. He enjoyed their sound and was proud of his expanding vocabulary. Joe was a simple working man in a time when few read but loved an exciting story. He believed that stories arose by experiencing life and conveying the experiences well in words. Telling these stories gave Joe a newfound sense of purpose.

When news reached London at 9:17 P.M. on Friday, the 18th of May 1900, that they had relieved the garrison at Mafeking, central London exploded. The Relief of Mafeking inspired many celebrations throughout the empire, out of proportion to its significance, they said. Someone coined the verb 'to maffick,' meaning to celebrate with extravagance in public. The newspapers telegraphed the news, and enormous crowds converged outside their offices to hear the latest rescue news first-hand. Thousands poured into the streets of Britain to celebrate this long-sought victory. The empire could hold its head high again as news of victory upon achievement reached it from its far-flung shores. And they honoured Colonel Robert Baden-Powell as a great British hero.

Back in the pub, Joe quoted Frederick Burnham from a piece of paper.

"Baden-Powell is a wonderfully able scout and quick at sketches. I do not know another who could have done the work at Mafeking if the same conditions had been imposed. All the knowledge he gathered has been used to save that community."

"I only understand half of that, but I got the important bits," said Mike.

"Victory at Ladysmith, then Kimberley, and now Mafeking!" Joe proclaimed. "The war in South Africa is finally turning in our favour. Total victory and the war's end can't be far off now. As I speak, preparations for a push for ultimate victory and an end to the war are happening. A massive army under Lord Roberts is on the march towards Pretoria. But I'll get to that the next time we meet here."

Saturday evening at the Rolling Mill Pub had become an institution, much to the pleasure of the publican. Emotions had run the full gauntlet since the South African War had begun, from disinterest to disbelief to dismay to depression. But with the sieges over and Lord Roberts taking command of a massive British Army, the mood had shifted to hope and expecting victory.

"The newspapers are praising the Field Marshal and saying they believe we will see triumph," announced Joe.

"It's about bloody time," said Mike.

Most of the men gathered that evening echoed that sentiment.

"What is happening now, Joe?" asked Billy.

"Lord Roberts is preparing to march to Pretoria, Billy," said Joe. "Now, we will see more action against those cheeky farmers."

---

1. William Hart-McHarg, *From Quebec to Pretoria with the Royal Canadian Regiment*, 1902
2. A spruit is a small watercourse, typically dry except during the rainy season.
3. S.G.P Ward, *Faithful, The Story of the Durham Light Infantry*, 1962

CHAPTER 4
LORD ROBERT'S PERFECT STORM
MAY 1900 TO FEBRUARY 1901

At first, Roberts brought the Orange Free State under British control. He occupied the state capital of Bloemfontein, but whether the whole of the Free State was under his command was debatable. His next goal was the South African Republic and its capital, Pretoria, 300 miles northeast of Bloemfontein. So, Lord Roberts organized his army into three columns—the bulk of the infantry following him in the centre, and the mobile mounted infantry and cavalry covered the flanks. Lord Roberts may have learned this from the great Zulu king, Shaka. Shaka was a ruthless military genius who had changed warfare in his time by using the same formation. He named the centre as the Head of the Bull. The flanks he called the Horns of the Bull, which closed around the enemy, not allowing them to escape. He used this tactic to enforce his rule over the Zulus and built a vast Zulu empire with assegais (spears) and shields, not rifles.

At the head of the central column, Lord Roberts took a more or less straight route along the railway line. Roberts recalled Ian Hamilton, who had done so well in Natal at Elandslaagte and Ladysmith and promoted him to general. He then gave Hamilton command of the right flank mounted column following a zigzag route from one significant town to another between the republic capitals. To Lord Roberts' left, leading a formation comprising

Canadian, Australian, and New Zealand mounted infantry, was Major-General Hutton, Commander of the 1st Mounted Infantry Brigade, who had pioneered the mounted infantry in the British Army.

And following their progress in England through the British press, as always, was the British public. The papers sent home hundreds of articles and illustrations on the war. They focused everyone's attention and imagination on the British Army of 45,000 men at arms, 18,000 horses, and 1,200 field guns in the columns, forming a net of over 40 miles wide. Military bands were raising the spirits and courage of the men they were leading. Scores of supply wagons creaked and bumped over the rough terrain, and there were long trains of mules and oxen, over which whips cracked in the air. Teams of horses pulled cannons, gleaming in the Highveld sun, and tens of thousands of rifles on the shoulders of the British and colonial infantry soldiers were ready for action. And as they marched, they created vast dust clouds, whipping up in the wind and showing their presence from a significant distance. It was an astonishing sight, a once-in-a-lifetime spectacle, lasting an entire month over 300 miles. At its head, Field Marshal Roberts, dressed in his best khaki field uniform, sat erect on his well-groomed, black-maned steed. And the troops, marching in tight formations of ten men abreast and ten rows deep, sang their favourite marching songs, including

> *We are marching to Pretoria, Pretoria, Pretoria.*
> *We are marching to Pretoria,*
> *Pretoria, Hooorah!*

> *You sing with me, I'll sing with you, and so we will sing together*
> *So we will sing together*
> *So we will sing together*
> *Sing with me, I'll sing with you, and so we will sing together*
> *As we march along. We are marching to Pretoria, Pretoria, Pretoria.*

> *We are marching to Pretoria, Pretoria, Pretoria.*
> *We are marching to Pretoria,*
> *Pretoria, Hooorah!*

The press conveyed the effect such a spectacle may have had on the hapless Dutch farmers witnessing it. Journalists claimed the cockiness and bravado that the Boers displayed in the early phases of this war was diminishing, but was that true?

Joe followed every move of the Roberts and Hamilton advance on Pretoria. Joe followed General Ian Hamilton's Army of the Right Flank, made famous by Winston Churchill, attached to watch and report on Hamilton's movements. Churchill sent his despatches to the *Morning Post*,[1] which Joe devoured. Hamilton left a few days before the general flow of the rest of the army. He was to protect the right flank of the central advance under Roberts, fending off any Boer commandos which had moved northwards during the operations in April. They marched and fought via Thaba Nchu through Winburg, Kroonstad, Lindley, Heilbronn, Johannesburg, and Pretoria. The Burmah Mounted Infantry, including the 2/DLI company, was part of this column. The right flank started at Bloemfontein in April 1900. As it wended its way north on several long roads, it met with predictable resistance from the Boers in skirmishes and battles. They fought Thaba Nchu on the 29th of April. And again at Hout Nek, 13 miles north of Thaba Nchu, General Christiaan de Wet attacked them from the 30th of April to the 1st of May. Then, there were engagements with generals de la Rey and Botha at Tabaksberg on the 4th and the Vet River on the 5th and 6th of May.

And every Saturday night, as always, Joe and his marras met at the pub, where he brought them up to date on the latest developments. For example, he recounted one incident he had just read and noted.

"A Captain Balfour of the 11th Battalion Imperial Yeomanry entered Winburg to meet Commandant Philip Botha and his commando as they were leaving," said Joe. "The captain went into town as an envoy under a protecting white flag to demand the town's surrender."

"However, the Boer leader, misunderstanding Balfour's words, raised his rifle and called out, 'Arrest that man!'" said Joe.

The audience became tense, waiting for what happened next.

"Well," said Joe, "the Landdrost, or chief magistrate of a district, and the mayor understood the potential danger of the confrontation and surrendered. Commandant Philip Botha then galloped off with his men to escape."

"That bastard, Botha!" Mike bellowed.

"Aye, but the mayor was a sensible Boer," said Joe. "There were enough stores of ammunition and forage in the town, which Captain Balfour confiscated. Don't confuse Philip Botha with Louis Botha, a Boer general causing us constant trouble, and you'll hear of him soon enough."

~

The Boers Bow to Roberts' Great Army

Meanwhile, unbeknown to Joe, the young but by then seasoned Boer fighter Deneys Reitz recounted his experience at the same battles in more detail, later published in his book, Commando[2]. Deneys and his brothers had survived the fighting in Natal with the Pretoria commandos. After spending two months in Natal recuperating, he heard a mighty army under Lord Roberts had captured Bloemfontein and was marching to Pretoria. He and his brothers decided they should return to the country of their birth, the Orange Free State, to defend it. They left the Pretoria commando with whom they had served for so long and rode through the valley to the train at Glencoe Junction.

They stopped a northbound train at the railway station, loaded their horses in one truck and themselves in another and left Natal behind them. After a three-day journey, including the usual delays at halts and stations, they arrived in Pretoria. Their father did not know they were coming until they approached the front door. But he approved when they told him they were heading to the Free State.

On the 30th of April, Deneys, his three brothers and their boy Charley caught a train for the Free State. Deneys knew the British had occupied Bloemfontein and were advancing towards the Transvaal, but they didn't know how far the railway line to the south was still open. They crossed the Vaal River that night, and after a slow journey over the rolling plains of the northern Free State, they reached a small station near the banks of the Vet River within fifty miles of Bloemfontein at eleven o'clock the following evening. But the train couldn't continue. The staff told them the British advance was two stations ahead. So they off-loaded their horses and camped beside the track until daybreak.

As they were preparing to start the following day, another train arrived from the north, carrying 150 men under Commandant Malan, a brother-in-law of Commandant-General Piet Joubert, who had died. Malan had recruited inexperienced men who he formed into a flying column called the Afrikander Cavalry Corps (ACC). They were on their way to the nearest fighting.

Deneys and his brothers enrolled themselves as members of the ACC. They spent the morning getting ready, and that afternoon, they began their forward advance, riding south through the Vet River toward the sound of distant gunfire.

By nightfall, they were on the vast plateau beyond the river, where they met hundreds of withdrawing horse riders. The retreating Boer fighters said they were heading to new positions, but Deneys suspected them of being on their way home. They reported that vast swarms of British troops were on the move and that it was useless to think of fighting them face-to-face. The ACC had ridden until midnight when they encountered General de la Rey and halted with his Transvaal commandos. Squatting by a small fire, the general was a splendid-looking older man with his hawk-beak nose and fierce black eyes.

"He gave us a hurried account of the state of affairs, which was bleak," Deneys noted.

General Koos de la Rey was one of the bravest Boer generals and a leader of Boer independence. He opposed the war initially, and President Paul Kruger accused him of being a coward. De la Rey said, "I will still fight long after Paul Kruger has given up and fled for safety." Doornfontein Farm in the Winburg District was De la Rey's birthplace, and he was now fighting on his home turf.

With Cronje and Bloemfontein captured and Roberts' army advancing on the Transvaal, the Boers were on the run. Because of the demoralized state of the commandos and the lack of defensive cover in this bare region, de la Rey saw little or no hope of stopping them. He said he had 4,000 demotivated Transvaalers who escaped the debacle at Paardeberg and were no longer interested in fighting. The Free State commandos had disappeared altogether. But he believed President Steyn and Christian de Wet were out of action for the time being and trying to reorganize themselves somewhere in the mountain country to the east. Meanwhile, the British were within a few miles and would doubtless resume their advance in the morning.

General de la Rey ordered the ACC to ride forward for half an hour and halt until daybreak. They were then to join the firing line and react according to the evolving state of affairs. Having arrived at their destination, they sat draped in their blankets, shivering till daybreak. It was late autumn, and the temperature was below zero, so they could not sleep.

They scanned the horizon at dawn and soon distinguished dense masses of British infantry on the plain. The horsemen arrived first, followed by infantry, guns and wagons, creating massive dust clouds.

They looked in dismay at the advancing army of over 40,000 men. They faced this massive enemy with so few Boer horse riders strung in a jagged line along a gentle ridge. From how the men sat on their horses, Reitz noted that they refused to stand against this advancing force. It must have been a terrible sight for this diverse band of Boer fighters. This grand British army was advancing across the dusty plain, trampling the grasses and everything else beneath their marching feet and under their rumbling wagons.

They were on the same plain that Reitz had surveyed at the start of his journey.

"One might wonder how such a small group of men could confront such a horde?" said Reitz. "But we did."

As the British scouts approached them, the Boers fired at them until the scouts fell back to their regiments. Then, the British unlimbered the batteries, and shrapnel was soon bursting over the Boer fighters, causing their line to collapse. The ACC stayed as long as possible but soon realized the futility of standing up to such odds. They galloped back in retreat with field guns and QF 1-pounder pom-poms showering them with shells as they rode. After a hard ride, they slowed at a deserted farmhouse to rest their exhausted horses.

By nightfall, the British had pushed the Boers back to the Vet River, a distance of 20 miles or more. They had just enough time to prepare a quick breakfast the following day before they saw the British columns advancing again. It was relentless.

General Louis Botha had hurried from Natal by rail to see conditions in the Free State and was waiting at a drift in the Vet River. Born in Greytown, Natal, he fought as a burgher under Lucas Meyer in Northern Natal and later became a general, commanding and fighting at Colenso and Spion Kop. On the death of P.J. Joubert and the end of hostilities in Natal, the Transvaal Boers made him their commander-in-chief.

He and General de la Rey now stretched their commandos along the Vet River from the railway bridge to a point four miles away. They were under orders to make a stand against the approaching British Army.

They positioned the ACC on the extreme right, seeking a suitable spot on the river bank. Leaving their horses in the riverbed, they took up their posts. Since Deneys expected trouble, he sent Charley to the rear with their spare kit loaded on the Basuto pony they had brought from Natal as a pack horse.

The British were advancing across the plain that descended to the river. Before long, the artillery was lobbing shells at the Boers from the tall grass. Then their guns came forward and shelled the Boers again, who couldn't see the British positions because of the thorn trees fringing the bank. They had to crawl to the outside edge of the bush to see the enemy, leaving them sparse cover.

"The British killed and wounded several men near my brothers and me," said Deneys. "Altogether, it was a beastly day." [3]

Heavy shelling ran along the Boer line as far as the bridge and back again. It continued until long into the afternoon, and only at three o'clock did they see the infantry preparing to charge.

The ACC had suffered six dead and 15 wounded by that stage. They lay the dead on the sand in the riverbed, placed the injured on their horses, and sent them on their way to survive as best they could. The rest stayed in holes and hollows they had dug into the sandy soil. But the British infantry advanced, and 300 cavalrymen rode with their swords thrust before them. The Boers fired a few shots, then scrambled pell-mell into the riverbed to get their horses. Leaving their dead, they mounted the opposite bank and raced across the open plain to the hills a mile behind them. The British pounded them non-stop with cannon shells. Then, just before sunset, the soldiers arrived to drive them out of the hills into which they had fled. One of the British regiments changed direction, and before the Boers could stop them, the British soldiers were climbing into the hills where the Boers were hiding. They worked their way towards the Boer fighters from 1,500 yards away.

It was utter chaos. The brave men who had besieged Ladysmith were experiencing their enemy's entire weight and might, and they could see that the tide was turning against them. The British legions were too many despite their "inferior riding and fighting skills." [4]

"One cannot imagine the depths of despair we were feeling by then," said Deneys.

But it got even worse for the Boers. Panic set in as they reeled around to meet the approaching British troops, and the remaining ACC took flight. Bullets were firing in every direction, and one bullet shot out the horse from under Deneys' eldest brother. The sun was setting and shining in their eyes, so they couldn't get any accurate shots off in defence. But they grabbed another horse from the dozens, bolting around the battlefield without riders. The ACC then joined the complete and utter rout of the Boer forces. Over 30 ACC men were dead or wounded by then, but the full Boer force had far more casualties. They fell well back behind the lines again.

As soon as dawn broke the following day, dust clouds rising south of the river showed that the British Army was getting near again. A counterforce of 600 burghers was looming under the personal command of General Louis Botha. He ordered them to open out, and each man stood before his horse, awaiting the onslaught.

Their wait didn't last long.

First, the English scouts crossed the river, followed by the infantry dropping into the drifts as more troops and transport columns approached. The British gun batteries opened fire, and the Boers mounted and retreated since there was no cover. The entire day long, the British kept driving them back.

"They herded us like sheep to the incessant shriek of shells and whizz of bullets," said Reitz. "By evening, we were a demoralized rabble fleeing across the veldt." [5]

It was a total rout that helped convince generals de la Rey and Botha that conventional war against such an army was futile—although not hopeless enough for the Boer fighters to give up. They needed to change their approach.

Joe completed his version of this battle as told by Churchill from a British perspective in his *Morning Post* despatches from the front, not repeated here.

"We were showing them who was in command," said Joe. "We were beating the shite out of them."

"That's how it should be," Mike snorted, "We are giving the Boers what they deserve—a good hiding!"

"Aye," said Joe, "We have them retreating now."

"They are still giving our army a hard time," said Billy.

"Aye, right, but their numbers are dropping," said Jack.

The following weekend, on Saturday, the 12th of May, Joe and his marras once again met at the pub for an update. As usual, after preliminary greetings and getting a few bottles of ale, Joe launched into another narrative, this time on the clash with General Louis Botha on the 10th of May at the Sand River. Once again, the British column defeated the outnumbered Boers. Joe concluded, "We have the Boers on the run, and this battle proves it. They must soon surrender."

The marras agreed. "It sure looks much better for us, doesn't it, Joe? Here's to Lord Roberts!" And they lifted their ale glasses in a salute.

"We are beating the Boers at every battle," said Jack.

"Victory is ours," Mike shouted, standing and raising his glass to another toast. And with that, the other pub patrons stood, raised their glasses and sang a stanza of *We Are Marching to Pretoria*.

"They won't give up," said Billy, pointing out the obvious.

"They are a very proud and stubborn folk," said Joe. "Not only that, but they are defending their country."

"They are stupid," said Mike. "Why don't they surrender?"

"I don't know, Mike. If an enemy invaded England, I, for one, would fight to the end."

"You're right, Joe; I get your point and would too," said Mike. "We all would."

For the next three Saturdays, Joe kept everyone abreast of where the army had reached on their march to Pretoria.

On Saturday, the 26th of May, they heard of the British occupation of the Orange Free State two days earlier.

"Lord Roberts is doing his job," Jack proclaimed.

"Aye," said Joe with enthusiasm. "They have conquered one Republic; one more to go—the so-called South African Republic."

"Aye, and we're missing it," said Mike.

"I'm doing what I can," said Joe. "But the family and Ruth are holding me back. Please give me more time. Otherwise, you guys just get going, and I'll catch up with you."

"No," said Mike. "I can wait. But for God's sake, hurry."

"Us, too," said the others.

Then, when the marras met a week later on the 2nd of June, Joe reported on the Battle for Johannesburg at Doornkop on the 29th of May, alias the Battle of Klipriviersberg.

The Battle of Doornkop and victory at Johannesburg

"The Battle of Doornkop this last week was a key battle to take control of the mining town, Johannesburg," Joe started. "Doornkop is a ridge of hills southwest of Johannesburg and the same place where Dr. Leander Starr Jameson capitulated on the 2nd of January 1896, following his raid against the Transvaal government. This week, we came up against the Boer General Koos de la Rey there, and a fierce battle followed. The Boers chose a suitable position. They waited among enormous boulders on a long ridge with heavy guns facing the British troops. Two other powerful forces occupied more ridges further west. The whole of the Boer position facing our troops was 6 miles long."

"Shite!" said Billy. "Which of our boys were there, and what happened next?"

"The 21st Brigade under Brigadier-General Smith-Dorien, supported by two field batteries, moved over to the left to handle the right of the Boer position," said Joe. "This force, containing the Canadians, Gordons and Cornwalls, under cover of two field batteries and 5-inch guns, moved forward for the major attack on the Boers. The Gordons were the outstanding regiment that day. They placed them in the centre, the Cornwalls on their left and the Royal Canadians on the right. The Shropshires [6] stayed behind with the baggage."

Joe's marras were getting accustomed to the military terminology such as battalions, regiments, batteries and the various weapons, but they were battling to keep up with the multiple units involved.

"Gordons?" asked Mike. "Who are they?"

"The Gordon Highlanders are from Aberdeen and the northeast of Scotland," said Joe, referring to his notes. "The Gordons have a history of being fierce fighters. They fought in Egypt, the Peninsula, Waterloo and Afghanistan. They were returning to England after many years overseas when the army rerouted the regiment to fight in the disastrous 1st Anglo-Boer War in South Africa. The Gordons suffered severe casualties at the Battle of Majuba Hill. My marra, Fred, once told me about the Gordons and that battle. And they involved the Gordons in the successful defence of Ladysmith during this war."

"I've heard of them," said Billy. "They're a fine Scottish regiment."

"Aye, they are," said Joe. "They proved themselves again at Doornkop. The three regiments moved forward in four lines, 150 yards apart. They spread them out behind a ridge with 20 to 30 paces between the men. As they advanced over the ridge, the ground dropped away and rose again to the opposite ridge. The distance between the two hills was two miles. The Boers set fire to the grass, and a light wind from the north fanned the fire towards our boys. It forced them to run through the flames halfway down the slope.

Soldiers in kilts singed their legs, beards and eyebrows. From then on, they were on the burnt ground, the khaki contrasting with the blackened soil."

"These bloody Boers are snakes," growled Mike. "Imagine using fire against your enemy?"

"Anything goes in war," said Billy.

"Anyway," said Joe. "Covered by the heavy shell fire from two batteries and the 5-inch guns, our boys descended the slope and climbed up the opposite ridge. And the front line established itself in an excellent position to open fire. The second line reinforced the first, and they held this location until sundown."

"What brave lads they are," said Jack. "They must have been sitting targets."

"In the meantime, out of sight of the Brigadier, the Gordons took matters into their own hands," said Joe. "They advanced nearer the top of the ridge, halting from time to time to return the fire of the Boers. And then, despite the heavy gunfire pouring upon them, they rushed the Boer positions with their bayonets. But as they reached the ridge, they saw the last Boers escaping on their horses."

"Cowards. Bloody cowards," said Mike.

"Aye, they ran away, they did," said Joe. "Then the City Imperial Volunteers, supported by the Camerons, attacked the left. The Derbys drove the enemy from the kopje on the west, so they cleared the positions just as it got dark. I read that one of the Canadian soldiers involved in this battle was full of admiration and praise on the day for the Gordon Highlanders, writing later that:

"The Gordon Highlanders earned the honours of the day. From a military point of view, I cannot imagine anything finer than the sight they presented on the 29th of May 1900 at Doornkop. They marched up to the Boer rifles, confident, with an even stride, earning the admiration of all who saw them. They were never steadier on the parade ground of Edinburgh Castle. Nine officers and eighty-eight men put out of action in a short time testified to the severity of the fire they endured. But even if only half the company was left, it would have engaged with its foe." [7]

"Howay, man," said Billy. "What a regiment."

"Aye, they are," said Joe. "I learned from my new marra, Fred, how they fought during the 1st Anglo-Boer War. They are a feisty lot!"

"What a battle it was," said Mike. "We're winning this war at last. But where are the Irish?"

"Which Irish?" Joe asked. "Irish-Irish, American-Irish, Boer-Irish or British-Irish? They're all over the bloody place."

The marras then broke into wild laughter, and Mike fetched another round of ale.

Joe concluded his story of the Battle of Doornkop. "The cavalry had taken the Doornkop ridge under the command of General John French. Seven infantry battalions took an adjacent ridge, including the Canadians, the City Imperial Volunteers and the Gordon Highlanders of General Ian Hamilton. And so, with this victory at Doornkop, not one month after they had left Bloemfontein, 250 miles away, Roberts' army entered the mining city of Johannesburg victorious. They didn't stay for long, though, for the primary goal remained Pretoria. They gave the troops two days to recoup their strength and to wait while supplies caught up with them."

Pretoria Capitulates

On the 3rd of June 1900, Roberts resumed the advance. The army again marched in three columns; as before, the Cavalry Division under French was on the left, and Ian Hamilton's force formed the right column. The central infantry column marched nearest the railway line, comprising the Seventh and Eleventh Divisions, the 3rd Cavalry Brigade under Brigadier-General J R P Gordon and the Corps Troops. They were under the personal command of the Field Marshal, who left one brigade behind to hold Johannesburg. Pretoria fell without a fight before midnight on the 4th of June, and the British troops entered the town unopposed the following day.

Joe had studied Churchill's description of this momentous day from the newspaper article. [8]

"By first light, the army moved forward," said Joe. "They despatched the Guards to the railway station, and Ian Hamilton's force swept around the city's western side. Churchill hurried ahead to enter the town among the first victorious troops and joined his cousin, the Duke of Marlborough. Together, they soon caught up with General Pole-Carew, who was advancing towards the railway station with his staff. Churchill's contingent passed through a narrow split in the southern wall of mountains, revealing Pretoria lying before them. For the first time, they viewed the picturesque town with red and blue roofs peeping out among masses of trees, here and there the occasional spire of a factory chimney. Behind them, on the hills they had just taken, they crowded the brown Pretoria forts with British soldiers. Two hundred yards away stood the railway station.

"They forced General Pole-Carew to wait while the infantry caught up with him. While they were waiting, a locomotive whistle sounded. Then, to their astonishment, a train drawn by two engines steamed out of the station on the Delagoa Bay line. They observed this insolent breach of the customs of war for a moment since the town had not yet surrendered. No mounted troops being at hand, a dozen staff officers, aides-de-camp, and orderlies launched into action at a furious gallop, hoping to force the train to stop. Failing that, they were to shoot the engine driver, sending it to its destruction. But wire fences and the gardens of the houses thwarted them. Despite their best efforts, the train escaped with ten train wagons of horses, which might have been of value, and one carriage load of Afrikanders. Three engines with steam up and several trains still stood in the station. The leading company of Grenadiers, rushing forward, captured them and their occupants. These Afrikanders tried to resist the troops with pistols but soon surrendered after someone fired two volleys. They hurt no one in the scrimmage.

"After a further delay, the Guards, fixing bayonets, entered the town. Marching through the principal street, crowded with people, towards the central square, they posted sentries and pickets as they went.

"Churchill was eager to know what had befallen his comrades from the train in Natal, held prisoner these long months. Rumour had it they had moved them at night to Waterfall Boven, 200 miles along the Delagoa Bay line."

"The Duke of Marlborough found a mounted Dutchman who declared he knew where the officers were, and he offered to guide him. They set off at a gallop without waiting for the troops to advance with due precautions.

"Within a few minutes, turning a corner and crossing a small brook, they saw an extensive tin building surrounded by a dense wire entanglement. Seeing this familiar building, Churchill raised his hat and cheered; then, a cry answered from inside the building at once. What followed resembled the end of a theatrical melodrama. Churchill had returned to the same building, the Model School, from which he had escaped not six months earlier. It was a triumphant moment for him, as he recalled."

"The Duke of Marlborough demanded that the commandant of the prison surrender," said Churchill. "Prisoners rushed into the yard, some in uniform, others in flannels, hatless or coatless, but all excited in their freedom at last. They flung the gates open, and a few guards surrendered their rifles. Another 52 Boer sentries stood by, uncertain of what to do. But the long-penned-up officers knew what to do: they surrounded the sentries and seized their weapons. Grimshaw, of the Dublin Fusiliers, presented a Union Jack he had made during his imprisonment. He'd made it from a Vierkleur, the green, red, white and blue Transvaal flag. They tore down the Transvaal emblem and, amid wild cheers, hoisted the homespun British flag over Pretoria. Time 8.47 A.M., the 5th of June 1900.[9]

"The commandant then formally surrendered 129 officers and 39 soldiers to the Duke of Marlborough, who he had in his custody as prisoners of war. He then offered himself four corporals and 48 Dutchmen. The Boers were confined within the wire cage and guarded by their liberated prisoners. But they decided since the guards had treated the British prisoners well, they could take the oath of neutrality and return to their homes.

"The anxieties the prisoners had suffered during the last few hours of their confinement were terrible. Nor did I wonder, when I heard the account, why their faces were so white and their manner so excited. But the reader shall learn the tale from one of their numbers. [10]

"At two o'clock, Lord Roberts, the staff and the foreign attachés entered Pretoria victorious. They headed to the central square surrounded by city hall, the parliament house and other public buildings. They hoisted the British flag over Parliament House amid cheers. The victorious army then paraded past it. With the Guards leading, Pole-Carew's division came from the south and Ian Hamilton's force from the west. For three hours, the river of steel and khaki flowed. The townsfolk gazed in awe and wonder at those endless, majestic soldiers.

"With such pomp and the rolling of drums, they ushered the new order into Pretoria. The former government had ended without dignity. One had hoped to find the stolid old president seated on his stoep reading his Bible and smoking a sullen pipe, but he chose a different destiny. On Friday preceding the British occupation, Kruger left the capital and withdrew along the Delagoa Bay Railway. He took with him a million pounds in gold. The old president left behind him a crowd of officials short of pay and far from satisfied with the worthless cheques they had received instead of pounds.

The Canadian William Hart McHarg of the Royal Canadian Regiment described the moment:

"Lord Roberts, with Lord Kitchener and all his staff, took up a position on the south side of the church, facing the Raadzaal. The only band that could be mustered was the Derbys, placed opposite, and the grand march past began.

"The Guards fixed bayonets and headed the procession, followed by the Warwicks, the Yorks, the Essex and the Welsh. Then our turn came, and we were followed by the 21st Brigade. It was the campaign's climax, even if not the war's end. I shall never forget that parade. Ragged and tanned, footsore and weary, dirty and gaunt, we trudged along the western road leading into the square, past the race course, where the British prisoners had been kept, past Paul Kruger's house, through lines of transport and mounted troops moving in different directions; past British sentries guarding piles of arms the burghers were busy surrendering; a 'Halt! Fix Bayonets!' and then on into the square.

"As we wheeled around the corner, the band struck up *'The Boys of the Old Brigade.'* I thought it was the sweetest music I had ever heard. We squared our shoulders, chucked out our chests, and put all the ginger we could muster into our step. I hope everyone else felt as stirred up as I did; if so, they experienced a sensation they will not forget.

"Out of a regiment of 1,150 men, we entered Pretoria with 438. We had marched 620 miles on scant rations since being brigaded on the 12th of February, helped capture ten towns, fought in ten general engagements and on many other days, and stood shoulder to shoulder with British regiments of a long and great tradition. But what thought we of perils and hardships?

"We stood on the 5th of June as the representatives of the Canadian people in the Grand Army of the British Empire in the surrendered capital of the enemy. And there was 'Bobs, a little thinner and somewhat browner than when we last saw him at Kroonstad but sitting on his horse in the same old incomparable style, and the light of his eye as undimmed as ever, while on one side of him sat Kitchener, and on the other our gallant brigadier, Major-General Smith-Dorrien, who had led us successfully and well during the past four months.

"It was one of those unique moments which only come to a man occasionally during a lifetime, and it will never be forgotten. Suppose anyone asks me what I consider the most extraordinary occasion. In that case, I say that it was when I marched past Lord Roberts in Pretoria on the 5th of June 1900 with the Royal Canadian Regiment."[11]

"But the war had not yet ended," said Joe. "So, on the 16th of June 1900, Lord Roberts issued a proclamation warning the Republican forces. 'We will burn houses near Boer activities, and the inhabitants will be made prisoners of war.' This policy became known as the British 'Scorched Earth Policy.' Henceforth, they would drive stubborn Boers and their families to hell on earth."

Determined to pursue his political career, Churchill returned to England on the RMS Dunnottar Castle in July 1900. This ship was the same one he had set sail for South Africa eight months earlier. Upon his return to England, Churchill published *London to Ladysmith via Pretoria* and the second volume of Boer war experiences in *Ian Hamilton's March*. These were both based on his collected despatches to the *Morning Post*. Churchill stood again as an MP in Oldham in the 1900 general election and won. This victory promised him a career as a British politician. After the 1900 general election, he started a speaking tour of Britain, followed by journeys to the United States and Canada. The trip earned Churchill £5,000, and he retired from the regular army in 1900.

"*The Times* wrote 4,314 men surrendered in Pretoria on the 9th of August," Joe reported.

"Because of the operations, they captured three guns, 2,800 head of cattle, 4,000 sheep, and between 5 and 6 thousand healthy horses. The British destroyed two million rounds of ammunition." [12]

"Are you going to tell me it's finished?" Mike asked.

"Aye, it looks like it," said Joe.

"Damn, does that mean we won't be going to South Africa?" asked a somewhat despondent Jack.

"Well, the Boers haven't surrendered yet," said Joe. "There have been no peace discussions yet. And although we've killed or captured many thousands, it still leaves thousands at large in the Republics."

And Joe was right. Even though the British believed that, through this ultimate victory, they had won the war, the Boers had other ideas. They realized that they couldn't beat the mighty army of the British Empire using conventional warfare. With the British occupying the former Boer Republics, the Boers retreated into the bush and hills across South Africa. They resorted to guerrilla tactics and gave the superior British Army real headaches.

What happened to the Royal Canadian Regiment then was documented by A.S. McCormick:

"From Pretoria, we went to Springs to guard the coal mines. After a 'sentry go' of 24 hours, men were black from the dust. This was the only place where we lived in buildings. The rest of the time, except for an occasional short period in which we had tents, we lived in the great outdoors in days hot and nights freezing cold. It is a healthy climate, and none ever caught a cold.

"Around the town were outposts with trenches where sentries were posted. It wasn't bad during the day, but the nights were so dark that seeing over 10 feet was impossible. A sentry watched less for the enemy than for the officer making his rounds, for if he failed to see and challenge him, he got hell. One hour before daylight, the battalion with loaded rifles fell at the square to prepare for a night attack. We were ready for a 'night attack' at daybreak.

"One night, an alarm called us out because 'heavy firing has been heard at the No.8 outpost.' A company hurried over and learned that there had been no firing; a black mule driver had drawn the end of his whip along the side of a corrugated iron house as he passed, and the 'rrrrrrrrrrrrrrrr' sounded like distant rifle fire to the main guard sentry. At another station, Silverton near Pretoria, a sandstorm arose every day at noon when 'come to the cookhouse door, boys' was sounded. We had to run into the tents and close every opening to keep the sand from getting into the food.

"On August 2nd, we left Springs for the Orange Free State to join a brigade and go after General De Wet, the cleverest guerilla. We missed him, but we gave him the run of his life for 21 days, driving him to the far north of the Transvaal, although we were on foot and his men were on horses. On the 10th, we crossed the Vaal River from the Orange Free State into the Transvaal. The river at this point is 500 to 600 feet wide, and we accomplished the almost incredible feat of crossing without getting wet. At high water, the river is a raging torrent. When we crossed, it was low water but just as damp, with many deep pools, so we jumped from rock to rock. At dangerous spots, two men stood where they could catch the jumper as he landed. Only one man fell in. The British officers were not as adaptable to the situation as were ours, and the men of the other four battalions splashed their way across with no chance of getting dry because the march, like a show, must go on. The other battalions in the brigade, commanded by Major General Fitzroy Hart, were the 1st Battalion Derbyshire Regiment, 2nd Battalion Dublin Fusiliers, 1st Battalion Somerset Light Infantry, and 2nd Battalion Northumberland Fusiliers.

"Marching day and night with only four hours of sleep, we averaged seventeen miles daily and did 301 miles in twenty days. One day, I went on sentry-go at midnight. The march started at 2:30, and we did not stop until 11:30, during which time I was still on sentry-go by the water cart, a record sentry-go of eleven and a half hours. We marched thirty miles, the last four hours under a scorching sun, up and down hills. When we finally halted, men of all the battalions straggled in for two hours, dropped everything and lay down. After four hours, we resumed the march but were turned back after going two miles. Then we learned that we had been on the way to relieve besieged Zeerust near Mafeking but that another force had reached the place.

"One day, when some careless boob in the mounted infantry ahead dropped a lighted match, we had to run like hell to get around the blazing dry grass. Food was short: weak coffee and biscuits for breakfast, tea and biscuits at noon; for supper, thin soup, some boiled meat, tea and biscuits. Very monotonous.

"Despite everything, the men of the RCR were a jolly lot and saw the humour in any difficulty. On the march, 24 singers sang in the middle of the battalion. Two popular songs were the lovely 'Blow Ye Winds in the Morning' and 'I'll Make Dat Black Gal Mine.' When a French Canadian member of F Company would start a French song, his company and E Company joined in.

MICHAEL G. BERGEN

"We left the brigade at Krugersdorp and moved by train to stations on the Delegoa Bay Railroad. On the 24th of October, we marched to Pretoria, arriving shortly before the darkness, which came quickly. We had no tents, and the night was very unpleasant sleeping on the ground in a wild rainstorm. After two days in Pretoria, we left for Capetown, the officers in comfortable coaches, the men in open coal trucks. The bully beef, biscuits, and tea were very tiresome and unsatisfactory.

"We reached Capetown on the 7th of November and immediately boarded the Elder-Dempster S.S. Hawarden Castle, which sailed at 4 P.M. Also on board was the Household Cavalry Regiment, a fine lot of men. We were 260 men, comprising A and B Companies, Col. Otter commanding."

Sargeant William Hart-McHarg was in that detachment and described their homeward journey.

"On the voyage, we passed through the Canary Islands and Madeira. We had 24 hours at St Vincent in the Cape Verde Islands, arrived at Southampton on the morning of November 29th, and reached London by the afternoon. The London streets were lined with cheering crowds as the Band of the Coldstream Guards led us to Kensington Barracks. We had comfortable quarters and good meals, but on the first night in a bed, many of us could not sleep after so many months of sleeping on the ground. Some rolled up in blankets and slept on the floor.

"On December 10th, we left for Liverpool, arriving in the early afternoon. The streets were lined so that we barely had enough space to march. The colossal square by the law courts and town hall was filled with at least 50,000 cheering men and women.

"We sailed on the 'Lake Champlain' on December 12th, stopped at Queenstown, Ireland, on the 13th, reached Halifax on the 23rd, and I was home the afternoon of the 24th. We arrived at our stations in complete marching order with all our equipment, which the government decided we should be allowed to keep.

"The Canadian Government also gave us scrip for 320 acres in Western Canada, and I sold mine for $700.00.

The 2nd Battalion, Royal Canadian Regiment of Infantry, had set a very high standard for British Empire units following them in the South African War. Four more excellent Canadian contingents, the 1st Canadian Mounted Rifles (Royal Canadian Dragoons), the Royal Canadian Artillery and the 2nd Canadian Mounted Rifles, and the Strathcona's Horse, soon followed the RCR returning home. The Dragoons left the next month, and the RCA and Mounted Rifles departed for Canada Canada in December 1900. The Strathcona's Horse left in January 1901.

John McCrae of the Royal Canadian Artillery returned to Canada with his regiment in January 1901. When he left South Africa, it was with mixed feelings about war. He was still convinced of the need to fight for one's country, but the young doctor was shocked by the poor treatment of the sick and injured soldiers.

More men died of disease during the war than in combat, partly due to foul water, poor hygiene, and poorly run field hospitals. McCrae wrote of the British hospital "for absolute neglect and rotten administration; it is a model. I am ashamed of some members of my profession; every day, from 15 to 30, Tommies die from fever and dysentery. Everyone who dies is sewn up in a blanket at the cost of four shillings out of their pay. The soldier's game is not what it's cracked up to be."

It would become a lifelong mission of John McCrae to improve the conditions of field hospitals in wartime.

The third Canadian contingent was the only one to take a field hospital to South Africa in January 1900, providing outstanding medical services during its stint there. 10 CFH numbered only 61 staff and 29 horses. It was organized into a hospital staff of five officers, a ward section of 35 other ranks, and a transport section of 21 others to pick up and transport the wounded. The hospital was based on British practice with Canadian innovations, including improved tenting, ambulances, water trailers, and an acetylene gas lighting system. Many among the staff of 10 CFH were veterans of previous tours in South Africa.

In South Africa, a section of the hospital unit accompanied the 2nd Regiment, Canadian Mounted Rifles, into the western Transvaal. The rest moved to Vaalbank, 60 kilometres away on the Lichtenberg blockhouse line, until 18 June 1902. There, it received sick and wounded from the columns operating in the area. This section of 10 CFH treated over a thousand British, Boer and Black South African patients. 10 CFH ambulances evacuated patients for longer-term care to Klerksdorp.

The 10th Canadian Field Hospital (10 CFH) stayed and offered vital services until after the war ended.

Outing to South Shields

Excursions to the beach were always an important and happy event for the workers of Tyneside. It was a rare diversion from the workers' arduous lives, only happening once or twice a year in the spring and summer. In August 1900, the Rutherfords joined in the exodus. The women prepared picnic lunches while the men gathered the children and any accessories they needed for such an occasion, such as beach pails, shovels and other sports items.

The next time the marras met, Joe described his family outing.

"On this Sunday, everyone dressed up in their best clothes, as always," remembered Joe, "They told the children to wear beach clothes under their Sunday dress. We had our baths the night before and looked our best. We men wore our finest shoes and clothes and straw boater hats, and the women dressed up in their Sunday finery, including their fancier straw bonnets. We headed to the train station in high spirits when everyone was ready. The men carried the lunches and any bags of extras packed by the women.

"My family comprised my father, Thomas James, and mother, Susannah Irwin, my four brothers, and seven sisters. Then there were the wives and husbands, five boys and three girls. It was a large clan of Rutherfords on the move that day. At the station, the working men bought return tickets to South Shields for the family. Then they waited for the train, which soon appeared, grunting and puffing its way into the station. It was a lovely sunny morning, and everyone was excited about the day ahead.

South Shields is a coastal town at the mouth of the River Tyne, England, 4 miles downstream from Jarrow. It sits on a peninsula where the River Tyne meets the North Sea. It has six miles of coastline and three miles of riverfrontage, dominated by the massive North and South Piers at the mouth of the Tyne. South Shields has excellent sandy beaches, dunes and coves, and dramatic limestone cliffs with grassy areas above, known as The Leas, which cover three miles of the coastline. It was a favourite Sunday destination of the miners and shipbuilders of the South Tyne urban and industrial sprawl.

"From the South Shields railway station to the beach was half a mile away, a pleasant walk along Ocean Road on such a beautiful day. But this wasn't a quiet outing on one's own. They packed the train with labourers and their families. It was deafening with the screams and laughter of children and the shouts of parents admonishing their behaviour in public. They filled the station as they left the train and strolled along the road to the beach. But when they got to the beach, it was so crowded there was no space to move. Yet nobody minded this. They were carefree, not working, away from the daily routine and out to have a lovely time with their families and friends. Sundays were peaceful family days in England, so far away from the war in South Africa.

"At the beach, we joined the crowd, but not before agreeing on a meeting place should anyone get lost in the crowd," Joe told his marras. "The children tore off their outer layer of clothes and raced to the water's edge. The parents shouted reminders not to venture too far into the sea since none could swim and to stay together. Then, the adults flung off their shoes and socks. We men rolled up our trousers, and the women lifted their skirts and wandered into the chilly water at the beach's edge to watch the children.

"After an hour of playing on the beach, we went to the Marine Park to find a quieter spot for lunch. Finding just such a place under a tree, the women spread the picnic blankets and emptied the contents of the bags into the centre. Everyone gathered to enjoy the tasty goodies the women had prepared for the picnic.

"After lunch, the children played within sight on the lawns of the Marine Park while we adults lolled away the afternoon. But soon, a nutter arrived near us with a soapbox, and he placed it on the lawn and stood on it. The stranger first only stood there, watching the crowds lying around or wandering around the park. Then, he yelled at everyone around him."

"Do you believe what we are doing in South Africa is right?" the nutter shouted. "Do you?

"Then he yelled again even louder, still not getting any reaction," said Joe.

"What the hell are we doing in that God-forsaken country killing farmers? Do you think it's right? Well, it's not. It is wrong! What is our great British Army doing going after a bunch of bloody farmers? What do they hope to achieve?'"

"Here we go again," I commented. "Another nutter on his soapbox. Why are there so many of these nutters?"

"He then launched into a long lecture on what was wrong with the British invasion of the Boer Republics," said Joe.

"Over 10,000 dead so far; for what?" the nutter yelled. "For what?"

"He paused and looked around the crowd before him," said Joe. "It went on and on for many minutes."

"We should look, instead, here at home, for what is wrong with our empire," the nutter continued. "Look at the slums. Look at the starving children living in Tyneside. Why does our government think it's necessary to fight a bunch of farmers at the bottom of the world? There are enough problems to handle here. How dare we interfere with the politics of that country? What is Lord Roberts doing there with his vast army of good British boys? Why?"

"Worried the man was insane, drunk, or both," said Joe, "most onlookers packed up their things and moved away, afraid of trouble. They shook their heads and gestured towards him as they discussed his words in their small groups. Men lectured him for his unpatriotic conduct, but that made no difference to him. He continued his criticism for the rest of the day until he was hoarse."

"We Rutherfords packed up and left, too. What a load of blather," said Joe as the pub closed.

The following day, Joe was with his family when his joining the British Army arose again.

"Well, Joe, do you still want to leave us for South Africa?" his father asked.

"Aye, Da, I sure do," said Joe.

"Isn't the war over?" said William.

"That is what the newspapers are saying," said Joe. "But that's not what I hear through the regiment."

"How so?" asked George.

"The Boers aren't giving up," said Joe. "They are still fighting."

"The fools," said George. "Don't they know we've beaten them?"

"I don't understand it either, George," Joe said. "They are now fighting what they call a guerrilla war, conducting ambushes and doing as much damage to our army as possible. They are killing our soldiers, blowing up the railway, bridges, telegraph lines and more while staying out of sight."

"What do you mean by guerrilla war?" asked William.

"Aye, I learned that word, too," said Joe. "Guerrilla war is where small groups of fighters spread out to use ambushes, sabotage, raids and hit-and-run tactics to fight a larger army. That, I read, is what the Boers are now doing against our mighty army."

"Why can't our generals stop them?" Thomas asked, losing patience with the war talk.

"I don't know, Da," Joe said, "I don't know. They don't seem to know how to deal with them. But it's time for me to help in any way I can."

His father gave a loud snort and quipped that Joe should have listened to the crazy man, but Joe had the full attention of his brothers, so he continued.

"The Queen needs as many soldiers as possible for this war, which has become an enormous problem for her and our country. We must do everything we can to end it," he said. "Any men of fighting age must join the army and offer their services to the British Empire. England is strong, and it must stay healthy if men like us are to keep our jobs, feed our families and enjoy such family days as this."

Silence.

"We can't allow the Boers, a bunch of farmers, to stand up to the empire."

"Rubbish," Thomas boomed. "Absolute bloody rubbish!"

"Well, Da, I believe it and will help our Queen. I'm going."

"What about Ruth? Your family?" Thomas asked.

"I discussed it with Ruth, and she has told me she might not be here for me when I return," said Joe. "I'm asking my family to understand. I want your blessing, Da. But I'm going, whether you give it to me."

With that, the mood changed. Joe's brothers realized that nothing would alter his mind or his father's, and that was that.

"Well, we'll back you, George and me," insisted William, "We'll be proud of our little brother marching off to protect the empire."

"Aye," echoed George, "That we will."

His mother remained silent, and his father refused to discuss it further.

Similar conversations were repeated tens of thousands of times across the British Empire. The war and foreign adventure excited and captivated youths, while their cynical elders questioned the sense of yet another imperial quest. Thousands of young British men still rushed to join the British military. The pull of the glorious British Empire was just too strong to hold them back.

∼

Kruger, Buller and Roberts Leave South Africa

Meanwhile, in South Africa, President Paul Kruger left the Transvaal by rail on the 11th of September 1900. They say he wept as the train crossed into Portuguese Mozambique. Oom Paul, the Uncle of the Transvaal, who had been so involved and instrumental in its creation and development, was fleeing South Africa forever. He planned to board the first outgoing steamer, the Herzog of the German East Africa Line, in Lourenço Marques. But the local British Consul asked the Portuguese governor to prevent him from leaving, insisting that Kruger stay in port under house arrest.

A month later, Queen Wilhelmina of the Netherlands agreed with Britain to evacuate Kruger on a Dutch warship, the HNLMS Gelderland. To Kruger's delight, they would transport him through non-British waters to Marseille. But it dismayed the president that his wife Gezina in Pretoria was not well enough to join him. The Gelderland left on the 20th of October 1900, and he received a rapturous welcome in Marseille on the 22nd of November, where 60,000 people turned out to see him disembark. He went on to an exuberant reception in Paris, then continued to Cologne, Germany, on the 1st of December. The German public greeted him with similar exuberance, but

Kaiser Wilhelm II refused to receive him in Berlin. Still harbouring hopes of German aid in the war, it shocked Kruger, who said, "The Kaiser has betrayed us."

On the 24th of October 1900, General Redvers Buller left South Africa for England. Since he was still famous as a military leader amongst the public in England, he had a triumphal return from South Africa. He spent the following months giving lectures and speeches on the war. They promoted him in November 1900 to a Knight Grand Cross of the Order of St Michael and St George (GCMG).

But he had damaged his reputation through his early failures in Natal. When public unhappiness over the continuing guerrilla activities of the so-called defeated Boers emerged, the Minister for War, St. John Brodrick, and Lord Roberts looked for a scapegoat. The many attacks in the newspapers on how the British Army was performing provided the perfect opening. The matter came to a head when a toxic piece was published by *The Times* journalist and Boer War historian Leo Amery. Buller responded to Amery's article in a speech on the 10th of October, 1901. Brodrick and Roberts saw their opportunity to pounce and summoned Buller to an interview on the 17th of October. With Roberts in support, Brodrick demanded his resignation for breaching military discipline. Buller refused, and they dismissed him on half-pay on the 22nd of October. They also denied him a court-martial and his application to appeal to the King.

At home, in Britain, news of the South African War was rampant; everyone was discussing it. The newspapers reported every battle won and lost at length, often with sketches illustrating various aspects of the fighting. They celebrated heroic generals and brave VCs, recipients of the highest military decoration awarded for "valour in the face of the enemy"—the Victoria Cross.

War correspondents despatched descriptions of weapons, uniforms, and the enemy, often with photographs or sketches, from South Africa to newspaper and magazine offices at home.

Joe was still in his relationship with Ruth and had obligations to the family income. So he joined the 1st Battalion Durham Volunteer Engineers to get started and learn the ropes at home.

The biggest news in mid-1900, when he joined the Volunteers, was Roberts' victory over the Boers and the capture of Pretoria. Celebrations broke out across Britain, and spirits were high. But as time wore on, the realities trickled home. They realized that the war wasn't over despite the victories. Britain still called thousands of recruits to South Africa to fight an ugly guerrilla war. It was a war that had spread its tentacles across the entire sub-continent. It could continue for many months against a deceptive and stubborn enemy. Guerrilla comes from the Spanish word for a war of ambushes and sabotage. In South Africa, the Boers instigated dozens of such clashes and acts of destruction daily. They broke out across the country, including deep into the British colonies of the Cape and Natal.

Joe had gained practical experience as a Volunteer but didn't believe he was helping England with its challenges in South Africa. So he and his marras decided they must join the thousands of other young men who had either gone or were still entering the effort there.

Just as the Canadians were taking their leave of South Africa, Joe and his friends offered their services to the war efforts of the British Empire. Joe enlisted with the 1st Battalion of the Durham Light Infantry on the 19th of November 1900 at the recruitment office in Newcastle, where the DLI shared premises with the Royal Northumberland Fusiliers at Fenham Barracks. His attestation recorded that he was 18 years and 11 months old, 5 foot 5 ½ inches tall and weighed 105 pounds. Joe had a fair complexion, blue eyes, dark brown hair, and scars on his neck. He gave his place of work at Hawthorn Leslie Shipbuilding Company in Hebburn and lived at 81 Salem Street, Jarrow. Joe was a fine specimen of a young man with a springy gait, a wonderful sense of humour, and the Irish gift of the gab.

Mike, Billy and Jack signed up with him. They would soon head to South Africa as soldiers to work for their new employer—the British Army.

It had been difficult for Joe to move away from his current life. First, he had to convince his parents and family that he and other young men needed to join the war effort and do their duty for the Queen and Empire. Joe was late joining the campaign, but they had no choice but to understand and let him go. He assured Ruth that he was to return to her when he had completed his tour of duty. Whether she believed him was another question.

"Why must so many join up?" she asked. "I'm sure most of the young man-servants of the grand houses of Britain have joined up and left, leaving us women to do most of the work. Why must you go too? And why for six years?"

"Because, hinny," said Joe, "young British men are duty-bound to protect the Queen and Empire, and six years is the standard tour of duty with the army."

She was right. So many young British men answered the patriotic call and joined the army, and she was just one of many young women losing their men to the war. But she, too, realized she had no choice but to agree.

After enlisting, he and the other recruits spent only 49 training days. The Army was in a hurry to send them to South Africa. The Army's training involved turning a bunch of miners, shipbuilders and farm labourers into a well-disciplined and well-turned-out company of British soldiers who followed orders without question, even under fire and in the worst of circumstances. They learned how to shoot a rifle and to use a bayonet in close combat. The training was tough from both a physical and mental perspective. When the recruits arrived at the camp, they spent 12 hours a day, and sometimes more, drilling and learning. They learned to march in step, to fall into various battle formations, and how to use and care for their weapons. Recruits learned the basics of first aid and how to survive in a land of extreme heat and scarce water. They were taught to care for horses, hitching up and riding a wagon. The army then reassigned them to the war effort in the 1/DLI on the 18th of February, 1901.

"I guess, in the beginning, we were a sorry lot," recalled Joe. "But after several weeks of drilling and yelling by the drill sergeant, it sunk in, and we acted like soldiers. It was punishing at first, but over time, we came to enjoy it and proud of our progress as soldiers of the Queen."

Officers had much longer and more involved education and training in military academies. Soldiers rely on their officers' superior knowledge when fighting, such as the approach to enter combat. The ways of fighting changed during the South African War. The Edwardian public felt the traditional cavalry operations with swords and lances were inhumane. In this war, the cavalry scouted the principal theatres of conflict. Under Major-General the Earl of Dundonald, they guarded the flanks of General Sir Redvers Buller's army. They entered Ladysmith first at the end of the siege of that garrison town. Under Major-General Sir John D.P. French, the cavalry charge at Klip Drift swept through the Boers to relieve Kimberley. But galloping in the heat of the South African summer was too strenuous for many horses. Horses needed to be hardy and well looked after to survive the South African conditions. Mobility was critical since the marching infantry could not effectively fight the fast-moving mounted Boers. The British Army needed more mounted infantry than cavalry. Men equipped and trained as infantry, armed with an infantry rifle and not the cavalry carbine or a sword or lance, but with the mobility provided by the horse. This need became more prominent as the war moved into the guerrilla phase. As with all wars, many mistakes were made, and they learnt many lessons in the South African War.

～

Lord Roberts left on the 11th of December 1900, one year after his arrival. He considered the war won and that he could delegate the mopping-up operations to his chief of staff. Roberts handed over command to Lord Herbert Kitchener on the 12th of December. Kitchener had arrived in South Africa the year before with Lord Roberts on the RMS Dunnottar Castle. Roberts mentioned Kitchener in Despatches several times during the former part of the war. In a despatch from March 1900, the Field Marshal wrote that he was "greatly indebted to Kitchener for his counsel and cordial support on all occasions."

Lord Roberts returned to England to receive yet more honours from a grateful Queen Victoria.

Field Marshal Lord Kitchener in Command

Henceforth, in this South African War, Field Marshal Herbert Kitchener was the man in charge.

Horatio Herbert Kitchener was an esteemed and decorated soldier. As commander-in-chief of the British-controlled Egyptian Army from April 1892, he won victories at the Battle of Ferkeh in June 1896 and at the Battle of Hafir in September 1896. These battles earned him national fame in Britain and promotion to major-general in September 1896. He achieved further successes in Sudan at the Battle of Atbara in April 1898, a turning point in the conquest of Sudan by a British and Egyptian coalition. Then, at the famous Battle of Omdurman in September 1898, Kitchener defeated the army of Abdullah al-Taashi, the successor to the self-proclaimed Mahdi, 'The Guided One.' This battle pitted a disciplined army equipped with modern rifles, machine guns and artillery against a much larger force armed with old weapons. It marked the success of British efforts to re-conquer Sudan and avenge Major-General Charles George Gordon, murdered by the Mahdi's followers in January 1885. The Battle of Omdurman earned Kitchener his early reputation and his future title.

In South Africa, Lord Roberts handed the baton to Kitchener, whom he had promoted to lieutenant-general in November 1900. At forty, Kitchener became the new South African Field Marshal. Kitchener stood 6 foot 2 inches tall with a slim, upright physique and squared shoulders, towering over most of his contemporaries, and a foot taller than Lord Roberts. He was a handsome man with thick brown hair parted in the middle, deep blue penetrating eyes under heavy brows and a large moustache that concealed his upper lip. Kitchener was the image of good health, strength and alertness that detracted from his shy and reserved manner. British administrator and diplomat Sir Evelyn Baring, whose 24-year rule in Egypt as a British agent and consul general profoundly influenced Egypt's development as a modern state, considered Kitchener, Egypt's de facto British ruler, the most competent soldier he had encountered.

But amid this change in command, the Empire received the news of Queen Victoria's death on the 22nd of January 1901 with deep emotions. In the South African Karroo, as elsewhere in the British Empire, her subjects mourned her passing. British gun salutes echoed across the veldt, and rumours of battles spread.

War correspondent Edgar Wallace received the news at the headquarters of the Cape Command at Matjesfontein in the Karroo. He wrote this poignant piece: "Queen Victoria had ever been sacred among the rank and file of the army. The men who serve and love her are broad-minded; Papist, Buddhist, or Jew are one with their Protestant selves. It governs their thoughts towards her by a love no one can command."

Upon his return to England, Lord Roberts visited Queen Victoria days before her death at her retreat at Osborne House on the Isle of Wight. He reported on their progress in the South African War, a conflict she had long concerned herself with and followed with interest. He extended his condolences for the death in Pretoria of her grandson, Prince Christian Victor, the son of her daughter Helena. Despite her weakened state, the Queen spoke to Roberts for half an hour, then conferred the Order of the Garter and his Earldom upon him. Henceforth, he became known as 1st Earl Roberts of Kandahar in Afghanistan, Pretoria in the Transvaal Colony, and the City of Waterford [Ireland].

With the death of Queen Victoria, one of the greatest eras of British history ended. She was the longest-reigning British monarch in history and reigned over an empire where the sun never set. Victoria ruled the United Kingdom for 63 years, from 1837 to 1901, restoring dignity to the English monarchy and ensuring its survival as a formal political institution. They mourned her death, at 81, around the world.

The Boers didn't mourn her passing. For them, nothing had changed, apart from another British monarch taking her place. And despite the change in the British monarchy, they soon discovered this was not a turn for the better for them. The British politicians didn't change, nor did the highest command of the British army. The war continued unabated as if nothing of significance had happened.

---

1. These despatches were later published in the book *Ian Hamilton's March* by Winston Churchill, 1900
2. Deneys Reitz, Commando – A Boer Journal of the Boer War, 1929
3. Deneys Reitz, *Commando – A Boer Journal of the Boer War*, 1929
4. Deneys Reitz, *Commando – A Boer Journal of the Boer War*, 1929
5. Deneys Reitz, *Commando – A Boer Journal of the Boer War*, 1929
6. Queen's Shropshire Light Infantry Regiment
7. William Hart-McHarg, From Quebec to Pretoria with the Royal Canadian Regiment, 1902
8. From *Ian Hamilton's March* by Winston Churchill, 1900
9. From *Ian Hamilton's March* by Winston Churchill, 1900
10. From *Ian Hamilton's March* by Winston Churchill, 1900
11. William Hart-McHarg, *From Quebec to Pretoria with the Royal Canadian Regiment*, 1902
12. *The Times History of the War in South Africa, 1899-1902*, Amery, L S (ed), 1909)

CHAPTER 5
WEATHERING THE WANING STORM
MARCH 1901 TO MAY 1902

Joe's Voyage to South Africa—the 15th to 31st of March 1901

The day the marras had waited for so long arrived at last. With their training completed, Joe's company of three officers and 113 men of the 1/DLI left England for South Africa from Albert Dock in Liverpool on the 15th of March 1901. His war stories were now to become a reality for Joe and his marras.

The entire Rutherford family converged on his parents' home at 81 Salem Street in Jarrow. There, his father, Thomas, mother Susanna, brothers William, George and Thomas James, and sisters Mary Ann, Esther, Margaret, Sarah Jane, Susannah Balance, Eleanor and Elizabeth turned out for Joe's departure. Then there were the wives and husbands, William's two boys, George's three girls and son, and Esther's two boys. Family friends, such as the Burgesses, Ruth Anderson and her parents, arrived too. Joe wore his elegant new Durham Light Infantry full-dress uniform—dark blue trousers, a bright red blazer, a white belt and a peaked cap. Standing at attention, he was a fine specimen of a British Army soldier.

They each went to Joe and commended him on his new uniform and persona as they arrived.

"You look the best example of a soldier I have ever seen, Joe," said his brother William as he arrived, confirmed by his other brothers. He thanked them with a slight smile but maintained his composure until his mother embraced him and, with tears in her eyes and a cracking voice, told him to look after himself and return to her as soon as possible.

"Please don't worry, Ma," said Joe. "I'll be fine. You understand that I have to do this, don't you?"

"I have no choice but to understand, Joe," said his mother. "Just make sure you return to me in one piece. And never mind your father. I'm sure he is just as proud of you."

His brothers and sisters and each of their friends wished him well. Only his father stood aloof, refusing to offer any compliments or show any emotion. But Joe didn't expect any goodwill from him.

To his forlorn girlfriend, he said, "Write to me, Ruthie. Six years may seem long, but it will pass in a flash. We must write and keep our ties to each other that way."

"I still don't understand why you must go, Joe," said a tearful Ruth. "There are enough other laddies who can fight this war. And six years is a very long time!"

"Aye, but please understand, Ruthie. I must go," said Joe while hugging her. "I've followed this war long enough and must now add actions to my reading and talking, and to find myself, to discover who I am, to see the battlefields and the world for myself. Please try to understand."

Then, pulling himself together, Joe waved goodbye to his assembled family and friends and made his way along Salem Street in his new uniform and carrying his army-issue kit bag. He was on his way to the 1/DLI meeting point in Jarrow. Joe may have missed the heroic march and battles of the early stages of the war, but that didn't matter to him now. He was heading out into the world to spend the rest of the war doing whatever they expected of him.

The army delivered them to Newcastle Train Station from the depot, where they caught a train to Liverpool. They marched to the harbour in Liverpool, where their ship waited to transport them to South Africa. And while they marched in step without a military band, shoppers and bystanders cheered on the 117 officers and men. This applause made them stand taller, holding back any smiles to look stern and fierce but not holding back their pride. They arrived at the ship as the last of the other soldiers were boarding. Joe and his marras had never been at sea. Apart from the occasional ferry trip across the River Tyne, they had never been on a vessel of any significance. But now Joe and his companions were boarding a ship of the high seas, the 3,445-ton SS Ebro (1896).

Besides the 1/DLI company, three other companies comprising three officers and 113 men each were on board - the 1st Northumberland Fusiliers, 2nd Northumberland Fusiliers and a joint company of the Scottish Rifles and the Argyll and Sutherland Highlanders. Two officers and three men from the Royal Army Medical Corps were on board, too. The full complement was twenty officers and 680 men, plus horses, weapons, wagons and other equipment in the hold.

They assigned the officers cabins with eating and socializing facilities in the spacious wardroom. They gave non-commissioned officers shared accommodation with an NCO mess, too. The rank and file bunked together in sizeable open cargo areas in the hold. The ship's captain provided army kitchens, eating and meeting messes, and improvised ablution areas in other storage areas. The troops had little room, but their training prepared them for rough living. They used the open main deck as an escape for fresh air, socializing and sports during the voyage.

"There's a bloody freezing wind out here today," complained Joe as the troops lined every ship railing for the departure. "But at least it's not raining."

They waved to the onlookers and gazed across the Mersey River to the shipyards of Birkenhead. It was still early in the day, and they looked forward to the unfamiliar sights and sounds as they headed out into Liverpool Bay. After a while, the ship rocked and pitched in the wild waters of the Irish Sea.

"I'm not sure of this sailing business, Joe," said Mike. "I feel shite with this ship rolling."

Joe, Billy and Jack expressed the same sentiment. And before long, the deck emptied of everybody but the bravest and most seasoned sea travellers. So began several days of absolute agony for most men, Joe among them. None could have imagined this torture continuing for the two weeks the journey was to take before landing in Capetown. But it soon passed as they started finding their sea legs.

Four days out, the first port of call was the island of Tenerife, where they took on fresh supplies. After they had lowered the anchor off the busy Santa Cruz harbour, a fleet of small boats surrounded the ship. The floating emporium offered various fruits, nuts and vegetables, tobacco, cigars, cheap wine, etc., and made a roaring trade.

"Just look at this," said Mike, sweeping his arm across the scene. "It's amazing!"

The island was mountainous, rising in the south to the summit of Mount Teide, with an elevation of 12,198 feet above sea level, dressed in snow. An officer on deck told the men, "Mount Teide summit is the highest point in Spain—Tenerife belonging to that country—and the highest point above sea level in the islands of the Atlantic." The men from the North East of England had never seen a prominence higher than hills, let alone mountains.

They could see a bustling town from the ship, filled with people, horses, and donkey-drawn carts. The harbour was teeming with goods and workers loading or offloading sail and steam-driven vessels of many shapes and sizes. Cranes on the wharves heaved huge freight lots to and from the ships.

The soldiers marvelled at the views.

"Look at the white two-storey buildings and magnificent churches every few blocks," said Joe.

"Look at those strange-looking trees everywhere," said Mike, pointing to the palm trees. "I've never seen those before, have any of you?"

"Never," was the response in unison. But they were most impressed with the scene before them.

Beyond the town, to the south, were vast fields of bright green sugar cane. They didn't know it was sugar cane until a deckhand told them. It surprised them to learn that sugar came from such large grass plants. To the immediate north of the town and harbour, it was rugged with small, jagged peaks devoid of vegetation. The soldiers on board marvelled at this unfamiliar sight. Most came from busy harbour towns in County Durham or the Highlands of Scotland. Santa Cruz de Tenerife was exotic and most enjoyable. Best for the men, the weather was balmy and sunny, which the boys from Scotland and North East England appreciated.

As soon as the ship had taken on its provisions, it set off and, in three days, crossed the equator. In another three days, they dropped anchor at St Helena, where they discharged part of the cargo and took on water, fresh fruit, and vegetables. Six more days of sailing brought them to Capetown.

During the voyage, there was no lack of amusements aboard the ship. They had various musical instruments onboard, including bagpipes, bugles, flutes and a piano in the wardroom. There were two informal bands with impromptu devices, including tin whistles, combs covered with paper, and an empty tin for a drum. Throughout the day, the soldiers took part in various sports, like the ancient game of quoits and a recent game from America called Mintonette, or volleyball.

On the equator, the ship's crew organized a line-crossing ceremony with initiation rites and an abundance of rum and ale for those who had never crossed this latitude. Everyone dressed in festive costumes, and the sailors danced the jig to entertain the newcomers. The first officer dressed up as King Neptune, complete with a robe, crown and trident, and abused the soldiers as Slimy Pollywogs without mercy. The alcohol-lubricated festivities lasted for two days, after which the Pollywogs received a certificate declaring their new status as Shellbacks. Soldiers and sailors bonded, discarding any nervousness among the recruits. And they partied until they collapsed into a drunken heap in the tropical heat.

"I don't think I've ever had so much fun," said Mike. "Despite the lack of female company."

"Aye," said Joe, "what a party! And think, lads, we have crossed the halfway line between north and south. What an honour, and what an exploit."

"Aye," the marras said in unison, "Champion!"

Along the way, the troops saw the most impressive sights. They saw whales and dolphins, sea turtles and flying fish, none of which they had ever seen. None of these fantastic creatures had even entered their imaginations, let alone their lives.

"How can such enormous animals as those exist?" asked Jack. "How can any animal get that big?"

"They call them whales," said Joe. "Who could have imagined that we'd see such things?"

"Whoever heard of flying fish?" said Mike when they first saw them. "I can't believe my eyes."

"My God, look at those enormous fish chasing them," called Jack.

The 12- to 18-inch-long flying fish emerged from the water and launched themselves into the wind with the help of their flapping tails, their long pectoral and pelvic fins extending as wings to catch the breezes. But large and colourful Dorado fish chased them, showing blue, green, silver and yellow flashes as they emerged from the water to swallow the fleeing gliders.

"Just look at them fly and glide," said Billy. "What a sight!"

"Aye, but look at those birds picking them off in the air. They can't win, chased and eaten from below and above," called Joe. "What a dangerous life!"

"Well, the fish and birds must eat, too," said Mike.

They were passing the westernmost bulge of Africa, where a host of incredible birds arrived from sea and shore to greet them. These visitors included giant gliding frigate birds effortlessly picking off the flying fish.

There were skuas, shearwaters, phalaropes, gulls and hundreds of petrels and terns skimming over the smooth surface of the water. The marras marvelled at the wildlife they saw out of sight of the shore.

"Could you have ever imagined that there were such belta[1] creatures in the sea?" Joe asked of his mates.

"You're the one who reads so much, Joe," said Mike. "I've never seen or heard of the likes of this, nor even dreamed of it."

"My Da was in the Transvaal War and often spoke of his time at sea, South Africa, and India. So, it's not new to me," said Jack. "But it's grand to experience it myself."

They also saw several ships travelling in the opposite direction, including tall sailing ships. Joe and his marras spent entire days on deck observing these fantastic sights or playing various sports.

Their travels into the wider world were off to an exciting beginning.

The Arrival in Capetown—31 March 1901

After an eventful two-week journey from Liverpool, the ship arrived in Capetown on the 31st of March 1901. It was a pleasant morning, and the sight of the mountain and the city was breathtaking. For men who had never seen a peak before, apart from Mount Teide at Tenerife, let alone one of such unique beauty, the flat-topped mountain rising above the city was a marvel. As they approached, the prominence loomed large, and the city stretched below it from the slopes to the harbour. A blustering south-easterly wind plummeted from the mountain, making their docking tricky for the pilot, and it propelled the "tablecloth" clouds pouring over its peak. It was an awe-inspiring arrival after 8,644 miles of a once-in-a-lifetime journey from their port of departure.

Joe could see many sizeable buildings stretching along the principal street descending from the mountain's lower reaches into the harbour. Trams running near the port were visible as dozens of carts, wagons, and scores of riders and pedestrians ambled along. It was a Sunday, so crowds gathered in their Sunday finery despite the wind to welcome the new batch of troops to this corner of the Empire so far from home.

Their arrival was not comparable to Winston Churchill's entry with General Redvers Buller on the *Dunnottar Castle* at the start of the war. They disembarked without the pomp and ceremony for General Buller this Sunday and marched straight to Green Point, a large encampment with 6,000 troops under canvas. They camped near the Royal East Kent Regiment (Buffs) and the Black Watch. These veterans received many valuable lessons on what to expect on the battlefield. Joe made a friend of one of the wounded Black Watch soldiers who had suffered in that terrible charge at Magersfontein in which they suffered such significant losses.

"He gave me lots of useful advice," recalled Joe. "For example, when on sentry, never challenge a Boer. When a Boer scout approaches the lines, he shoots on being challenged. So it's better to shoot first and challenge afterwards."

"I've heard these Boer farmers are cunning," said Mike. "We had better learn as much as we can about our enemy before we meet them on the battlefield."

"Aye," said Billy, "Who ever heard of an anthill? What the hell is that?"

"I suppose we'll discover that and much more out here," said Joe.

They remained in camp for a week and had an easy enough time.

"There aren't too many drill exercises," said Joe to his marras. "I was expecting more. It's a doddle, and there's plenty of free time to visit the city. But the meals aren't great."

They got coffee and bread for breakfast, bread and tea at teatime, a tin of jam every three days, and bread and meat for dinner. But they started adjusting to army life "in the field."

They had a march through the town one day to impress the inhabitants of Capetown. The parade numbered 1,000 cavalry riders, two artillery batteries with their guns and 4,000 infantry, plus the army medical corps. Joe and his marras said it was "the grandest march in which they had never taken part."

And then, on the same day they were to entrain, the 5th Queensland Imperial Bushmen arrived in Capetown. They had sailed from Australia on the 6th of March 1901 on the SS Templemore. Another Australian detachment followed a few days later on the SS Chicago. They selected these men based on height, it seemed. None was to be above five foot ten inches or below five foot six inches. They were to travel straight to Pietersburg in the northern Transvaal, a journey of twelve days, and then attached to Colonel Plumer's force.

"A fine-looking bunch of lads," said Joe.

"Aye, and I love their hats," said Jack. "I wonder what fur that is."

"Kangaroo?" suggested Billy, to everyone's amusement.

The 1/DLI company marched through the city with the Australians and other companies from various British and colonial regiments to the train station. It was a sunny autumn day with a comfortable temperature—and the wind had dropped. The men, free of the confinements and monotony of the lengthy ocean journey, stretched their gait in the march and soon struck up the song 'Marching to Pretoria.' They sang various other regimental and well-known marching songs as they strutted the short 3-mile distance from Green Point to the train station on Adderley Street, Capetown's principal business street.

The recent arrivals felt elated. They were far from their departure points and felt genuine excitement, freedom and pride as they waited for the train at Capetown station. Most were young recruits; this was their first venture into the glorious British Empire. The usual onlookers, more of them on a Sunday even at 8 A.M., bid them adieu from the platform as if they were family. A military band played various uplifting marches. Because of the importance and solemnity of the occasion, station officials surveyed the proceedings with purpose. They determined the train's readiness before signalling the locomotive to start its journey.

"Well, we are here, at last, lads. On our way to the action," said Joe with excitement.

"Aye, and what a sight," said Mike. "Look at those lassies."

"Not for us yet, alas," said Joe.

"Look at that lass, Joe; isn't she sweet?" said Mike.

"Aye, that she is," said Joe. "A real beauty."

"I prefer that chocolate one over there," said Billy.

"Ready for danger, are you," quipped Jack?

Then they roared with laughter.

∼

The Train Ride to the Karroo—April 1901

A few snorts later, the locomotive exited the station, travelling east. They soon moved through an industrial complex with workshops, warehouses and dozens of carts just beyond the city limits. Beyond that, they passed through a shantytown filled with Uitlanders who had fled the Transvaal and newcomers from foreign lands in search of the riches of Africa—diamonds, gold and ivory. Further out of town, they travelled through suburbs for a distance and were soon out into rolling green farmlands. They crossed dirt tracks and roads with wagons pulled by oxen or donkey carts and coloured agricultural workers of mixed races waiting for the train to pass.

Before long, Joe and his companions caught sight of the Cape Coastal Mountains, soaring into a dark blue sky. By now, the tablecloth seen on Table Mountain was flowing from various peaks of the coastal mountain range. They picked up speed on turning north to run parallel to the mountains.

"What a grand place this," said Joe. "Do you suppose the entire country is as spectacular?"

"We don't know, Joe, we only just got here, my marra," someone said, and everyone laughed.

"I've seen drawings of this in books," said Joe. "It looks so much better in proper life."

"That it does, Joe," said Mike. "We've never seen the sky and mountains as they are here."

They looked up at the peaks in complete awe. These were men from the rolling hills and dales of County Durham, the coal mines and shipyards of Tyneside and Wearside, with the North Sea nearby but no mountains. None of them had seen such vertical peaks. Their first experience with cliffs and a high mountain was the volcano on the island of Tenerife. But this was their first brush with something as exotic as the southern tip of Africa. They had never encountered such a sight and were full of exhilaration and wonder.

"Pinch me," said Joe. "I can't believe I'm here."

"Aye, Joe," said Billy, "I know what you mean."

They passed through towns such as Paarl, its sentry mountain, a granite rock formed into three rounded outcrops gleaming like pearls, hence the Dutch name Paarl, then 35 miles from Capetown by 9:30 A.M., and Wellington 45 miles out by 10 A.M. Around these settlements, they saw the vineyards dripping with the harvest. Being a Sunday, no one was harvesting; the farming people of the Cape are a religious, God-fearing folk of Dutch and French Huguenot descent. Sunday was the day for worship and family, rest and prayer as they passed through Wellington, named in honour of the great General Arthur Wellesley, 1st Duke of Wellington, of Battle of Waterloo fame.

"I guess they named this town after the Iron Duke," said Mike.

"Aye, I'm sure they did. I've read the farmers make wine from those grapes we've seen here," said Joe.

"Have you noticed how brown the people are?" asked Billy.

"Aye, do you think they are slaves?" said Mike.

"That's not allowed at home," said Joe. "I wonder whether it's allowed out here?"

The train inched parallel to the mountain range, through farmlands and whistle-stops with names such as Hermon, Voelvlei and Gouda. As the mountain range became smaller, the train found a gap through a narrow gorge into another parallel valley past Tulbach Road. After that, they reversed direction, heading southeast, and were in a broad scenic valley with mountains on either side, rising and rising. Soon, they realized that they had circumnavigated the high mountain range they had first confronted when leaving Capetown. They were travelling faster towards another gap further along, which the train followed, heading north again.

The valley was so peaceful, disrupted only by the huffing of the locomotive. The mountains on both sides were bare and majestic, their undulating folds visible from time to time on cliffs hundreds of yards in height, like giant, tormented frowns. They crossed many small streams and dry riverbeds. In places, they crisscrossed large riverbeds running more or less parallel to the train tracks the length of the valley. They learned the rains only arrived in this part of South Africa in winter, and that little rain fell in summer—a strange phenomenon for men who had lived in England their entire lives. To balance this lack of rain in summer, the farmers created dams everywhere that collected water in the winter to irrigate the farms in the dry season. And as they passed roads and farms, the farmworkers and children waved to them with enormous smiles and shouts.

"Look at the names of these places we are passing now," noted Joe, as the passing signs announced Wolseley, La Plaisante, Romans River, Breede River, Botha, Goudiniweg and Chavonne. "Apart from Wolseley, most are strange foreign-looking names and hard to pronounce."

In time, they came to another substantial town—Worcester. There, the train stopped to take on coal and water and a second locomotive, allowing the soldiers to survey the settlement, but only from the train. By now, it was noon and hot under the uninhibited autumn sun. Army details passed through the train, handing out lunch packets and water. Even with the windows open, they were wilting in the heat. But no one minded; they were so busy looking at their surroundings and the various onlookers, including more gorgeous young ladies.

"What are they giving us to eat?" asked Mike. "Bread filled with shite!"

"I think it's sausage, Mike," said Joe. "It doesn't taste too shabby."

"Where's the ale?" asked Billy, to agreement and laughter all around.

"We're not officers, Billy," said Mike. "Only the officers get fine food and drink. But never mind that. Look at those sweet lassies over there."

But those were the last young ladies they would see for a long while. When the train had taken on its fill, it lurched forward again and inched out of the town. Then, the rails turned to the northeast and entered a winding gorge that became narrower and narrower as it scaled the mountains, the train climbing a slight incline. After a while, the chasm opened again into a lush valley planted with fruit trees and grapevines. They travelled through these farms briefly, passing more whistle-stops called Hex River, Orchard and De Doorns. Then, the track left the valley floor and started a steep climb up the side of the mountain ridges. The train passed through a long tunnel, and when they emerged from it, the track twisted and turned while climbing higher. They passed through more tunnels as they rose through the pass. Most soldiers on board this train had never experienced a mountain climb on a train. So, they were apprehensive of the steep slopes dropping away from the tracks in places.

"This is getting more and more dangerous," said Billy.

"Aye," piped up Jack, who had been dozing off to the gentle rocking movements of the train. "I wonder if the trains ever leave the tracks?"

"There's your answer," said Joe, pointing to rubble far below them in the gorge.

"What's that?" asked Jack

"I don't know," said Joe. "What do you think, Mike?"

"That wreckage is from a train for sure," said Mike with a huge grin.

After a while, they left the gorges behind them and arrived at another compact town called Touws River, a village with the same name as its river. They stopped there for a proper break at the station, detraining and waiting in a desolate spot while the train got a single locomotive replacing the others. They spotted a sign showing that it was at 2,530 feet.

"Howay," called Mike. "That was a proper climb!"

"Aye, that it was, Mike. We've never been so high," said Joe in astonishment. "Look over there. There's a shunting yard filled with old locomotives and other types of old and battered cars, most in a terrible state and victims of the war. I reckon it's a railway graveyard."

"There's not much else here but dried-out earth and scrub," said Mike. "Where is the town?"

"I saw a few houses and a wee church back a bit," said Billy.

At Touws River, the steep climbing had ended, and the terrain opened into a wide, flat valley lined on either side by low weathered ridges. After that town, they passed through many little whistle-stops, deserted and with more strange names, as they moved into a vast barren landscape of scrubland known as the Great Karroo.

Empire Discovered | The Rutherford Chronicles - Part 1

The Cape Command Remount Camp at Matjesfontein—April 1901

After an hour of travel through this desolate region of kopjes and dry riverbeds with little sign of life, they arrived at a simple tin-roofed train station called Matjesfontein [2]. There was a sign declaring its name and its elevation of 3,349 feet. They couldn't pronounce that strange name, but it didn't matter; the soldiers of the British Army knew it as the Cape Command Remount Camp. Behind the station was a single short street running parallel to the tracks with a half dozen cottages, an elegant house and a sizeable building resembling a castle, the lot surrounded by well-maintained gardens. It was an unexpected oasis arising out of such a barren land.

The hamlet of Matjesfontein owed its existence to the Cape Government Railways. Once launched in 1871, its founder, Cape Colony Prime Minister John Molteno, rapidly pushed the rail line inland. As it progressed, they built a remote station at Matjesfontein and opened it on the 1st of February 1878. Matjesfontein was only a tiny depot and farm until the industrious Scotsman James Douglas Logan became superintendent of this stretch of railway.

Logan was a dynamic and unorthodox man. Shipwrecked near Simonstown, to the south of Capetown, and with only a few pounds in his pocket, he walked the 28 miles to Capetown. There, the youth got his first job on the fledgeling railways. In Capetown, he met and fell in love with Miss Emma Haylett, of English and Afrikander descent, and married her a year later. He had just turned twenty-one, and she was nineteen. Soon afterwards, the railways sent Logan north into the interior. Arriving at Matjesfontein, he fell in love with the Karroo.

Matjesfontein then was a stark place. A simple iron shed stood next to rails that appeared to vanish northwards into the shimmering semi-desert plains. But Logan looked past the barren landscape. He saw a way of making a fortune from the Karroo's scarcest commodity, water. As an experienced railwayman, Logan knew every locomotive needed 70,000 gallons of water to cross the Karroo. He knew there was no reliable source between Touws River and De Aar, a distance of 340 miles. So, it placed him between those two locations. Logan spent over £1,000 finding a source capable of delivering 11,000 gallons an hour and piping it to Matjesfontein.

Matjesfontein appeared on the barren vastness of the Karroo as if by magic. Logan imported the materials to build his hotel and cottages and sourced skilled Scottish and Irish stonemasons and carpenters as builders and artisans. Most stayed in the region when their contracts expired or moved elsewhere in South Africa. They built a row of elegant cottages, the Logan residence Tweedside Lodge, culminating in a sizeable and stylish building, a modern and comfortable hotel resembling a castle with turreted towers—The Milner.

Always ready to try something new, Logan built a wind-powered mill to crush wheat and generate electricity for Tweedside Lodge, his and Emma's elegant home. Tweedeside Lodge was the first private dwelling in South Africa to have electric lighting. He pioneered water-borne sewage and South Africa's first flushing toilets in his home. Logan opened the first artesian well in South Africa on Tweedside Farm and sank several drill holes. Each time he found a good water supply, he planted fruit trees. His cherry, pear and peach orchards prospered, and Logan sold the harvested fruit as far away as Kimberley and Capetown. He laid a 13-mile telephone line, the longest in South Africa, from his Tweedside farmhouse to his Matjesfontein residence. And he imported electric street lamps from London.

The Castle Steamship Company, one of the leading shipping companies of the time, issued a poster in England offering a round trip to Matjesfontein. By the outbreak of the Anglo-Boer War, Matjesfontein had become a popular health and holiday resort. Aristocrats from Britain and the continent flocked to the hamlet to convalesce from various actual or imagined ailments. The resort caught the interest of doctors sending patients to Beaufort West but found that the town was too dusty and had too much grass pollen. Matjesfontein proved to be perfect.

When the Anglo-Boer War broke out, Logan equipped and outfitted a private corps of 100 men. The enemy wounded him twice and shot out a horse from under him. They mentioned him in despatches, and the British awarded him two medals and clasps for bravery in action. The British Army established Matjesfontein as its officers' command headquarters, hospital and home. It was the furthest north the Army allowed wives and sweethearts to travel. One saw many strolling on officers' arms and dining in the hotel. Soldiers used the hotel's turrets as lookout posts and often spotted bands of Boer fighters moving through the hills. On the outskirts of the hamlet was a vast remount camp for over 10,000 British troops and 20,000 horses. It was an enormous and complex labyrinth of tents on the opposite side of the railway to the hotel. There was a constant commotion, with 10,000 men rotating as sections and companies came and went their ways. The army had transformed Matjesfontein from a quiet health resort to a vast, bustling army encampment overnight.

The Cape Command had moved into the hotel as their headquarters, accommodating senior officers within its elegant walls. It also served as a temporary hospital for wounded officers. They stationed crack British regiments at Matjesfontein. Among them were the Coldstream Guards, the Seventeenth Lancers, the Middlesex Regiment, and the esteemed but ill-fated Highland Brigade under the command of Major-General Andy Wauchope.

Even though the train was to continue north, Joe's company had orders to disembark at Matjesfontein, march to the camp and report for duty with the 3rd Battalion Durham Light Infantry (3/DLI). The company commander, Major Hawkins, reported to the 3/DLI Commander, Lieutenant-Colonel Wilson. Hawkins had orders to guard the lines of communication up the railway line to Laingsburg, at 18.5 miles, relieving another company of the 3/DLI.

The army provided the company with mules, wagons, and other equipment. Engineers joined them to carry out any repairs on the telegraph line and railway as needed when attacked by commandos, a frequent occurrence in this war. Wilson told Hawkins that his team should carry out this duty for three months, after which they would get new orders.

Hawkins asked, "Are the Dutchmen active around here, Sir?"

"They are," confirmed the colonel, "We are dealing with commandos under the command of Boer generals P.H. Kritzinger, J. B. M. Herzog and Jan Smuts. They are capable chaps and very devious. We have observed Kommandant Gideon Scheepers and his commando south at Touws River and north at Laingsburg, but they have been active throughout the Karroo."

Gideon Scheepers had become something of a legend. At age sixteen, he joined the Staatsartillerie in the Transvaal Republic and was soon a first-rate heliographer and telegraphist. He later became a scout prized by General Christiaan de Wet. He took part in the Battle of Magersfontein and avoided capture when General Piet Cronje surrendered at Paardeberg. They gave him the rank of kommandant at twenty-two, leading a commando of 150 men. He made the lives of the Cape Colony British soldiers miserable. Scheepers disrupted the British War effort by damaging communication networks and railway lines. He gathered many of his recruits from the surrounding country, and his commando was able, through the sympathy and help of the farmers, to keep themselves well-mounted and supplied.

One might consider it the most straightforward military operation to hunt these small, scattered rebel bands, but it proved far from easy. Operating in a vast and challenging country, the Boer fighters were outstanding, well-informed and skilled riders well-supplied with horses. It proved impossible for the slow-moving British columns, with their guns and wagons, to overtake them.

As a result, Scheepers had many successes, and his bravery was legendary. His mere presence in the Cape Colony inspired more Boers to take up arms against the British. Up to 80% of Scheepers' commandos were Cape Rebels.

"The Boers avoid such large concentrations of British soldiers as we have here at Matjesfontein," said the colonel. "They are out there. Ready to hit anywhere and then disappear. Keep that in mind."

"Right, Sir, thank you," said the sergeant. "We'll be on the road first thing in the morning, extra cautious and observant."

Hawkins then found his way to the company's allotted section, deep within the hundreds of tents of the camp, to brief his men.

They distributed the new 3/DLI company under ten Indian tents of the khaki-coloured, double-roofed and square-shaped canvas. These, they assured them, was the best the army offered in the heat extremes of the Karroo. They assigned one for Major Hawkins and his field desk; the two lieutenants shared one, and the men had the rest, fourteen to a tent.

They had equipped the camp with ablution facilities, where one could occasionally wash, shave, and shower. Water was scarce in the Karroo, except at Matjesfontein, so it was a rare treat for the men at the camp. The company had cooking facilities and a mess tent with field tables and chairs.

"They will serve supper at 1900 hours, after which I will give you men a briefing," said the major.

The men organized their cots and kits for the night, washing and preparing for supper. They heard the first news from home during the meal when the major remarked on the Newcastle football fans.

"I hope you lads will behave better than your lot in Newcastle."

Surprised by the comment, they stared at him, trying to determine whether he was serious or joking.

"I don't suppose you've heard, being on your journey here," said the major. "Last week on Good Friday, there was a major derby between Newcastle United and Sunderland."

They nodded, saying, "Aye, we know, Sir. Tyneside versus Wearside. D'you know who won?"

"They stopped the match," said the major. "70,000 fans descended on St James' Park, which can only handle 30,000. There was a huge crush, and the fans broke the gates and clambered like cats over the walls. With thousands of fans jammed inside the ground, the pitch became awash, while hundreds teetered on the roof of the grandstands."

The men stood shaken, full of curiosity about what might follow. So, the major continued his story.

"Only twenty-five policemen were on duty at first, so it was impossible to empty the pitch. So, at 3:30 P.M., they abandoned the match before it had started, resulting in a full-scale riot. The rioting fans tore down the goalposts, ripped the club flag to shreds and uprooted barriers and fences while throwing bottles and stones in every direction. Wagonloads of police and officers on horseback needed two hours to remove the rioters from St James' Park. They only injured twelve people, including one fan who'd plunged from the stand's roof. It was a nasty state of affairs and put football and Newcastle in a horrible light."

The men looked at each other and grinned. They knew how Northeast football fans could get themselves so worked up.

"At least they killed no one, a miracle," said the major, "including the idiot who fell from the roof." Then the soldiers burst into hysterical laughter, the major included.

After an excellent supper of beef and potatoes, they helped themselves to tea, and the major began his briefing.

"Right, men, there's no time to relax. Our next job will be to guard the lines of communication between here and Laingsburg, a distance of 18 ½ miles. That isn't an enormous distance, but the colonel assured me we'd be busy over that section of the railway. This year alone, they have had over fifty incidents of sabotage and action over that same section, with five deaths and two dozen wounded. The railway ran parallel to the road and a dry riverbed, crossing many dongas where the Dutchmen could conceal themselves. They hide in those hills during the day and descend at night on raids."

"We need to guard our section 24 hours a day," said the Major, "so we will break the company up into watches under the lieutenants. You will be on the lookout for eight to ten hours, alternating between you. A company of Cape Mounted Riflemen will join us under Major Harding and lieutenants Smith and Higgins."

The Cape Mounted Riflemen, or CMR, was a multiracial unit with a long and distinguished tradition and an excellent regular military force of the Cape Colony. They were at one time in the service of the British government, but from 1870, the colony bore their expense. When the Anglo-Boer War started in October 1899, the corps numbered 924, with a total supply of horses and eight guns.

"You will form patrols with the CMR leading the way, followed by your men in the reinforced wagons they have assigned to us. They have entrusted us with engineers knowledgeable on communication lines, railway tracks and sleepers.

"Your job is to keep the Boers away from the railway line. And to correct any damage to the railway or telegraph lines should they get through our defences. They are the primary means of transport and communication between Capetown, Kimberley and Pretoria, so we must keep them open.

"Right, you're dismissed. Don't stay up too late; we'll muster the first watch before dawn. We need to relieve the last watch of our companions who have been out there since January."

And with that, a great commotion arose, with chairs shuffled as the men stood up, excited at their first proper assignment in this South African War. Many weren't new recruits and were experienced in warfare. Several more senior NCOs had either been in South Africa, having returned to Durham to recover from injuries or had experienced earlier conflicts in Africa or elsewhere. They were the mentors for the men and the junior officers, for whom this was their first assignment outside England.

"Well, lads, we're in the thick of it at long last," said Joe to his marras. "This is exciting, don't you think?"

"Aye," said Jack. "Let's hope that Gideon bloke doesn't appear here."

"You heard the colonel, Jack," Mike reminded him. "They avoid large gatherings of British soldiers such as this camp."

"Aye," said Joe, "Just wait until we are out in the open starting tomorrow. We must watch our backs, I reckon."

Billy grunted instead of voicing any further concerns.

∼

An Introduction to Boer Fighters—April 1901

They awakened the soldiers at 5 A.M., even though it was still dark and chilly.

"Sunrise is at 7 A.M., but we'll leave long before that, laddies. Coffee, tea and rusks are ready in the mess tent. Hurry," bellowed Sergeant on Duty Munroe, another Scot from County Durham.

With that, Lieutenant George Smith arrived and added his urgency.

"What are rusks?" someone asked.

"South African morning biscuits," said the sergeant. "Good with tea or coffee."

With that, they gulped their tea and ate as many rusks as possible, which were sweeter and softer than hardtack and not too shabby, they thought. They then headed to the mustering point, where the engineers were hooking the mules to the carts. Minutes later, the CMR arrived, and the Durhams mounted the wagons and set off on their way out of the camp onto a trail that ran parallel to the railway track. There were more stars in the night sky than Joe had ever seen on Tyneside. They had never seen the Milky Way, which was bright and omnipresent across a glassy night sky, and they were full of awe. A faint glow of dawn appeared on the eastern horizon.

Their patrol made Laingsburg within the eight hours of the watch. Along the way, they met the company they were relieving returning to Matjesfontein. They stopped and exchanged greetings, then asked the retiring patrol questions about their experiences, who responded with their most memorable episodes over the past three months and gave the recruits a few tips to note well.

"Keep your eyes and ears well peeled, lads," called one. "The Dutchmen are invisible, fast and cunning. Watch your backs!"

"Thanks for that, me marras," called Mike. "Me rifle's ready."

The terrain between Matjesfontein and Laingsburg was rough. Ridges and kopjes surrounded them with small, dry dongas cutting into them and making their way to lower ground. They could see evidence of flash floods and deeper dongas with ragged edges. Mid-way between Matjesfontein and Laingsburg, they dropped 100 yards.

There was a small British camp at Laingsburg between two dry riverbeds. They pitched their tents there, grabbed food from their emergency rations, and bunked. The following squad covered a stretch to the north and used the same camp. The sunset was at 6:41 P.M., so they slept a few hours in daylight before their next watch started at 8 P.M.

Rising in the dark at 7:30 P.M., they ate tinned beef and biscuits with a strong cup of coffee before the watch started. Whereas the day had been pleasant, it cooled quickly after sunset. They walked with the wagons for a while to exercise and get warm.

The terrain was flat, the moon was bright, and the soldiers made excellent progress. At ten miles out, they came to a whistle-stop called Skeiding. The terrain there was irregular, with a dry riverbed and a rise to the right, and it was just visible in the moonlight. Then they heard riders approaching.

"Boers!" shouted the lieutenant. He ordered them to leap out of the wagons and seek shelter. They peered into the darkness toward the intruders. Then they heard shots from not far away, and the bullets ricocheted off the carts.

"Shite, lads, the bastards are shooting at us," yelled Mike.

"Dive for cover," ordered the lieutenant.

The Boer fighters were coming from the hills to their right. They returned fire towards the riders. They shot into the night for five minutes toward the flashes of the Boer weapons. The last watch had told them that this was a favourite trick of the Boers: to distract while they prepared mischief elsewhere. And that's what happened. They heard an explosion at the station within a few minutes, followed by silence!

"What the hell was that?" Mike called, whipping around towards the explosion.

"Sounds as if our Boer friends are bent on causing damage to the neighbourhood," said Joe.

"OK, let's get ready for a fight," said Mike.

In the meantime, the CMR had ridden out to investigate the dongas and rises. They found nothing and reported back that the Boer fighters had fled. The lieutenant ordered a detail to study the damage at the station. They found the track had lifted off the sleepers but was undamaged by the explosion. The engineers set to their task, and within half an hour, the rail was back in place, ready for the next train. They had to work with little light since they were otherwise vulnerable to attacks, and they put the wagons between them and the last direction of the Boer attack.

They didn't have to wait long. Without warning, the Boers opened fire again from somewhere else in the darkness. One of their bullets ricocheted off the wagon and over Mike's head.

"Shite, laddies, I felt that," cried Mike. "It only just missed my head!"

The CMR and British soldiers responded toward the Boer rifle flashes. The battle raged for another ten minutes, after which the shooting stopped. Joe felt a burning in his right leg during the shooting but neither cried out nor complained of being shot. The adrenalin had set in, and he felt nothing more, continuing his shooting as required until the skirmish ended. They could hear the Boer mounts galloping away at top speed and listened until silence returned.

The calm was restored, the engineers finished their work, and the soldiers righted the wagons. They mounted and moved on, arriving at the Matjesfontein camp by 6:30 A.M. at first light.

"Well, laddies, that was your first confrontation with a Boer commando," proclaimed the sergeant, "First of many, I'm sure."

"Aye," said Joe. "It looks as if they have damaged me."

Joe had felt no pain as the bullet passed through the muscle of his leg and out the opposite side. With adrenaline flowing through his veins, blood had been oozing from the wound without him seeing it until now. The pain had set in, and he was limping.

"Well done, laddie," said the Sergeant. "The Boer has christened you. Let's hope that's the worst that will happen to you."

"Aye," said Joe. "So, now what?"

"Off to the sickbay you go, laddie; I'll show you the way."

"Well done, laddie," his marras called as Joe followed the sergeant to get his treatment, "You're a true veteran now."

With that, the sergeant led Joe through the labyrinth of the tented camp's walkways to a large, open tent used as a field hospital. A nurse, who hurried past beds occupied by recovering soldiers to the treatment centre, received him. There, to his amazement, they handed him over to a nurse he recognized from home.

"Jenny? Jenny Ambler?" he said. "I don't believe it."

"Joe?" she blurted, startled. "Aye, it's me. Fancy us meeting here in the middle of the Karroo. As usual, you are in a spot of bother, Joe. Now come here. Lie on this table. The doctor wants to check you out."

After examination by the doctor, nurse Jenny cleaned and bandaged the damage and gave Joe a new pair of trousers and socks to replace his bloodied clothing. Jenny gave him a shot to sedate him and led him to a bed where he could recover from the shock of being shot for the first time. The pain had crept in, and he had become most uncomfortable, but before five minutes were over, he was in a deep sleep.

When he awoke, he realized it was time for his next watch and readied himself to rise. However, before he could, Jenny was upon him. She told him the doctor ordered rest for a day or two before returning to duty.

"We want to ensure no infection sets in, Joe," she insisted. "Infection is a killer out here; more soldiers die of infection and disease than the bullet."

This development upset him since he didn't want to disappoint his company, but Jenny assured him they understood.

"Joe, the Boers have shot and injured you," she said with sympathy. "Your mates will see you as a hero, but you must rest. They'll be serving you soup and biscuits soon."

"Oh, I'm looking forward to that, Jen. I'm starving and have had no decent soup since I left the ship," he said.

Joe observed Jenny as she went through her tasks. She wore the standard dress of British war nurses of the time—a light blue, neck-to-ankle cotton dress with long sleeves and wide, white, starched cuffs. Over the dress at the front of her uniform, Jenny wore a long white apron flowing from her neck to her ankles. The apron was smeared in places from the blood of soldiers. She wore a short dark blue cape over her shoulders, a white starched collar and a white bonnet flowing over her shoulders to the middle of her back. It was a handsome uniform, thought Joe, which made Jenny the picture of a perfect British nurse.

"Jenny, when I saw you, I couldn't believe my eyes," he said. "I thought I was in heaven and that you were an angel."

She laughed. "Your wound isn't that serious, Joe. You're still alive, and I'm not an angel. But it surprised me to see you too, a friendly face so far from home."

"How long have you been here?" Joe asked.

"I've only been at Matjesfontein a few weeks," she said. "But I've been in South Africa for over a year now. The Princess of Wales, Alexandra of Denmark, organized a group of nurses from the Royal London Hospital to work in South Africa, and I was among them."

"Well done," said Joe. "Where else have you been, then?"

"I've been around, Joe," she said, "Wherever I'm needed, I suppose. I started in Natal, then on the Great March to Pretoria with Lord Roberts, then with the Brandwater Campaign in the Orange Free State, then De Aar, and now Matjesfontein."

"My word," said Joe. "Has it been tough?"

"Not for me, apart from a few sleepless nights during battles," she said. "I've seen lots of blood, deaths, maiming, and disease. It's not been pleasant, but that's the job."

"I'm sure," he said.

"It's not for me to say, Joe, but I don't know why you lads are here in this God-forsaken place."

"To protect our King and Empire."

"Oh yes," she said, giving no clue of her displeasure. Field nurses disapprove of wars, but their profound sense of duty and compassion takes them to where the army needs them on the battlefields. "Here is your soup coming, Joe. I'll check in on you before I go off duty."

Joe, who was ravenous, much appreciated the soup and biscuits. "Jenny Ambler," he thought, "What a surprise meeting her way out here, but an enjoyable one."

Jenny came back before the lights came out and checked Joe's bandage. "Everything looks fine, Joe," she said. "I'm sure the doctor will release you tomorrow morning."

Joe thanked her and said he wanted to see her again soon, and she then disappeared into the darkness which had befallen the camp.

His marras visited him that evening, and they recounted the events of their first engagement with the Boers for the longest time.

"Sneaky bastards they are," said Mike, "Sneaking up like weasels in the dead of night."

"Aye, that they are," Joe said. "They are working now under guerrilla warfare rules."

"I wonder whether we shot any of those Dutchmen," Jack questioned.

"Who knows?" Joe said, "I couldn't see a bloody thing. But I doubt it; we couldn't see them."

"Do you think it will happen to us often?" Billy speculated.

"From what the colonel told us, the answer is yes," Jack said.

"That's the nature of guerrilla warfare," said Joe. "It's a nasty business."

"Well, Joe, you are our hero, laddie," said Mike. "Taking the first bullet. Well done!"

"Ahh, it was just a muscle wound," said Joe. "No catastrophe."

"Aye, and a splendid thing, too," said Mike. "We don't want to lose you, our good marra, so soon."

The next day, Joe checked back in with his company. But his section had long since gone out on patrol. So, he reported to Lieutenant Guthrie, who commanded the other watch. They told him to rest and join the following day's vigil. The patrol left at 8 A.M., so they wouldn't return until 7 A.M. the next day. The next departure was at 3 P.M. tomorrow; he had free time.

He washed the blood off his puttees and cleaned and polished his boots, ready for the next watch.

The following morning, his wound became painful, so he returned to the hospital tent to have it checked. Sure enough, Jenny was there and pleased to see him again. But she noticed at once that he was in pain.

"Hello, Joe," she said. "I see the wound has become infected, just as I feared. That happens here often, and I'll have the doctor check it."

"It's a bother, me ending up in here again," said Joe, half-embarrassed, sweating and shivering simultaneously. "I feel sick, Jenny."

"We'll get you right; don't worry," said the concerned nursing sister.

The doctor arrived and examined the wound, then turned to Jenny. "Nurse, this wound needs thorough cleansing and excision. Give this man a powerful shot of whisky, dig into that wound, and find and remove any foreign matter and infected flesh. Soldier, this will not be pleasant. But it could get much worse for you if we don't do it. Nurse, you will need help. I'll send a male medic or two to hold him while you clean his wound and will come back and check it when you have finished and before you bandage it again."

Jenny gave Joe not one but three good snorts of whisky, and two stroppy male medics held him until he passed out from the pain. Then Jenny cleaned and treated the wound with iodine. The doctor approved her work, and she bandaged her patient again and let him sleep. The night duty nurse checked in on Joe, and Jenny arrived the following day.

"How are you feeling, soldier?" she asked him.

"Much better for seeing you, thank you, nurse," said Joe. "I'm still feeling pain and woozy in my gut."

"I will watch over you for a while, Joe. We don't want to lose such a valuable Durham lad. Your temperature was at a dangerous level from that infection, and you know we are losing more men from infection and disease than from weapons out here in Africa?"

"Oh? I didn't know that. Thank you, Jenny, and as I promised, once better, I will watch over you. Are you on duty on Sunday?"

"No, why?."

"I thought it might be nice to get together."

"Aye, that is an excellent idea," said Jenny. "If you are feeling better, that is."

"Good, I'll collect you right after lunch," called Joe after her as she left.

Rendezvous at the Matjesfontein Stream—May 1901

On Sunday, Joe collected Jenny as promised.

"Alreet, Jenny?" asked Joe.

"Alreet, Joe," said the nurse.

"I know a lovely spot where we can be alone and talk in peace," said Joe, leading her out of the camp, across the railway track and through an alley next to the hotel to an oasis of trees and grass lining a flowing stream.

"I don't believe this. How can this be in such a dried-out place?"

"Amazing, isn't it?" said Joe. "The Laird says this stream is why he built the town here."

"Well, I never," said an astonished Jenny.

Joe then led her to a spot he had picked out for them. It was a small patch of grass surrounded by trees and shrubs, making it very secluded and private. There, they reclined on the grass and stretched out.

"It's pleasant here, isn't it?" said Joe. "I discovered it while out for a walk recently. Just look at the many birds in the trees. And I saw a deer here; I think they're deer. Very few come here, so no one should disturb us. So tell me, how did you end up in this camp?"

She then repeated what she had told him earlier. "I've only been at the camp a few weeks, but I've been in South Africa for over a year. When the Princess of Wales organized a group of nurses from the Royal London Hospital to work in South Africa, I was among them."

"No, Jenny. What I mean is, how did you become a nurse and join up for war service?"

"Oh. I have wanted to be a nurse since I was a wee girl. I had a cousin who knew Florence Nightingale."

"Who?" asked Joe.

"Florence Nightingale. She was the founder of modern nursing, and they train nurses now to follow in her footsteps. She first became famous while serving as a head nurse and trainer of nurses during the Crimean War, in which she cared for wounded soldiers. It's because of her that nursing has such an excellent reputation. She became known as 'The Lady with the Lamp' when she made rounds of wounded soldiers at night. My cousin, much older than me and a nurse, learned much of what she knew from Florence Nightingale when she was an old lady but still teaching at St Thomas' Hospital in London."

"Wey aye, that's canny," said Joe. "I didn't know that. But I know of that Crimean War. That was in the 1850s, where that terrible charge of the light brigade happened."

"Aye, that's it," said Jenny. "So, when I saw my cousin in her handsome uniform as a child, I was always envious, and I started pretending I was a nurse, treating my dolls and friends whenever we played together. And when I was old enough, I asked my cousin to help me apply for nursing training, which she did. And that's how it happened. I trained at St Thomas' Hospital. And here I am, an army nurse following the British Army from one trouble spot to another, doing what I can for you soldiers."

"That is such a canny story, Jen," enthused Joe. "Amazing!"

"Well, not so amazing. But I do what I can. The worst is seeing so many young men dying from their wounds. You grow used to it, and that's my job. But tell me how you got here."

"Aye, well, I suppose mine is a similar story," said Joe. "The British Army, Royal Navy and the great British Empire always interested me. Since leaving school and working, I wanted to become a soldier and join the British Army. I enjoyed reading, so I started collecting newspaper stories on whatever the British Army was doing worldwide. And when this war started, I read everything I could about it. I even started a scrapbook on the war. And I repeated what I had read to my marras, family and pub patrons. None of them read, so I became their only source of information on the war."

"That is so unusual for a working-class boy, Joe. Your parents must have been proud of you."

"Nee. My brothers were, but my Da hated the British, the Queen and everything British. He was a bitter old Irish miner and never lost his Irish hate of the British. He gave me a hard time when I said I wanted to join the army, and that's part of the reason I only joined up so far into the war."

"Well, maybe he was right on that point, Joe. And maybe it was because he didn't want to lose you."

"Nee, he didn't want to lose my money."

They then fell silent while they collected their thoughts and enjoyed the cool breeze wafting through the wood and the trickle of water in the stream.

"What do you think of the war now, Joe?"

"That's a good question, Jen. It's not what I expected. The first part of this war was more of the British Army fighting, with columns of thousands of troops, flags waving in the wind, bands playing and cannons firing. That's what I followed before I came here. But now we are fighting what they call guerilla warfare. You can't see the enemy. And they pounce on you when you least expect it. It's a dirty war."

"Aye, well, any war is dirty and wrong for me," said Jenny. "I know what you mean."

"Aye, but let's not talk of wars now, Jenny. Let's enjoy what's around us. I have grown to love this barren land, with its bright blue skies and starlit nights. And you?"

"Aye, now you're talking, Joe. I love it, too. It's much cleaner and more natural than the filthy mines and factories at home. When you breathe in this clean air, you can fill your lungs with oxygen, not the dirty air and soot of home."

"Aye, whatever oxygen is, if you say so. And we see amazing sunrises, sunsets, and a sky so full of stars you can see your way at night even when the moon isn't shining. It's pure belta!"

"Do you know that many of these little plants of the Karroo are medicinal plants that can cure many diseases and health problems?"

"Nee. How do you know that?"

"One of our fellow nurses is a South African girl," said Jenny. "She learned of these plants from her nanny, a Cape-coloured woman who learned the ways of the bushmen."

"Well, I never!. Plants that can cure you?"

"Aye, and they can cure many problems. The bushmen knew how to cure everything that happened to them, including snake bites."

"You know, Jenny," said Joe, in a near whisper, "It's grand to have found you here, and I'm very fond of you. And you're doing so much good in your work."

"That's so nice of you to say that, Joe. I'm fond of you, too."

"Well, we must keep seeing each other. We make a good pair."

"That we do. That we do."

"It'd be so nice to talk to a woman from home instead of just my marras. I miss my Geordie women, mother, sisters, and Ruth."

"Aye, I remember them, including Ruth," said Jenny. "I'll be your Geordie girl away from home, Joe. You can count on me."

∼

More Patrols and Skirmishes—May 1901

From the moment the principal battles had been won by the British Army under Field Marshal Roberts, the Boers had resolved to disrupt the peace wherever and whenever they could.

By September 1900, the British High Command purported to control both Boer Republics. But they soon realized that they only controlled territory where their troops were present in numbers. With each conquered territory, they had to leave behind enough forces to support the peace. But despite losing their two capital cities and a half of their army, the Boer commanders adopted guerrilla warfare tactics—raids against railways, troop concentrations and army supplies—hitting wherever they could cause pain and disruption to the enemy. They were disrupting the operational capacity of the British Army and avoiding the painful and costly battles of the early phases of the war.

The Boer commandos returned from the battlefields to their home districts and relied on local support and personal knowledge of the terrain and the towns. They could live out of sight of British troops and survive off the land. Their orders were to attack the British forces and to strike hard, causing as much damage to the enemy as possible and then to withdraw and vanish before enemy reinforcements could arrive. They had the freedom to move over the vast distances of their homeland, making it near impossible for the 250,000 British troops to control the territory using columns alone. British control faded after a column left a town or district.

So, despite Roberts' belief that the war ended with the capture of the Boer capitals and the defeat of the Boer armies, the war continued undeterred. Attacks and skirmishes spread out across the entire sub-continent wherever

British troops assembled. They focused these attacks on the western and eastern Transvaal, the Orange River Colony and the Cape Colony. This guerilla war and the new Boer tactics became Kitchener's most significant problem to overcome. By the time Joe and his marras had arrived, the Boers had established guerilla warfare throughout southern Africa, and they were to learn of their tactics and the consequences daily. News of other districts' sabotage, attacks, battles and engagements arrived daily. The Boers were relentless in their plan to win back their Republics.

Incidents such as the one described above were often happening and causing injuries and even deaths among the troops based at Matjesfontein. On another day in May 1901, they despatched Joe's patrol to guard the railway between Matjesfontein and Laingsburg. They left the camp at 8 A.M., monitoring the hills, dongas, and horizon as always when, 5 miles out, they saw a sizeable group of riders appear on the horizon before them.

"Steady, men," cautioned the lieutenant. "This doesn't look good. Form defences. Tip and use the wagons as protection and keep yourselves and the horses down."

They leapt into action as the riders gained speed in their approach, identifiable now as Boers.

"It's unusual for such commandos to attack during the day," called the lieutenant. "They are counting on their numbers to overpower us."

"Bring them on," growled Mike.

"Yeah. We're ready for the Dutchmen," echoed Jack.

"Mine is the one with that white horse," called Billy.

"Keep your heads down," called Joe. "Don't let them bury a bullet in your forehead."

The fighters were bearing on them at speed in a cavalry charge. They counted 20 as they lowered their rifles and began firing. Bullets were ricocheting off the wagons and boulders behind the patrol when the first

British soldier slumped in his position, then fell back while spilling blood onto the soil. Then, more and more bullets slammed into the wagons and whizzed past their heads.

"Shite, lads, let's get a few of them, quickly now, before they get us," shouted Mike as he made his mark on a rider who fell hard from his saddle.

"Look, the CMR is coming to our rescue," shouted Joe.

Unnoticed by the footsoldiers crouching and shooting from behind the wagons, the CMR had split into two at first sight of the Boer riders, then peeled off to attack them from their flanks.

"Aye, what a bunch of good laddies," called Billy.

"Look, the Dutchmen are dropping," called Mike.

Seeing the CMR attacking from both sides, the Boer fighters halted their firing and fled in the opposite direction. The CMR didn't slow their attack and soon routed the Boers, dropping a few more.

When the battle was over, the Boers vanished into the hills, and the CMR returned victorious to a much-diminished group of soldiers huddled behind the wagons. Of the original contingent, only the marras, three other soldiers, and the lieutenant had survived. The rest were dead or wounded. So, those who could righted the carts and loaded the dead and injured into them. They then returned to camp as fast as they could.

There awaited the medical staff to take the wounded into their custody while others off-loaded the corpses and took them to the field morgue. There, too, was Jenny, who greeted Joe with an enormous smile.

That evening, the marras mourned their fellow soldiers killed in the attack.

"They were top-notch laddies," said Joe.

"Aye, that they were," said Mike. "But that's our work. It could have been us, so we've been lucky once more."

The others agreed and called it a day. Joe went to the medical tent to see Jenny and hear how the injured soldiers were doing.

"One is in a serious condition," said Jenny. "We're not sure whether he'll make it. But the others are stable and should survive their ordeal."

"That's excellent news, Jenny," Joe rejoiced. "But we lost five men. That was our worst attack since we arrived and a close call for me and my marras. They showed up from nowhere and ambushed us. But we got some of them, too. The CMR was grand!"

"This war isn't over by any means, Joe, regardless of what the generals say," said Jenny. "Please take care."

"Aye, Jenny, you're right on that count, and yes, I'll try to take care," said Joe as he waved and left for something to eat and his bunk.

A Sunday Bicycle Outing and Picnic—June 1901

On one mild autumn Saturday, the marras borrowed bicycles for an excursion to a slight ridge of undulating hills rising out of the Karroo two miles due south of Matjesfontein. Bikes were popular at the turn of the twentieth century, but the army had only just introduced them to warfare. South Africa was the testing ground for the bicycle in war. It proved to be a most valuable auxiliary means of personal transport compared to the horse. The distance a cyclist can cover and the weight he can carry is three to four times greater than that possible for the infantryman. And they cost less to buy and keep than a horse. They appeared to have a glorious future. Mike, an avid cyclist at home, had become friendly with a few of the soldiers of the Cape Cycle Corps, a new unit just formed in January 1901. The CCC agreed to lend him four of their spare bicycles for the Sunday excursion but warned him to take care of them.

They rose at dawn the following day and had breakfast in the mess tent. With Jenny's help, they had arranged for the cook to prepare sandwiches. He had made thick slices of fresh bread stuffed full of corned beef, wrapped in brown paper, which they fetched on their way to get the bicycles. Joe and his marras filled their water canteens with safe drinking water. They had learned to be very careful with the water they drank.

The marras dressed in their usual field uniforms but only took one rifle in case they "saw a hare or two to shoot along the way for the cook." Setting off together in friendly spirits, apart from Mike, unsteady on the bikes at first, they launched themselves into the Karroo. The sun rose on a crisp autumn morning as they wound through the vast camp. Before long, they were out into the wide-open spaces of the barren Karroo.

They followed a trail in the direction of the ridge. They were in no rush, so they settled into a slow, steady pace. It was a comfortable ride and a gentle but steady incline despite the need to avoid obstacles. They bantered, sang, and observed their surroundings as they travelled and had a good old time. They didn't concern themselves about straying too far from the camp and getting in harm's way.

In less than an hour, they reached the bottom of the ridge where the trail split east and west. They followed the path west for a quarter of a mile. Then, as they rounded a bend, the route turned south again and started a steep ascent after crossing two dongas. Near the summit of the highest hill, they stopped to admire the view of the camp before them and surrounding Karroo in the distance.

"Just look at that sight," said Joe.

"Aye, Joe, that's a fine sight, for sure," said Mike. "Can you believe the size of that camp? It's huge!"

"With those hundreds of white tents, it looks like a field of snowdrifts," said Jack.

"Aye, it does, Jack," said Billy. "Look at that herd of horses. There must be thousands of them."

"Aye, thousands of them, Billy," said Mike. "Look at the huge piles of hay. They ship that up from the coast."

"I love looking out over that plain," said Joe, "You can see forever. Forever nothing except for that scrub only goats and wild animals can eat."

"I don't see any trees except for those few by the stream behind Matjesfontein," said Mike.

"Aye, it's a bloody dry and uninviting place," said Joe. "Still, I'm enjoying it. There's nothing out there but scrub and wild animals, but it's special."

"I know what you mean, Joe," said Jack. "I've grown fond of it too. And I love the sounds of those strange birds and the wind swooshing through the scrub."

"Aye, I'll second that, Jack. Well, laddies, we had better continue exploring," said Joe. "Let's see what else we can find out here."

The marras followed the path around the hill, not knowing what they might meet ahead. But they stopped in their tracks at once; they suddenly realized they were not alone. They could hear talking and laughing from over the top of the hill. Dismounting, they hid their bicycles and continued on foot. Taking a circuitous route to the top of a rise, they peered at a small group of men camped just over the summit of an adjacent hill.

The voices became louder on a slight breeze until they could distinguish the words as being English. They felt relieved until they realized that at least one of the voices was American, and the others had a foreign accent even though they spoke English.

"That's bloody strange," said Mike in a whisper. "I don't think they are ours."

"Then who the hell could they be?" Joe murmured

"Boers!" Jack said with a hint of panic. "There are Yank sympathizers amongst them."

"No doubt still annoyed by the tea tax they revolted against," said Joe.

"What?" asked Mike with a grimace.

"Never mind," said Joe.

"Shite," Billy said, "Let's get the hell out of here!"

Everyone agreed with that sentiment since they did not want to battle Boer fighters. They backtracked to their bikes in haste and returned to the fork where, well out of earshot, they stopped to discuss their next course of action.

Billy wanted to return to camp to alert the major. But Mike felt they were well away from the fighters and should take the east fork to explore the Karroo more. "Let's find a pleasant spot for lunch and relaxation before heading back to camp," he suggested.

They eventually agreed, mounted their bikes again, and set off on the other trail. Not too far along the path, they crossed a donga with shrubs and low trees growing in it. There, they stopped and broke out their lunch under a tree.

"Cook made great sandwiches for us," said Mike.

"Aye, and Jenny played a part in that," said Joe.

"Aye, she did," said Jack. "No doubt adding a measure of a woman's touch."

Over lunch, they recalled their encounters with the enemy and reminded Joe that, had the Boer not injured him, he might not have met up with Jenny. He had to agree with that. They had a few laughs and lamented the loss of their other marras.

The sun was dropping to the west over the camp and hills to the other side of the valley when they packed everything up and headed back toward the fork. But as soon as they arrived at the division and turned north towards the camp, they heard horses galloping in their direction.

"What the hell? Quick," Joe called, "Let's get back to camp as fast as we can."

And with that, they crouched forward on their bikes and pumped the pedals as fast as possible. They made sure that nobody shouted or otherwise alerted the commando approaching from behind them. But despite their caution, they soon heard shouts and the sounds of galloping horses gaining on them.

"We can't let these bastards catch us," Mike yelled. "They'll kill us!"

"Aye, or take us prisoner. But we'll get in trouble with the officers in the camp too, never mind the Boers," Joe yelled back.

They heard shots and bullets whizzing overhead.

"Bastards," yelled Jack, holding their only rifle back over his shoulder, releasing a few volleys. The horses were getting closer, and the Boer firing continued at first.

They pumped harder on the pedals, harder, faster, faster.

Then, Billy's bike hurtled off a large rock in the trail, and he somersaulted into the veld, landing face first. Bloodied, he howled invectives as he scurried to recover his bike and saw it had suffered no damage. Remounting, he pushed as hard as he could to catch up with his marras, the blood pouring from his nose.

But the commando decided that riding into this huge British camp wasn't a marvellous idea. So they abandoned the chase and vanished before they became the prey.

The Boer shots hit no one, and as far as they knew, Mike's bullets hit none of them either. Within half an hour, Joe and his marras were back in camp. They decided it wasn't helpful to report the incident since they had left on borrowed bicycles without explicit permission. When they arrived, the marras returned the bikes with thanks and returned to their tent in time for tea. They heard no talk of gunshots in the veldt, so they surmised that the incident had gone unnoticed. Billy peeled off at sickbay along the way to have his nose seen to, claiming he had slipped on horse dung in the road.

∽

The Bridge Skirmish—July 1901

There were ongoing instances of action with the Boers over the next few weeks. On one occasion, they surprised a commando trying to destroy a railway bridge over a donga. They found them in daylight again, so they could see them in the distance as the CMR rode out to meet them. The Boers took flight and disappeared without a shot fired.

But that night, they returned to complete the deed. Joe's patrol had camped out there for just such an eventuality. The lieutenant had assigned watch duties to guard the bridge "just in case the bastards return." Joe and Mike were on the first watch while the rest bunked for a few hours of sleep. The lieutenant stationed them on either end of the short bridge, and they could see each other outlined by the feeble light of the stars despite the lack of a moon. Winter was fast approaching, and the temperatures dropped after sunset.

"Bloody chilly out tonight," said Mike quietly.

"Aye, that you can bloody well say again, my marra," said Joe while he settled in and hauled his coat around his ears.

After an hour, they heard the gentle approach of horses. The marras became alert and peered into the frigid darkness. Joe could make out the approaching group of men and beasts from 100 yards, sounding the alert and ducking for cover.

Then, pandemonium broke out. The riders fired in the general direction of the bridge, and Joe and Mike returned fire in rapid succession while the rest of the patrol leapt out of their sleeping blankets and, gathering their weapons, ran to back up the guards.

"Where are they?" called one.

"Straight ahead," called Joe, pointing in the fighters' general direction. But rising from a deep sleep left the backup soldiers confused and afraid.

"There, look," called Mike, pointing out the horses.

The Boer riders dismounted and surrounded the bridge and its British guards. A fierce firefight ensued, the shots coming from several directions, the flashes visible in the moonless night.

"The bastards are firing at us," yelled Mike, the fighters' positions now shown by their rifle flashes.

The lieutenant took command and issued commands to his men.

"Fire at the flashes," he commanded, which they did. But the commandos returned the favour, and within a few minutes, their sharpshooting had dropped two British soldiers.

"Shoot their horses," the lieutenant ordered with greater urgency. But his men couldn't equal the shooting skills of the Boers, and firing into the night, they missed most of their targets. The lieutenant's command alerted the Boers, who heard and understood it, and they mounted their horses and retreated. The British patrol continued firing, hitting one or two fighters. Within half an hour, the skirmish had ended, and the Boers had fled. One soldier was dead, and three were injured. They collected the wounded soldiers and treated them as best possible. They also found two wounded Boer fighters they took as prisoners and gave them first aid.

"You men need more target practice when we get back to camp," scowled the lieutenant. "If you don't get better with your shooting, we may not survive these skirmishes."

The men agreed, and no one slept for the rest of the night.

"Well, Lieutenant, we got two of them," Mike commented.

"Aye, we did, chaps, we sure did," said the Lieutenant. "When I watched you before the Boer fighters arrived, it reminded me of a poem by our esteemed Poet Laureate, Rudyard Kipling, called Bridge-Guard in the Karroo. We know him as the 'Poet of the Empire'; he is writing poetry to support the British cause in this war.

"Kipling was born in Bombay to English parents, a child of the British Empire, so to speak. In early 1898, he and his family travelled to South Africa for their winter holiday, beginning an annual excursion. They always stay in The Woolsack, a house built for Kipling by Cecil John Rhodes on his Groote Schuur Estate, within walking distance of Rhodes' mansion.

"He has made many visits to South Africa, and on a visit last year, he became a correspondent for *The Friend* newspaper in Bloemfontein. Lord Roberts commandeered this newspaper for his troops when he occupied that city. You may know it. Rudyard Kipling travelled throughout South Africa in the early stages of the war and told stories of these places through his poetry, such as Bridge-Guard in the Karroo, written just this year and ending:

> '*More than a little lonely*
> *Where the lessening taillights shine.*
> *No—not combatants—only*
> *Details guarding the line!*'"

"Aye, that sounds right for us," said Mike, and the others nodded in agreement.

Then, as dawn broke over the Karroo, their relief unit arrived to take over while they returned to camp to deliver their wounded comrades to sickbay for proper treatment and the prisoners to gaol.

Such encounters were frequent in this guerrilla war.

"They never let up, the bastards," complained Mike.

"They don't," said Joe. "They are everywhere. There is nowhere to hide in this war where we can be safe."

"I'm enjoying it," said Mike. "It's exciting!"

"Aye, but getting shot, or worse, killed, is not exciting," said Joe.

"Aye. But if the Boers kill you, your worries are over, laddie," joked Mike.

"I'm not ready for that yet, Mike," said Joe.

They all laughed, then turned in.

The Move to De Aar & the Visit to Springfontein—August 1901

After a few months at Matjesfontein, the army ordered Joe's company north to De Aar, so they entrained and continued their journey northwards. Beyond Matjesfontein, the Karroo stretches flat and wide, as far as one can see. A ridge of weathered hills with horizontal rock ridges stretches off to the right of the rail line for many miles until it, too, retreats to the horizon.

There were frequent stops along the way at this stage of the war because of rail sabotage carried out by the Boers. On his trip along the same route, Churchill had seen natives with flags guarding strategic points. Now, at regular intervals, British encampments and blockhouses defended the line. The British Army fortified the bridges. But they heard the Boers had sabotaged a few bridges ahead of them and were under repair. Apart from the occasional civilian railway foreman, they saw no combatant Boers. But they saw many coloureds and a few natives.

"I love this Karroo," said Joe on one of these stops. "It seems to go on forever and forever."

"Aye, and so flat," said Jack, "except for those flat-topped hills we see now and then.

"I divven know how anything can survive out here," said Mike. "There's no water except where they have those windmills."

The British soldiers, originating from the lush green of their homeland, marvelled at the vast expanses of hot, arid scrubland of the Karroo. They saw a few sheep and goats, a few antelope, which they thought were deer, and occasionally other creatures in the wild terrain, unrecognizable to them. There was no barbed wire apart from around the British encampments in those days, so sheep, goats, ostriches and buck alike could wander wherever they wished. Joe wondered what they ate in the barren landscape with so little grass.

"What the..." called Joe. "Do you laddies see the size of those birds? I think they are birds. What do you think?"

"Aye, Joe," said Jack. "What the hell are they?"

The lieutenant overheard them and responded. "Those are called ostriches, and they grow wild here, but the farmers grow them too for their tail feathers we use back home for ladies' hats."

"Oh, now I get it," said Mike. "These must be from one of those ostrich farms we've heard of, then."

"I know the hats you are talking about, Sir," said Joe. "They are too costly for our women."

"Aye, Joe," said the lieutenant. "They are only worn by upper-class ladies."

They had occasional stops where now well-established army posts made food and freshwater rations available. Civilian canteens at these stops had more precious items from time to time, such as savoury and sweet food items and sometimes even alcohol, for sale. At one such pause, the marras got off the train and bought a bottle of beer each.

"Now that's right useful," said Mike. "A bar in the desert!"

"Aye," said Joe. "With a sizeable beer garden," which caused a few laughs.

They wandered to the donga ahead of the train, where engineers were working to fix the damaged bridge, and the noise had frightened away any wildlife.

"I wonder what these holes are we are seeing?" asked Mike.

"Might they be dug by animals to find water?" asked Joe.

Mike then looked for a branch strong enough to dig deeper into one hole.

"Howay, man. Just look at that," called Mike to his marras. "There is water down there!"

They ran to where he stood over a hole with a small puddle at its bottom.

"They must have had rain here," said Joe. "What a find, Mike."

They walked farther along the donga bed, where chicken-sized brown birds exploding in flight from beneath scrub caught them by surprise.

"Haddaway, man. That scared the shite out of me," cried Mike. To which the others laughed.

"My God, they shouldn't do that to us," said Joe. "We could have thought it was an ambush!"

They all had a nervous laugh and returned to their car. An hour later, the train continued its journey. They crossed many more dongas where the vegetation changed from low scrub to bushes and even a few hardy trees. A sergeant told them that the taproots of these shrubs and trees could find water deep beneath the surface of the dry riverbeds. The fauna changed near these dongas, and in the more extensive wooded riverbeds, they spotted large and majestic antelopes with magnificent corkscrew horns. The soldiers later learned they were called kudu.

It was August and late winter when they arrived in De Aar, which was nothing more than a farm, the name meaning the artery because of its abundant underground water supply. When the Cape Government founded the railways in 1872, they chose a route through De Aar to connect the Kimberley diamond fields to Cape Town on the coast. Because of its central location, the government selected the site for a junction between this first railway line and the other Cape railway networks running further east in 1881. Then, in 1899, the brothers Isaac and Wulf Friedlander, who had erected a trading store and hotel at the junction, purchased the farm. By this time of war, the rail intersection had become one of the most important in the country, and the British Army had a sizable camp there. So, the entrepreneurial brothers saw an opportunity to increase their wealth despite the dangers inherent in the conflict.

Joe's company continued sorties from there for several weeks, many by armoured train across the border into the Orange River Colony 60 miles away. On one such raid, they despatched Joe's company to cross the Orange River to eradicate Boer commandos in the region. They loaded their wagons and horses onto protected flatbed cars and stopped off wherever the Army ordered them to patrol along the line. Crossing the river at Norvalspunt into the Orange River Colony, they travelled north and patrolled the region of Philippolis in the Free State, thirty miles north of Norvalspunt, Cape Colony. The London Missionary Society, under their representative, John Phillip, founded Philippolis in 1823 as a mission station for the local Khoi people. It is the oldest settlement in the Orange Free State since most others only grew after the Great Trek of the 1830s and 40s.

The town and surrounding farms lay in ruins from Kitchener's scorched earth raids, and they saw no Boer commandos anywhere in the region. But they searched the flattened ruins for any survivors.

"Can you believe this?" asked Joe. "How can we lay ruin to a farming town?"

"Because this could be a town that harbours Boer fighters, soldier," said the Sergeant. "So Lord Roberts and Lord Kitchener have ordered the army to destroy any town we meet. But another patrol cleared this one."

"Where are the people?" asked Joe.

"We captured them and put them into camps," said the Sergeant.

"Women and children, too?" asked Joe in disbelief.

"Aye, soldier, women and children too. Many members of the families of the Boer fighters," said the Sergeant. "That was supposed to stop the Boers from fighting this war. But the bastards are still fighting, even with their families locked up in our camps."

So, after a few days of searching the region for Boer fighters but finding none, Joe's company followed the road from Philippolis to Springfontein. Springfontein was another critical railway junction on the main railway line to Johannesburg, where the Bloemfontein line converged with the East London and Port Elizabeth lines.

As the patrol moved past an encampment, what they saw shocked them. Hundreds of women and children were malnourished and wasted to near skeletons from months of internment. [3]

"What the hell is this?" asked Joe. "What are these women and children doing here? Look at them."

It was their first introduction to a horror concentration camp, and no one had warned them of their existence. As they passed, the indigent inmates stared at them with expressionless faces from behind the fence surrounding the camp, too afraid of the soldiers to raise their voices to ask for help. Even the wasted children were silent.

"My God, the stench," said Mike. "These people are dying, and that is the smell of death! What the hell is going on here?"

The stench was too much, even for the most battle-hardened soldiers. So, they increased their pace and continued hunting for the elusive Boer fighters.

That night, around the campfire, the soldiers were mulling over what they had seen when the lieutenant joined them.

"What was that camp for?" asked Mike. "Those people were starving in there and dying like rats. Did you see and smell that?"

"I did, Mike," answered the lieutenant, repeating what the Sergeant had told them. "Those are the families of Boer fighters. Lord Roberts long ago ordered the British Army to impound or destroy these fighters' homes, farms, and livestock and put the Boer families into these camps. Lord Kitchener has been carrying out his orders. The army set up camps across the old Republics to house those families. What else could we do?"

"I know it's not our place to question Lord Robert's orders, Sir," said Joe. "But couldn't the army feed them and look after them better? They are women, children, and old men, with nothing to do with the war except that their men are fighters."

"We are feeding them, Rutherford," said the officer. "There's too many of them. We want their menfolk to stop the war, and then we could free them and let them go home and look after themselves."

The men were dumbfounded, and it had become a massive shock that their army treated innocent women and children this way. But they could find no other polite words for the lieutenant and dispersed to their tents for the night.

One day, when returning from a sortie, Joe discovered that Jenny had transferred to De Aar to be near him. They picked up their relationship where they had left off in Matjesfontein.

"It's so good to see you, Jenny Ambler," said Joe. "I thought I'd never see you again."

"I wanted to see you again, Joe, before you vanish into the Transvaal," she said. "So I arranged a transfer to your camp here at De Aar."

"Are we going to the Transvaal too? I've not heard that. Well then, we had better take advantage of this time, hadn't we?" said Joe. "I'm so surprised and pleased to see you here."

And so began a few precious weeks of enjoying each other's company again between Joe's sorties and Jenny's hospital duties. Joe had grown fond of Jenny and her of him. So, they had many pleasant hours together at De Aar, taking walks out into the Karroo or sharing intimate moments in secret nooks and crannies discovered in and around the camp. They made tentative plans for when they returned to Jarrow.

"Will you return to your hospital work after the war, Jenny?" Joe asked one day.

"Aye," said Jenny. "Sherburn Hospital is in the countryside, Joe. I may look for a job closer to Jarrow."

"Well, I'll find work at Hawthorne Leslie."

"We must try to find jobs near each other, Joe, don't you think?"

"Aye, we must."

"Stay positive, Joe. This war will end, and we will survive it and return to County Durham. I could go back to Sherburn, and you could find work on a farm there. Farm work in the fresh air isn't bad, and the air is clean."

"Aye, I could, I'm sure," said Joe. "But I still have five years in my tour of duty no matter what happens. I can only then return to County Durham."

He then thought back on his time so far in South Africa.

"I haven't been here long, Jenny, but I see things in another light. I've seen and heard enough to wonder why we British are here."

"Why are we here?" she asked. "What do you mean?"

"I used to think it was to grow and protect our British Empire," he said. "But how can I agree with destroying homes, farms, and animals, rounding up thousands of women and children and putting them in terrible camps across South Africa, no matter the reason? I saw one of those camps the other day, and it was disgusting. They say it protects women and children, but I don't believe that. They want the women and children to suffer so their men will surrender. Where is the honour in that? I can't agree with treating innocent people as animals; they treat their horses better."

Jenny sat listening to him, not wanting to interrupt the flow of his thoughts. It surprised but pleased her to hear these sentiments, and they differed from the words of defiance she had heard from him when they met. Jenny considered

Joe intelligent and observant of what was happening around him, which was rare among ordinary soldiers. Then she picked up on Joe's points.

"I agree with you, Joe. I've heard of a British woman, Emily Hobhouse, fighting the politicians and generals to stop this horrible crime. So many women and children are dying from diseases such as measles, enteric fever and dysentery caused by the terrible hygiene conditions in these camps. I haven't seen this, but I know fellow nurses who have. But the British Army in South Africa has lost more men to disease, particularly enteric and typhoid fever, than to the Boers. Africa is a dangerous place."

"You should have seen them, Jenny," said Joe. "Skin and bones. Women and children. And the stench of disease and death. It was horrible! I've never seen such misery at home, even in our worst slums."

"I can only imagine, Joe. I've heard Emily Hobhouse visited the Springfontein camp in March of this year. During her investigations into the conditions within British camps, she also visited the Norval's Pont, Kimberley and Mafeking concentration camps. She was so angry that she brought the British public's attention to the conditions inside these camps. Many sympathetic people at home have been complaining and want it stopped."

"Who is Emily Hobhouse," asked Joe. "Imagine a woman confronting those powerful men."

"Aye, she is strong," said Jenny. "She's an exceptional woman, a welfare campaigner, anti-war activist, and pacifist from the middle-class family of an Anglican minister. Her sister and a cousin were also activists. But she has taken up the important cause of these concentration camps, impacting many influential men back home."

"You know, Jenny," Joe said after a moment's silence, "my upbringing didn't prepare me to understand the actions of important men, but I cannot imagine why they would wage such a war. Nor can I figure out why the Afrikander men cannot end this war and the misery of so many of their wives, children, and parents; it makes no sense."

They sat in silence for a while, pondering this surprising discussion.

"You know, Jenny, I still believe in my King and country. But things are different out here. I think the empire here differs from how we live it at home; different rules, don't you think?"

"Aye, that it does, Joe," said Jenny. "I've seen too many young British lives maimed or snuffed out because of this war on both sides."

"They want to grow the Empire at any cost, Jenny," said Joe. "Even if it means killing innocent women and children. Is it the same in India and other parts of our empire? I hope not."

Over the next few weeks, Joe and Jenny saw much of each other and spent many pleasant hours discussing life and their future together. Joe grew in maturity and stature in her eyes, and her fondness for him increased by the day. Joe also developed a deep affection and respect for this caring and thoughtful woman through their discussions.

"Army nurses are angels sent to help us when we are in need in this war," said Joe to Mike while on one of their forays. "I've never thought of how important our nurses are. Jenny is a pure, belta woman who cares for us soldiers."

"Aye, that she is," said Mike. "You two are close. But what of Ruth?"

"Her letters have stopped arriving, Mike," said Joe. "So I guess she's found another man."

"How can you carry on together during this war?" asked Mike. "How can you make it work?"

But make it work, they did. Between Joe's sorties and her hospital shifts, they saw each other as often as they could and talked over and over about home in Jarrow or the war and life in the army. And as they saw each other, even for short stints, the relationship grew.

"She is a gorgeous lass, so sweet and caring and helpful," Joe said to Mike another day, "I long to be with her when I'm away, and I hate to leave her when we are together. I think I'm in love with her."

"Ah, Laddie, what you need is a good cuddle," said the Sergeant who had overheard the conversation.

"Well, maybe," said Joe, "but she's worth more than that. I might marry her one day."

"What about Ruth?" asked Jack.

"I loved her, too," said Joe. "But she's given up on me."

"Well, you're a lucky gadgie, my marra," said Jack. "I should have one hinny, never mind two."

"Well, who knows for how long?" said Joe. "Women have an uncanny knack for changing the match rules." Which got chuckles from his marras.

~

Jan Smuts' Commando Enters the Cape Colony—August 1901

By mid-1901, it had become more challenging for the Boers to evade the British troops, and they had run out of military successes. So, the Boer generals met in secret and discussed peace. Botha and Smuts said they had underestimated the resolve of the British politicians and sent a telegram to Kruger in Holland to ask for his advice. Without the full knowledge of the dire predicament in which the Boers found themselves, he responded that they should continue fighting. The Orange Free State's two representatives, President Martinus Steyn and Christiaan De Wet, ridiculed the peace proposal. They wanted to launch one last major assault on the British and chose Smuts to lead it.

At the onset of the war, Smuts, 28, a British-educated advocate, served as Paul Kruger's eyes and ears. He handled propaganda, logistics, communication with generals and diplomats, and whatever the president required of him. In the second phase of the war, he served as a fighter under Koos de la Rey and proved his prowess in hit-and-run warfare. So, they made him a general.

The Boer plan required General Smuts to secretly lead a commando of 340 men unseen into the Cape Colony. From there, he could find support from the Afrikanders of the Cape, the so-called Cape Rebels. His goal was to instigate a general rebellion against the British government in Capetown, just as Christiaan de Wet had attempted before him but failed. Just getting near British territory was tough for Smuts since Kitchener had launched a campaign to rid the Orange River Colony of Boer commandos and General Smuts, who was as notorious as De Wet by then. He escaped capture by the British a dozen times, and his forces rendezvoused on the border after a month with only 240 men left.

Deneys Reitz, meanwhile, was still under 20 but a seasoned Boer fighter by then, hardened and wiser from his experiences in Natal and the Transvaal and was heading to the Cape Colony, too. It was the end of August 1901, the time of the spring thaw in the Basutoland mountains, and the rainy season could soon begin. The Orange River rises in the Drakensberg mountains along the border between South Africa and Basutoland, 120 miles west of the Indian Ocean, at an altitude of over 9,800 feet. The river then makes its westward journey of 1,400 miles across the entire southern African sub-continent to the Atlantic Ocean. It was the border between the British Cape Colony and the Boer Orange Free State, by then called the Orange River Colony. There was a concern among the fighters that if they waited too long, a deluge or flash flood could make the Orange River impassable. So, since they were within fifteen miles of the river, they hastened for the drift.

But on the morning they had hoped to cross, they spotted horse riders appearing over the crest of a distant hill. By their formation and manner of riding, they could see they were Boers, but they knew of no commando of that size in the region. So, they waited for them with keen interest and curiosity. After an hour, the column caught up with them.

"That's General Smuts leading them," called Deneys.

"Hello there, brothers," called Smuts to Deneys and his compatriots, "I'm on my way to the Cape Colony with these 240 honourable men. Why not join us?"

Through an ironic comment on their tattered clothing and ragged appearance, this group that Deneys Reitz had joined called themselves the *Rijk Section* or the *Dandy Fifth,* as one of their members had dubbed them.

"What a stroke of luck," said Reitz to his little band. "Meeting up with the Rijk Section was lucky enough, but now joining this full commando making for the river is our greatest fortune."

"Excellent," called Smuts, pleased to welcome more fighters into their ranks. "You can be our scouts."

Joining this commando was a distinction they accepted with honour. Deneys considered it the best fighting unit with which he had ever served. They were keen young farmers from the western Transvaal, the pick of De la Rey's fighting men. And General Smuts was the one man in South Africa who they considered could lead them through the perilous days ahead.

General Smuts halted his men and ordered them to off-saddle, allowing Deneys to mingle with them. The general was a handsome man, he thought, and older than most of his young fighters. He had a well-tended beard, pointed beneath the chin. The general was a slim man and stood firmly erect, two bandoliers crisscrossing his chest.

"He is as sharp as a whip," said Deneys, "A confident leader who commands respect."

Deneys had another pleasant surprise. His Hollander uncle, Jan Mulder, whom he had not seen since Natal two years earlier, was among them.

"We have endured great hardships and dangers on our way through the Free State," said Mulder. "The British got wind of our intention to invade the Cape Colony and are making strenuous efforts to prevent it. Many troops chased us from every side, giving us no rest, night or day. It was only by hard riding and fighting that we survived. But we lost many men and horses."

General Smuts proposed a flying raid into the Cape central districts to rehearse a later, larger-scale invasion. It would be a diversion, pulling in more British forces to relieve the increasing pressure on the Boer commandos in the north.

Deneys and his companions met General Smuts' commando near the village of Zastron, fifteen miles from the Orange River. Smuts intended to march nearer the river that day and cross at night. They set off by noon, and towards five in the evening, they could see the gorge's edge. The Orange River ran at the bottom of this deep ravine, rushing between steep mountainous walls.

Zastron was in the district of Rouxville, where another Boer general, Pieter Hendrik Kritzinger, had settled. After encountering a troop of 2nd Brabant's Horse, who tried to stop him near Zastron on the 13th of December 1900, Kritzinger crossed the Orange River with 300 men and a Maxim Machine Gun on the night of the 15th of December 1900, at a point five miles west of Odendaalstroom.

General Kritzinger was with Generaal De Wet during the battle of Sanna's Post. Commandant P.H. Kritzinger, J. B. M. Hertzog, Captain W.D. Fouche and Captain Gideon Scheepers, among others, caused much pain for the British forces in the Cape Colony. When Hertzog and Kritzinger invaded the colony in December 1900, a revolt against British rule arose. They were enemies hated by the British, who hunted Kritzinger for many months until they caught up with him. The feelings of hatred were mutual.

As the Smuts commando was preparing to cross the river, they saw that a cordon of British troops was holding their side of the canyon for miles in each direction, stationed there to bar the way of any Cape invaders. Wherever a footpath descended the cliffs, there was a tented camp. Active groups of mounted men informed of their approach patrolled the entire region.

So, General Smuts led them back into a range of hills, where they waited until the next day. They then sought nearby friendly outpost people to act as guides. At dusk that same day, a young officer named Louis Wessels arrived with a hardened crew of fifty men, with whom he had been operating in the field for over a year.

Wessels reported that British columns were closing in on them from the rear and said they could trap them unless they crossed that night. He warned that the depth of the gorge and the perpendicular cliffs meant that the river was challenging to ford everywhere. But he had brought a veteran of the Basuto wars who knew of a better path.

General Smuts ordered them to start at once, and in the falling dusk, their force rode out, accompanied by Wessels and his men, who agreed to enter the colony with them. They travelled over rough ground, hour after hour in the dark, and then, towards three in the morning, they caught sight of a glint of white far below them. There, the Orange River boiled and eddied in its narrow channel. Night still enveloped them as they embarked on the final descent, guided by their leader. After navigating the treacherous path, they arrived at the water's edge. Because of its difficulty, they were confident that any other mounted troops had never used the path. They crossed the river in a single file. It was a raging mountain torrent, not extensive but so swift that their horses struggled to keep their footing. As dawn lit the cliffs above them, the last man was through, and they finally stood in the Cape Colony.

War historian L.S. Amery wrote of the future exploits of this commando: "The adventures of this handful of resolute men led by General Smuts forms one of the most interesting episodes in the entire course of the guerrilla war."

Meeting the Smuts Commando at the Stormberg—September 1901

Early in September, the Cape Command ordered Joe's company to join a patrol, leaving the following day to go towards the east. Rumours soon circulated that General Jan Smuts and hundreds of Boers were heading for the Cape Colony, and they were to ride out to intercept and repel them.

Instead of the usual route north from De Aar to Kimberley, they first travelled by train southeast to Noupoort, an essential junction for the line from Port Elizabeth north-west to Bloemfontein and Johannesburg. They then switched trains north toward Colesberg, the site of fierce fighting between the British and Boer commandos early in the war but now under complete British control. The train passed Colesberg, reaching Norval's Pont [4] not long after.

Norval's Pont began as a hamlet in 1848 when a Scot named Norval built a ferry ("pont") to cross the Orange River at this point. But on the 17th of December 1890, a new bridge for the railway line from Colesberg Junction to Bloemfontein opened, making the boat redundant. They considered it the best viaduct in South Africa, 500 yards long, with eleven massive solid concrete columns made in Britain and shipped out for assembly at the river site.

Norval's Pont was a major railway stop for passengers travelling to Bloemfontein and the Witwatersrand goldfields. On the 1st of November 1899, Boer forces from the Orange Free State captured this town and held it until the 3rd of March 1900, when they retreated. As they left, the Burgher Forces of General De Villiers blew up the bridge. But the explosions had been ineffective since the British engineers hoisted the blown-out sections back into place, reattaching them to the columns. Within a short time, the railway line was operational again.

Joe's company detrained at Norval's Pont and readied themselves and 600 other infantry and mounted infantry (MI) troops to continue patrol along the river towards the east. They packed the infantry into wagons, two cannons, and other supplies and equipment and set out at sunset. As they settled in for the long, bumpy, dusty trip ahead, they wondered what adventures awaited them out there in the blackness of tonight.

"Well, Here We Go Again, laddies. Off to find more bloody Dutchmen," commented one.

"Not just any Dutchmen," said Joe, "We are going after the Boer General Jan Smuts, who I've heard is a clever leader. And his fighters are exceptional horsemen and bloody excellent marksmen, too. Never forget that."

"That they are, Joe," said Mike. "I have to give them that."

They continued along the river and through Aliwal North for three days, where they headed south. Then, one evening, they were near a village in the eastern Cape Colony called Jamestown. There, they caught sight of a bedraggled Boer commando and readied themselves for battle. But no sooner had the Boers appeared than they disappeared again, so they ordered the MI to remount and push on to find them.

As Deneys Reitz and that disappearing commando approached the village of Jamestown towards sunset one evening, they saw the British column to their right, so General Smuts moved them forward. It grew dark, and driving rain struck their faces. It was impossible to see even the men right ahead of them, plus it was so cold that the brave fighters became stiff and numbed.

"Dismount, men," ordered Smuts. "Let's continue on foot to conserve our horses' strength."

They dragged their beleaguered horses along with great difficulty, but none of the fighters said a word in their misery. At first light, they counted over thirty horses lying dead from exposure and abandoned many others. The optimism of Smuts' fighters was now at its lowest ebb. The rain continued unabated until noon, when the sky cleared, and the warm sun shone upon them again. They moved forward and soon saw a large farmhouse and outbuildings. They warmed their numbed bodies and cooked their first hot meal in days.

The housewife at the farm gave Deneys a pair of old elastic-sided boots. Deneys found an empty grain bag in the barn, into which he cut an opening for his head and one at each corner for his arms. He thus tailored a crude but valuable greatcoat, which caused much mirth among his fellow fighters. But during the next few days, they searched for grain bags whenever they passed a barn, and soon, many men were wearing them.

"That was an excellent idea, Deneys," called the general. "It does the job right."

"Aye, thank you, general," said Deneys. "I learned that one from our male servant."

After their meal, they continued for an hour and then halted in a valley. While the fighters rested in the grass, two British field guns fired at them from a hill, lobbing shells over their heads. More rounds followed, and, taken by surprise, the fighters leapt into their saddles and made off for the cover of a line of hills to the rear. But the British artillery was off its mark and hit neither man nor horse. Once in safety, the Boer fighters put their animals out of harm's way. They then climbed a hill to spy on the British. A British column, at first hidden from view, was coming towards them. They estimated the column comprised 600 British soldiers, and they had two fifteen-pounder Armstrongs and several pom-poms with them, which they unlimbered to open fire on the Boers.

Meanwhile, the British horsemen approached the fighters with caution. After a while, they picked up their pace as though to attack, but coming under heavy Boer fire, they took cover behind farmhouses and other buildings. Despite the shelling and rich exchange of rifle fire, there were no casualties on either side. The action ended after dark. Reitz didn't fire a shot on account of the shortage of ammunition, and the others fired only as necessary to stave off the enemy. The commando's store of ammo had become precarious.

The Boer fighters withdrew to a nearby farm when darkness fell, hoping for rest. They had not enjoyed a complete night's sleep since they had crossed the Orange River a week earlier.

But they got no rest that night. Smuts ordered them up at three o'clock in the morning, and they started on a record march in an icy drizzle. Weakened by their long privations, their ammunition reduced, and their horses exhausted, they set off again.

During the trek south to the Orange River, Smuts' commando lost thirty-six men. He crossed at Kiba Drift on the 3rd of September 1901. But a Basotho armed body of warriors attacked them on the 4th of September, too, near Wittenberg Mission. The Basotho warriors killed three and wounded seven with spears and antique guns before being driven away. On the 7th of September, Smuts' force went on a recce near Mordenaar's Poort, near Dordrecht, but the British ambushed them. They shot three of his companions, and Smuts escaped by a whisker.

The spring rains carried on, tormenting both Smuts' raiders and their horses while British columns, under the overall command of Major-General Sir John French, closed in on them. On the 13th of September, General French cornered the Boers on Stormberg Mountain, and they escaped only when a local farmer, Hans Kleynhans, led them on a steep descent route to safety. The night of the 15th of September finished the raiders, as freezing rain killed over sixty ponies, and fourteen men went missing. The Boers also learned that the British held every mountain pass ahead of them.

Soon after this episode, on the 17th of September, General Smuts' commando threaded through a gorge that opened out into the Elands River Valley. A seventeen-year-old farmer named Jan Coetzer told them that a British force held the pass at Elands River Poort in the next valley. Smuts commented, "If we don't get those horses and a supply of ammunition soon, we're finished."

Joe's company now found itself in the camp below the Stormberg Mountains in a thick mist, out on patrol with General French's columns. They were in pursuit of General Smuts' commando, which had just descended from the mountains and was heading towards Elands River Poort.

The battle that followed, known as the Battle of Elands River, was brief, bloody and decisive. It took place on the Modderfontein Farm near the

Elands River Poort mountain pass on the 17th of September 1901. During the battle, a Boer raiding force under Jan Smuts destroyed a British cavalry squadron on the Modderfontein farm. They know this battle, too, as the Battle of Modderfontein. The burghers' shots were deadly; they were De la Rey's veterans, honed by two years of fighting in the Transvaal. Their opponents were the famous 17th Lancers, the Death or Glory Boys, under Captain Sandeman, a cousin of Winston Churchill, and Lord Vivian. The 17th Lancers (Duke of Cambridge's Own) was a cavalry regiment notable for participating in the Light Brigade during the Crimean War.

The Boers exploited the darkened conditions to encircle the British camp. When Smuts' advance guard encountered a Lancer patrol, the British hesitated to fire because many Boers wore captured British uniforms. They wore these uniforms despite an order from Lord Kitchener decreeing immediate death by firing squad if caught in them. The Boers opened fire and attacked in front, while Smuts led the rest of his force to attack the British camp from the rear. British soldiers suffered further casualties at a closed gate that slowed them. The Boers hit six British officers, of whom four died; only the commander, Captain Sandeman, and his lieutenant, Lord George Vivian, survived. The Boers executed 29 Lancers and wounded 41 before the cavalrymen surrendered. The Boer fighters had revitalized confidence in their leader and themselves. They lost only one man, killed when they rushed the camp and had six wounded.

Deneys Reitz gave his account of the aftermath of this brief battle from his perspective.

"We weren't sure of the number of British soldiers, but there must have been at least 200," said Deneys. "We knew we had attacked the 17th Lancers, one of the crack regiments of the British Army, and we were proud of our achievement. Among their wounded was their commander, Captain Sandeman. And I found Lord Vivian among the rocks where we had first rushed them."

A calm and collected Lord Vivian pointed out his bivouac tent and said it might be worth Deneys' while to look inside it. Reitz took the hint and re-emerged in a bright British cavalry tunic and khaki riding breeches instead of the grain bag he had been wearing as his main outer garment. Reitz was now at risk of execution should the British ever capture him. But in place of an exhausted horse, an old rifle and two cartridges, he now sported a Lee-Metford, full bandoliers and a sturdy grey Arab mount, the property of Lieutenant Sheridan, whom Field Cornet Jack Borrius had shot through the brain. Pleased with his extra equipment, Deneys tested the smooth bolt action of the rifle a few times and detached and reinserted the magazine. He also chose a strong riding mule in preference to another horse. He then walked around the British camp and saw the dead gunners and other men he had shot. Reitz looked at them with mixed feelings since even though he had never hated the English, a fight was a fight. And although he was sorry for the affected men, he was proud of his share in the day's work.

Reitz then went to look for his faithful roan mare. The horse was still waiting for him where he had left her. On each side of her lay a dead horse, but she had escaped unharmed. But when he tried to lead her away, she struggled to walk. So Deneys unsaddled her and, removing the bridle and halter, turned her loose, hoping a neighbouring farmer could find and look after her.

"She too had shown the mettle of her Free State pasture and the marvellous endurance of the South African horse," murmured Deneys to a companion with a tear in his eye.

General Smuts ordered them to burn the tents and wagons and destroy the mountain and machine guns. They destroyed surplus ammunition and other supplies they could not take with them. Then, leaving the prisoners, mule drivers and native servants to fend for themselves, they rode off triumphantly.

"When finished, we were as giants refreshed," said Deneys. "We had ridden into action that morning on our last breath, and we emerged refitted from head to heel. We had fresh horses, new rifles, clothing, saddlery, boots and more ammunition than we could handle, and supplies for every man compliments of His Majesty, the King of England." [5]

The Cape Command ordered Joe's company to quickly march the 60 miles from the Stormberg to Craddock, where they caught a train to De Aar. Back in camp, they mulled over their experiences in the eastern Cape Colony and their contact with the Boers.

"We had a close call the other day," Joe mentioned to a companion back in De Aar who hadn't been with them on that sortie. "We encountered a large Boer commando under the leadership of General Jan Smuts."

"Jan Smuts? Where? That man is a legend," said his companion.

"Aye," said Joe. "He dodged us in the Stormberg. But the state of his men and horses was pitiful, and many wore grain sacks as coats, which we only see in the poorest neighbourhoods back home."

"Ah, then we must have them on the run now."

"I suppose so," Joe said while deep in thought, "but they're not done for yet, not by a long shot. We heard later they had slaughtered our Death and Glory boys at Elands River Poort in the Stormberg."

"How did they do that?" asked Mike, turning to the passing major who had overheard them and stopped.

"By deception," said the major. "They were wearing our khaki uniforms, so the 17th Lancers thought they were British soldiers and held their fire until it was too late."

"Bloody hell," called Mike. "That's not fair!"

"Well, as they say, it's war," said the major. "But they killed 29 of our finest cavalrymen and injured another 41 out of 130! The 17th Lancers lost more men that day than in the famous charge of the light brigade during the Crimean War."

The Move to the Transvaal—October 1901

After these and many more exciting and tragic episodes, the Army again ordered Joe's company to move, this time attached to the 1/DLI in the northeastern Transvaal. The 3/DLI company had spent six months in the Cape and the southern Orange Free State, and it had encountered a lot of scattered action, and the men were ready for a change of scenery. But now, the most challenging part for Joe was to leave Jenny. He had his last rendezvous with her before leaving.

"You and your marras have had a few challenges of late, Joe, haven't you?" asked Jenny during their conversation.

"Aye, that we have," said Joe. "The Boer commandos have been active, Smuts in particular."

"I treated many of our wounded brought here by train, including the 17th Lancers," said Jenny. "The Boers made a mess of them."

"Aye, that they did," said Joe, "The major said by deception, wearing our uniforms. Bloody bastards!"

"Well, I've heard many Boer fighters are dead or injured, too," said Jenny to Joe's comments. "This war is hard on both sides."

"Aye, I suppose you are right," said Joe. "But soldiers are one thing, and locking up women, old folk and children makes little sense. I can't support that, even if Lord Roberts had ordered it."

"Well, I may talk myself out of a job here," said Jenny, "but as you know, I can't support any war, no matter who started it."

"Aye, well, we can only hope this one will soon be over," said Joe. "But in the meantime, they have ordered my company to the Transvaal."

"Nee, Joe," said Jenny, distraught. "Not another move?"

"Aye," said Joe. "That's the army for you, always thinking of ways to separate us. I've grown so fond of you and will miss you terribly. I'm unsure how I will live up there without you being close. And I mean that."

"That goes for me too, Joe, and I'll miss you so much, too," she said, "But this war can't go on for much longer, can it?"

"God only knows," he said. "I hope not. We must write to each other, and no matter what happens, we mustn't lose contact with one another."

"No, we mustn't," she said, "Let me know when you know your base, and I'll try to get there."

They embraced and kissed for the longest time, then parted ways.

The following day, Joe's company entrained once more at De Aar with many other troops for the trip to Pretoria. Joe was heavy-hearted as he waved goodbye to his sweetheart, who waved and blew kisses in return from the station platform.

As they had done before, the marras travelled together with their company by train towards the Orange River Bridge at Norval's Pont. But this time, instead of disembarking in the town, they continued their journey and traversed the bridge into the Orange River Colony. As they progressed north, they noticed the vegetation gradually transforming from scrubland to grassland. They saw many more antelope as the grasses grew longer and greener since the rain started. But they noticed something strange and eerie, something they had seen at Philippolis and Springfontein while on patrol. The farms were devoid of life, bar a few wretched abandoned coloureds and natives hanging around at a loss of what else to do. They noticed that many of the farm buildings were in ruins, burnt and useless to any living creature. Joe surmised they were again witnessing the results of Lord Kitchener's scorched earth policy.

And so, the train trundled for hours across the vast grassy plain of the northern Karroo, punctuated with the occasional kopje and, less often, by a flat-topped mesa.

"Those hills look the same as the ones you see in comic books of the Wild West of America," said Mike.

"Aye, Mike, they do," said Joe. "But without the cowboys and Indians."

"Do you suppose the Boer fighters lived and farmed cattle here, too?" asked Jack.

"Maybe," interjected Billy. "But you'd never see those gigantic birds or goats in the Wild West."

"Aye, but I can imagine the Wild West of America looks the same as this," said Joe.

The monotonous journey continued while the troops amused themselves with card games and songs, exchanging stories of themselves and their families and where they had originated. Reliving the action they had experienced, they told jokes and heckled light-hearted taunts towards one another for hours, laughing and enjoying themselves. They drifted off for an occasional nap to the constant rocking and rhythm of the train's clicking wheels on the tracks.

"Hey, do you notice that the land is changing here?" asked Mike.

"Aye, there's less scrub and more grass," said Joe. "Look at those antelope and ostrich birds. But no cattle or sheep, and not even any goats anymore."

The farther north they travelled, the longer and thicker the grasses grew, and the scrub disappeared. They were moving through a vast sea of flat, spring-green grassland. They saw the occasional kopje or dry donga and flowing streams with green shrubs and trees from time to time. But soon enough, they were no longer in the Karroo but travelling through the vast grassy plains of the Orange River Colony. The farms became more frequent but were burnt-out ruins farther into the Orange River Colony. They were moving through the war zone of the two-year-old conflict. The army stopped for a night outside Bloemfontein and fed them thick slices of roast meat and potatoes instead of the usual bully beef and biscuits, spoils of the war?. They couldn't wander far from the train but could see portions of the city and its surrounding hills and kopjes from the platform.

They travelled far across the northern Orange River Colony grasslands the next day. The day after that, they crossed the Vaal River into the Transvaal.

"This river is the border between the Orange River and Transvaal colonies," said the lieutenant. "That's why they call it the Transvaal."

"This river isn't as wide as the Orange River," said Joe. "But it's still a major river."

"So, they use rivers as their borders, Sir," said Mike.

"Yes, it's common down here. The Limpopo River starts in South Africa and divides the Transvaal from Bechuanaland and Rhodesia in the north. The Limpopo is the second-largest river down here, emptying into the Indian Ocean in Portuguese East Africa. The Vaal River starts 19 miles north of Ermelo in the Eastern Transvaal and flows into the Orange River southwest of Kimberley. And the Orange River empties into the Atlantic Ocean in the west."

"I'm getting the picture," said Mike. "Good thing that we have bridges. I'm not good at swimming." To which the surrounding troops gave a hearty laugh.

As they entered Johannesburg, the train stopped for coal and water at a siding near the station. But after a brief period, they continued the journey to Pretoria without stopping at Johannesburg station. They could view far more people as they travelled through Johannesburg and its surrounds than Cape Town or Bloemfontein. Many were Uitlanders who had returned in droves to the gold mines of the Witwatersrand under British protection. They could see the mine dumps, too, scattered as they were high above the many mines outside the city. Now and then, they saw a few young lovelies in lovely clothes waiting at stations. An hour and a half after leaving Johannesburg, they arrived at Pretoria's central station, under the firm control of the British Army.

~

Train Incident in the Eastern Transvaal—October 1901

The army had assigned Joe's company to the eastern Transvaal. They took a train waiting on the Pretoria to Delagoa Bay platform at Pretoria Station to get there. They were joining an ever-growing mass of British soldiers from various regiments heading towards this last major theatre of activity.

President Paul Kruger opened this line only six years earlier, on the 8th of July 1895. It was of utmost importance to the South African Republic since it opened a channel for freight between the landlocked Transvaal Republic and the only non-British port available to them—Lourenço Marques, Portuguese Mozambique. It was the same line Winston Churchill had used to escape from Pretoria earlier in the war. Once the British Army units were on board, the train pulled out of the station, starting its journey towards Middelburg in the eastern Transvaal.

Beyond Pretoria, the landscape was much the same as that experienced across the northern Orange River Colony and the southern Transvaal. There were vast vistas of green grasses on a flat or rolling plateau. On their trip south of Pretoria, any farms they saw lay in ruin, and they saw few people and no livestock or crops along the route.

"Do you notice the dead and rotting animal carcasses here?" asked Mike.

"Aye. It seems the clearances have been more recent here," said Joe.

"But more blockhouses," said Jack. "Every few hundred yards, more barbed-wire, and more troops guarding them too."

In this guerrilla phase of the war, the British built many fortifications across South Africa, known as blockhouses. They weren't unique to South Africa; they were introduced in the fourteenth century in England. They used them in America during the Civil War, too. But in South Africa, the British had built close to 8,000 blockhouses during this war, joined by 3,700 miles of barbed wire. They used a range of designs for these fortifications, but most were two- or three-storey structures built using quarried stone. Around 440 of them were sizeable masonry blockhouses. However, the enormous scale of this British strategy forced them to develop cheaper, bullet-proof, double-skinned, corrugated iron structures costing £16 compared to several hundred pounds for the masonry structures. These were prefabricated and delivered to sites by armoured trains, and the soldiers packed rocks or rubble inside the double skin to improve protection.

An officer on the train explained what he knew of these South African blockhouses.

"Blockhouses protect the railway lines and bridges. They're crucial to our military supply lines," said the officer. "But they need many troops for support, tens of thousands of British soldiers on blockhouse duty. They use a few thousand native Africans as armed guards patrolling the lines between the fortifications at night."

"The Army has linked the blockhouses with barbed-wire fences to partition the vast veldt into smaller sections. We then mount drives, under which a continuous line of troops sweeps a section of veldt bordered by blockhouse lines. Hunters use this technique to locate and shoot game birds in England and tigers in India. It's much more efficient than the earlier scouring of the countryside by scattered columns."

"Hunting men like animals, Sir?" asked Joe. "Is that just?"

"Aye, soldier," said the lieutenant. "Just as blowing up our troops and garrisons in the night! They protect the blockhouse with a small wall built of stone or sandbags and a trench. They erect wire entanglements around the fortification, many strands twisted together and anchored to the ground with stays, and stretch a wire to the next outpost 1,000 yards away. Bells and tin cans hanging on the fence act as alarms, and sometimes they connect trip wires to a loaded rifle aimed along its length."

"Aye, I guess that gets a few," said Mike.

"But a blockhouse line isn't straight," said the lieutenant. "They build them in waves, so one blockhouse doesn't accidentally fire on its neighbour. The blockhouses have connecting fields of fire, making the area around the outpost and along the wire a killing zone. They connected the fortifications along the railway by telegraph or field telephones connected to the principal telegraph lines, which the Boers cut. We are always reconnecting those wires and guarding them. The typical blockhouse garrison comprises seven men: a junior NCO and six other ranks. They put a lieutenant in charge of 3 to 4 outposts and a captain for every 10 to 12. A battalion can occupy up to 60 fortifications."

"When did they build these blockhouses, Sir?" asked Joe.

"They built the first blockhouses around Pretoria just after we occupied it on the 5th of June 1900. Then they built the first line of circular fortifications in January 1901, right where we are going in the eastern Transvaal," said the officer. "In July and August, they extended the blockhouses across the whole of South Africa, but the new, less expensive ones."

Joe and his marras listened to the officer's explanation since they suspected they might end up in one of these blockhouses soon. Then, the officer focussed on their current situation.

"I don't know about now," he said after a while, "but we started having enormous problems along this railway line a year ago. The Boers blew up and wrecked everything, and many British soldiers died."

The entire car became silent while listening to what the officer was saying.

"On the 1st of October 1900, for example, twenty-three British troops died in an attack on a train at Pan Station, east of Middelburg. And on the 8th of October, they wrecked a train at Vlakfontein, near here."

The men looked at each other with growing apprehension.

"My God, they could have warned us," said Mike.

"Aye, well, the derailment of trains along the Pretoria-Delagoa Bay line continued throughout January this year," the officer said. "Not a day passed without the Boers attacking a train along the line. On the morning of the 17th of January, they blew up the engine of the westbound train and derailed it near Brugspruit. These attacks are the work of a notorious train-wrecker, Captain Jack Hindon, among General Ben Viljoen's forces. He has become an expert at destroying trains and manufacturing an improvised explosive mine for that purpose."

"I've heard of him," said Mike. "He's a Scot, Billy."

"Bloody traitor," grumbled Billy! "Why does a Scot fight for the Boers?"

"There are many Scots who hate the English," said Joe. "He must be one of them."

"Aye, that's right," said the officer. "The enemy recruited disgruntled Irish, Americans, Scandinavians, Germans, French, Poles, Greeks, and even Australians. Those who hate us are many. I know something about Oliver Jack Hindon. He's a Scottish turncoat born in Stirling, Scotland, in 1874. He joined the British Army at 14 as a band boy, and they sent him to Zululand. There, he deserted and went to live in Wakkerstroom in the eastern Transvaal. I suppose the army branded him a deserter and was hunting for him, so he joined the other side, even learning their language. During the Jameson Raid of December 1895 to January 1896, he fought on the side of the Boer forces, and they made him a full citizen, something they rarely do for Uitlanders. Four years later, at the start of the Anglo-Boer War, Hindon joined the Middelburg Commando and was first in Natal Colony before returning to the eastern Transvaal as a fighter. He is a dangerous person to have on the other side!"

"Then he deserves whatever he gets from us," said Billy.

"The next big railway attack took place six days later, on the 23rd of January," the officer said. "When Lord Kitchener was travelling from Pretoria to Middelburg to meet General Smith-Dorrien, as his train approached Balmoral Station, there were signs that the enemy was in the vicinity, and they took special precautions to protect the Field Marshal's train. Lord Kitchener ordered that they attach two laden freight wagons to a pilot locomotive to precede his train without personnel. The weight of the train wagons and the engine was enough to trigger a mine planted on the track. The explosion blew the wagons sky high, and the pilot engine derailed. Hindon and his train wreckers emerged to admire their work, but their victims had escaped this time. They watched Lord Kitchener's train reverse along the line to safety."

"As a result, the Field Marshal ordered our forces to sweep through the sector south of this line," the officer said. "They used over 500 wagons to carry sheep, cattle, and other supplies to the British troops. They laid waste to acres and acres of crops and slew thousands of sheep and cattle daily. By the 14th of February, they had reached Amsterdam, near the Swaziland border."

"But Hindon didn't stop. On the 11th of March this year, Dynamite Jack, as we were calling him, struck again between Wilge River and Balmoral stations, where we are now. When the mine exploded under the engine, derailing it, our troops took cover in the ditches alongside the track. There, the high banks offered protection, and a twenty-minute firefight took place at a distance of 400 yards. Hindon realized that his men could never reach the train unless they were to make a desperate charge under fire. So, he called for volunteers, and 10 men came forward out of his 100 fighters. With these, he stormed the train. They forced 35 British soldiers and 30 Africans to surrender. The rest of Hindon's men impounded clothing, blankets, foodstuffs and saddles from the train. Seeing our soldiers charging from the blockhouse while others were approaching from Balmoral Station, Hindon made his getaway. He set the train alight and escaped. Lord Kitchener has said Hindon has caused him more problems than any other Boer, including Gideon Scheepers. Hindon and his men have become notorious train wreckers along this Delagoa Bay Railway Line."

"Now you tell us," mumbled Mike, inaudible to the officer. The men glanced at each other as the officer spoke of the dangers of this railway line. They glanced at the veld, too, watching for signs of the enemy as the train moved them over it.

"Those bastards could be anywhere out there," said Mike.

"Aye, or just ahead of us," said Jack.

"Yes," said the officer. "They could be. Be alert. But here's the point where we started this discussion. By June of this year, we were using our blockhouses and armoured trains on the Delagoa Bay Railway to good effect in a plan to entrap the Boers. The troops operated in smaller and smaller pockets of veldt and then closed the net, capturing as many Boers as possible. General Ben Viljoen's forces were keen to cross over the Delagoa Bay Railway to escape the trap. So, on the 22nd of June, Viljoen sent Hindon a message asking him to mine the railway near Uitkyk Station. He wanted to cross the line with his commando the next day."

"But as Hindon's men were on their way to lay the mine on the track that night, the British surprised them with two cannon shots from Balmoral. Later, our men caught up with Viljoen's men attacking a blockhouse to prepare for their dash across the line. Then, an armoured train appeared on the scene, lighting up both sides of the line with its searchlights and attacking the Boer forces with field guns and Maxims. Several of Viljoen's men crossed the line with a loss of ten casualties, forcing Viljoen to stay on the south side of the line."

"By July, a massive British force of 25,000 men had cleared the region in the eastern Transvaal south of the Delagoa Bay Railway. So, the focus now lies to the north of the railway line where General Viljoen's men had retired after crossing the line at last on the 27th of June. So watch out on the left side of the train." [6]

"Welcome to Hindon territory, laddies. And get ready for it," said Joe. "That's where we're heading, and that's what we'll be doing for the next few months." In return, he got a smile from the officer and a few scowls from the men.

The train continued its slow eastward journey for a few hours, rocking side to side and lolling the men into dozing in their seats. They passed stations on the way, most of which had unpronounceable names until they recognized Balmoral Station, halfway to their destination of Middelburg. And on and on, they trundled for at least another hour. Apart from the sound of the wheels, the carriage had become quiet. Occasional snores and grunts of the soldiers suggested they were catching up on lost sleep.

Then they awoke to a powerful explosion somewhere in front of the train. Regaining consciousness, the soldiers struggled to place or understand the sound of the blast. Then, half a minute later, the locomotive came to a sudden halt and left the tracks. The soldiers heard a second explosion as the locomotive itself rolled over and exploded. The cars then lurched, throwing men in every direction, including against the windows and the ceiling, as the carriage they were in twisted and turned with loud groans and metal screeches. Other carriages were doing the same, a few landing on top of others. After what seemed to be an eternity, the movement stopped, and the men in Joe's carriage lay in silence, catching their breath and wits, except for a few who were screaming or moaning in pain. Coals from the locomotive had spilt into the veldt and started a raging fire. The smoke from the fire was filling the carriages. It was complete chaos.

"Mike, Jack, Billy... where are you?" called an unharmed but shaken and bruised Joe, trying in his desperation to find his marras.

"Over here, Joe," called Mike. "That bastard Hindon caught us napping!"

"I'm here," called Jack while climbing out of the overturned carriage. "That's three of us. Where is Billy?"

More soldiers spilt and stumbled out of the wreckage, bloodied and stunned. The marras searched but could not see Billy among them. Then another Durham yelled out in dismay, calling for help since he had found someone crushed under their carriage. They rushed to the scene, but only the legs of the soldier were visible. A rattled lieutenant arrived and took control.

"Right men, we need to roll the carriage back if we can," he called, "at least far enough to extract this poor sod."

The uninjured men leapt to the call and lined up along the overturned carriage.

"On my count, push with everything you can muster," called the lieutenant. "Come here, laddie, and help me pull this chap out from under the carriage."

On the lieutenant's order, the men heaved. The carriage rolled just enough to remove the soldier, but it was soon clear he was dead, his head crushed beneath its weight. The Marras could see it was their lost friend, his red hair thickened with blood from the wound. They stood rigid, bowing their heads in sorrow while they held back their tears.

"Nee Billy, tell us it's not you," called Mike.

"Are you sure it's Billy?" asked Jack.

"That's him, Jack," said Joe. "No doubt about it."

The marras had grown up together and had been friends for so long. So, for Billy to die in such a horrible way was too much for them to bear. As the lieutenant ordered the body carried to a triage collection point, the marras bowed their heads and fought back the tears. When the chaos settled, and the men mustered, they counted three dead and another twenty injured. Medics were doing everything they could to treat the wounded until they could move them to the nearest field hospital. The marras were in shock. They had lost a lifelong friend to a murderous enemy train-wrecker and a Scot to boot.

"He was a good laddie," said Joe, holding back the tears.

"Aye, that he was," said Mike. "We'll miss him a lot for sure."

"We were the best of marras," said Jack. "He was an awkward laddie but had a good heart."

And then gunshots and the sound of horses galloping towards them shocked them out of their mourning. Those able to move dove for cover, and those with rifles shot back at the approaching riders. The agony of war continued for the bombing victims until the Boer fighters retreated into the veldt and vanished again.

The British troops on this train soon realized they had suffered a double blow from the Hindon gang. Fear and panic turned to anger and determination to strike back at the offenders. The officers mustered their uninjured men and marched ahead to the next station, where they signalled ahead to ask for another train to complete their journey. After three hours, the train arrived, and they continued to their destination, a sore and miserable lot.

They arrived at their first destination, Middelburg, by evening. This central town of the Highveld farming region of the eastern Transvaal had served as the headquarters of Eastern Transvaal operations of the British Army since their victory at the Battle of Bergendal.

Joe's company joined the many contingents pouring from the train. The company major directed the Durhams to muster outside the station, a handsome building of rough, red stone with elegant little gables on its roof. The various companies then assembled in quarter-column formations for the march to the camp on the edge of the town. Once the train was empty and the units had gathered, they began their march without musical accompaniment, except for drummers beating the pace. A half-hour later, they arrived at the camp, were given their mail and were shown their tented living quarters.

The camp was large but not as big as Matjesfontein, and the structure and types of aligned rows of tents were familiar.

Sure enough, there was a letter from Jenny.

"My darling Joe,

I found out from an officer at headquarters where your company is in the eastern Transvaal, so I wrote this letter to find you. Things are much quieter here these days. So, I requested a transfer to a more active theatre of the war where I could be of more use. They have granted this, so I'll be arriving in Middelburg as soon as I can organize myself. I couldn't go on another day without you.

"All my love, Jenny."

Beaming from ear to ear, Joe settled himself into his quarters. He couldn't wait to tell his marras of Jenny's pending arrival. When he considered it, Jenny must have arranged this and sent the message just after his departure. How else could the note have been waiting for him? His heart quickened at the thought. He hoped he'd still be in camp when she arrived, not out on patrol.

That night, the remaining marras discussed the day's events.

Mike was the first to comment: "I'll miss that poor Geordie."

"Aye, me too," said Joe. "He was a wee bit odd but a great marra."

"Ha, do you remember our bicycle outing in Matjesfontein?" Jack asked. "He, nee, we, almost lost it then."

"Aye," Jack said, "He was always in the wrong place at the wrong time. Do you remember how he almost died in the pit when that cart broke loose and barrelled downhill when we were kids?"

"Aye," said Joe, "that's true. I remember that. He was always clumsy and in trouble. But today was his last bit of poor luck. I'll miss him too, for sure."

"But we had the luck today," said Mike. "It could have been any of us."

"Aye," *said* Jack. "We're at war, and it can happen to any of us. Keep your noses out of sight of the Boer."

"You know, lads, this war is not what I expected out here," said Joe. "Lining up to confront an enemy is one thing; an enemy who fights using ambush and sabotage is another. We've got to end this guerrilla war."

"Agreed, Joe," said Mike. "It's a bloody dirty war! I didn't sign up for that either."

"Well, I don't know, laddies," said Jack. "I don't suppose that enemies lining up at close quarters and shooting at each other is much fun either."

"Aye, true," the others nodded, agreeing with a snicker.

"It's bloody difficult to carry on a relationship with a woman out here, what with us moving around so much," said Joe. "I wonder when my Jenny will arrive?"

"You should complain, Joe," said Mike. "At least you have a woman who loves you."

But before Jenny arrived, they assigned his company to a column on its way to Ermelo to join the blockhouse drives.

The March to Ermelo and the Blockhouse Drives—October 1901

At the start of October 1901, the 1st Battalion of the Durham Light Infantry in Natal re-entered operations. They had a relatively calm period following the Natal phase of the war, where they played an active role in the Relief of Ladysmith. On the 3rd of October, a party of four officers and 196 NCOs and men, under Major Mansel, joined Colonel Rawlinson's column at Greylingstad, near Standerton and Bethal in the eastern Transvaal. By the end of October, the rest of the battalion left their Standerton headquarters to join another column. They were to take part in Kitchener's summer offensive against a still active General Louis Botha and the Highveld commandos, a vast undertaking using twelve columns.[7] These columns were to hem in and destroy any Boer commandos active in the eastern Transvaal. And Joe's company was to join up with them.

Early the following day, they mustered the column his company belonged to on the camp parade square to prepare for a long march. Over 1,000 men gathered, half of whom were MI units. They kitted out the infantry with the usual field items. A small haversack contained 50 rounds of ammunition plus odds and ends and a mess tin, often carrying hardtack and a piece of ox-trek, or biltong as it's called in southern Africa. There was a water bottle, a blanket and an overcoat too. Then, they stored a bayonet and a trenching tool in a leather pouch. And they had bandoliers containing more rounds of ammunition and the Lee-Enfield rifle.

After a formal muster with a ceremony raising the Union Jack to the rousing tune of 'Rule, Britannia,' the companies moved out of camp and were soon on their way into the open veldt. The infantry settled into a comfortable but well-paced 120-step-per-minute march, or three and a half miles per hour. The mounted infantry matched this slow pace. Since their intended destination was Ermelo, sixty miles away, they had eighteen hours of good marching ahead of them, covered in two days with ease.

The first night, they camped without tents in a veldt near Bethal. They arrived at Ermelo the following day, where a distressing sight confronted them. Only one building was still standing in the destroyed town. During the march, they'd also noted that they had seen few living beings, human or otherwise. The army had cleared the region of its civilian population and either rounded up livestock as supplies for the troops or shot them where they stood.

"My God, this emptiness is so bloody strange, laddies," said Joe. "We haven't seen a soul so far on this march, and I can't get used to it."

"Aye, and no animals either," said Mike. "Apart from the dead ones rotting along the road, of course. What a bloody stench!"

"It bothers me," said Jack in a muted voice. "Are they hiding, waiting for us out there somewhere?"

"Aye," said Joe. "Keep your eyes peeled."

The commanding major told them that several thousand Boer combatants were still out there somewhere, most under Louis Botha, dangerous and waiting to pounce despite their reduced numbers.

"Well, I've heard rumours we're supposed to come up against them during the drives," said Mike.

They were soon to experience such a drive. At Ermelo, they spent another night in the British camp, where they dined on a heavenly meal of roast meat with potatoes and corn captured in the civilian clearances. They slept a few hours before being awakened early to muster for action in 30 minutes.

The officers now spent the entire day spreading mounted infantry and foot soldiers along the line from Ermelo to Standerton 50 miles to the southwest. They placed 1,000 men and 500 horses 40 to 50 yards apart across 25 miles. Another column met them mid-way by coming up the line from Standerton. There was alternating mounted infantry and standard infantry every forty to fifty yards, armed and ready for action over the entire fifty-mile stretch. They separated the marras for the first time since arriving. They also commanded the soldiers to stay silent to avoid betraying their presence.

That night, they received the order via pre-determined light signals to move along the line. As one coherent unit, 1,000 men and 500 horses began the drive through the pitch blackness of the night. They did not quieten their steps since they aimed to flush the enemy along the blockhouse line from Volksrust on the Orange River Colony border to Piet Retief on the Swaziland border. There, fifty miles away, another 2,000 British troops were waiting for the catch like hunters in readiness to catch their prey emerging ahead of the sweep.

They marched the entire night, with the mounted infantry galloping ahead to flush out the Boers while the infantry followed to complete the work. Any fighters the MI had flushed out, the infantry cornered and captured, including those missed by the MI. And so, it continued through the night. At first, they heard or saw nothing. Then, they heard shots and the shouts of men in the distance. The net appeared to be working. That night, the British killed five Boers wounded and captured another fifty. But they lost one soldier, and the skirmishes injured another two.

At dawn, the drive halted, and they rested until the following night. They ate from the meagre rations in their mess tins and dozed until nightfall when the order to prepare for the next drive passed along the line.

"It's a lonely pursuit, these drives," Joe wrote in a letter to Jenny later. "But that's the job, so we get on with it."

"After dark, we saw the signals and started the march in a lengthy line. I could just make out the MI soldiers in front of me. But I couldn't see my nearest infantry companions most of the time. The MI set the pace so we could orient ourselves to them. The night was inky since it was moonless, but the stars cast a little light on the way ahead."

"A long way back, wagons followed as a backup for any required task, transporting prisoners and wounded, for example. We marched, making as few noises as we could. It wasn't a problem in the veld, but the going got more difficult as soon as we entered the bush."

"We had been marching for four hours when I heard a commotion in front of me. I could hear galloping horses approaching, and our MI prepared to meet whoever it was."

"Out of the bush crashed a small group of armed Boers on horseback. When they saw our MI, they reared and tried to escape. But their noise had travelled far, so more groups of MI closed in on them rapidly from every side. We soon surrounded them, and they threw up their hands. We told them to dismount and discard their weapons, which they did. But one of their numbers made a dash towards me with a carbine. I prepared my rifle and shot above his head as quickly as possible. But he ran towards me! So my next shot hit him, and he dropped."

"Once the smoke and dust had cleared, we found we had captured a dozen Boer fighters and wounded one. We tied their wrists and guarded the men while a wagon was called in to take them away. We soon completed our task, and once loaded, the cart trundled back to its position with its prisoners and three infantry guards. Then spreading ourselves in a line and moving to catch up with the rest of the line, we continued our pursuit."

"There were no more incidents that night. But along the line, other events had been occurring throughout the night. By the time we reached the blockhouse line, we had rounded up two hundred prisoners. The officers said It wasn't a great 'bag,' but maybe not too shabby."

"In the dawn light the next morning, I could not believe what I saw. They were a bedraggled, weathered, thin, and battered bunch of weary farmers. I thought what a ragtag army we are fighting, their filthy bearded faces and hands scarred and pocked with nasty sores, their clothes in tatters."

By this stage, the British Army had reduced the number of Boer combatants from 88,000 to 20,000. Those who weren't casualties were prisoners shipped to remote prison camps around the Empire or had vanished into the surrounding bush. War had exhausted those still fighting and in danger of being wiped out by a superior military machine.

Their column carried out these drives for several days and took the men to the limits of their patience and tolerance for such a sad duty. They then marched back to Middelburg and rested for a few days before their next assignment.

Attack on the Blockhouse Line at Badfontein—24 October 1901

In late October, Joe's company again found themselves on an armoured train on the Delagoa Bay line. This time, they were heading to Machadodorp, below the first escarpment of the Drakensberg. They were on their way to help with a new blockhouse line on a farm called Badfontein[8], between Machadodorp and Lydenburg, in the eastern Transvaal.

They passed a settlement called Belfast, which at 6,170 feet was higher than Johannesburg. There began a drop over the escarpment of over 1080 feet to Machadodorp. The distance from Belfast was only seventeen miles, but the train applied its brakes and descended at a crawl to avoid the train running away. It was such a slow descent that many men jumped off the train and walked beside it.

"At last, a chance to stretch our legs," said Joe. "I'm getting stiff and sore from these lengthy train rides."

"I can only agree with that, Joe," said Mike. "But let's watch for Boer fighters... or we'll be dead stiff!" Men guffawed but increased attentiveness to their surroundings as they walked next to the train.

The next station after Belfast was Bergendal, the site of the now famous pitched Battle of Bergendal from the 21st to the 27th of August 1900 between 7,000 Boers under Louis Botha with 20 cannons, including their four 25 foot 6.1 inches Creusot Long Tom guns and the British forces under generals Redvers Buller, Reginald Pole-Carew's infantry and John French's cavalry, a total strength of 19,000 men and over 80 cannons.

The Battle of Bergendal was the last set-piece battle of the first phase of the 2nd Boer War, where both armies chose the fighting location and time. It was the only occasion on which the Boers used the four Long Tom canons in the same fight.

Before the battle started, Gun A was at Dullstroom above the escarpment, at 6,890 feet, the highest village in South Africa. The fighters then moved it to a hill northwest of Belfast. They positioned Gun B on the farm Waterval on a ridge called Witrant above Bergendal. They first mounted Gun C on a railway flatbed. But by the 23rd of August, the Boers had transported the gun southwest of Dalmanutha station, the next station beyond Bergendal, and then moved it to a hill behind the Boer forces. Gun D remained on the farm Driekop above Dalmuthia throughout the battle. These guns had 94-pound shells with an effective firing range of 30,000 feet (5.7 miles). The British answer to the Long Toms was the 5-inch (127mm) 40 cwt BL gun with a percussion distance of 6 miles.

The Battle of Bergendal lasted an entire week, costing 385 British casualties to 78 Boers. Because of this victory, the British breached Boer's line of defence, and on the 28th of August, Buller's troops marched into Machadodorp. The Boers escaped to Nelspruit in the Lowveld below the second escarpment. A few days later, on the 1st of September, Lord Roberts proclaimed the entire South African Republic British territory. General Buller chased the Boers and two Long Toms retreating towards Lydenburg, which the British captured on the 6th of September 1900. No sooner had it been occupied than the Boer Long Toms on the mountain pass to Spitskop opened fire on the town. On the 8th of September, Buller, with 12,000 men and 48 guns, started ascending the pass in pursuit of Botha and the Long Toms. But by the next day, the Long Toms had passed the summit of the mountain and stopped just beyond the part of the pass known as the Devil's Knuckles. From there, they fired their parting shots at the enemy and disappeared into the mist. The Boers later destroyed the four Long Toms to avoid them falling into British hands.

Three hours after they had left Belfast, Joe's company arrived in Machadodorp. From there, they marched the 30 miles north on the road to Lydenburg, dropping another 1260 feet to Badfontein Farm. Even though it was spring, it became hot on their march. The gravel track they were on followed the magnificent escarpment running north, with its buttresses and deep gorges, many adorned with waterfalls cascading from the Highveld. The soldiers stopped along the way and drank from the fresh mountain streams.

"Look at those mountains," said Joe. "Like the Cape Mountains, but greener."

"Aye, they are grand," said Mike. "Have you ever seen such clean streams as these in this country?"

The lieutenant overheard their conversation and said, "I have heard that Scottish fishermen have introduced trout fish to these streams in the last few years. Trout fish were never here before they tried that. Most African waters are too warm, but these streams are cool enough for trout, so they breed and farm them here, just as in Scotland."

"What is a trout fish, Sir?" asked Mike.

"Oh, sorry, lads. I thought you knew them," said the lieutenant. "They are a northern hemisphere fish that live and breed in the clean, cool waters of England, Scotland, and elsewhere. Many gentlemen and lady anglers enjoy fishing them for relaxation. They taste good too, especially when smoked like a salmon."

The men looked at him blankly as if he was speaking a foreign language, but Mike said, "Oh, thank you, Sir. I don't think I've ever tried one of those." To which the marras chuckled to themselves. They held back on asking what a salmon was but assumed it was also a fish.

Along the way, they saw antelope and zebras, a sight they were by then accustomed to. The lieutenant told them there used to be lions and elephants, too, but the farmers had killed most of them to protect their livestock and crops. But the men couldn't see any farm animals or cultivated fields on this march. The British had been clearing the region and burning farms there too.

"There are still leopards around, though," said the lieutenant. "But they only hunt at night. So, you'll never see them during the day until they attack you!"

"Well, that's canny," said Mike. "I guess we're safe for now, then."

"Aye," said Joe, "but maybe not so safe tonight."

"You won't catch me leaving my tent tonight," said Mike. Everyone laughed.

They arrived at the farm on the evening of the 20th of October. There, they pitched camp next to the blockhouse line under construction. They were to relieve the company working there for the past month after a week-long handover. Work was progressing well, and they could see completed blockhouses as they approached the site. They pitched their tents next to those erected there. Then, the lieutenant led them on tour. After the visit, they prepared field food and settled for the night.

The next day, refreshed from a peaceful sleep, the men arose and enjoyed a hot cup of coffee, bread and jam before mustering to receive their instructions for the day. Joe and Mike were assigned to a blockhouse several hundred yards away under construction. The existing team members led them there and then showed them what they needed to do on the building site. They pointed to the equipment and tools they required for the job stored inside the structure. The old guard stayed for the rest of the day to pass on their work techniques and watch over the new team as they picked up the tasks. Midday, a black helper from the camp arrived with sandwiches for the men on site. The day passed well and without incident; both teams returned to camp for supper. After supper, the men congregated around a bonfire where the new unit could ask questions of the outgoing team before retiring for the night.

At the crack of dawn the following morning, the men arose, had breakfast and went their separate ways, the old team marching toward Machadodorp while the new group dispersed to their various construction sites.

"This isn't so bad," said Mike. "There's no one around except us, and we have enjoyable work to do. No fighting!"

"Aye, not to mention that view," said Joe, gesturing toward the mountains. "Pass me that bucket of cement, will you, Mike?"

Another day passed without incident while the men carried out their tasks. The lieutenant made frequent rounds to ensure everyone was working hard on finishing the remaining blockhouses, and he inspected the quality of work, which was progressing well.

But on the fourth day, they heard galloping horses and rifle shots as they rose from their bunks. Stumbling out of their tents, they saw a Boer commando of 20 men attacking and firing their rifles towards the awakening troops. Chaos ensued. The British soldiers grabbed their firearms and began returning fire as best they could while seeking cover. The attack lasted for several minutes before the Boer fighters vanished as quickly as they had arrived. They left a scene of destruction and death in their wake.

"Bloody Boers," shouted Mike. "Come back and fight, you bastards. You are always hitting and running. Bloody cowards!"

"Jack, are you all right?" called Joe. "Come, Mike, give me a hand. Jack is on the ground over there."

"I'm all right," said Jack from a distance. "Just shot through the leg. Nothing serious."

The marras ran to Jack's side and started applying basic first aid. But they saw several other injured men and a few who looked dead. The lieutenant instructed a soldier to climb the nearest telegraph pole and call for help. Then he organized the company to clean up the camp and care for the dead and wounded until help arrived a few days later—a mounted troop accompanied by an ambulance cart. In the interim, they cared for the injured as best they could and buried the dead in a makeshift cemetery, erecting handmade wooden crosses with the names and IDs of the departed carved into them.

The rescue troop went, and the remaining men returned to their tasks and waited for their replacements to arrive in three weeks, keeping a constant eye out for Boer fighters.

The Battle of Bakenlaagte, Transvaal—30 October 1901

A few days later, a British patrol passed the Badfontein blockhouse construction site and told them of the Battle of Bakenlaagte, a major Boer raid that had taken place 100 miles southwest of them on the 30th of October 1901. While marching to its base camp, Eastern Transvaal Boer commandos attacked the rear guard of Lieutenant-Colonel George Elliot Benson's much-feared No. 3 Flying Column. Generals Louis Botha, Ben Viljoen, Grobler and Brits led these commandos.

"I've heard of Benson," claimed the lieutenant. "Is he all right?"

"No, Sir," said a sergeant of the patrol. "He died in the struggle, and our generals are fuming! I fancy we'll see an increase of British activity over the next few weeks to catch the remaining Boer generals and Botha in particular."

Benson's British No. 3 Flying Column of 2,000 men specialized in night raids and terrorized Boer commandos in the eastern Transvaal. They had become so victorious that General Botha ordered his forces to muster at Bakenlaagte to attack Benson and get revenge.

The Flying Column was returning to a camp after performing farm-clearing operations. It was a wet day blanketed by mist, causing reduced visibility and challenging travel conditions. The British column spread out into clusters of troops, and it became further extended when Colonel Benson deployed detachments to take out any Boer sniping teams.

After riding hard for twenty-five miles, General Botha arrived at Bakenlaagte with 800 reinforcements. On arrival, Botha noticed that the extended column of British men was an ideal opportunity for his overwhelming force to pick off the dispersed bands of British troops. He ordered a sizeable mounted Boer force to attack the column's small, remote rear guard.

The column's rear guard of 210 British troops, outnumbered four to one, set up a defensive position on Gun Hill. They fought the 900 Boers in a close-quarter 20-minute gunfight. When they had obliterated the Boer column rear-guard, the battle ended.

The men on both sides showed great bravery. Of the 210 officers and other ranks of the rear guard, they killed 73 and injured 134. The Boer casualties were 14 dead and 48 wounded. Colonel Benson, a veteran of the Battle of Magersfontein in December 1899, was to die the following day from wounds received on the battlefield.

"My God, I don't believe it," said the lieutenant. "Benson was a genuine hero, one of our best!"

"Is there still a long way to go in the war, Sir?" asked Joe.

"Aye, it sure appears so," said the lieutenant. "If they can still muster that many fighters, we have lots more work to do, lads."

"Just what we want to hear, Sir," said Mike. "Let us go after them. I'm ready to fight." A sentiment echoed by the rest of the team.

It was another severe blow to Lord Kitchener, for it was not going well at that stage of the war. The Boers thwarted them wherever the British tried to subdue the fighters. The Boer commanders were eluding his forces at every effort to capture them. Losing Colonel Benson, his best commander, at Bakenlaagte was a further blow. For example, Kitchener was attacked at home in The Spectator for his "incompetence." He took too long to end the war, so the home wolves were baying at the door. Field Marshal Kitchener feared the government had lost patience with him. The cabinet's overriding priority, he knew, was to cut the cost of a far too expensive war by reducing the number of troops in South Africa. But he was requesting more troops to end it.

The British had cleared the eastern Transvaal of its human population. So, Louis Botha's men escaped into the hills around Vryheid in the Natal Colony, where Botha had fought in the past days of the war. In the western Transvaal, Koos de la Rey still attacked British columns and convoys whenever the opportunity arose. Jan Smuts was in the Cape Colony's northwest, standing against the small number of British troops around O'okiep. Hertzog, Malan, and others operated in the eastern and northern Cape, defying every effort to surround and capture them.

On the 1st of November, Lord Kitchener sent an urgent despatch to Lord Roberts.

"It would be admirable to send any troops you can spare," he pleaded. Later, he telegraphed Roberts confidently, "Perhaps a new commander might hasten the war's end?"

Long a Kitchener supporter, Roberts quelled any suspicion of sacking Kitchener and even promised more reinforcements. "The cabinet is not considering sacking you!" Roberts reassured.

Kitchener then resolved to push harder to bring the remaining troublemakers, Botha, De la Rey, Steyn, Smuts, De Wet, Viljoen and others, to their knees.

Returning to Jack and Jenny at Middelburg—November 1901

Towards the end of November, Joe's company returned to the Middelburg Camp. There, he and Mike visited their marra, Jack, to see how he was doing in his convalescence. Jack was in the field hospital at Middelburg Camp, where the marras found their way to his bedside.

"Howay, Jack," called Joe as they arrived.

"Howay, Jack," echoed Mike. "Alreet?"

"Aye, I'm canny, my marras," said Jack! "It's grand to see you."

"How're yee feeling, Jack," said Joe, then "So sorry."

"I'm fine, laddies. Sorry for what, Joe," said Jack?

"Sorry for bringing yee here, my marra," said Joe. "I'm sorry about the fighting, getting injured, and our marra Billy's death. I'm sorry for the bloody mess," he repeated, tears welling up. "It was a crazy idea!"

"What are you talking about," said Jack. "You didn't bring me here. I brought myself here."

"Aye, and that goes for Billy and me, too," said Mike. "I don't know where you get that idea. We decided ourselves."

"It wasn't my talks on the war?" asked Joe.

"Are ye mad?" said Jack, laughing.

"In no way, Joe," said Mike. "Not on your life, man. Aye, you helped us understand what was going on here. But we made up our own minds. Billy, too."

"You're joking, aren't you?" Joe asked.

"Nee. We're neet funnin yee, Joe," said Jack. "Why'd we joke with you over that? We worried that Yee didn't want to come with us!"

Then Jenny appeared out of nowhere. "You are fools to be here. But so are the hundreds of thousands of other boys out there. Let's look at your wound, shall we, Jack? How is that infection doing?"

Joe spun around to face her. "Jenny, you're here. Laddies, isn't she a wonderful sight? I told yee she'd follow me here..." Jenny only smiled.

"Well, yee told me that in your letter," said Joe.

"Aye, that I did," said Jenny. "Here I am. I've been here a while and looking after your marra Jack. You, laddies, are never here and always out fighting Boers."

"Aye, that's true," said Joe. "But we've got a few days here for now."

Satisfied with Jack's progress, Jenny disappeared again, doing her rounds. So, the marras caught up on the days after they took Jack to Middelburg, joking over Joe's apologies. Relieved, Joe relaxed and joked with his remaining marras.

"These bloody Boers won't surrender," said Mike. "Two years of war, and they're still giving us grief. Lots of grief!"

"Aye, how true, Mike," said Joe. "But it's us who won't admit defeat. We are in their lands, and the diehards are still trying to eliminate us. They are up against a giant Empire, and many soldiers and civilians have died. They call them Bittereinders, and they'll never give up."

"Oh, I know what you're saying, Joe," said Mike. "But who are we to question why we are here?"

"Aye, who are we to question that?" Joe sighed.

Back in camp with Jenny, they couldn't find a private place to meet. So, they had to content themselves with talking wherever they could, finding a quiet spot to dally and taking walks outside the camp when they could. As the drives cleared the Transvaal of fighters, there were fewer and fewer casualties, too. So, Jenny became concerned with how long the army still needed her services there. They consoled each other by saying that the war was soon over, and they'd be back in Jarrow together once Joe had served his time.

On the 5th of December, they informed Lord Kitchener that British troops had forced Boer General Christiaan de Wet to abandon his final try to enter the Cape Colony. Other excellent news for Lord Kitchener included information on Commandant Kritzinger. While he was crossing the De Aar-Noupoort railway with a force of 150 men, on the 16th of December, the British fired upon Kritzinger and his men from a blockhouse, wounding five before they retreated. Kritzinger, a citizen of the Orange Free State, aged 27, and a seasoned commander, returned under fire again to carry off one of his wounded men. The British soldiers in the blockhouse hit him, too, injuring and capturing him, together with his five wounded companions. The British treated them well in their local hospital and sent them to the coast. Kritzinger had been the most successful of the many commandants who had invaded the Cape Colony in retaliation for the British farm-burning and looting measures in the Orange River Colony. The British put him on trial on four charges of murder and one for damaging the railway. The court acquitted him, but he remained a British prisoner for the rest of the war. One less commandant for Kitchener to consider. De Wet, Botha, De la Rey, Smuts and others had eluded him, causing him more pain and distress.

At the end of 1901, Kitchener reversed his concentration camp policy. The continuing tumult in England at the death rate, led by Emily Hobhouse, helped change his mind. By mid-December, he instructed column commanders not to bring in women and children, leaving them with the guerrillas. It was an astute political move as a gesture for the Liberals. It made excellent military sense, too, as it handicapped the guerrillas now that the drives were in full swing. And it was perhaps the most efficient of the anti-guerrilla weapons.

Contrary to liberal convictions, it was less humane than the camps, though Kitchener was not significantly concerned. [9]

By the end of 1901, the war had drifted into its final mechanical phase of coercing the Boers by brute force. The army mounted as many men as possible to occupy the enemy. Field guns not being needed, they formed the Royal Artillery into a corps of Mounted Rifles. Ian Hamilton, who had gone home with Lord Roberts, returned to South Africa a year later as the Chief of Staff to Lord Kitchener, much to Kitchener's delight.

~

More Struggles near Ermelo—January 1902

The Boers fought to the bitter end as the war continued into its third year. Skirmishes, encounters and battles continued into 1902 across the new and old British colonies of Natal, the Cape, Orange River and the Transvaal. Joe's company took part in a skirmish at Bankkop (Onverwacht), Ermelo, Eastern Transvaal, on the 4th of January 1902 and engaged with the enemy at Spitskop, Ermelo, Transvaal, on the 18th.

January 1902 saw the end of the notorious Boer raider Gideon Scheepers. Although the British captured him in October 1900, he was too ill to bring to justice until 1902. By December 1901, Scheepers had recovered enough to go to the jail in Graaff-Reinet in the Cape Colony for trial. He faced sixteen charges in a court-martial: seven of murder, one of attempted murder, one that he placed a prisoner in the enemy's line of fire, one of maltreatment of a PoW, three of assault, two of malicious injury to property and one of arson. The court called fifty-four witnesses to testify for the prosecution, and Scheepers appointed his attorney, Carl Auret, to defend him. The court convicted Scheepers on all counts except one of the murder charges and sentenced him to death. On the 18th of January 1902, the British executed Scheepers by firing squad while tied into a chair.

The execution was yet another reason for Lord Kitchener to rejoice. From the war's earliest days, Gideon Scheepers had been a real thorn in the British side.

The Army also involved Joe's company in the celebrated capture of Boer General Benjamin Johannes "Ben" Viljoen at Lydenburg on the 25th of January 1902. The general remained a prisoner-of-war until May 1902 at the Broadbottom Camp on St. Helena.

This minor victory was of great importance to Field Marshal Kitchener. Now, he'd drive hard towards the end. By the 5th of February 1902, the Army had completed Kitchener's blockhouse lines. He then sent 9,000 men on a massive sweep through the countryside. In the first sweep, they captured 285 Boers, but De Wet, President Marthinus Steyn, and their men escaped the trap. The second drive lasted from the 16th to the 28th of February. Once more, De Wet got away, but they forced him to abandon his cattle this time. On the 27th of February, the column of Colonel Henry Rawlinson encircled and captured a 650-man Boer commando at Lang Reit, northeast of Pretoria. This success brought the British 'bag' to 778 surrendered Boers. They considered the third drive, by Major Elliott's division, from the 4th to 11th of March a failure with only 100 Boers captured. De Wet escaped and continued the fight with General Koos de la Rey in the western Transvaal.

De Wet didn't have a high opinion of the British blockhouse lines. "On the 27th of February 1902, the English made one of their biggest catches in the Free State," said D Wet. "They had made a great kraal they call a drive. Narrower and narrower, the circle becomes, hemming us in more at every moment. The result was that they bagged an enormous number of men and cattle without a solitary burgher captured by their famous blockhouse system." [10]

From then on, until the last days of the war, De Wet remained quiet since the British had left the Orange River Colony desolate by their sweeps. In late 1901, De Wet overran an isolated British detachment at Groenkop, Orange River Colony, inflicting heavy casualties and prompting Kitchener to launch the first New Model drives against him. De Wet escaped the first such drive but lost 300 of his fighters. Later attempts to round up De Wet failed, too, and most of De Wet's forces avoided capture. The British never caught Christiaan De Wet.

Joe and Jenny saw each other seldom in those last days of the war. Joe's company returned to Middelburg occasionally for re-kitting and rest. But they sent them back out into the field after brief stays.

On one sortie, they introduced Joe and his fellow soldiers to one of the most unusual inventions the Boers used during this war—their moveable forts.

Relieving Fort Hendrina, Northern Transvaal—20th to the 28th of March 1902

During February, Joe's company was part of a column sent north via Pretoria by train to the Soutpansberg in the northern Transvaal. The Boers assembled many of the remaining north Boer commandos returning from other parts of South Africa around Louis Trichardt. Louis Trichardt is a town at the foot of Songozwi, in the Soutpansberg mountain range 230 miles northeast of Pretoria. There, the Boers had erected Fort Hendrina, named after the wife of Commandant-General P.J. Joubert. This fortified military shelter was one of three moveable iron forts ordered by the Transvaal Government in 1887.

Czech-Austrian immigrant Adolph Zbořil (pronounced "Sbor-shil") designed and built these mobile forts. On the 8th of February 1886, Zbořil, who had served time in the Austrian Artillery, became a captain of the Transvaal Artillery. On the 1st of July 1886, the Transvaal Artillery appointed him as acting administrator and adjutant, the second-highest rank in the Transvaal Artillery. Zbořil discovered that the Transvaal artillery and the police corps needed modern weaponry and resources. He put pressure on Commandant-General Piet Joubert to gain new weaponry. In 1887, he designed "yzeren forten" (iron forts) that they could dismantle and transport wherever needed. They made the forts of heavy armour plates, and they were octagonal. Each fort section was light enough for two soldiers to carry it. Between 20 and 25 soldiers could find refuge in each fort. The Boer military moved the Hendrina Fort north and installed it on the farm Klipdam, owned by Oscar Dahl, the Native Commissioner for the northern Transvaal. The Commissioner had fortified the double-storeyed house on the farm with cannons at two of the corners. He took these measures following attacks by local Venda natives. Transvaal President Paul Kruger was the commanding officer who ordered Schoemansdal to evacuate in 1867, following a guerrilla war that the Venda King Makhado had waged against the settlers.

Fort Hendrina was still in Louis Trichardt when the Anglo-Boer War broke out. The Soutpansberg saw little action early in the war, and most northern burghers who joined the Transvaal's forces did duty in other parts of the country.

They went north after the British forces took over Pietersburg in May 1901. When the British invaded Louis Trichardt, they moved Fort Hendrina back to its old site. They renamed the region Fort Edward after the British monarch of the time. The infamous Bushveldt Carbineers renamed the Pietersburg Light Horse on the 1st of December 1901, then defended it and used the fort as a base for their operations. The Bushveldt Carbineers (BVC) was a short-lived, irregular mounted infantry regiment of the British Army, raised in South Africa during the Second Boer War. They formed the 320-strong unit in February 1901, commanded by an Australian, Colonel R. W. Lenehan. Based at Pietersburg, they saw action in the Spelonken region in the far north of Transvaal from 1901 to 1902. Forty percent of the men in the BVC were Australians, and the regiment included forty surrendered Boers, too, known as "joiners," which they had recruited from the internment camps. The British later charged several of the officers of this unit with war atrocities. Lieutenants Harry "Breaker" Morant and his sidekick, Peter Handcock, were court-martialled and judged guilty of murdering a civilian and Boer prisoners of war in August 1901. The Queen's Own Cameron Highlanders executed them by firing squad on the 27th of February 1902.

From the 20th to the 28th of March 1902, a Boer commando laid siege to the fort. The Army called upon Joe's company to support the relief of the fortress. They had just arrived at a raised promontory a distance above Fort Hendrina and could see both the fort, manned by a small group of British soldiers and the Boer fighters hiding behind shrubs surrounding the fort.

"What the hell is that?" asked Mike, somewhat astonished.

"That, my laddies, is a moveable fort," said the lieutenant. "The Boers have three of them. They call this one Fort Hendrina. Several soldiers of the Bushveldt Carbineers are inside it and can't get out. So, our mounted boys will charge them at dusk, and we will follow them to complete the job. Hide and be silent until then. The Boers haven't noticed that we are here."

Following the lieutenant's orders, the marras found a shielded spot that looked out onto the Songozwi, Hanglip, and the rest of the Soutpansberg mountain range and hid.

"No matter where we go, we see views like that out there," said Joe in a whisper.

"Aye, Joe, you make an excellent point there," said Mike. "There's better weather than in England, too."

"I can't get over that moveable fort we saw there," said Jack. "I want to get closer to it."

"Well, it looks as if we might soon get there," said Joe.

After two or three hours, the sun vanished over the Soutpansberg, and the men could hear the rustle of mounted infantry moving in behind them.

"Howay, my marras," said Mike. "Here we go...." They could see in the failing light that the Boer fighters were rustling, too, readying themselves to attack the fort after dark. And then, with no audible signal, the mounted infantry moved forward through their midst towards the Boers. The marras looked up from their position as the MI crept past them.

"Oh my God," said Mike quietly. "What an amazing feeling."

"Aye," said Joe. "I don't think I've ever been this near moving horses."

The MI attacked at once, launching themselves through the bushes on the Boers below, which they took by surprise, shooting one fighter after another. The MI was out of the gates, and the infantry company poured over the slope behind them, shooting cautiously to not hit anyone from the same side.

"Let's go, men," called the lieutenant. "Let's finish these bloody Boer fighters!"

"We're with you, Sir," shouted Mike as he tumbled through the bush. "Let's get the bastards."

Within 10 minutes, they had finished the struggle. Surviving Boers threw their weapons on the earth and raised their hands. Joe's company arrived within seconds of the surrender, herding the enemy into the open and rounding up their firearms. The besieged Bushveldt Carbineers poured out of the fort to support the attack. The British had won the battle, liberated Fort Hendrina, and regained complete control of Louis Trichardt.

"Ha. That was champion!" called Mike. "That was a fantastic engagement, the closest we have experienced. Amazing."

"Aye. Amazing," said Joe. "Attacking for a change instead of being attacked!"

"Agreed," said Jack. "What a victory! Small, but a victory still."

"Well done, men," said the lieutenant to his troop as they mustered when they had completed the episode. "Now, we must collect the wounded and bury the dead before returning to camp."

And with that, they carried out his orders at once. They handed the wounded over to the Carbineers to care for and buried the dead in shallow graves marked with crosses engraved with their IDs. They returned late to camp and ate a hearty supper before falling exhausted into their bunks.

On the 26th of March 1902, Cecil John Rhodes died. He wasn't a healthy man for most of his life. His parents sent him to Natal at 17, hoping the climate might help the problems with his heart. But when he returned to England in 1872, his health deteriorated with heart and lung problems. His doctor, Sir Morell Mackenzie, believed he would only survive six months. He returned to Kimberley, where his health improved for the next two decades. But from age 40, his heart condition returned with increasing severity until his death from heart failure in 1902, aged 48, at his seaside cottage in Muizenberg, near Cape Town. [11] South Africa's richest man, the founder of De Beers diamond mines, politician and champion of the British Empire and the Cape to Cairo Railway, was dead.

In his will, he provided an endowment for the Rhodes Scholarship, the world's first international study programme. The scholarship enabled students from territories under British rule or once under British influence and from Germany to study at Rhodes's alma mater, the University of Oxford. [12] Rhodes aimed to promote leadership marked by public spirit and exemplary character and to make war impossible by fostering friendship between the dominant powers. [13]

MICHAEL G. BERGEN

The Canadians at the Battle of Hart's River

On the 31st of March 1902, a British column under Colonel Cookson was pursuing a force of 2,500 Boers under the command of generals Kemp and De La Rey, believed to be operating in the Western Transvaal, and came into contact with an advance party of Boers. The primary force of the column took off after the Boers, but around 1:30 in the afternoon, encountered the Boer force and was encircled. The Boers began shelling the British positions, using the artillery as a screen to push forward mounted troops.

The 2nd Canadian Mounted Rifles, guarding the baggage train, rushed towards the fight and attacked the Boer positions to relieve pressure on the primary force. Twenty-one Canadians from 3 and 4 Troops, 'E' Squadron, under the command of Lt Bruce Carruthers, became cut off from the central column during a charge. Still, rather than surrender, they decided to fight to the last, eventually running out of ammunition and being overrun. Around five P.M., the Boers called off the attack and withdrew, having inflicted significant damage on the British force and escaping with minor losses.

The Canadian Mounted Rifles suffered the most casualties, with thirteen men killed and over forty injured, the second most significant loss of life in battle for Canada after Paardeberg at the beginning of the war. A telegraph to the Minister of Militia of Canada stated: "The regiment and field hospital have undergone a severe test and have acquitted themselves most creditably. I regret the heavy losses." Lord Roberts congratulated the Governor-General of Canada and the men in the field.

Hart's River was one of the last significant battles of the Boer War, and although it was a British defeat, the Boers could not fight on much longer and were forced to come to the negotiating table, with peace finally being signed in May.

On the Brandwater Basin Blockhouse Lines—April and May 1902

In early April 1902, they ordered Joe's company south to the blockhouse lines in a region where the Transvaal, Orange River, Natal and Basutoland colonies met. Up against the soaring Drakensberg was a massive gathering of British troops, which had just completed the last sweeps in the region. Those under Colonels Nixon and Garratt headed northward to the Transvaal. Lieutenant-General E.L. Elliot, with the columns of lieutenant-colonels Henry de Beauvoir De Lisle, Hew Dalrymple Fanshawe and Lieutenant-Colonel Michael Barker, retired to Harrismith, Orange River Colony, where they soon parted ways. General Elliot moved westward to Bethlehem, and Barker headed for Frankfort. At Harrismith, Lt Colonel De Lisle, a renowned polo player who had started his career with the 2/DLI in India, relinquished command of his men and passed the baton to Brigadier-General Little. [14]

Joe's company travelled the extended distance from Middelburg by train via Pretoria and Johannesburg to Harrismith, then marched to Fouriesburg in the Brandwater Basin of the Orange River Colony on the border of Basutoland. This mountainous region was the site of a significant rout by British forces of Boer commandos earlier in the war. After the British march under Lord Roberts through the Orange Free State and the Transvaal, the Boers sought refuge and regrouped there.

By April 1902, the British Army had cleared the region of Boer fighters and their families. But as luck had it, just as Joe's company arrived and the Army was about to spread them along the blockhouse line between Bethlehem and Ficksburg, it was being attacked every night by a Boer force. These blistering attacks almost eliminated the British ability to halt the movements of Boer fighters at night. Before dawn on the 8th of April, the Boers attacked four blockhouses at Steenkamp's Kop, just south of the mountain pass of Retief's Nek. In surrounding the outposts, the Boers opened an intensive rifle fire, which resulted in the capitulation of these fortified posts. They killed three soldiers, wounded five and took fifteen British prisoners, a minor victory for which they were soon to pay.

No Boer attacks were on the line for the next eleven days, and the Army restored the vacant fortifications to strength. General Elliot's force returned to Bethlehem and headed northward, taking part in multiple engagements with the remaining Boer fighters. By completing these operations, they had captured 311 Boers and killed ten, including those who had attacked the blockhouses at Steenkamp's Kop.

With the close of this exercise, fighting in the eastern half of the Orange River Colony ended. Survivors of both Boer republics had capitulated and chosen their representatives for a peace conference they were soon to hold at Vereeniging on the southern border of the Republics. The British forces then dispersed. The columns under Elliot, Barker, Garrett, Nixon and Rimington spread over an Orange River Colony region, including Lindley, Heilbron, Frankfort and Majors Drift. Within this sector, they cleared whatever crops or supplies remained. On 15 May, they suspended these activities, and the troops returned to the railways to await the outcome of events at Vereeniging.
15

By the middle of May 1901, Joe and his four companions had been in their outpost for several weeks. Since no more Boers had shown up, they suffered from severe boredom. Nothing happened for weeks, apart from visits by the supply wagon. The war had moved from constant excitement to total drudgery. The life of a soldier was dull at the best of times, although Joe had survived his share of drama. But being on the blockhouse lines was monotonous to the extreme.

Joe's small blockhouse unit devised an action plan comprising minor tasks for maintaining the blockhouse and its surroundings. Two stood guard, monitoring every direction from their upper perch, while the others carried out their duties. They gathered firewood and water, cooked, laundered, cleaned their living space, and tidied their surroundings, which they completed in no time. They passed their time for the remaining weeks doing their simple chores, playing cards, writing letters or journal entries and talking about whatever interested them, no matter its relevance. Since they had each entered the war simultaneously and spent the past year in close quarters with one another, experiencing the same perils, they had bonded into close companions.

They lit a small fire in the blockhouse in the cool evenings to warm themselves and occupy the hours when they relaxed and discussed various topics. These idle chats included descriptions of their home life, stories of family, lovers and friends, past jobs, the war, their particular battle experiences, lost companions, and the Boers.

"It's been an exciting year... apart from losing friends," said Joe one day. "But not what I expected."

"Aye," said another, "The same for me."

There was silence for a while.

"What did you expect, Joe?"

"Well, at the start of the war, I wasn't here, but I read a lot on it—the battles, the great marches, the generals and heroes, the defeats and the victories. I expected to experience the same glory when I joined, but it's been very different."

"Aye," said Joe's fellow guard. "I know what you mean."

Then another piped up, "Did you not have enough battles?"

"Oh, aye," said Joe, "But small, nasty ones, ambushes, skirmishes, most often at night when you can't see them. That's not what the British Army is used to, is it? Britain built the Empire through pitched battles and conquest, where armies faced each other and fought as soldiers at an agreed time and place. We're not used to pouncing on each other from behind boulders or bushes."

"Aye," said another, "We shouldn't have to fight such cowards."

"We aren't cowards. And the Boers aren't cowards either," said Joe. "They fought too in the beginning. But once they lost against such a massive force as our army, I wager they felt the only way of surviving was through this guerrilla war."

"But why did they fight in the first place?" asked Joe's companion. "They could have just let the foreigners be, to mine their gold and pay their taxes. Why did they need to fight?"

"That's the right question," said Joe. "They've lost so much because of it—their women, children and parents, homes and farms, livestock, friends. They've lost everything!"

"So have we," his companion said. "20,000 soldiers, I hear."

"Aye, I can't make any sense of it," said Joe. "But we might have done the same thing if an army invaded our country, mightn't we?"

"Aye, maybe," said the others in agreement. "In a flash!"

And so passed the hours, days, and weeks until the war's end: idle talk, minor maintenance tasks and seeing nothing but the supply wagon, which brought supplies and mail once a week. There was also the random inspection by their lieutenant and roasting of the odd buck or bird they had trapped for the pot.

But one day, they noticed a lone rider approaching them. Startled after weeks of seeing no one, they drew together, peering through the observation slits, guns ready for action. Occasionally, the horse stopped for a few moments, then stumbled onwards. They could make out a mounted figure, its head nodding. As far as they could see, the rider was skinny and weak - another wretched victim of the war.

"It's a Boer," said the corporal.

"Aye," said Joe. "A Boer fighter."

"Is he alone?" asked the corporal. "Or is he a decoy, the others hiding in those bushes?"

"Should we shoot him?" asked the other.

"He doesn't have a weapon," said Joe. "So, why shoot him?"

"Good question," said the corporal. "But what if he isn't alone?"

"Let's wait and see what he wants with us," said Joe.

So they waited silently, with only their heavy breathing heard, while the horse and rider inched ever nearer.

"I can't see a weapon," said Joe. "Why is he here?"

The horse stopped in front of the blockhouse, and the rider slid off the horse onto the ground. They ventured out with caution to investigate. The man seemed lifeless, and the horse hung its head low over the body. On closer investigation, they could see he was a young man in tattered clothes, and his skin and hair, where visible, were covered with dirt and sores. But seeing he was still breathing, they concluded he was alive and needed help.

After quickly scanning the surroundings to ensure he was alone, they carried the emaciated rider into the blockhouse and laid him on a bench. The corporal inspected the man and instructed one soldier to bring water and smelling salts from their first aid kit and another to wash the man's face and hands.

Cleaned up and regaining consciousness, they gave him meat from a buck they had cooked that morning. He revived and soon sat upright, murmuring a few words in English.

"You speak English?" the corporal asked him, surprised since he was a Boer.

"Yes," the Boer youth said, then paused while he chewed on the meat.

"My name is Jan Marais," he said. "I belonged to the Bethal Commando but separated three weeks ago by falling off my horse. When I came to, my comrades were no longer there. I found my horse and have been wandering ever since, but I am tired and finished. I don't want to fight anymore. What does it matter? We have lost the war. I want to search for my family and take them home."

With that, he drifted out of consciousness again. So the men threw a blanket over him and let him sleep. He only awoke the following morning. The soldiers were having their breakfast when he rose, so they offered him strong coffee and a mess tin of porridge and invited him to join them. He polished off the coffee and oatmeal in no time, so they offered him more.

Jan's fear had dissipated, but only once had he asked them whether they'd kill him, and the corporal assured him they had no such plans.

"Have you been a fighter?" the corporal asked.

"Yes," he said. "I've been a fighter since my father told me to join the commando when the war started."

"How old were you?" they asked.

"Fifteen," said Marais.

"They pulled you in at fifteen?" asked Joe.

"Yes. Even though the official age to join was seventeen, the Boer leaders told every male who could ride and use a rifle to join the commando. You couldn't do anything else. My father and Oom Paul commanded it."

"Is your father still alive?" they asked.

"I don't know. My father and brother disappeared during the battle of Ladysmith, and I haven't seen them since then."

"What about your mother and the rest of your family?"

"Gone," he said, shaking his head. "My ma and younger sisters and brothers are in a British camp. I had two older brothers who joined when I did, but I heard they are both dead."

The conversation stopped as they prepared a hot bath for Marais in a large tub. The men asked the corporal what they should do with him.

"He is our prisoner-of-war," the corporal said. "So, we must get him right and decide what to do with him. The lieutenant will have to decide. In the meantime, we should help him get back on his feet. That's the Christian thing to do, isn't it?"

They agreed and looked for clothing for him. They found an extra pair of trousers and a shirt to replace the rags he had been wearing for months. The problem was that the clothes were British Army-issue, and Kitchener had issued an order to shoot any Boer fighters caught wearing British Army clothes.

"Well, we didn't catch him wearing army clothes," said Joe. "We have loaned him our clothes for the time being. What is he supposed to do, walk around naked?"

They then threw the fighter's rags into the fire to kill the vermin living in them.

After his bath, he dressed and slept again. They then met for a late afternoon meal of antelope and potatoes, which he devoured. After that, they made tea and sat around to talk.

Marais told them of his exploits during the war. He was in the first wave of commandos descending on Ladysmith in October 1899. Jan explained that the Boers had been moving since the British took back Ladysmith and chased them onto the Highveld. He had been with Louis Botha's column until things had fallen apart in the last few months. The British had chased his commando non-stop, but Botha escaped their clutches. The rest of his commando, he believed, were dead or captured. He had not eaten or slept for two weeks, always keeping one step ahead of the British troops until he arrived at this blockhouse, starving and exhausted.

"I didn't care whether I would live or die. Your fellow soldiers finished us. By now, my entire family might be dead. I don't even remember how I got here."

"Well, Jan," said Joe. "You are very much alive, my boy. And the corporal says we should take care of you until you are back on your two feet."

"This has been a bloody war," the corporal said. "It hasn't been right for any of us. The sooner it's over, the better, I say."

Everyone agreed with that statement.

On the lieutenant's next visit, they discussed what they should do with their prisoner.

"You are right in what you are doing," said the officer. "Let's get him back to health. Then I'd put him to work as soon as he is able. He should pay for his upkeep!"

Then he added just what they had been waiting months to hear. "I know that the leaders from both sides are meeting in Vereeniging now," he said. "Let's hope this terrible war will soon end."

---

1. Fantastic
2. Pronounced Mykeysfontain, and spelled Matjiesfontein today.
3. The Springfontein Grave Register recorded 568 people of various ages as having died there between the 4th of April 1901, and the end of the same year – Stanley, Liz. *Mourning Become: Post/Memory and Commemoration of the Concentration Camps of the South African War 1899-1902*. Publisher: Manchester University Press, 2006.
4. 'pont' being the Afrikaans word for a ferry and the French word for bridge, both in a sense having the same purpose.
5. Reitz, Deneys; JC Smuts (2008). *Commando: A Boer Journal of the Boer War*, first published in London, 1929.
6. D.W. Aitken, *Guerrilla Warfare, October 1900-May 1902*: Boer attacks on the Pretoria-Delagoa Bay Railway Line, *Military History Journal Vol 11 No 6 December 2000*; SA Military History Society
7. S.G.P Ward, *Faithful, The Story of the Durham Light Infantry*, 1962
8. Now flooded by the Kwena Dam.
9. *The Boer War*. Thomas Pakenham. New York: Avon Books, 1979
10. *Three Years War*, C.R. de Wet, 1902
11. "Death of Mr. Rhodes." The Times. 27 March 1902
12. Rhodes, Cecil (1902), Stead, William Thomas (ed.). The Last Will and Testament of Cecil John Rhodes, with Elucidatory Notes, London.
13. On Rhodes's leadership and peace goals for the Rhodes Scholarships see Donald Markwell, "Instincts to Lea: On Leadership, Peace, and Education," Connor Court: Australia, 2013.
14. S A Watt, *Harrismith – A Military Town During the Anglo-Boer War, and After: Part II; The South African Military History Society Military History Journal Vol 8 No 2 – December 1989*.
15. HARRISMITH, *A Military Town During the Anglo-Boer War, and After: Part II* Military History Journal, Vol 8 No 2 – December 1989 –

CHAPTER 6
THE END OF THE STORM
MAY TO OCTOBER 1902

Smuts and Reitz journey to Vereeniging

Meanwhile, 700 miles away, General Jan Smuts and his much-reduced commando, including Deneys Reitz, were still hiding out in the arid north-west wilderness of the Cape Colony.

"Five months ago, we came into this western country hunted as outlaws," remembered Reitz. "We now command the entire region from the Olifants River to the Orange River, four hundred miles away, except for compact garrison towns here and there."

These towns included Concordia, O'okiep and Springbok.

Concordia started as a German Rhenish mission station for the Nama people in 1852; the same year European prospectors discovered copper in the area. Although first identified by the Dutch settlers in 1685 when a group of Namaquas visited the Castle in Cape Town and brought along pure copper implements, they did nothing much to mine it for 200 years. Then copper mining began there in 1853, and by the 1870s, the region had the most productive copper mines in the world, launching the lucrative mining industry that transformed South Africa into an industrial country. A railway to Port Nollath on the Atlantic transported the copper ore for shipment. Mules and horses first pulled the train carriages, which they later replaced with steam locomotives. By the time Smuts arrived, this vast region of South Africa was bordering on German South-West Africa, a colony of Germany from 1884, with the Orange River forming the border between them.

From the mountains of Basutoland, the Orange River travels through this hot region where it seldom rains and empties into the Atlantic after a journey of 1,040 miles. But after the sparse winter rains in the desert and highland thaws of spring, it comes alive with multi-coloured carpets of flowers. They founded a town on the site of a spring known in the Khoekhoe language of the Nama people as U-gieb (large brackish place), which the European settlers translated into O'okiep.

Once abundant in copper, the mines ran dry, and the unemployed miners who had settled in the region started farming endeavours using their meagre water supplies before General Smuts and his raiders arrived in early 1902.

General Smuts laid siege to the mining town of O'okiep, a small copper mining town, and the nearby settlements of Concordia and Springbok on the 4th of April 1902 for 30 days. He surrounded 700 officers and men of the 3rd Battalion Queen's Royal Regiment, 5th Royal Warwickshire Regiment, Namaqualand Border Scouts, the Town Guard, the Cape Garrison Artillery, and a sizeable number of Black and European miners. Colonel Shelton, the commander of the British garrison at O'okiep, refused to surrender, even though he only had enough provisions for holding out for three weeks.

The village of Concordia, with a garrison of 100 men, surrendered a day after the encirclement started. Most English settlers of the region fled to Port Nolloth on the South Atlantic coast. There two British gunboats arrived and evacuated them. The nearby town and the garrison of Springbok gave stiff resistance to the Boers, with British losses of four men killed and six wounded. Even after the settlements of Concordia and Springbok had surrendered, the siege of O'okiep continued.

On the 1st of May 1902, the commandos launched an attack on O'okiep, using the commandeered locomotive "Pioneer" of Concordia's Namaqua United Copper Company to propel a waggon with a load of dynamite into the besieged town. Smuts didn't mean to harm the women and children within, but only to frighten them into surrender. The protective defences at O'okiep were little more than a barbed-wire fence, which they erected across the railway line at Braakpits Junction, just north of the O'okiep. They tied the points at the junction to it causing the waggon to derail, spilling its load of dynamite on the ground, where it burned out without exploding. [1]

Because of the small number of British forces in the region, Smuts and his commando had free rein there. They had forced many British outposts, often forgotten by the British High Command, to evacuate and blew up their blockhouses.

Then early in May, Deneys Reitz rode out one afternoon with two companions to snipe at the English posts on the other side of O'okiep. As they were returning to their horses, they saw a cart coming along the road from the south, with a white flag waving over the hood. Galloping up, they encountered two British officers who said: "We bring a dispatch from Lord Kitchener for General Smuts".

"Follow us, gentlemen," said Deneys, full of curiosity as to why the British were sending envoys deep into the Northern Cape.

The Boer fighters escorted the officers to Concordia where General Smuts took them into his house and shut himself away with them for a while. He later came out and walked away into the veldt by himself, deep in thought. The letter from Lord Kitchener stated that they were organising a meeting between the English and Boer leaders at Vereeniging, on the banks of the Vaal River south of Johannesburg. The purpose of the meeting was to discuss peace terms, and the Boer leader General Smuts should attend. They enclosed a letter of safe conduct, under which he was to go through the English lines to Port Nolloth. From there, the British were to take him by sea to Capetown, and on by rail to the Transvaal.

The general considered this news as ominous.

"The British have offered to give safe conduct to me, a secretary and an aide to go with me," said the general. "Reitz, you come along as my aide."

"Yes, sir," responded Deneys becoming excited at the prospect of such a journey. He and his fellow fighters had grown weary of the war and dreamed of a peaceful life once more.

The general set to work making plans and dictating orders. He sent a messenger to O'okiep the next morning to tell the garrison that both sides were to refrain from active operations while the Peace Congress lasted. The two British officers went on ahead to Steinkopf, to warn the relief force gathering there that the Boers would be soon passing through their pickets.

On the next day, the fighters came in from the outlying posts to bid their goodbyes to their leader. They paraded past the courthouse, each man sitting with his rifle on his thigh, while General Smuts addressed them. He informed them of the purpose of his departure and asked them to prepare for disappointment if need be. But there were only cheers and shouts of courage as they pressed in to wish him farewell.

Smuts and Reitz set off for Port Nollath the next day, escorted by a small British patrol, and reached Capetown on a steamer in five days. The British transferred them from Capetown around Cape Point to Simonstown on board the HMS *Monarch* (1868), an ironclad masted turret battleship, where they spent a week in comfort. HMS *Monarch* was the first seagoing British warship to carry her guns in turrets, and the first British warship to carry 12-inch calibre guns. The officers and men of the ship vied with each other in their efforts to make them welcome. Deneys later reported that the British, for their many faults, were a liberal nation. Not only on the man-of-war but throughout the time they were amongst them, they spoke not a word that could hurt their feelings or offend their pride, even though they knew the Boers were on "an errand of defeat".

They headed north by an armoured train, reaching Matjesfontein the next day. There, General French came to see them, "a squat, ill-tempered man, whom we did not like". The awkward General did his best to be friendly. He sat talking to them for an hour or more, attempting to draw information out of General Smuts, who had "no trouble parrying his awkward questions", said Reitz. When General French made no headway, he became more open and spoke of his experiences during the war. The British general mentioned how the Boers missed capturing him that night below the Stormberg Mountains.

General Smuts and his small delegation then started their train journey north, stopping first at Matjesfontein. From Matjesfontein, they continued their journey, travelling only at night, an armoured train puffing ahead of them the entire way, its searchlight sweeping the veldt to spot Boer fighters. Each day they parked on a siding at a lonely spot till dark and thus made slow progress. They took the better part of a week to reach Kroonstad in the Northern Orange River Colony where Lord Kitchener met them. Soon after their arrival, the Field Marshal rode up to the station on his great black charger, followed by a large entourage, including turbaned Pathans [2] in their Eastern costumes and gold-mounted scimitars. To the Boers, it was a show of opulence and superiority.

His retinue waited outside while Kitchener entered their compartment to talk to them. It was apparent the Field Marshal was keen to end the war since he referred again and again to the hopelessness of the Boer struggle. Kitchener told them there were 400,000 British troops in South Africa against 18,000 remaining Boer fighters. He said he'd let the burghers keep their horses and saddles. The British Government would help to rebuild the farmhouses, which they had destroyed on "military grounds". General Smuts complained that they had executed Boer fighters in the Cape without moral reasons. But Lord Kitchener rationalised this as justified since the Boer fighters had used khaki British uniforms to decoy his soldiers. He cast an eye at Deneys, who was still wearing his British clothes from Lord Vivian.

Once they arrived at Vereeniging, a tiny mining village on the banks of the Vaal River, General Smuts first continued to the eastern Transvaal to meet General Louis Botha, the conference at Vereeniging only taking place after that meeting of Boer commanders. Still escorted by an armoured train from Kroonstad, they crossed the Vaal River into the Transvaal. They then travelled through Johannesburg at night before turning east on to the Natal line to the town of Standerton. There they travelled by cart along a blockhouse line that ran straight over the Highveld. They passed small British camps at intervals where the troops turned out and greeted them as a courtesy. After journeying for a day and a half, they reached a point where a party of horsemen sent by General Botha was awaiting them.

The next day, the Boers held elections. Even in adversity, their instinct for speeches and verbose wrangling came to the fore. By evening, they had elected thirty delegates to represent the Afrikander people.

The following morning the gathering dispersed, riding off on their hungry-looking horses to re-join their remote units. General Botha and the deputies set out for the British blockhouse line. They returned along the blockhouse line to Standerton, the soldiers everywhere standing to attention as their tattered cavalcade passed. At Standerton they entrained for Vereeniging, where the British had prepared a sizeable tented camp for the reception. The first man Deneys noticed as they entered the encampment was his father.

"He was shaggy and unkempt, but strong and well. Our greeting after so long a parting was deep and heartfelt," recalled Deneys.

Then the delegates from the Transvaal and Free State converged on Vereeniging. Every leader of note was there: General de la Rey, Christian de Wet, President Steyn, General Smuts, Beyers, Kemp and many others, the best of the Boer fighting-men. Deneys learnt from General de Wet that his younger brother had been serving under him for over a year and was in safety. So, Deneys had accounted for all the Reitz men, including two brothers who were prisoners of war. His brother Joubert, with whom he had ridden to Natal in 1899, was in a British PoW camp in Bermuda. They considered themselves luckier than most Afrikander families who were mourning their dead.

The outcome of the Peace Conference was as they had foreseen. Every representative had the same disastrous tale to tell of starvation, lack of ammunition, horses and clothing. They spoke of how the blockhouses were strangling their efforts to carry on the war. Added to this was the massive death toll among the women and children, of whom twenty-five thousand had died in the concentration camps. Universal ruin had overtaken the country. The British had burned every homestead in the Republics to the ground, impounding or destroying the crops and livestock.

As Deneys Reitz said, "There was nothing left to do now, but to bow to the inevitable."

General Botha, General de la Rey, F. W. Reitz and other essential dignitaries travelled to Pretoria to conclude the final treaty with Lord Kitchener and Lord Milner.

"On their return, peace was an accomplished fact."

And so, the end of this war had arrived at long last. The British declared themselves victorious, and the Boers defeated. Christiaan de Wet remembers:

"On the evening of the 31st of May 1902, the members of the Governments of both Republics met Lord Kitchener and Lord Milner in the former's house at Pretoria. They were to sign the British Proposal which the National Representatives had accepted. It was a never-to-be-forgotten evening. In the space of a few minutes that was done, which could never be undone. There was nothing left for us now but to hope the Power which had conquered us could draw us nearer and ever nearer by the strong cords of love."

Deneys Reitz added, "Of the sting of defeat I shall not speak, but there was no whining or irresponsible talk."

The Afrikanders present at the conference accepted the verdict. The delegates returned to their commandos to inform the burghers of the terms of surrender. Deneys' father spared him the ordeal of returning to break the news to the men in the Cape, by insisting he stay with him while General

Smuts returned to Concordia. When the general said goodbye to Deneys, he stated that he dreaded telling the men.

Deneys and his father travelled to Balmoral Station. When they arrived there, they found a message from Lord Milner confirming the British planned to deport them. His father had a fortnight in which to settle his affairs in Pretoria. And so, father and son returned to Pretoria after two years. They found their home occupied by a British general with sentries outside who blocked their approach. Had it not been for the hospitality of a friend, they'd have gone roofless for a fortnight. During that time Deneys' younger brother rode in from the Free State, six inches taller than when Deneys had last seen him, and none the worse for his ordeal. Their business in Pretoria finished, they went into self-imposed exile at the end of June. Reitz concluded his accounts of the war with these last words:

"As we were waiting on the border at Komati Poort, before passing into Portuguese territory, my father wrote on a piece of paper a verse which he gave me."

"Whatever foreign shores my feet must tread,

My hopes for thee are not yet dead.

Thy freedom's sun may for a while be set,

But not forever, God does not forget."

"And he said until liberty came to his country, he will not return." [3]

End of the war and repatriation

Of the 88,000 combatants including foreign fighters and Cape Rebels who started in this war, 7,000 died in battle, and the British sent 24,000 prisoners of war overseas to far-flung PoW camps. A further 28,000 Boer civilians died in concentration camps along with 20,000 black servants and combatants. At the end of the war, 21,000 irreconcilable Bittereinders[4] surrendered.

The British had a moral responsibility to move 200,000 men, women and children back into the old Republics devastated by war. It was another vast undertaking for the British forces in South Africa. They redeployed the concentration camps for peaceful purposes, filling them with burghers from the bush and prisoners of war from prisons in South Africa and overseas. They then reunited the prisoners with their families. The starving Afrikanders relished the British rations they received compared to their meagre rations in the field. British troops then returned the Boer families to their farms, providing each household with a tent, bedding and a month's rations. They offered tools, agricultural implements, seeds, livestock and vehicles from repatriation depots.

The dry season of the South African Highveldt winter had just started as they started repatriating the Boer families back to their destroyed farms began. They assigned Joe's company, waiting for its battalion to arrive, to repatriate the Standerton Camp. It wasn't a pleasant experience, except that it gave Joe immense satisfaction to be part of freeing the inmates of a concentration camp that had so appalled him. The British soldiers directed the operations as the hundreds of families loaded their goods onto army-supplied waggons over several weeks.

"My God, Mike, just look at them," commented Joe. "How will they make their journeys? They look so weak!

"Aye, and sick too, many of them," observed Mike.

"Help me with these people," called Joe, to which both Mike and Jack complied.

"Here, people…" called Joe to a struggling family. "… food for a month, and bedding, and a tent. No, you're a large family, so here is more food, bedding and two tents."

They didn't understand him but received the goods with such gratitude. The old lady among them had a heap of broken furniture and food that she had collected over her many months of incarceration.

"Hand that stuff to me, Mike," called Joe. "They don't have the strength to load it."

Joe noticed the woman's elderly husband, who had various curios and other items from his months of imprisonment overseas.

"Throw me that, Jack," called Joe. "And help up the old man. You can see he is struggling even to walk."

They helped the children too, who had books and toys from the camp school. They piled the dray high with various belongings, on which the family sat on precarious perches. The long columns of oxen and mule spans hauling hundreds of waggons pulled out of the tent camp, on their way into the veldt back to their distant homesteads. Clouds of dust rose into the skies as the cracks of long whips, and the familiar shouts of the native drivers urging forward their beasts of burden rang out across the Highveld. [5]

Joe and his marras felt genuine compassion for each of the families of wretched souls they had helped as they embarked on their journeys home with their meagre possessions.

"Good luck, people," called Joe, echoed by his marras.

"My God, laddies," called Joe to his companions. "What have we done to these people?"

They established the Standerton concentration camp in December 1900 as Lord Roberts issued his command to destroy the farms. General-Superintendent Goodwin reported in February 1901 that the condition of the people was "pitiable in the extreme". To add to the woes, a Doctor Leslie from Cape Town, took one look at the camp and refused to take up his duties, "causing considerable inconvenience". [6]

By the end of May 1901, Standerton Camp had reached 3,000 internees in size, and they continued to arrive. Accommodation ran short, so they housed families in the local Dopper church too. They allowed others to live in the town. There was a black camp alongside the whites as well. In the bitter winter of 1901, people became ill and died, most from pulmonary complaints and a high incidence of typhoid fever. A severe measles epidemic struck in September of that year, contracted by children from a group captured by Colonel Colville's column. There wasn't a family which had not lost someone in the measles epidemic. And many children developed pneumonia after recovering from measles. By the end of the war, 716 prisoners had died, of whom 609 were under the age of 15.

The Standerton camp was just 1 of the 45 tented camps built for Boer internees and 64 made for black Africans across the two Boer Republics. The authorities mismanaged encampments from the outset, and they became overcrowded when Kitchener's troops implemented the internment strategy on a vast scale. Conditions were terrible for the health of the internees, because of neglect, poor hygiene and inadequate sanitation. The supply of needed items was unreliable because of the constant disruption of communication lines by the Boers. The food rations were meagre, and there was a two-tier allocation policy, whereby they gave families of men who were still fighting smaller rations than others. [7]

"Well, at least they are on their way to their farms," replied Mike. "And we are helping them get there."

"Aye, and so we should," replied Joe. "God knows they have suffered enough."

"And the fighting is over," added Jack. "Hurrah!"

On arrival at their homesteads, the Burghers off-loaded their goods, and the repatriation waggons lumbered away for their next load. The Boers then found themselves alone on the plains with the ruins of their old homes and barns, stark and silent on the veldt. Faced with the results of the three-year war, the Boer fighters and their families only now understood the full meaning of the guerrilla war. But they pulled themselves together and began the work restoring habitable rooms if they still existed, building new homes and farm buildings and restoring any furniture they could salvage. They repaired fences, dams and kraals, and prepared for ploughing and planting in the following spring. They were a hardy and industrious people who then put their energies into building an alternative life and nation.

The total number of British Empire combatants in that war were 347,000 British and up to 150,000 colonial forces. Of these, 6,000 died in combat, 16,000 died of disease, 23,000 injured, and 1,000 missing. Besides human losses, the war cost the British Crown over 200 million pounds, a vast sum of money then. [8]

The breakup of the army of half a million took many months. The 1/DLI troops did not arrive at the British garrison at Standerton until the 30th of June 1902, a full month after the hostilities had ended. Demobilisation began the very next day. They first sent the men who had completed their time and reservists in detachments of 100 to Eden Dale, near Pietermaritzburg in the Natal Colony. Of those, the first detachment reached Southampton by ship from Durban on the 24th of August and the last on the 9th of October. The Volunteer Service Company embarked at Capetown on the 9th of July and landed at Southampton on the last day of that month. But the much-reduced permanent 1/DLI, including Joe and his marras, remained at Standerton until the 26th of October.

Planning for the future

But the 1/DLI delay at Standerton was important news for Joe since Jenny caught up with him while his unit was waiting there for re-deployment. The Army had sent Jenny to Standerton when she asked to be the battalion nurse.

The war over, they could pick up from where they left off in Middelburg. They met often and could soon catch up on their news. Jenny arranged private accommodation where they could meet undisturbed.

They took long and frequent walks together too when they talked of whatever popped into their minds. One lovely winter's day they sat in a copse of trees on the outskirts of Standerton, a small settlement established in 1876 and named after Boer leader Commandant Adriaan H. Stander, who owned the farm Grootverlangen where they founded the town. They had waded across Stander's Drift through the upper reaches of the Vaal River, which flowed past the village.

"I think back on what I've seen and lived through here, Jenny," said Joe, "so far from home."

"Tell me, Joe," replied Jenny.

"Well, we've seen things we could never have dreamt of in Jarrow," he continued while including her. "Deserts, high mountains, wide plains with wild animals roaming everywhere... strange plants, fruit and wine farms in the Cape Colony..."

"So true," agreed Jenny. "It is an amazing place."

"... And there's none of the smoke and filth of our collieries or factories in this land. Just wide blue, sun-filled skies and nights so full of stars they light our way on their own. It's been belta! I could never have imagined what I have seen out here."

Jenny smiled and nodded her head in agreement while gazing at him.

"I've fought in battles and lived through injuries and disease and boredom," continued Joe. "And I have grown, Jenny. I feel much wiser now than before I got here."

"Aye, that you are, Joe," she nodded in agreement. "You are a man now."

"But beyond the wide Karroo? What we saw was so terrible. Detention camps for women and children, disease, everywhere hundreds, no, thousands of innocent people dying! Dead farm animals were rotting in the fields or on the roadsides. Ragged Boer fighters were attacking us wherever and whenever they could, right to the end."

Jenny listened to the man she loved with the compassion of a nurse. She had noticed subtle changes in his stance towards the war throughout their relationship as Joe's experience in the field transformed and moulded him. He was no longer the brash and idealistic youthful man she once knew who had spoken of the glory of the British Empire and his duty to protect it.

"And aye, I agree with you now, Jenny. This war was horrible; it made no sense," continued Joe. "There was no glory! At least, I saw none. And I believe that more soldiers died since the first glorious battles before Lord Roberts returned home in victory. I may be wrong on that, but we had one skirmish after another right from our arrival. And we weren't alone. There were skirmishes and battles over the whole of South Africa. Thousands more died on both sides during the guerrilla war."

"Aye, you're right, Joe, for sure," agreed Jenny. She could see that Joe wanted to vent his feelings. And he did, to her surprise.

"Despite the grand parades and puffed up stories and the well-dressed generals at the start of the war, the guerrilla war saw no such glory... The newspaper stories fooled me, and I see that now. I've seen only the ruins of farms and towns, death and shame in this war. Aye, I know wars cost lives. But why have we given up the lives of so many of Britain's sons?" continued Joe. "I know I keep saying this over and over, but we killed old men, women and children too on this far-away land, Jenny. We built the blockhouse lines and rounded up the Boers like animals. Why? As a simple working man and soldier, I ask, what have we won and was it worth all the dying? Are the gold and diamonds in those mines worth the deaths of so many men, women and children? And I'm not just blaming the British for this disaster, nee. The Boer fighters were as much to blame! Why didn't they stop fighting when we started burning their homes and putting their families in those terrible camps? Why were they so stubborn against such an enormous army?"

Jenny empathised with her disillusioned British soldier. She had seen it coming in Joe, as she had seen it with so many of her other patients over the last three years. She saw them arrive as innocent young laddies, full of pride and energy in their brand new uniforms, then change over time into disillusioned men. Jenny understood Joe's change of stance and delighted at his arrival at the same conclusion as hers.

"My dearest Joe," she responded after a long silence between them, "I am so sorry that you… that we had to live through this. You and Mike are right too that we working folk are always struggling to make a decent living, while the politicians and grand generals lead us into wars where we lose so many good young lives on both sides. As a nurse, I came to those conclusions long ago. That's why I joined the Army Nursing Service. Florence Nightingale inspired me as an adolescent girl to help those who suffer because of these horrible wars. But I've seen too many youthful men die, Joe. Far too many."

Joe continued verbalising his bottled-up thoughts. "Aye, and it was finding the gold that did it. When they found gold, so many miners from around the world came here to find their riches. I suppose that's normal. But the Boers saw it as an invasion. They didn't want hundreds of foreigners here upsetting their way of living. Would we not have felt the same in England? The Irish invaded England looking for work, my parents among them. But the British needed and welcomed the Irish workers for the mines and factories and shipyards. But the Boers just wanted to farm without outside interference. But more and more miners came, and the mining towns grew and grew, full of foreigners. And the arguments started and grew into a reason for war. The Boers tried to push us out, and the Queen and politicians didn't allow that. And there you have it – three years of a terrible war that should never have happened."

"Aye, Joe. I can see that you understand it now," she continued. "You're a wonderful person, Joe. And a knowing and caring man who I don't want to lose again. Let's learn from what we've seen here and use that to guide us in life going forward."

Joe nodded his agreement. He was a changed man; a matured, questioning working man and soldier who had experienced and survived a colonial war; a war that he had considered justified and glorious as a younger man. The reality of the battlefields had taught him much and opened his eyes.

"Aye, well Jenny, enough of that," he said, changing the topic. "I'm sorry to have dumped my thoughts on you. Who are we to question the reasons for our vast Empire? The King, the politicians and generals must have excellent reasons for what we are doing. Let's instead plan our future together, as you say. I have heard a rumour they may post my battalion to India soon. I still have another four years to serve, and I want to make the best of it. And from what I've been reading, India is an interesting place, and very different from Africa. Do you know, Jenny, they have tamed elephants, imagine that. They ride them and use them for heavy work the way we use teams of horses or mules. And, I have heard it's peaceful over there right now. Are you willing to join me?"

"For sure, Joe," she responded with a smile. "That should be grand. When do we leave?"

On the 26th of October 1902, the 1/DLI left by train for Durban in the Natal Colony and embarked on the P. & O. ship SS *Assaye* on the 29th of October, destination Bombay. They were a complement of 14 officers and 422 men on board heading for unknown adventures in the great British Empire.

For his service in South Africa, the British Army awarded Private Joseph Irwin Rutherford the Queen's South Africa Medal with four clasps: South Africa 1901, Transvaal, Orange Free State and Cape Colony.

---

1. Bagshawe, Peter (2012). *Locomotives of the Namaqualand Railway and Copper Mines* (1st ed.). Stenvalls.
2. The Pathans of Punjab (also called Punjabi Pathans or Saraiki Pathans, depending upon the region of the Punjab from which they originated) are Pashtun people who settled in the Punjab region of Pakistan and northern India.

3. Deneys Reitz, *Commando: A Boer Journal of the Boer War*, 1929.
4. A faction of Boer guerrilla fighters, who resisted the forces of the British Empire to the bitter end of the war.
5. *The aftermath of War*, G.B. Beak, 1906
6. Published camp reports
7. Pakenham, Thomas, *The Boer War*. New York: Random House, 1979.
8. Roughly equal to twenty-two billion pounds sterling today or 75% of the cost of Britain's involvement in conflicts in Iraq and Afghanistan, and 63% of Britain's involvement in all wars in the 30 years since the fall of the Berlin Wall.

CHAPTER 7
BEYOND THE STORM IN INDIA
NOVEMBER 1902–JUNE 1906

The Voyage from Durban to Bombay

Five months had passed since the end of the war. It was a pleasant spring night on a flat and peaceful southern Indian Ocean, late on the 29th of October 1902. Full of excitement and unable to sleep, Joe and his marras Mike and Jack had lingered on the upper deck since leaving Durban harbour. They were in no hurry to descend into the ship's bowels with the cramped conditions they had seen there. The SS *Assaye*, which they had boarded in Durban, South Africa, glided through the transparent surface of the sea, destination Bombay, India. The throbbing of her two massive steam engines well below the upper deck provided the rhythm of a giant heart for this steel creation from Greenock at the mouth of the River Clyde in Scotland. She was a new ship, launched in October 1899 for the Peninsular & Oriental Steam Navigation Company as an intermediate passenger service. Advertised for a commercial voyage to Calcutta in January 1900, the army requisitioned her on completion as a Boer War troopship. One of her first and most notable passengers during that conflict was the Boer General Piet Cronjé, who she took to St Helena as a prisoner-of-war along with his wife and 500 other Boer prisoners of war.

The marras could see the phosphorescence-illuminated outlines of enormous fish and dolphins torpedoing at top speed just below the surface or through the bow wave. A bright, rising full moon cast its extended, glimmering reflection across the sea's surface to the east. They were heading northeast toward northern Madagascar Island.

"This is grand," said Joe. "Have you ever been anywhere as peaceful as this? No wind. No waves. Warm. A sea so flat you can see the moon in it."

"Aye, Joe. What a life. I should have been a sailor. Look at those fish," said Mike. "This doesn't look real. They look like ghosts!"

"Aye, and no war. And it's hard to believe we are heading to India," said Jack after a lengthy pause.

"Aye," said Joe, "an unknown land to explore, more of the British Empire and a new adventure. It's a pity Billy couldn't be with us now. He would have loved it."

"Aye, that he would have," said Mike.

"We can see from the number of our fellow Durhams on board that many more died back there in that South African War," said Jack. "Hard luck that! We knew so many of them. They were good laddies."

"The gamble of being a soldier, I guess," said Joe. "We were lucky, laddies."

Half the 800 military passengers on board were from the much-reduced 1st Battalion of the Durham Light Infantry (1/DLI). The 1/DLI landed in South Africa in November 1899 with 26 officers and 920 NCOs and men, and it now numbered 14 officers and 422 men, less than half their original strength.[1] Now, the Durham survivors of that war were on their way to India to relieve the 2nd Battalion of the Durham Light Infantry (2/DLI). The 2/DLI had been in India since 1862 as the 106th Regiment of Foot, the Bombay Light Infantry. The Honourable East India Company created it in 1839.

"I'm glad to be leaving South Africa behind me, though!" said Mike. "It was bloody dangerous out there!"

"Aye, Mike, that it was," said Joe. "It's a great place, though. I liked that part."

"Aye, and it was a splendid adventure," said Jack. "One we'll never forget."

"Whey aye, man! But those bloody Boer fighters," said Mike as usual.

"Aye, they caused us lots of problems," said Jack.

"Aye, they did. But we caused the Boers much pain, too," said Joe.

"Two more British colonies for the King," said Mike. "The Empire is a little larger. I guess we did our job."

They fell silent while gazing at the peaceful scene before them.

"But what the hell, we've had a grand time out of it so far, haven't we?" said Mike in a change of spirit. "At least we're not freezing our buttocks in the pits or yards."

"Aye. Fresh air. Blue skies. Star-filled nights. I loved the Karroo," said Joe.

"That's because you met up with Jenny there," said Mike.

"Aye, that's true, but the wide-open spaces, the wild animals, the heat and dryness, the desert. It agreed with me. We won the war. And now we are on our way to explore more of the Empire in India," said Joe excitedly. "I think we should stop rehashing that bloody war. I'm looking ahead, and it looks exciting. But I'm paggered [2] now; time to find my scratcha[3]."

The marras agreed with Joe, then called an end to their memories of the war on the upper deck and went below to catch a few hours of fitful sleep in their hammocks.

The following day, an incident occurred on board that caused an unexpected distraction. Joe was on deck on his own, enjoying a fresh breeze, when he felt a severe shudder of the ship. The vessel stopped its engines and slowed to a halt on a becalmed sea. Joe ran forward to see what the commotion was. There, seamen and soldiers peered over the ship's bow into the sea. He ran up to join them. Looking over the bow, he saw the lifeless form of an enormous animal—which an officer said was a whale. He watched as the form drifted out of sight into the depths.

When the engines and ship stopped, many more soldiers and sailors emerged onto the upper decks to discover what was happening. Joe's marras soon found him.

"What happened, Joe?" asked Jack.

"We hit a whale," said Joe.

"So, what's the commotion? Why did the ship stop?" asked Mike.

"It's a gigantic animal, Mike," said Joe. "But even such a creature is no match for 5,000 tonnes of steel colliding with it. I guess the Captain halted the ship to get away from it. But it died and sank into the deep. Very sad!"

The whale was no longer visible, and the ship resumed its journey while Joe silently reflected on the incident. He had read that men were hunting for their blubber and spermaceti without mercy. They used these substances in oil lamps, cosmetics, candles and much more. They prized their meat, bone and ivory, too. Whales were such valuable creatures that whale hunters hunted them to extinction. Joe and his marras had seen a few pods of whales while sailing from Britain to South Africa. But this was the closest that Joe had ever come to one. And the death of such a harmless creature saddened him. Even though he had often enough seen the end of men and horses and other animals in the past, he felt profound remorse for the death of this enormous animal. It affected him for an unexplained reason and stayed with him for the rest of his life.

"Sad? It's just a bloody fish, Joe," said Mike.

"No, Mike, it's not a fish," said Joe. "Its young drink milk from their mothers. It's a sea mammal that breathes on the surface and gives birth to its young in the sea, just as elephants do on land or us."

"Oh, a mammal, aye, now I understand," said Mike. Joe grimaced but didn't pursue the topic any further. He knew he threw out words he had learned through reading that his marras didn't always understand.

By 1902, the northern whale populations were vanishing through excessive whaling, and despite strong demand, many whalers couldn't supply enough and were threatened with going out of business. So, they headed to the southern oceans to hunt the still abundant whale populations there. From 1903 onwards, they killed the Southern Right Whales without mercy, so named because the whalers considered them the right whales to kill. But Joe's behaviour was unusual for a working man, and most people didn't care for whales then.

"I can't explain it," said Joe. "But I'm sorry for these creatures. I've heard they can think like us! The whalers even believe they can talk to each other and say they've heard them singing. They've been around longer than we humans, but how long will they last now? How many more of God's creatures will we wipe away off this earth because of our greed?"

This incomprehensible perspective on Joe's part fell on deaf ears. He wasn't a regular church-going man, but he believed in God and God's creatures as they had taught him since Sunday School. But his marras couldn't understand. Who worried over whales in 1902?

On another evening, the marras met on deck as usual but in a curious frame of mind. Questions soon started about the land to which they were heading.

"Tell us what you've learned of this place we are going to, Joe," asked Mike, suspecting that his friend had done his usual research.

"Well, I don't know that much, but I've read that it's very different from what we know, even after being in Africa. They call it exotic, meaning different from our country. India is not as large as Africa. It's like Africa in some ways, but from what I've read, it's very different. It has jungles and deserts and the highest mountains in the world. India has scorching places and icy places. It can be bone dry in the deserts or flooded during the rainy 'monsoon' seasons. The skins of Indians are dark but not as dark as the African natives we now know."

"The Karroo in South Africa was bloody dry too, lads," said Mike. "Not only that, but those Highveldt summer thunderstorms dumped plenty of water on us, too."

"Aye," said the others in unison.

"India's history is old, much older than ours, and it has many languages and religions. It has majestic palaces and places of worship for their religions called temples. And it has always had powerful armies and many wars and invasions."

"What are we doing there? Us British, I mean?" asked Jack.

"Because it has lots of valuable things England wants," said Joe. "They have spices, jewels, silk, and many other valuable things. England arrived long ago and started a trading business called The East India Company, known as the John Company."

"Jewels, I understand," said Jack. "But what are spices and silk?"

"I don't quite know," said Joe. "But I believe the gentry toffers use spices in their food, and silk is a fine cloth they wear. None of that interests us working folk, not that we could afford them."

"So?" said Mike. "They started a bloody company. Is that all?"

"Aye, Mike. But that company ruled over much of India with an iron fist for a hundred years and traded for precious goods all over the Far East. These goods ended up in England and Europe, where the gentry paid a lot of money to have them. John Company had a vast army, too. But they had big troubles almost fifty years ago—the Indians rebelled. So, the Crown stepped in to help stop the mutiny and took over the running of India, now a British colony and part of the British Empire," said Joe. "They say the sun never sets on the

British Empire, Mike. They say it's the world's biggest and most powerful empire ever known."

"Aye, I've heard that too," said Mike. "So, who is the toffer in charge there?"

"I read he's a viceroy," said Joe, "appointed by King Edward himself as his representative. Right now, it's Lord Curzon."

"What's a viceroy," asked Jack?

"The viceroy speaks for the Crown, for the King and Emperor, in India," said Joe. "He is what they call a Governor-General in charge of the Indian States too. The Governor-General and the Raj are in charge in India now."

"What the hell is that again, Joe?" asked Mike. "Raj?"

"It's what they call the British administration ruling India," said Joe. "That officer on board told me that Raj means Reign or Rule, as with our Government."

"My head is hurting from this talk of an Indian Raj, viceroys and John Company," said Mike. "Let's watch the sunset behind us on this wonderful evening."

The days stretched beyond a week and into a second one until, at last, the Captain announced that SS *Assaye* was arriving in Bombay the next day. Days at sea had become dull. Soldiers didn't have work tasks assigned to them as the sailors did and had little to amuse themselves with, apart from deck games on a cramped upper deck and impromptu music sessions. A few onboard musicians entertained them from time to time with songs or dance music, such as jigs. But that only went so far to keep the men amused. A few more curious, such as Joe, borrowed books from the ship's library and broadened their knowledge horizons. But apart from these activities, they had little to occupy them. They became bored and restless.

So, they met news of their pending arrival in Bombay with cheers and excitement. A few jugs of gin and rum appeared on deck as if by magic, no doubt through the ingenuity of the sailors. Passed around by the thirsty soldiers, who hadn't drunk alcohol since they left Durban, they emptied the jars in no time. The soldiers passed around a hat for financial contributions, and with that, the sailors replenished the empty jugs. Spirits grew, and the party became alive and boisterous. Soon, soldiers were dancing with each other and singing on deck as the gin loosened their otherwise more disciplined military behaviour. Night fell on wild and chaotic festivities on the aft deck, far from the eyes of the captain.

Then, the unthinkable but inevitable happened. A drunken soldier lost his balance and fell overboard into the ship's wake.

"My God," yelled Joe. "That gadgie just fell into the sea."

"Help him, somebody," yelled Mike. "He'll drown! Help!"

"MAN OVERBOARD," called a nearby sailor, repeated a score of times by many drunken soldiers to ensure the captain heard. They looked for any buoyant object to throw and help him. Most of these men couldn't swim, so they feared for the man's life. A practised and sober sailor threw a lifebuoy as hard as possible towards the soldier, hoping it could reach him in time. But by then, he had already disappeared.

"Look. The ship is turning hard," called Joe. "The captain is heading back to save him."

The ship's captain raised a general alarm, and the ship turned hard to starboard to reverse direction. Then, the vessel slowed and aimed for its dissipating wake and the lifebuoy. Sailors brought powerful spot lamps and swept the sea in search of him. They could see the lifebuoy and retrieved it, but there was no sign of the soldier. At that point, the captain declared the man lost at sea and resumed the original course for the ship to arrive at its destination on time.

"My God. Poor gadgie."

"Aye, Joe. And I knew him, a gadgie from South Shields," said Jack.

"I knew him as Charlie," said Mike. "It's a bloody shame! He was a fine lad."

The regimental chaplain led a brief funeral ceremony of remembrance and wished the lost soldier Godspeed on his way to heaven. The men grieved for their comrade in silence for a while. But they soon resumed their deck party, which became a well-lubricated wake for the dead soldier until dawn when the drunken soldiers slept it off wherever they had collapsed.

The battalion commanding officer must inform another mother or wife that their beloved one "had died in the line of duty."

The SS Assaye reached Bombay at midday on the 11th of November 1902. As it entered the busy harbour, packed with ships and boats of various sizes, they could see a magnificent city spread out before them with many elegant buildings. Many were ancient buildings, exotic temples, and newer and grander structures built in the British style but with unfamiliar spires and accessories added. They could see an old fort jutting into the harbour at the end of the docks. One of the ship's officers nearby told them the Portuguese had built the fortress long ago. He then pointed out Custom House next to the old fort, a large and impressive building with a clock tower.

"To tax the riches that flow into this magnificent land," said the officer.

"It's grand," said Joe.

"Aye. We British built many of the newer ones," said the officer.

The ship tied up at the Government Dockyard, and from there, they could see the entire city stretching out before them. It was an impressive view.

"Look at those men," said Joe. "They aren't wearing very much."

"Aye, and they are doing the work of asses too, look," said Mike.

They saw men in scant clothing, pulling carts loaded sky-high with various produce everywhere. Smaller vehicles called rickshaws taxied British gentlemen, ladies, and exotic wealthy Indian merchants. It looked like they had replaced horses and donkeys with little men of colour.

"Aye, but horses too, look," said Joe. "Look at those strange-looking oxen pulling those huge wagons, too."

They could see British and Indian soldiers and sailors among the crowd. Occasionally, they saw gentlemen and ladies walking on the quays and streets in their finery, the women sporting colourful parasols. Above the sounds of the ship docking, there was a loud din on the dock. Shouts, laughter, the racket of the horses, and rickety carts on the cobblestones filled the air. Behind them, they could see the Yacht Club. It had an imposing building with watchtowers at either end, many private sailing boats, and a few very impressive yachts.

They didn't get an order to disembark immediately and spent another night on board. In the evening, the commotion died, and the harbour became very peaceful. But in the distance, the soldiers could hear strange chanting, singing, drums and the sounds of other unfamiliar instruments, continuing deep into the night. They noticed the peculiar and exotic smells of spices drifting from the warehouses or the cooking smells from public eateries and private kitchens. After supper, Joe and his Marras went on deck again to enjoy the atmosphere and the more comfortable temperatures once the sun had set.

"It's grand to reach dry land again," said Mike. "Well, close enough to it."

"At least we had our sea legs this time, so it wasn't as bad as the trip to Africa," said Joe.

"Aye, that's true," said Jack. "Just look around us, laddies. I thought Africa was strange, but this land is stranger still!"

"Aye, but I'm looking forward to it," said Joe. "So much British, but so different and exotic to see and take in!"

"No war," said Mike. "I hope nobody is hiding behind a building waiting to shoot at us the way it was in South Africa."

They talked until well after nightfall, trying to guess the identity of more magnificent buildings within view. One just visible above the other buildings between them had spires and a massive tower in the middle. They speculated that it was a cathedral but found out the following morning it was the railway station.

The troops disembarked early the following day and mustered on the quay. They were to transfer on foot for their onward journey to the Indian troopship Royal India Motor Ship (R.I.M.S.) Clive. A local army honour band had arrived to guide them and beat the stride for them to their destination. When the soldiers had assembled, the "quick march" command cried out, and they stepped out into an unfamiliar country on a new and exotic sub-continent. R.I.M.S. Clive was at another dock two miles away. So they got much-needed exercise and fresh air and could get an excellent look at the strange and exotic sights around them along the way.

"I thought Newcassel and Capetown were impressive," said Joe, "but these buildings are pure belta!"

They marched along Marine Street through the heart of Bombay past many grand buildings, including the Post Office building, the Great Western Hotel and the Custom House. They trooped around Elphinstone Circle with its curved, multi-storeyed, arcaded terraces that exhibited Italian facades enriched with cast ironwork. Manicured gardens with statues, a large circular pond, and a fountain adorned the circle's centre. Above them loomed the monolithic Town Hall. Designed and built in 1833, Greek and Roman styles of architecture inspired this edifice, spanning 200 feet with a height of 100 feet. Beyond a flight of thirty steps was a grand entrance to the building, adorned with a Grecian portico and eight impressive Doric-style columns. Their lieutenant told them the Raj built the entire edifice of stone brought from England.

"Why'd they do that?" asked Mike. "Isn't there any stone in India?"

"I don't know the answer to that," said the lieutenant marching alongside them. "I suppose the Raj wanted it made of a stone they knew. But I agree with you, it's strange. They call it the Tondal; it also contains an extensive library and a museum, and the Literary Society of Bombay raised the money to build it."

Beyond the Circle, the battalion marched along Eastern Boulevard past the Mint and the Port Trust Office. Then, they marched past the European hospital and into the Esplanade Market Road. They marched past the most magnificent building they had ever seen—the Victoria Terminus railway station.

"I can't believe it's a train station," said Mike. "It looks like a palace."

"Aye, a palace. It's not like our train station in Newcassel, that's for sure," said Joe. "It's much grander. And look at those towers. They must be Indian."

"Look, there's a statue of Queen Victoria below the clock," said Jack. "That's grand to see!"

"Have you ever seen a railway station like that?" asked Joe.

"Never," they said, none of whom had seen the grand train stations of London.

"This must be a wealthy country," said Joe. "I guess the British Raj is paying for this. But look at those poor people running around here. And those lying at the side of the road? Are they asleep or dead?"

"Well, it must have cost a colossal sum of money to build this city," said Jack. "It's somewhat like home, except different. Grand British buildings built by the poor people of this land."

The builders constructed the massive station in 1887 with influences from Victorian and traditional Indian Mughal architecture. It was the hub of land-based travel into and out of Bombay via the British-built railway network. By the early 1900s, India had the fourth most extensive rail network in the world, with 25,000 miles of track joining the principal centres of the country, built over 70 years. Opposite the railway station, they marched past the Gothic-style Municipal Corporation Building, with its central dome rising to 234 feet. The men saw a magnificence created by the marriage of British Victorian and Indian influences and were in awe.

They soon arrived at the quay where their next ship, R.I.M.S. Clive, awaited them. Laird, Son & Co. of Birkenhead, England, launched the Clive on the 15th of November 1882. That was the same shipyard that built the ill-fated, 1,400-tonne paddle frigate HMS Birkenhead (1848) that sank off South Africa in 1852 with a loss of 450 British troops. [4] But none of these passengers knew of that disaster.

∼

Sailing Down the Malabar Coast

Men, livestock and material on board, R.I.M.S. *Clive* then sailed out into the Arabian Sea and headed 500 miles south along the Malabar Coast, a long and narrow coastline on the south-western seaboard of India. This coastline is one of the wettest regions of southern India. It captures the moisture-laden monsoon rains on the west-facing mountain slopes of the Western Ghats, a 1,000-mile-extensive mountain range that runs parallel to the western coast of the Indian subcontinent. The shoreline has pleasing sandy beaches backed by coconut palm trees and occasional villages. Halfway to Cannanore [5], the Portuguese colony of Goa was cut into British possessions. But the Durhams saw none of this alluring coast until they approached Cannanore since the ship had travelled too far out at sea. And they were wondering whether they would ever arrive at their destination. They arrived at Cannanore in the Madras Presidency on the 15th of November, 1902.

The following day, one company landed and relieved a unit of the 2/DLI at Cannanore. Headquarters and the remaining seven companies sailed to Calicut [6] in the Madras Presidency. The Malabar Coast monsoon season had ended, but a strong gale blew as the Clive approached Calicut. They arrived in the evening as darkness befell a city which didn't have a harbour deep enough to accommodate the Clive. The storm pounded the ship, but the crew manoeuvred it into a safe anchorage far from the dangerous reefs and sandy beaches.

The entire battalion disembarked via small craft at the Port of Beypore at the mouth of the Challyar River, south of Calicut. This city had a British past, reaching back to the seventeenth century. By 1792, the whole Malabar Coast, including Calicut, was under the British administration. The region had a long and diverse history of relationships with Europe. Before the British, the Dutch had ruled there, and before them, the Portuguese Vasco da Gama landed near Calicut in 1498, providing a sea route between India and Europe.

The 1/DLI remained there for the night, with one company detached to West Hill Barracks. They relieved another unit of the 2/DLI on the 16th of November, an unusual event since the two battalions of the same regiment hadn't met face-to-face for 30 years.

At this meeting, Joe and his marras saw their first incident of British belligerence in India. An unfortunate lower-caste Indian had erred between the two battalions meeting in a ceremony for the first time in Calicut. A gruff and seasoned 2/DLI sergeant-major screamed at the bowed older man, "Get the hell out of our way, you wog," raising his swagger stick to hit him.

But the 1/DLI colonel saw the incident and addressed the sergeant-major. "Steady on sergeant-major. The man hasn't committed a crime. The poor creature strayed into our midst. Show him the way out and don't beat him. We don't want a scene here."

"Aye, aye, Sir, but we don't need this scum ruining our historic meeting, do we?"

At that point, a 2/DLI lieutenant on hand offered a weak excuse. "Sorry, Sir, but you will understand the sergeant-major's reaction once you've been here a while."

"Maybe," said the colonel. "I have just come from Africa, not England, so I understand the reaction in principle. But I don't think we can condone such rage upon such an innocent and pathetic old coolie as this."

With that, they dropped and forgot the matter. But it was not the last such incident that the marras saw in this exotic land, far from home. They discovered that treating humans as animals was a favourite sport for the British in India. Nor, they reflected, was it any different from how they handled the wretched street urchins and vagrants back home.

Arrival in the Nilgiri Mountains and Wellington Cantonment

On the 16th of November, the 1/DLI boarded a train and headed across the scorching plains of the Madras Presidency. One company detached 30 miles inland at Malappuram, and the remaining five units were to continue to Coonoor and the Wellington Cantonment in the Nilgiri Mountains the following day.

From Malappuram, the 1/DLI travelled to Coimbatore and then on to Mettupalayam. From Mettupalayam, they continued to Coonoor on the Nilgiri Mountain Railway, known as the "Toy Train." The railway hadn't opened the line to the public yet, but it was complete enough to travel, so they made a train available for the army. Nilgiri Mountain Railway is a single-track, 29-mile-long narrow-gauge single line through 208 curves, 16 tunnels, and 250 bridges built by the British using cheap local labour.

The uphill journey lasted five hours, 1,000 feet above sea level on the hot plains below the Nilgiri Mountains. It then travelled across the plateau toward the Nilgiris for the first five miles. Then, for the next twelve miles, it ascended to over 4,300 feet through nine tunnels along cliff edges and many bridges. The marras marvelled at the magnificent and breathtaking views of the eastern slopes of Nilgiri. Stations they passed on the route included Kallar, Adderly, Hillgrove, Runnymede and Kateri Road.

As they climbed into the Nilgiri Mountains at a snail's pace, the marras found themselves in a vibrant and exotic world of lush forests, stunning cliffs, crystalline streams, rivers and waterfalls. As the train traversed dozens of bridges and dove into tunnels that cut through the mountains, it passed through a reserve rich in wildlife. There were lion-tailed macaques, Nilgiri Langer monkeys, orange-breasted Nilgiri Martins, wild goat-like Nilgiri Tahr, and even small family groups of Asian elephants. They heard tigers there, but they hid from sight most of the time. A large variety of exotic birds came into view in the trees. The radiant blue and green adorned Malabar parakeet, blue-shaded Nilgiri flycatchers, and fluorescent sunbirds with bright scarlet throats and bright blue spots on their heads and tails. There were orange and black Scarlet Minivets, Black-chinned laughing thrush, familiar-looking wood pigeons and the spectacular blue peafowl they had seen in the zoo back home. But many more unusual birds were out of sight, filling the forests with melody. They marvelled at many flowering plants, including multi-coloured orchids and exotic trees they had never seen. And they noticed that closer to the communities, the towering Australian eucalyptus trees, familiar to them from South Africa, were gaining ground here, too. In its entirety, this brief journey came together as a spectacle of unforgettable sights and sounds.

The train stopped at railway stations painted in various shades of blue with red roofs where small gatherings of local natives were out to greet them with fruit for sale. It passed little hillside meadows offering sustenance to wildlife and livestock. They saw wetlands, home to more birds and the Indian water buffalo. After a while, they emerged into more open landscapes with pasture land and scattered tea plantations, with scores of women harvesting the tea leaves. They saw small hamlets and villages with terraces mounting the hillsides with the houses of farmworkers and other working-class residents.

Joe and everyone aboard the train were dumbstruck by the quick ride's beauty and tranquillity despite the steam locomotive chugging, pushing them into the heights.

"Well, I'm blown over," said Joe. "Never have we experienced such a rich forest. I wonder whether that is what they call a jungle?"

"Look at those birds," said Mike. "Amazing!"

"What of the elephants?" said Jack enthusiastically. "There are monkeys everywhere, including at the stations, looking to us for food, and elephants everywhere too."

"Aye," said Joe, "Have you noticed that they use elephants for everything—for transport and heavy lifting? In a book I read, I saw that the army even uses them in war. We saw no such use of African elephants. We saw fantastic landscapes and many wild animals in Africa, but never such a rich forest as in the Nilgiris."

"Who'd have thought tea grew in hedges? Enormous gardens of tea hedges!" said Jack.

"I think I will enjoy my time here," said Joe.

"Aye, and with luck, we'll meet a few of those gorgeous chocolate women," said Mike, not realizing that traditional Indian women were taboo to foreigners here and English women were considered too exclusive and out of bounds for regular soldiers.

"The natives dress better here than those we saw in Africa," said Jack.

"Aye, the women cover themselves with those colourful costumes despite being poor. And the men sometimes cover their bodies up, too," said Mike.

"Not all of them, Mike," said Joe, "I have seen women naked from the waist up and men in nothing but cloth wrapped around their middles."

"Aye, on the coast when they were fishing in the day's heat," said Jack. "The men wear little there too. But it's cooler in the mountains, so everyone covers up against the cold."

"I am so excited by what we see here, laddies," said Joe. "We are far from the smoke and dirt of Tyneside. And we are getting to know a wholly unfamiliar world. I read up on it in books on the ship, but being here is much better. It's an excellent thing we joined the army."

"Aye, now that the war is over," said Mike.

After a short while, they pulled into Coonoor station, and the Sergeant was barking out orders on what should happen now.

Coonoor is well over a mile above sea level and was the second-largest hill station in the Nilgiri hills after Ooty. As elsewhere in the colonies, the British built their hill stations at higher elevations than the surrounding plains and valleys. They found these refuges from the summer heat at cooler altitudes of 3,500 to 7,500 feet. The region has a mild and healthy climate throughout the year. Seasonal temperatures vary from 37°F to 85°F but are usually pleasant. The Nilgiris receive rainfall from the southwest summer monsoons from June to mid-August and the northeast winter storms from the Himalayas from October to November. Aggregate annual rainfall is among the highest in India at 11 feet, compared to England's 2 feet.

"Gather up your things, laddies," barked the Sergeant, "Disembark in a hurry when the train has stopped. We will muster on the street opposite the station for our march to Wellington Barracks. Get your asses moving, now!"

Wellington Cantonment is nine miles from the hill station resort of Ootacamund, known by most foreigners as Ooty, and was the summer capital of the Madras Presidency. Wellington is 12 miles from Ooty but only 2 miles from Coonoor. So, the troops marched to the new and impressive barracks in no time. The Sergeant showed them to their quarters, bunks and storage lockers, and they heard an orientation talk by the Sergeant on the "dos" and "don'ts" of Wellington Barracks. Among the "don'ts" were ominous warnings on brothels surrounding every cantonment catered for soldiers. They learned that cantonments were the large military garrisons or camps built by the British around India and the Far East.

As a result, brothels and bars sprang up as soon as the troops arrived.

"Dip your wicks here, laddies, and you'll come to regret it," scowled the Sergeant. "But don't despair; the army has just finished an excellent new hospital should you get into trouble, not to mention an enlarged gaol."

The Sergeant warned the soldiers to ensure they didn't drink alcoholic beverages from "questionable sources."

"Don't try the Indian beer, horrible! But I can recommend Lion Beer. It's brewed in the Himalayas by Dyer Breweries of Kasauli and is a genuine pale lager as we know it at home. Dyer also started a distillery in Kasauli with a fine whisky you might try. And a new brewery has just started in Ooty, although I haven't tried their beer yet."

The large barracks occupied a slight rise in a shallow valley surrounded by gentle hills. They could see higher peaks a short distance beyond them. The terrain there was grassland with few trees, reminiscent of the edge of the Highveldt in the Drakensberg Mountains of South Africa and at a similar elevation. Joe and his marras were most impressed by this charming hill station and its comfortable barracks. They warmed to the thought of spending relaxing peacetime duty there and hoped for easier working time in such agreeable surroundings. They felt sure they had earned it after what they had gone through in South Africa.

"I heard from one officer on the ship that Lord Curzon has been changing India," said Joe. "Lord Kitchener is making changes as Commander-in-Chief, India."

"Kitchener?" said Jack. "Is he the same bloke who ran the war in South Africa?"

"Aye," said Joe. "That's him. He has followed us."

"Aha," said Mike. "He's a tough bastard."

"Aye," confirmed Joe, "He was the Field Marshal, our commander-in-chief in South Africa, the hero of the Boer War and the hero of Omdurman, Sudan. The king was pleased with his work in South Africa, so he put him in charge of the army in India."

The new Commander-in-Chief, India, was by now one of Britain's most celebrated soldiers. At the successful conclusion of the Second Anglo-Boer War, the Army promoted Kitchener to the permanent rank of general on the 1st of June 1902. They hosted a farewell reception for him at Capetown on the 23rd of June, and he left for England in the SS Orotava on the same day. He received an enthusiastic welcome on his return to England. On the 28th of July 1902, they renamed him Viscount Kitchener of Khartoum and the Vaal in the Colony of Transvaal and Aspall in the County of Suffolk. On the 28th of November 1902, Lord Kitchener arrived in Bombay to assume his post as commander-in-chief of the Indian Army.

"I've heard strange rumours of his private life," Jack mentioned with a chuckle.

"That means nothing to us," said Mike. "He is so high up; the clouds will hide him. They don't care about us swaddies. Nor do I care about his private life."

This last statement received agreement as usual and a grunt or two from his marras.

"Well, I've heard that Lord Curzon is just as tough a haughty bastard as Kitchener," said Joe.

Lord Curzon was a self-centred and proud man who never tolerated interference with his work and decisions. When criticized for his changes to the Indian administration, he became infuriated. Curzon also involved himself in military matters, such as the Imperial Cadet Corps (ICC), an elite corps of selected youths between 17 and 20. He created it in 1901 to give Indian princes and aristocrats military training, after which they received officer commissions in the British Indian Army.

The military organization proved to be the final issue addressed by Curzon in India, and it involved a clash of two formidable personalities. A significant disagreement arose between Curzon and Kitchener on the status of the military member of the council that controlled army supply and logistics. Kitchener wanted the counsellor under his control. Curzon did not.

"Aye. But I'm not surprised that Curzon is coming a cropper with Kitchener here," said Mike. "Arrogant, ruthless bastard!"

"How do you know this stuff on India, Joe," asked Jack.

"I found an interesting book or two at the library," said Joe.

"Library? What library out here?"

"Back on the ship," said Joe. "They had a few interesting books and nothing else to do. So, I spent time there looking at them and reading. They have a library here at the barracks, too. I love this travelling we're doing. So much new to see and learn!"

"Aye, me too, Joe," said Mike. "We're learning the women are exotic and exciting."

"Ha, aye," said Jack with a laugh. "Let's go for them, Mike!"

"We've seen that they have lots of cattle and pigs and dogs wandering in the streets of the cities," said Joe. "I have heard the cows are sacred, and the Indians won't kill them for food."

"That's odd," said Mike. "Why do they do that? Why have cattle, then?"

"No idea," said Joe. "I've heard the cattle are important in their religions. And for milk, I reckon."

"Another interesting book I found in this library is on the British Army in India," said Joe.

"It had many pictures of army regiments and uniforms that were belta. Most Indian soldiers wear uniforms such as ours, red or khaki-coloured, many with turbans. Others wore colourful and strange uniforms and extravagant headgear, but I reckon these were most likely dress uniforms for parades."

"What are turbans?" asked Jack.

"Those cloth scarves they wrap around their heads," said Joe. "The Sikhs, one of the Indian religious groups in the north, must always wear them. Another interesting thing I learned is that the khaki colour of our uniforms in South Africa came from India. Khaki means soil-coloured in India. And the puttees we are wearing came from India too. What do you think of that?"

"Hmm," said Mike. "So, they can be useful, after all! Wearing the old red and blue uniforms in South Africa was dangerous. We might have been dead by now!"

"As in the 1st Anglo-Boer War," said Joe, remembering his discussions with Fred McRae. "Oh, and the book had pictures of the Gurkhas too."

"What's that," asked Mike? "How many more strange things will you tell us, professor?"

Joe chuckled, saying, "The Gurkhas are special army regiments from Nepal, northern India. They wear dark green or khaki uniforms and little round hats. They arm them with rifles and curved knives called Khukuri. Vicious-looking blokes. The British Army took them in after the Gorkha War between the Gorkha Kingdom and the East India Company. Legend has it the Gorkhali soldiers made such a powerful impression on the British in battle, they recruited them into our army but called them Gurkhas by mistake."

"I'm looking forward to meeting those blokes," said Mike.

"Well, where we are going, you'll see lots, I suppose," said Joe.

"I wonder how many British soldiers are in India?" asked Mike

"Many," said Joe. "I've read dozens of British regiments and scores of Indian regiments with British commanders. And the Princely States have armies, too. It's a massive army!"

And such was the marras' introduction to yet another vast holding of the British Crown, an exotic land filled with amazing sights and smells for them to explore. It filled them with awe and anticipation of the exciting experiences still in India.

Wellington Cantonment and Barracks

At Wellington Barracks, the army sounded reveille at 6 A.M. or sunrise, whichever came first. That was when they hoisted the regimental colours. Since these rituals signalled the start of the daily training parade, they awakened the soldiers half an hour before reveille to wash and dress hastily. The parade ground was large and surrounded by six barrack buildings 100 yards each in length. They adorned the double-storey buildings with many arches, beyond which covered outer corridors ran the length of the buildings. In the centre of each building, facing the parade ground, were two staircases rising toward a single central landing on the top floor. It was an impressive barracks, typical of those erected at the height of British rule.

There was room for several battalions, with officers, NCOs, and other ranks quartered in varying comforts. Besides the dining room, they gave officers a bar complete with billiard and games rooms.

They claim that one Colonel, Sir Neville Chamberlain, but not the future Prime Minister, invented the now-famous snooker game in Ooty in 1875. He added the coloured balls to the fifteen red balls of pyramids, a favourite game. [7] The game became more involved, and they called players who missed tough shots 'snookers,' slang for recruits at the Woolwich Military Academy in south-east London. Chamberlain had various postings throughout India and introduced the game wherever he went. They stationed him in Madras from 1881 to 1885, and the game became popular at the Ootacamund Club. That is where he first developed the detailed rules. During a visit to India in 1885, the world billiards champion, John Roberts, sought Chamberlain to learn the snooker game. He then introduced the game to England upon his return. [8] Chamberlain was a famous snooker inventor and a distinguished soldier who served Lord Roberts in South Africa from December 1899 as First Aide-de-camp and Private Secretary, commended by Roberts in despatches from that war.

Back at Wellington, the soldiers spilt into the parade ground and lined up abreast in front of their building and behind their commanding officers. They raised the various regimental colours and the Jack to the national anthem sound, after which the battalions each began their marching exercises. They built one side of the barracks with a tunnel through which the troop columns could march into or out of the parade ground. This tunnel provided access to the cantonment's outside roads and sports fields. There were passages between the ends of each building through which troops could march.

After the parade, they dismissed the troops for a breakfast of beef and bread. The working day began after the exercises and a hearty meal in the belly. The men changed out of parade uniforms into their work clothes. Then, gathering in small groups, their corporals completed their daily tasks. They sent Joe and his marras to the Gymkhana Club to clean out the stables first. Later, they instructed them to scrape and paint the barns' wooden outer walls and doors. Although not raised to care for animals, they had grown up with horses in everything they did at work or on the streets of Jarrow. They had close and frequent contact with animals during their time in South Africa and had grown to respect and even love these magnificent creatures so familiar and vital throughout their world. They had a pleasant working day. And they were in peacetime! There were no sounds of explosions or attacks by fighters, no need to listen or look over one's shoulder for an approaching enemy. It was a strange feeling they only knew after being in a war. They soon settled into Wellington and felt at home in this peaceful environment so far from home.

"Howay, man! Now, this army life here appeals to me," said Mike.

"Whey, aye. As the soldiers say over here—cushy!" said Jack

"Cushy, aye. It's not a terrible life," said Joe. "Let's hope we have no more wars to fight while we're here. I have read the Pashtuns on the North-West Frontier are always causing troubles."

"Well, let's hope our regiment stays far from that," said Mike.

Then, after a shortened working day, the many sports fields of Wellington filled with excited soldiers. The army believed in keeping their troops fit through sport. They played hockey and soccer, which were favourite games in particular among the ranks, with polo or shooting and hunting the favourites among officers. Many matches had a mixture of officers and men. Sometimes there were competitions with Indian teams, for as long as the Indians didn't win!

Jackal hunting replaced fox hunting. Shooting as a sport was prevalent among officers of the British Army in India as in England, and there was lots of game. Pig-sticking, the wild boar hunt on horseback with a lance, was also a favourite and dangerous sport among officers.

The army organized sports such as gymnastics and running. As cricket declined and became less popular, badminton and lawn tennis gained popularity, and they converted many cricket grounds into badminton and tennis courts. [9]

They reserved afternoons after tea for various pastimes, including boxing, wrestling, gambling, reading, arts and crafts, and even knitting. A few soldiers developed their knitting skills as a source of extra income by selling sweaters, money belts, scarves, etc. [10]

The marras thus settled into their unfamiliar army environment with verve. It was beyond their wildest imaginings.

The Marra's Introduction to Two Boer POW Camps in India

But just when the marras thought they had left the South African War behind them forever, the 1/DLI assigned them to a work party to clean up or dismantle the empty Boer POW camps in the region.

The British captured 32,500 Boers during that war. Because of security concerns over keeping them in South Africa, they sent 24,000 abroad to camps in St Helena, Ceylon, Bermuda and 17 encampments in India, which imprisoned over 9,000. The first batch arrived in Bombay on the 23rd of April

1901, with the last group coming on the 28th of May 1902, three days before they signed the peace agreement.

The Australians captured the older brother of Deneys Reitz, Joubert, in the eastern Transvaal in late 1900 and exiled him to a POW camp in Bermuda, where he remained for three years. He wrote a poem on the grief and longing of the Boers sent to these camps, forts and jails in Natal, the Cape Coast, St. Helena, Bermuda, Ceylon and India as prisoners of war:

> *The Searchlight*
> *When the searchlight from the gunboat*
> *Throws its rays upon my tent*
> *Then I think of home and comrades*
> *And the happy days I spent*
> *In the country where I come from*
> *And where all I love are yet.*
>
> *Then I think of things and places*
> *And of scenes, I'll ne'er forget*
> *Then a face comes up before me*
> *Which will haunt me to the last*
> *And I think of things that have been*
> *And happiness that's past*
> *And only then did I realize*
> *How much my freedom meant*
> *When the searchlight from the gunboat*
> *Cast its rays upon my tent.* [11]

In January 1901, St John Brodrick, Secretary of State for War, wrote to the India Office asking whether it was possible to set up a POW camp on the Nilgiri plateau as the camps in St. Helena and Ceylon were full. Lord Curzon was not pleased with this proposal. He informed the India Office that the site earmarked for the POW camp had an inadequate water supply and frequent diseases such as typhoid. He suggested the War Office look at other places in the Bombay and Madras Presidencies. So, the British established three more camps in the Madras Presidency: Bellary, Kaithy-Nilgiris (Ketti) and Trichinopoly (Tiruchirappalli).

They opened the camp near Ketti, in a valley between Ooty and Coonoor, late in the war on the 15th of May 1902 and closed it on the 5th of August 1902. They sent 821 inmates to a parolees' camp in Wellington before sending them home to South Africa.

The Boers, housed in corrugated iron huts, described Kaithy-Nilgiris as cold and damp. Camp authorities, who weren't strict, gave them the same rations as the British troops and the prisoners could buy alcohol. The camp commandant reported they behaved well as prisoners, with only occasional cases of drunkenness. But while the Boer PoWs survived the rigours and disease of the war in Africa, several died by contracting typhoid, and they were buried in the windswept cemeteries of the Nilgiris. [12]

After the war, most of the camps closed. But the army waited several months before checking on them. So, when Joe's work party arrived, they found it occupied by local vagrants. Once, proud Boer fighters had languished here, far from their South African farms. Now, Joe's group saw creatures of the lowest Indian castes seeking refuge in these vacated huts. On seeing this, the corporal in charge barked out his orders.

"Right, men, let's get rid of the vermin in this camp before we clean it."

They charged in and started the unpleasant task of chasing the wretched occupiers out of the huts.

"What's the army doing with these huts?" asked Joe.

"That's none of our business, soldier," said the corporal. "Get on with it."

"These are only fit for pigs," said Mike, laughing. "So, maybe that's what the army wants to use them for—pig farming."

Most vagrants ran for their lives, but a few refused to leave. The corporal grabbed a spade that the work party had brought and threatened the stubborn ones with a cracked skull if they refused to budge.

"You bloody swine," he yelled, raising his spade. "Get the hell out of here."

Soon, they were scattering to the winds, allowing the men to get on with the disagreeable task of cleaning up their excrement and rubbish behind the huts.

"There are toilets and ablution huts over there. Why didn't they use them?" asked Mike.

"Aye, but I reckon they don't know what the toilets are for," said Joe. "We've been seeing many of these people on the sides of the roads here. They don't seem to have anywhere to live. So how would they know how to live in huts?"

"Oh, look at that lassie over there, my friends," said Mike, pointing toward a young Indian girl. "I reckon there's beauty beneath that dirt. Can we take her home to clean her?"

"Are ye out of your mind, private?" asked the corporal. "Ye can't touch these people. They call them untouchables for a reason, you know."

It took a few days for the work party to clean up the camp, after which the corporal said they were transferring by train to another encampment a distance away. The army created a Ketti camp guard duty to keep the vagrants away while they decided what to do with it.

The following week, the British soldiers embarked on the Nilgiri Mountain Railway back to Mettupalayam, and from there on, by train, they went to Trichinopoly [13] 145 miles away.

Trichinopoly POW Camp differed from Kaithy-Nilgiris. To begin with, Trichy, as they called it, was on the plain 200 miles south of Madras and only 300 feet above sea level, so it was hotter and more humid than Wellington year round, but in summer, the temperatures rose into the high 90s and low 100s. The huts were long thatched barracks with separate doors leading into sizeable rooms every 8 to 10 yards. At first, the camp only housed 500 POWs, but they later enlarged it to accommodate 480 men in an area of 550 x 300 yards. They closed the encampment on the 10th of September 1902, when they sent 437 irreconcilables, who refused to sign the oath of allegiance, north-west to Bellary, another POW camp for 821 prisoners from May 1901 and August 1902. The last group of POWs at Trichy only left in October 1902. One can deduce their treatment at Trichy was decent from a positive thank-you note the POWs handed to the camp commandant Major Ivatt on the 20th of October 1902.

When Joe's work party arrived at the end of November, a few freed Boers were still living in the camp, and they had opted to stay on to try their luck in India. Joe and his marras found time to socialize and exchange experiences with the Boers.

"Hello, I'm Joe. Why are you still here?"

"We have no one to go back to," said one. "No farm either. Your army destroyed everything."

"Aye, we know about that," said Joe, feeling guilty. "Sorry, but your fighters refused to stop fighting. We are just soldiers and didn't make the rules of war. Our generals and yours did that."

"Yes, I know. It was a disaster," said the Boer. "I'm not blaming you. It should never have happened. But it did, and now, here we are. We speak English, have nothing to return to, our families are dead, and we are staying in India and want to make an alternative life here."

"What's your name?" asked Joe.

"Jacques," said the Boer. "Jacques de Vos, but you Brits can call me Jack."

"Well, Jacques, we have a Jack amongst us, so we'll stick with Jacques," said Joe.

Then Mike and Jack introduced themselves, as did the rest of the work party. The corporal remained aloof and introduced himself as "Corporal Williams."

"It's over," said Jacques. "So, we find ourselves together here in southern India. You English rulers and we lost Boers, so far from our homes, how about that?"

"Aye, here we are together," said Joe. "Who would have thought?"

"Where have you come from?" asked Jacques.

"If you mean here in India, we're from Wellington, near Coonoor," said Joe. "It's in the Nilgiri Mountains, so it's not as hot here. And it's comfortable there. You should come and see it."

"I might do that," said Jacques. "I want to look around more."

Jacques impressed Joe. Even though he was a Boer and an old enemy, he had a pleasant disposition, and Joe concluded he could get on well with him.

"We're in the Wellington Barracks," said Joe. "So, if you get to Coonoor, look for us."

When they finished their work at Trichy, Joe's work party returned to Wellington and its usual work routine.

The 1903 Delhi Coronation Durbar

Back in Wellington, one day in early 1903, the soldiers discovered a few newspapers and journals, such as *The Illustrated London News,* circulating the barracks that portrayed and described an elaborate event the British Raj had just held called the Delhi Coronation Durbar. They marvelled at the magazines' black and white photographs and colour illustrations. There were pictures of an elephant procession through lines of uniformed soldiers with white pith helmets in front of an extended covered stand for the visiting dignitaries. Joe explained the photos from their captions for those who couldn't read.

"Look at those elephants wearing large golden coats," said Mike. "Are they covered with jewels? Look."

"Aye," said Joe, "they are; look at how the aristocrats are riding on top of them in chairs with umbrellas to protect them from the sun."

"Look at the Indian soldiers walking next to them," noted Jack. "Can you believe their fancy uniforms?"

"Look here, a picture of them moving past a fort in the distance," said Mike. "What do you suppose that is?"

"Aye. It says here the procession came out from Delhi, past the Red Fort to Coronation Park, where they held the ceremony," said Joe. "Look at that elephant at the front with the fancy guards carrying Lord Curzon and his wife."

The Viceroy of India, Lord Curzon, led the 1903 Coronation Durbar spectacle on the 1st of January 1903 in Delhi called the Delhi Durbar. They held it to celebrate Edward VII and Alexandra of Denmark as Emperor and Empress of India two years after the death of Queen Victoria. This durbar was a mass assembly at the new Coronation Park.

"So, what is a durbar?" asked Mike

"They say here that it's an Indian court," said Joe, "where the king and his aristocrats and dignitaries meet. So, the Delhi Durbar is the Delhi Court."

"So, where is the king?" asked Mike. "No pictures of King Edward!"

"They say here he didn't come," said Joe.

To Curzon's frustration and disappointment, Edward VII did not attend but sent his brother, Prince Arthur, Duke of Connaught, the seventh child and third son of Queen Victoria and Prince Albert. He arrived in Delhi by train from Bombay with a mass of dignitaries. Curzon and his government came in the other direction from Calcutta, the capital of the British Raj, in 1903. The assembly awaiting them displayed the most magnificent jewels ever seen in one place. The Indian princes were each adorned with their most spectacular gems collected over centuries. Maharajahs came with great retinues from every corner of India. Massed ranks of the Indian armies, under their Commander-in-Chief Lord Kitchener, paraded, played their bands and restrained the crowds of ordinary people. [14]

"Look, there's Lord Kitchener," called Mike. "I'd recognize that bastard anywhere."

The first Imperial Durbar took place on the 1st of January 1877 to proclaim Queen Victoria as Empress of India. The 1st Earl of Lytton, the Viceroy of India at the time, attended along with maharajas, nawabs and intellectuals, culminating in transferring control of much of India from the British East India Company to the British Crown. That Durbar was a restricted event without the widespread appeal of later durbars.

The Raj celebrated the 1903 Durbar with an even grander ceremony. It was a spectacular and elaborate festival organized by Curzon's government and attended by a much broader audience, including the public. Lord Curzon designed the two full weeks of festivities in precise detail. [15] It was a show of power, pomp and split-second timing. In a few months at the end of 1902, it transformed a deserted plain outside Delhi into an elegant tented city. This vast complex of accommodation was complete with a temporary light railway to bring dignitaries and crowds of spectators out from Delhi. It had a post office with its stamp, a police force with uniforms designed for the event, and telephone and telegraphic facilities. There were various stores, a hospital and a magistrate's court, and sophisticated sanitation, drainage and electric light installations. They sold souvenir guidebooks and maps of the camping ground. They exploited marketing opportunities such as striking the first Delhi Durbar Medal, firework displays, exhibitions and glamorous dances.

On the first day, the Lord and Lady Curzon entered the festivities at the head of a long procession that included a line of maharajahs and Indian princes riding bejewelled elephants. They held the Durbar ceremony itself on New Year's Day. They followed it with many polo days and other sports, dinners, balls, military reviews, bands and exhibitions. Newspapers worldwide dispatched their best journalists, artists and photographers to cover proceedings. They now credit the popularity of movie footage of the event, shown in makeshift cinemas throughout India and the empire, with launching India's film industry. [16]

They culminated the celebrations with a grand coronation ball attended only by the highest-ranking guests, reigned over by Lord Curzon in his elaborate dress uniform and Lady Curzon in her glittering jewels and regal peacock gown. [17] The stunning Mary Victoria Curzon, Baroness Curzon of Kedleston, was a lovely British peeress who, as with Winston Churchill's mother Jenny, came from a wealthy American family—the Leiters. As the Vicereine of India, she held the highest official title in the history of any American woman up to her time.

As far as the soldiers could tell, the pageantry outstripped even the Royals' pomp in London.

"The only place you can see elephants in England is in zoos," said Joe.

"Where could you see so many jewels?" asked Mike.

"Well, our King has his crown jewels," said Joe. "However, I don't think he has as many as were at this durbar."

"So many jewels, so much wealth," grumbled Mike. "All collected from the hard work of men like you and me and the poor Indians we have seen everywhere."

So, once again, there was grumbling among the common folk in India. And at home, they complained about the outrageous extravagance of the British Raj and Aristocracy. The exotic grandeur of this Indian ceremony had impressed the marras and many of their fellow soldiers, but the extravagance angered them. They later learned that the 1903 Delhi Durbar cost the Indian Government £1,000,000, an unimaginable sum for them. [18]

Although many criticized the viceroy for the excesses and cost of the Durbar, a few even calling the 1903 event the "Curzonation Durbar," the public viewed it far and wide as a spectacular success for the British Empire. But the *Hindoo Patriot* called the 1903 durbar "an extravagant waste" and considered its exhibition nothing more than a "symbol of Britain's power and glory in the East." [19]

But the Raj did not invite the 1/DLI to take part in this grand spectacle, which disappointed them.

~

Precarious Encounters

The marras concluded that life was agreeable for the British soldier in India, so far at least, as long as no uprisings or wars started. After South Africa, it was a paradise for the ordinary soldier. Regardless of religion, Thursdays, Sundays, and other holy days were off-duty, valued by those with a few spare pence. Outside the boundaries of the cantonment, all hell could break loose! Beer and gin, the latter called "satinette" or "white satin," were cheap and plentiful, and the men were thirsty and filled with sexual urges. Across India, bars and brothels sprang up around cantonments to satisfy the soldiers' lust and empty their pockets. Wellington was no different. Prostitutes were many and exotic for the troops who, once plied with enough beef and beer, filled the brothels well into the night. [20]

For the South African contingents arriving in India, "beef, beer and lust" was a revelation. There had been no room for such extravagance in the field during the war in South Africa. Beef for hunger, yes, sometimes. Beer for thirst, seldom. But they could never satisfy their lusts because of the shortage of accessible women in the wild expanses of that country. Even Majesfontein was free of passion for most of the 10,000 men stationed there. But despite the warnings, the marras looked forward to their first foray into Coonoor, where they opened their minds to fun and satisfaction, not to the potential dangers.

"Right, lads, are you ready for our first outing into town?" asked Mike enthusiastically.

"For sure," said Jack. "I'm ready when you are! Joe?"

"Try to stop me," said Joe.

"Are you ready for sweet chocolate ladies, Joe?" asked Mike.

"No, Mike, I'll give them a miss. I'll wait until my Jenny arrives for warm female comfort."

"Ah, come on, Joe. Don't be a shirker," teased Mike.

"I'll partake in a wee bit of drinking and socializing. Although I'm sure the pubs won't have any Newcassel Broon over here," said Joe. "But I'll give the chocolate ladies a wide detour. I have heard they can be dangerous to your health."

They met this last comment with loud derision and laughter as the marras and many of their fellow soldiers sauntered out in their finery at 11 A.M. into a warm, sun-filled day. They didn't get far, stopping at the first bar they found a few hundred yards along the road toward Coonoor. They pushed through the swing doors into a dark, smoke-filled room that reeked of old beer and body odour, where loud shouting, laughter and singing welcomed them. Forcing their way to the bar, they ordered their first round of many. Then, they settled back into a vacant bench and table. They sipped their beer and took in the surroundings once their eyes had adjusted to the darkness. After a short while, the first young ladies emerged from the gloom. Long manes of pitch-black hair tumbling the length of their backs dramatized their slight Indian features.

"Aye, now I'm more at home," shouted Mike. "In a pub with women and alcohol and other goodies, so far from Tyneside."

"Aye, me too," said Jack.

"Not the Rolling Mill," said Joe, referring to their favourite pub back in Jarrow, "or any other English pub I know, but it'll do."

"Aye, well, we had brown ale there, but not these lovely chocolate sweethearts here," joked Mike, drooling.

"Give it a rest, Mike," said Joe. "You have the entire day and night for that. Let's first enjoy a few of these good Indian beers together!"

"Aye, excellent idea, aye," said Mike. "I've got to get used to this Indian beer before I try these Indian girls."

After a while and several beers, they adapted to the noise, although they could only communicate by yelling.

"So, we are halfway around the world protecting the British Empire," said Mike and then guffawing.

"Well, not here in this pub," said Joe.

"What do you mean, Joe?" asked Jack. "Are we not protecting the empire from these dangerous beauties here?"

They all laughed.

"Aye, and what a joy being in this wonderful country," said Mike as he slumped back on the bench with his beer raised, ignoring the foolish conversation.

"Lots of sunshine, excellent brew, women and no war," said Jack.

"Aye, I have to agree with that, lads. And I'm the one who convinced my marras to join me on this adventure," said Joe. "Aren't you glad I did that?"

"Aye, you did, you did, Joe," said Mike. "We're grateful for that. But remember too that we made our own decisions on that. Think of it; we could be hammering rivets back in the cold and wet of Tyneside right now. Instead, we're in an exotic land with excellent accommodation, wonderful food, decent beer and chocolate ladies. Ooh, what a pleasure!"

"It sure beats the tents and field food of South Africa," said Joe while ignoring Mike's last comment. "The lust is taking over Mike," he thought to himself.

As the evening wore on, the conversation between the marras and everyone else in the bar became slurred, louder and incomprehensible. Mike and Jack edged towards two young ladies next to the bar. Then Joe slipped out of the noisy gloom of the bar into the murk of a moonless and mist-filled night. He then weaved his way back to the barracks. The weather in Wellington was pleasant; the monsoons had passed, and the temperatures in November and December hovered day and night around a comfortable 70°F. So, it was a lovely, meandering stroll. It had been an exotic first outing, although he was still somewhat concerned for his marras' wellbeing. Just before dawn, they stumbled back into barracks with a few 1/DLI companions and headed for the ablutions to freshen up before reveille. They would catch up on sleep the following night.

That first night defined a behavioural ritual that continued in India whenever the lads had a few pence burning holes in their pockets. Between these debauched outings, they whiled away their dull but restful days in the barracks or explored the sights of Wellington, Coonoor and Ooty on their free days. Joe waited for his sweet Jenny to join him on such explorations. He was missing her!

~

Jenny Joins Joe at Wellington

Jenny arrived in India in mid-February 1903. She took up her post at once at the vast Wellington Military Hospital, a quick walk from the barracks on the opposite side of the major road. She and Joe met on that first afternoon.

"A young lady is waiting to see you at the road, Joe," piped up another nurse that Joe knew well from her frequent visits to the barracks.

"That must be my hinny," said Joe, and he rushed to meet her. As he rounded the barracks closest to the military hospital, he saw her and stopped awhile. She stood as if at attention in her nurse uniform. Her feet pressed together, and her arms folded to meet in front of her long white apron while she beamed from ear to ear. He rushed forward and embraced her. She felt so good and smelt so good! He kissed her long and hard; she tasted so good, too! She was not just a mirage and was with him at last. With that, they wandered off to find a quiet spot where they could be alone together, catch up on the news and enjoy each other's company again.

"I'm so glad to be with you again, Joe," gushed Jenny.

"That's for sure, dear Jenny. I am a whole man again, too," said Joe with genuine affection.

"Now, please, God, your regiment doesn't move on again," she said. "I don't know whether the army will allow too many more of my moves in peacetime."

"Was that a warning?" Joe asked himself. "I hope not, too, Jenny, but I can't guarantee that. The army does whatever it pleases and cares little about the loves and lives of us soldiers. But let's not worry about that now. We are back together again in this exotic country. And it's in peacetime. Let's make the most of it while it lasts!"

Jenny agreed, and Joe brought her up to date on his journey from South Africa to Wellington, and Jenny did the same. She told him how the British were still helping the Boers recover their farms. She said Jan Marais, the junior Boer soldier that Joe and his fellow guards at the blockhouse had saved from starvation, dropped in to see her. He sent his greetings to Joe and the others. She told him Jan had returned to his farm and his parents had returned home alive. Joe was proud of that act of kindness during wartime and pleased to know Jan, his parents, and South Africa were returning to normal. They discussed their future together, and when Jenny found a private room in the hospital that night, they spent the night together. They could do that here with no worries. India was a relaxed place compared to what they lived through during wartime, and Jenny had the full support and cover of her new colleagues.

"But I'm just a wee bit worried of me marras going too much astray," said Joe. "They have become wild and careless, particularly with the local ladies."

"Oh, dear," said Jenny. "In my briefing this morning, I heard most of the soldiers in this hospital are suffering from venereal disease. They have assigned me to those wards, so I may meet them again there."

Venereal diseases were a massive problem for the British Army in the nineteenth and twentieth centuries. When Lord Kitchener became Commander-in-Chief India in 1902, he ensured that officers paid enough attention to the consequences of these diseases. Kitchener, who had never desired a woman, felt that drink and idleness led men to impure thoughts. It was commanders' duty to ensure they kept their men busy and out of temptation.

After breakfast on the Sunday following Jenny's arrival, they attended a St. George's Garrison Church service. The British built this church and hospital in 1885 as a place of worship for the troops stationed there. It was the largest church in the district, accommodating up to 600 persons. Its impressive buttressed-style structure had the outer walls of the lower floor painted in red with seven white peaked gables framing stained glass windows on either side. They decorated the front of the church in white with three tall red doors beneath a round stained glass window with three more peaked stained glass windows above that. They painted the corrugated iron roof red, too, and it had a lofty spire with an imposing cross at the top. The interior was adorned by imported oak choir stalls, pulpits, and brass altar railings from England. Known for its perfect acoustics, St George's had a magnificent pipe organ imported from England and erected from 1900 to 1902 in memory of Her Majesty Queen Victoria. When played, the music reverberated and filled the church, and residents heard it throughout the cantonment.

"That is such a grand church, Joe," said Jenny as they exited the service. "It's as impressive as any of our churches in England."

"Aye, you don't expect something like that out here, do you?"

"That was a lovely service," said Jenny, "The organ and army choir were excellent!"

"They were wonderful singers, weren't they?" said Joe, not knowing what more to say.

After the church service, they changed into more comfortable attire and walked to Droog Fort. Bakasura Malai is a historic fort used as an outpost by

Tipu Sultan in the eighteenth century. It is located nine miles outside Coonoor at 6,000 feet elevation. The fortress was in ruins, with only one wall remaining, but to Joe and Jenny, it was impressive. The ruins reminded them of the monastery ruins in Jarrow. Droog Fort is an ideal spot to survey the valley far below and even the houses and churches of Coonoor.

Joe and Jenny learned from a visiting historian that Tipu Sultan, the Tiger of Mysore, was a ruler of the Kingdom of Mysore from 1782 to 1799. Tipu introduced administrative innovations during his rule, including coins, a new calendar and a land revenue system that ushered in the growth of the Mysore silk industry. They consider him a pioneer in rocket artillery. He deployed the iron-cased Mysorean rockets against the British forces and their allies in their 1792 and 1799 Sieges of Srirangapatna. Legend has it that in Tipu Sultan's last battle with the British, his French military advisers had pleaded with him to escape through secret passages. Tipu said, "One day of life as a tiger is far better than a thousand years of living as a sheep." The British shot the Tiger of Mysore that day as he rushed into the breach.

"Those were interesting and exciting times," said Joe. "Just imagine those Indian soldiers under Tipu Sultan fighting a British army far superior to them, and they were brave men."

"Yes, and stupid as always! Why are men going to war so often?" asked Jenny.

"They follow their leaders, fighting for lands, power, riches or revenge. It's always the same."

"Well, that doesn't make them any smarter," she concluded. And with that, the conversation moved to more pleasant talk as they strolled home.

"That was a magical day, Joe," she said as they approached the barracks.

"Oh, I agree, hinny. I loved our day together. Let's do that often."

And so began an incredible period in Joe's life. Every evening and night, as they finished their working day, and every Sunday, they were together. Apart from morning parades, work parties, and occasional excursions, Joe's marras saw little of him except at work. He was in love and enjoying every minute of every day. Joe and Jenny spent hours together talking, laughing, and exploring every corner of their adopted new home—Wellington, the hill stations of Coonoor and Ooty, and surrounding areas. They toured on foot, on borrowed bicycles and by train. The couple came to love the allure of the region and the gentle, hard-working people who, despite their poverty and daily suffering, always smiled and laughed and greeted them as if they were part of the family. They trekked the nearby hiking trails, discovering magnificent vistas and temples, and sampled the exotic but delicious local fare cooked and served at the roadside as they went on their journeys.

Jacques Arrives in the Nilgiris

One day, a few weeks later, Jacques de Vos, the Marras' new Boer mate from Trichy, showed up with friends in Ooty. He and two other freed Boer POWs who weren't ready to return to South Africa had followed Joe's advice to escape the heat of the plains. Jacques and his fellows explored the area for a few days to get their bearings, and then Jacques bumped into Joe and Jenny near Wellington.

"Hello, Joe," called Jacques from across the road. "What a coincidence finding you here."

"Hello, Jacques," said Joe. "It's not a coincidence. You followed my advice, I see."

"Yes, I'm escaping the heat. Just as you English do," said Jacques. "You were right. It's much more pleasant up here. Two of my fellow inmates followed me here too, and it reminds me of the eastern Transvaal Drakenberg."

"I've been there, Jacques, and I agree with you. Meet my friend, Jenny," said Joe. "She is a British Army nurse and followed me here from South Africa; she and I are from the same town in England."

"Pleased to meet you, Jacques," said Jenny. "It's hard to believe we were enemies a short time ago."

"It's a pleasure meeting you too, Jenny. And yes, it's wonderful the war is over, don't you think?"

"That's for sure. Joe told me he had met a few Boer POWs at Trichy. It's so strange meeting you here, our old enemy. Well, not my enemy—as nurses, we care for everyone, not just our soldiers. When and where were you captured?"

"They captured me a few weeks before the war ended. I was with a commando under the command of General Christiaan de Wet in the Orange Free State near Bethlehem. The English caught over 300 of us. Joe and I discussed it the other day. He was there too, and we almost met on opposite sides when he was on the blockhouse line there. That was in April, but the war had almost ended when we arrived in Trichy. So, I haven't been a prisoner for long."

"Were you treated well in the camp?"

"Yes, Jenny. We were in dire condition when they caught us. But the English at the camp treated us well. British Army doctors examined us, and medics helped us overcome our ailments. We ate well and had time to rest. Our guards knew the war was almost over, so they looked after us. That impressed me. Then, they freed us POWs once the war ended. The British Army shipped most of the POWs home, but a few of us stayed. Our families died in the war, and we didn't know what to do with ourselves in South Africa. So, we are staying here for a while. The British Army gave us money to get home when we wanted. They were very generous."

"I'm glad to hear that," said Jenny. "What are your plans here?"

"No plans," said Jacques. "I am here with two of my fellow POWs, and we have found decent lodging in Ooty for very little money. Joe told us about the pleasant weather, so we thought we'd visit you. We will look for work when we have used up our money. For now, we just want to explore and enjoy our freedom again. And after three years of war, we are looking forward to peacetime."

"Aye, well, you are no longer an enemy of the British, so you are most welcome here," said Joe. "You are most welcome to explore with us."

When they next met, Jenny invited a fellow nurse to join them. Her name was Alice, and she and Jacques hit it off at once. Jacques was a tall and good-looking man. And he possessed the Afrikander courteousness that impressed Alice and Jenny alike. Alice was an attractive young woman who had been nursing with Jenny in South Africa and then transferred to Wellington. So, out of curiosity more than anything, she agreed to join Jenny, Joe and Jacques on this Sunday outing. And it soon became a recurring event.

Through the following weeks and months, they explored the surroundings of Wellington and Coonoor, sometimes together as a group or alone as couples. They visited Dolphin's Nose, six miles from Coonoor, where they saw a view of Catherine Falls, a double-cascaded 250-foot waterfall in Kotagiri, the second-highest of the Nilgiri Mountains. As they climbed to the top of Dolphin's Nose, they could see both falls on their descent into the deep valley. They visited Lamb's Rock, five miles from Coonoor, with its spectacular view of the tea plantations and the distant Coimbatore plains.

On another day, they visited Laws Falls, six miles from Coonoor on the roadway to Mettupalayam. This thirty-foot waterfall on the Coonoor River tumbles through multiple cascades in the forest, with its vast stretches of undisturbed nature. Changing into their bathing costumes, they languished in the pool, enjoying the force of the water on their bodies where the falls plunged into the pool. They were on their own, so the couples slipped out of the water, separated and found concealed moss beds nearby, where they chatted and became intimate.

On another occasion, they wandered into the nearby Upper Bhavani. Thick forests and untouched wild habitats abound with wildflowers such as magnolias, orchids and rhododendrons. They had heard wildlife in the Upper Bhavani, including tigers, leopards, jackals, jungle cats, wild dogs, sambhar, giant squirrels, and Nilgiri langurs. But most of these magnificent creatures stayed out of sight to the casual visitor.

At this beguiling place, they encountered a holy man—a sadhu who had renounced the worldly life. He was daunting with a painted face, long entangled white beard and hair, and colourful robes covered in dust. He was squatting barefoot near a small temple. The sadhu talked to no one and didn't flinch when offered food or money. The Indian passers-by showed much respect for him, but Joe and Jenny only passed him by without an offering. He didn't react to that snub either.

"We've seen nothing like that in England or South Africa," said Jenny.

"Aye. Sadhus are Hindu religious men. We saw a few of them as we were coming here, and we don't have any of those back at home," said Joe. "But I heard Hindus are in South Africa, in Natal, they say. I remember reading that the Indians in Natal had volunteered in an ambulance corps during the war there."

"He didn't even notice us," said Jenny. "He was far away in his holy place, far above us human beings here on earth."

On another Sunday, they prepared a picnic and explored the enchanting Pykara Lake, village and river region twelve miles from Ooty. The local Toda people consider the Pykara River very sacred. It rises at Mukurthi Peak and flows over more cascades known as Pykara Falls. The last two falls are 180 feet and 200 feet in height. There, they discovered the vast grassy meadows and abundant wildlife habitats of the Toda settlements. The Toda people are a small pastoral tribal community whose men and women dress in uniform white, grey and red-striped robes and live on the isolated Nilgiri plateau. They live in traditional settlements comprising three to seven tiny thatched houses constructed like beehives. The Toda have scattered their communities across the pasture slopes of the hills, on which they tend their domestic buffalo. They base their entire economy on the buffalo, from which they trade dairy products with the neighbouring peoples of the Nilgiri Hills. The buffalo is sacred to them and central to the Toda religion, so they carry out rituals of milk activities and the ordination of dairymen-priests. They compose and chant complex poetic songs of the cult of the buffalo in their religious and funerary rites. Brothers share wives, including having equal sexual access to them. The Toda are peaceful folk, so Joe's group could easily pass through their lands.

After a pleasant picnic lunch, Jacques and Alice, who had grown fond of each other, wandered off independently. Joe and Jenny remained behind and enjoyed each other's company as always.

"Imagine. Such a peaceful and industrious people living and trading in such a perfect place," said Joe.

"Those people are amazing. They're so calm in this environment." Said Jenny, "I am full of admiration for them too."

"I wonder if our ancestors lived that way before the factories arrived? They were farming people."

"Maybe. But I don't think it was as tranquil or peaceful in ancient England."

And so, the months slipped past. The army called away Joe and his marras from time to time for one or other army duty, but this happened seldom. While they were absent, Jenny sometimes joined Alice and Jacques on their wanderings.

Meanwhile, Mike and Jack kept up their debauched lifestyles in the brothels of Coonoor and paid the price. They soon ended up in Jenny's and Alice's ward at the military hospital in a horrible physical state, sores covering their entire bodies. Joe visited his marras at the hospital after they admitted them for crabs, pubic lice and gonorrhea. They looked horrible, with nasty sores around their mouths, eyes, and entire bodies, including out-of-sight ulcers and pain in their genitals. They were miserable in their suffering. Joe was as caring as ever and refrained from saying, "I told you so," saying instead, "Jenny will soon have you back to normal laddies that I can promise you. You are lucky you don't have syphilis, which can be deadly." They talked for hours about their exploits. After that, the patients swore to return to a healthy and chastened lifestyle once cured. Joe doubted that but smiled without comment. Jenny checked in occasionally while on her rounds, providing them with various treatments. They realized what they had missed as Joe described his and Jenny's excursions into the surrounding areas. They had also become mates of the Boer visitors and swore to catch up just as soon as they were out of the hospital. But alas, that never happened. The hospital released the patients only days before the next regimental move—a total shock to everyone!

The battalion received orders in October 1904 to transfer to Lucknow in northern India. Jenny heard of the next move before Joe could tell her, and even though she knew it was inevitable, she was angry.

"Where have you been?" she asked him. "Have you not heard the news of your regiment? When were you planning to tell me?"

"Jenny, hinny," he said, trying to appease her, "I was out for a work party, and we only just heard of it when we returned to barracks!"

Jenny was sobbing as he wrapped his arms around her to offer comfort.

"I don't want you to go," she cried. "We have been having such a wonderful time together here, and I don't want it to end."

"Nor do I, Jenny. I'm every bit as upset as you are," said Joe, attempting to console her. "I had hoped I could continue here with you until they released me to return home together."

But she was inconsolable and ran back to the hospital as a helpless and wretched Joe watched her disappear. What could he do? Would she calm down and follow him again? How he wished that she would. Jenny had been so loyal to him. She had followed him through South Africa and into India. They had enjoyed such beautiful days and nights together. And now it was to end? It devastated him.

That night, he sought her out, but she wasn't available. She had instead turned to Jacques for consolation and advice. Joe met Jacques the next day and told him the grim news.

"Please look out for Jenny, Jacques," said Joe. "She is very cross with me, but what can I do? The army has ordered us north, so I can't stay here without deserting. I won't do that and end up in jail."

"Yes, Joe. She told me all about it. It upset her, but she'll calm down," said Jacques. "I know she loves you. She told me that, so she'll follow you to Lucknow, you'll see."

"Well, I hope so. But why won't Jenny talk to me? It is not my fault. But please look out for her in the meantime."

"I'll do that with pleasure, my English friend."

Joe recognized the irony of asking a past enemy to look after his sweetheart. But Jacques was the only person Joe knew, apart from Jenny and Alice, who was staying behind in this beautiful part of the world. Jacques was a polite soul, whom even Mike had grown fond of, and he was a gentleman, so Joe had no qualms about leaving Jenny in his care.

Joe's Battalion Transfers to Lucknow

The force first travelled in two parties to Secunderabad in the Indian state of Telangana, on the opposite side of Hussain Sagar Lake and the city of Hyderabad. Hyderabad and Secunderabad have unique histories and cultures. In the nineteenth century, Hyderabad was the capital of the Nizams' princely state. The British founded Secunderabad in 1806 as a British cantonment. Winston Churchill served there in 1896 and fell in love with the daughter of the British Resident of Hyderabad - Pamela Plowden. [21]

Joe and the Durhams arrived on the 22nd of October 1904, but the battalion only spent a brief time in Secunderabad, continuing on the 24th of December 1904. Headquarters and four companies were entrained for Lucknow, the capital city of Uttar Pradesh and the site of the Lucknow Siege during the

Indian Mutiny of 1857. On the 6th of January 1905, the 1/DLI arrived at Lucknow. Four days later, the remaining four units joined them.

Lucknow was the largest city in Awadh, or Oude as the British called it, now in the modern Indian state of Uttar Pradesh. Lucknow is the anglicized spelling of the local pronunciation of 'Lakhnau.' It's another historical city of magnificent buildings of different architectural styles. They built these iconic buildings during both British and Mughal rule. There are religious buildings such as Imambaras [22], mosques, and other Islamic shrines and secular structures such as enclosed gardens, baradaris and palace complexes. More than half of these buildings lie in the old part of the city. Joe and his marras spent many free time hours exploring this famous city, although, for Joe, it was not the same as his outings with Jenny. His heart was aching.

The battalion camped at the Lucknow Barracks in the colder months from their arrival in January 1905 until March. Then, during the hotter months from April to September 1905, it moved to Naini Tal, a hill station northwest of Lucknow in the Kumaon foothills of the outer Himalayas. At 6,800 feet above sea level, the hill station sits in a tranquil valley containing a pear-shaped lake surrounded by mountains. From the tops of the higher peaks, magnificent views of the vast plain to the south or the many convoluted ridges lying north filled the panorama. Beyond them lies the enormous snowy range, which forms the central axis of the Himalayas. It was colder and wetter than on the plains, with an average rainfall of thirty-five inches from the southwest monsoon winds from July to mid-September and snowfalls in December and January.

∼

The letter

In September 1905, almost a year after leaving Wellington and while at Naini Tal, Joe received a letter from Alice.

Dear Joe,

I'm hoping you are well in the north of this grand country. I'm sure getting a letter from me will surprise you.

I don't know whether Jenny has written to you, but I am sure you would like to know how we are. So, I am writing to tell you everything is always well here. But things have changed, and I thought you might like to know.

Jacques and Jenny have taken a keen interest in each other, so I am not seeing him anymore. Jenny and I are still friends, and I can't hold anything against her. Jacques and I were friends and lovers but not linked formally. It was not your fault, but you left, and Jenny felt she needed male company.

So, there we are. Life takes these turns. Take care of yourself. I wish you well.

Yours, Alice.

It stunned Joe. But once he recovered from the shock, he realized it was inevitable. He had left her, even though it wasn't his fault. Jenny had a right to continue her life as she saw fit. But he had hoped she would wait for him, and they could still realize their plans to get together again back in Jarrow.

"We had many wonderful times together, in the Nilgiris in particular," he thought. "I loved her. And she followed me throughout South Africa. So, I believed she loved me. We had been apart before, and she always waited before now. Maybe she hadn't loved me? Or perhaps she had just become weary of following me again and again, damn Army? Or worse, tired of me?"

But Jacques had disappointed him, although he had his rights too.

"The Army runs my life," thought Joe. "There's nothing I can do about it. So, maybe Jenny isn't to be my life partner."

So, he was soon to head home alone. And Jenny and Jacques would do whatever they needed to do. He resigned to this reality and looked forward to his new life beyond the army back home on Tyneside.

The Battalion returned to Lucknow in October 1905 and stayed there until early March 1906. On the 12th of March 1906, Major-General Sir E. Locke Elliott inspected the 1/DLI. Sir Edward Elliot was a veteran of the Boer War and Inspector-General of the Cavalry in India from 1898 to 1904. As major-general, he commanded the Indian Army 8th Division from 1905. There were 22 officers and 874 non-commissioned officers and men on the parade that day. The battalion was approaching its full complement once more. This ceremonial parade was Joe's last ceremonial dress parade in India.

A Brief Visit to Kasauli in the Himalayas and Home

But before he left, he briefly visited his battalion in Kasauli, north of Delhi. Kasauli is another hill station and cantonment that the 1/DLI escaped during the hottest months from April to September. The British established Kasauli, which has a moderate climate, in 1842. They built a parsonage in 1850 for priests of the Anglican Church there, and they inaugurated the Anglican Christ Church of Kasauli on the 24th of July 1853.

But of more relevance for the soldiers was the Kasauli Brewery and Distillery. Edward Abraham Dyer established the Kasauli distillery and brewery, the first in India, long before the hill station in the late 1820s. Edward Dyer located his distillery there because of the clear spring water available. And at that altitude, the climate was like that of Britain. There was a ready market of British troops and civilians in Shimla for his products. His ambition was "to produce a malt whisky equalling Scotch whisky." He brought brewing and distilling equipment with him from England and Scotland. This paraphernalia came by sailing the ship as far up the Ganges River as possible. They then loaded it onto ox carts and muscled them up into the Himalayas via the route through Shimla.

Dyer started by making India Pale Ale and malt whisky. The original whisky brand of the Kasauli distillery was a well-regarded single malt named "Solan No 1." Named after the nearby town of Solan, Solan No 1 was the best-selling Indian whisky well into the twentieth century. It remains the only malt whisky made in the Himalayas.

Dyer's products weren't as expensive as the imported versions and proved popular with the British, who consumed them in enormous quantities. They became popular with Indians, too. The distillery was a favourite destination for the men and officers of the British Army in Kasauli; every Thursday evening, they opened the bar for a "tasting." The soldiers of His Majesty's service pursued perfection in these tasting sessions! In his temporary stay in Kasauli, Joe even developed a taste for the Kasauli India Pale Ale, replacing his favourite Newcastle Broons by necessity.

Joe, Mike and Jack spent one last Thursday night together before Joe left for England. They got off duty early, arriving at the brewery and distillery in time for a tour. Their hosts opened the pub doors, and a robust, ruddy-faced Scot dressed in full Scottish regalia, who introduced himself as Hamish MacTavish, greeted them.

"Welcome through our doors to our Himalayan paradise, laddies. What would yer names be?"

The marras introduced themselves, "Joe Rutherford. Mike O'Brien. Jack Williams. Pleased to meet you, Sir."

"Nay, yee don't have to call me Sir, soldier. Just call me Hamish. Go on in there and make yourselves at home. A bonnie wee lassie named Annie will fix you with one of our prize-winning Indian Pale Ales. We'll get you onto the hard Solan No. 1 whisky juice later," said the jolly, rotund Scot with a big laugh and a bigger heart.

A delightful buxom redhead lassie met them in a long tartan dress and white short-sleeved blouse. A tam cap made of the same tartan as her dress sat on her head.

"Welcome, laddies," she purred in the most delicate Scottish accent, "Sit ye doon on this bench and table, and I'll get yee the ales. Whit's yer names, laddies?"

The marras looked at each other in a semi-state of shock, not believing what they saw and heard. But they introduced themselves to Annie.

"Where on earth are we?" asked Mike.

"You're in a wee Scottish corner of the Indian Himalayas," said Annie. "Our wee paradise!"

They were the first to arrive that afternoon at the mile-high pub. Within no time, Annie appeared again with three foaming Indian Pale Ales, setting them before her recent friends. Then she sat too and asked them, "Whaur dae ye come fae?"

The same question in Geordie is, "Weor are yee from?" So the marras understood, and Joe said: "Jarrow, County Durham, across from Newcassel, Annie and yee?"

"Oh, I don't know it," said Annie. "Is it a pleasant place?"

"We used to think so, Annie," said Jack, "But after what we've seen over the last six years, including here, no."

"But it's home," said Joe.

"Aye, and I'm from Glasgow," she said. "So I know what you mean."

And so started a friendly conversation which put the friends at ease, assisted by the India Pale Ale, which they agreed was a great brew.

"We're with the Durham Light Infantry, Annie," said Mike with pride, a wink and a smile. "Joe here is returning to England after six years in South Africa and India, but we are staying longer."

"Well then, have a pleasant trip home, Joe," said Annie. "You laddies are welcome back here any time you'd wish." At that moment, another group of soldiers arrived, so Annie slipped off the bench and greeted her other recent visitors.

"What a lovely lassie," said Mike. "I will be back here for sure."

"Aye, and me too, Mike," said Jack, "to make sure you behave yourself."

That raised a laugh from his now more relaxed marras. The ales kept coming as more visitors arrived. Before too long, they packed the pub full. A few more bonnie wee lassies appeared to help Annie. With the burgeoning gathering of 'tasters,' the noise level increased. Then, without warning, the lassies sang *I Love A Lassie,* only written by Scottish singer Harry Lauder the year before and a big hit in Scotland.

Before long, the entire pub sang the song, holding their mugs of ale on high. The songs *'The Bonnie Banks o Loch Lomond'* and *'Auld Lang Syne'* followed, and so on. The lassies served everyone the first of many glasses of Kasauli's fine grain Himalayan whisky, Solan No. 1, and the singing went on deep into the evening.

Among the singers was a local Scottish tenor by the name of Alistair MacDougall, decked out in his red plaid kilt, complete with a belt, sporran, sgian-dubh[23], tartan socks, garters, kilt pins and clan badge. As the evening faded, Alistair reached the marras' bench and sat beside Mike.

"Another round, lassie," he called. And sure enough, another round appeared. By this late hour, they had become drunk, so the conversation wasn't very coherent. But in no time, Mike felt a Scottish hand exploring his leg and edging towards his crotch. Without thinking, Mike shouted, "What the hell are ye doing?" and swiped at Alistair with a powerful force, sending him flying back off the bench, his kilt spreading to the winds, revealing his pulsating caber.

The shouting drew the entire pub to that sight, sprawled in its glory in the smoky air. At first, hysterical laughter broke out, but then Alistair's mates wouldn't take the insult, napping. So they hauled him up and shoved Mike towards the now wide-open doors. As they exited the pub, the entire patronage joined them in the courtyard, spoiling for a fight. But the chilly Himalayan winds had descended upon the town. The cold, fresh air and alcohol ensured that the inebriated tasters were nothing more than a pile of collapsed flesh and bones on the cobbles. Finished for the night, they were in a safe place.

At that moment, Hamish reappeared. "Gentlemen, I thank yee most sincerely for your visit. Please ensure that you find your way home safe and sound, and don't forget to tell your mates about our good Kasauli India Pale Ale and our finest Solan No. 1 whisky. Guid luck, and here's tae ye!"

Hamish was the last and only man who raised a glass that night. Most of the others slept where they lay until the wee hours before finding their way home.

Kasauli Brewery and Distillery is still the highest brewery and distillery in the world and the oldest in India and Asia today.

The army released Joe from his duties at Kasauli in June 1906, and they sent him on his way to travel home and finish his military assignment in County Durham. Mike and Jack extended their stay by a few months until the battalion returned to Lucknow in October 1906. Mike had a grand time with Annie, and Jack found his wee Scottish lassie.

It was time for Joe to leave behind India's exotic landscapes, people, buildings, and customs, just as he had done when leaving Africa. But Jenny was not with him. Nor, from what Alice was saying in her most recent letter, would she be joining him in Jarrow soon. He travelled from Kasauli to Lucknow in the company of a small group of fellow Durhams and then on to Bombay by train, where they were to catch a steamer back to England. Saddened to leave behind his incredible experiences in the British Empire and Jenny, he was grateful for the past six exhilarating years but homesick and glad to be heading home.

The Return to Bombay

An unusual man accompanied Joe and his companions on the train trip to Bombay. He had the qualities of a gentleman but was travelling in Second Class. He was in his fifties, rotund, well-dressed in a three-piece suit and a wide-brimmed felt hat, and sporting an enormous handlebar moustache, he wore a monocle. Sitting with an elegant polished wooden cane with an elaborate ivory head in both hands in front of him, he looked most sophisticated, as though he could afford to be travelling First-Class Sleeper and seemed so out of place. As they sat down in the few empty seats they could find, Joe sat opposite the gentleman.

"Greetings, soldier," said the gentleman, tilting his hat. "On your way to Bombay? My name is Major Peyton, emeritus."

"Aye, Sir," said Joe, "that we are. We are heading home."

"Where is home?" he asked. "I'm sorry to be so audacious, but I'm just curious."

"For me, it's Jarrow, Sir," said Joe. "On Tyneside, County Durham."

One or two of the others responded, while the rest didn't. The major's persona and boldness took them aback.

"Where have you been, soldier," he asked, looking straight at Joe, "if you don't mind me asking?"

"Well," began Joe, "I was in South Africa during the Anglo-Boer War—Cape Colony, Orange Free State and the Transvaal. Then I was in India in Wellington, Lucknow, Naini Tal and Kasauli."

"Excellent, soldier. Protecting the Empire, eh? Excellent," he said with an enormous smile. "Well, we've got many hours to reach Bombay, so I'd love to hear about your adventures in our glorious Empire. I'm a writer, and I love an enjoyable story. So, tell me all about it. I'll arrange the drinks and eats."

They then settled into the journey while Joe recounted his many adventures in Africa and India. He gave his impressions of what he had seen and experienced and voiced his disappointment with war. He spoke for hours. Most of the time, the gentleman sat motionless, listening to every word and making comments or explanations from time to time. Then, as Joe drew to a close, he commended him again for his contributions to protecting the British Empire.

"You were right in your belief in our Empire and the need to protect it, soldier," the major began. "It's been a long time and a lot of effort and brilliance to get to where we are today. We started late. The Romans started long before us and even colonized England for a few hundred years. Genghis Khan created the mighty Mogul Empire, and other empires have arisen and vanished. In more recent times, the Spaniards and Portuguese began their empires before us, even dividing the world in two between them. But once we started in the sixteenth century, we expanded England's possessions while competing with the French, Spanish, Portuguese and Dutch. By the time Queen Victoria's reign was well underway in the 1860s, we had built an empire of over 8.5 million square miles. But in the last forty years, we have added another four million square miles to our British Empire. That is a big number and hard to comprehend, but our Empire is now 100 times the area of the British Isles. Even the great Russian Empire is smaller. We are now the greatest and wealthiest empire in the world. And what's even more amazing is that we have done that without significant wars—the American Revolution and South African War were the major exceptions. It has been a significant achievement, soldiers. A substantial success! So now we must protect it. And that's where they involve you, lads. Bless you, risking your lives to keep us safe."

"Thank you, Sir. But why must so many innocent people die?" asked Joe. "Thousands of women and children died in our camps in South Africa. I saw one such camp, and it was horrible."

"Sadly, that is one of the unfortunate side effects of war," said the major. "There are always innocent civilians who die during a war. But I know what you are discussing with the South African War, and I never agreed with that strategy. It has given us a terrible reputation at home, thanks to that woman Emily Hobhouse and worldwide. Most unfortunate. Most people don't realize that building an empire like ours is difficult. Not everyone agrees that we should grow and prosper together. The Boers and the American revolutionaries were fine examples of that. We meet resistance from time to time and have to quell their hostility. You understand that, don't you, soldier?"

"Aye, Sir," said Joe. "I can understand fighting between armies. But I don't understand why they involve innocent women and children."

"Yes, most unfortunate," repeated the major. "Hopefully, we learned from that."

They had travelled for many hours when nightfall came. The gentleman ordered drinks and food from an attendant, and they chatted for a while longer before becoming silent, and Joe fell asleep. Most of Joe's companion soldiers had either fallen asleep to the train rocking or moved off to seats elsewhere. Joe woke up during the night, seeing the major had disappeared.

The following day, after washing and a cup of tea with biscuits, the major reappeared refreshed, and the conversation continued.

"I hope you slept, soldier," he asked Joe.

"Aye, Sir. I did, thank you. And you?"

"Refreshed too, thank you. And looking forward to the rest of our trip together."

Joe looked out leisurely at the arid landscape they were moving through. They were travelling south-east through the state of Rajasthan.

"This looks like the Karroo of South Africa," said Joe. "Only drier and with more villages and people."

"Yes, soldier," said the major. "This is the Great Indian or Thar Desert. You will see magnificent palaces and fortresses along the way. Why they wanted to build them in this inhospitable place is a mystery to me. But then the whole of this country, no, the whole of Asia, is a mystery."

"Have you seen much of the Empire, Sir?" asked Joe.

"All of it, soldier," the major said. "I have travelled from the west of Canada to the Maritimes, through the Caribbean Islands, North, West, East and Southern Africa, Egypt, Arabia, Malta, Cyprus, India, Burmah, Hong Kong, Singapore, Australia, New Zealand and our possessions in the Pacific. I haven't seen everything by any means. But I've seen much of it."

"How can you do that, Sir? Is it your job?"

"Yes, I earn a living by writing about the British Empire and the people I've met. It's a wonderful job."

"Well, soldiering is a splendid job, too, if you can stay out of wars and not get killed," said Joe. "I suppose I could have seen more of the Empire if I stayed in the army. But it's time for me to go home."

"I wish you all the best in your fresh life, soldier," said the major. "Stay out of trouble."

"Aye, thank you, Sir," said Joe. "I will, and I'm looking forward to being with my family and old friends again. I'm longing for peacetime in England. And I'm hoping to get my old job back in the shipbuilding yards. I don't know what my life there has in store for me, but I'm keen to find out."

---

1. S.G.P Ward, *Faithful, The Story of the Durham Light Infantry*, 1962
2. Exhausted
3. Bed
4. HMS Birkenhead was wrecked off the southern tip of South Africa with the loss of over 400 soldiers in 1852. The sinking of the Birkenhead started the maritime tradition of ordering "women and children first" to save the few women and children of officers on that voyage.
5. Now Kannur in the south Indian state of Kerala
6. Now Kozhikode in the south Indian state of Kerala
7. Pyramid pool, also called pyramids, was a form of pocket billiards (pool) mainly played in the 19th century. It was one of several pool games that were popular at this time (so called because gamblers pooled their bets at the start of play). This game had fifteen red balls that were racked in a triangle.

8. Peter Ainsworth, *The Origin of Snooker: The Neville Chamberlain Story*, https://www.s-nookerheritage.co.uk/normans-articles/days-of-old/origins-of-snooker/
9. Byron Farwell, *Armies of the Raj*, Norton & Co, 1989
10. Ibid
11. Anglo-Boer War Museum, https://wmbr.org.za/ under Prisoners of War
12. Nina Varghese, *Prisoners' Tales From The Nilgiris*, 15 September 2016 https://blog.teabox.com/prisoners-tales-nilgiris
13. Now called Tiruchirappalli in the Indian state of Tamil Nadu
14. De Courcy Anne, *The Viceroy's Daughters: The Lives of the Curzon Sisters*, Harper Collins, 2003
15. Nayar, Pramod K., *Colonial Voices: The Discourses of Empire*. John Wiley & Sons., 2012
16. Holmes Richard, *Sahib: The British Soldier in India 1750-1914*, HarperCollins, 2006
17. Cory, Charlotte, Sunday Times, 29 December 2002, *The Delhi Durbar 1903 Revisited*
18. £120 million equivalent in 2018
19. Codell, Julie. "Gentlemen Connoisseurs and Capitalists . . . in the 1903 Delhi Durbar Exhibition of Indian Art." *Cultural Identities and the Aesthetics of Britishness*. Ed. D. Arnold. Manchester: Manchester UP, 2004..
20. Byron Farwell, *Mr. Kipling's Army, All the Queen's Men*, Norton & Co, 1981
21. KSS Seshan, *Where Churchill loved and lost*, The Hindu, Living Hyderabad History & Culture, 10 July 2017
22. A congregation hall for Shia commemoration ceremonies, especially those associated with the Remembrance of Muharram.
23. A small, single-edged knife worn as part of traditional Scottish Highland dress along with the kilt.

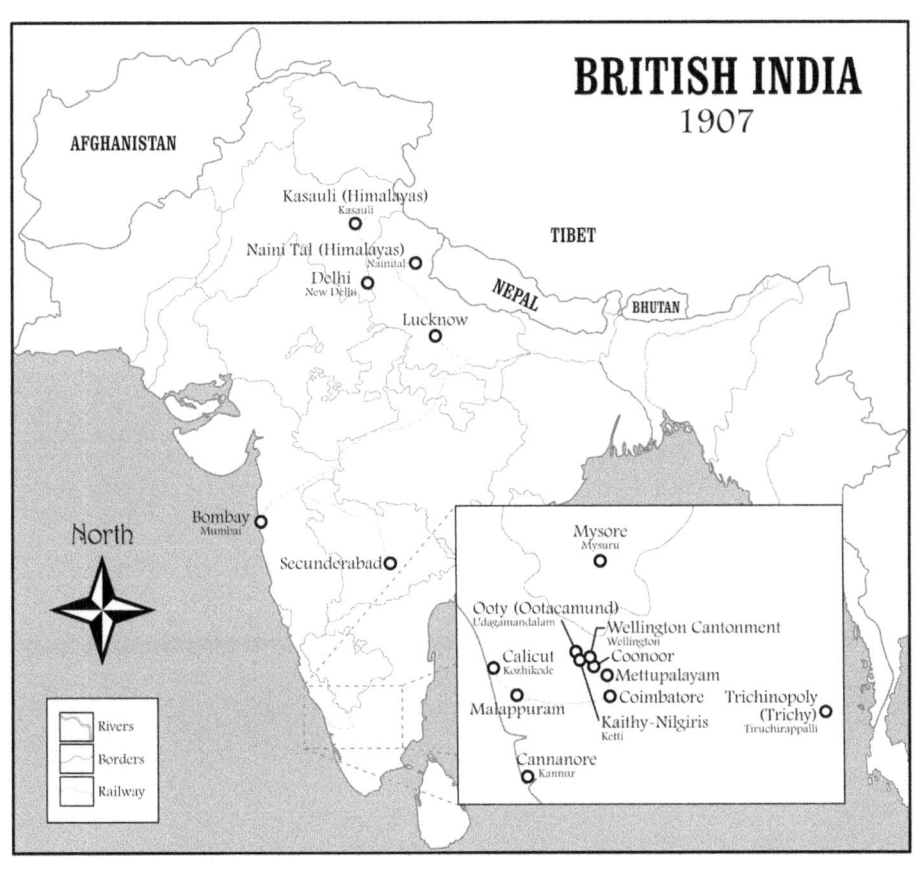

Michael Bergen was born in England and grew up in Canada, though he has lived in Europe and South Africa for most of his adult life, and it was here that *The Rutherford Chronicles* first sprang to life.

History was always Michael's first love and sparked an interest in his own family heritage. This led, following meticulous research, directly to his writing of *The Rutherford Chronicles*, a series of four books based on the lives of his ancestors, their friends and families and the broader world in the turbulent years of the early to mid 20th century, and culminating in the final novel, based on his own experiences during the Cold War of the second half of that century.

The Rutherford Chronicles follow the lives of ordinary people thrust into extraordinary circumstances, and events controlled by their much better known and more powerful contemporaries on all sides of the conflicts, many of whom are referenced within the pages of the books.

Book one, *Empire Discovered*, begins during the Second Anglo-Boer War in South Africa and continues into British India.

Book two, *Empire and War*, takes place in the trenches and German POW camps in WWI.

Book three, *Empire and Tyranny*, is the story of a soldier of the Canadian Artillery during WWII.

The last book, *Empires Lost*, follows events during the Cold War, based on Michael's own experiences during the later years of the 20th century.

www.michaelgbergen.com

Milton Keynes UK
Ingram Content Group UK Ltd.
UKHW040133030224
437175UK00006B/737